F
H36   Helmreich, Helaine G.
              The chimney tree.

DATE	ISSUED TO

F
H36   Helmreich, Helaine G.
              The chimney tree.

Temple Israel Library
2324 Emerson Avenue South
Minneapolis, MN. 55405

Please sign your name and telephone number on the above card.

Books and materials are loaned for a period of three weeks and may be returned to the Library or Temple reception desk.

Fines will be charged for any damage or loss of materials.

DEMCO

The Chimney Tree

Helaine G. Helmreich

THE CHIMNEY TREE

The Toby Press

Toby Press Edition 2003

The Toby Press LLC
POB 8531, New Milford, CT. 06676-8531, USA
& POB 2455, London WIA 5WY, England
www.tobypress.com

A previous version of the first part of *The Chimney Tree* was published
in 2000, by the University Press of Colorado. The text has been
substantially changed by the author for this new edition.

This is a work of fiction. The characters, incidents, and dialogues are
products of the author's imagination and are not to be construed as
real. Any resemblance to actual events or persons, living or dead, is
entirely coincidental.

ISBN 1 59264 031 1, *hardcover*

A CIP catalogue record for this title
is available from the British Library

Typeset in Garamond by Jerusalem Typesetting

Printed and bound in the United States by
Thomson-Shore, Inc., Michigan

To my husband and children

Part One

Chapter one

Miriam Rutner, known in her village as "Miriam Rote," *Dubnitz, Poland, 1935* or "Red Miriam," because of her bright red hair, stood in front of the mirror combing the long, thick tresses that had earned her the nickname. Her earliest memories involved her hair. Red hair was considered ugly, a misfortune to have befallen a Jewish daughter. Her mother, Chaya Rochel, had always cut it short, the better to hide it under caps and bonnets. Since she had turned twelve however, Miriam had insisted upon letting it grow, placating her mother by braiding it and winding the heavy coils around her head.

"Miriam! Open the door already!"

Miriam slid the chair away and allowed her sister, sixteen-year-old Dina, to enter the room. The two girls had always shared the cozy back bedroom, but for the last two years, since Miriam had turned sixteen, she had insisted upon her privacy when dressing and undressing. This enabled Miriam to spend more time in front of the tall, gilt-edged mirror. When and how had her body changed so much? The transformation had been gradual, but Miriam still saw it as miraculous.

As a child she had been fat. Memories of the red welts on

3

her wrists and thighs from the overly-tight elastic in her sleeves and stockings were as vivid in her mind as the taunting voices of her classmates. Then, finally, at fourteen, she had started losing weight. Chaya Rochel had worried that she was ill, God forbid, and had rushed her to the village doctor. That's how it started, after all, with Zeeva Buchsbaum, first the weight loss, and now the poor girl was bedridden. It was whispered that she had diabetes. But the doctor had pronounced Miriam healthy, and she had grown tall and slender, with long, graceful limbs and softly rounded breasts. Unlike many redheads, her skin did not have a sickly pallor but was rosy with no freckles. Her hair had darkened since childhood, turning from a carroty hue to a burnished auburn that set off her large, almond-shaped green eyes.

"Dina, do me a favor and button up the back of my dress, please."

"All this time locked in here and you're still unbuttoned?" asked Dina incredulously. "And your hair isn't even done up yet!" Dina had little patience with her sister's frivolities in dress and grooming. Short and plump, with a round, good-natured face and chin-length chestnut hair, she spent much of her time sewing, knitting, and helping their mother, or Katya the maid in the kitchen. She considered her status as a *kalla moid*, a soon-to-be bride, very important. Young Jewish girls in the village were called *kalla moiden* once they turned thirteen or so, and Dina, like most girls her age, spent a lot of time preparing for marriage and children.

It was a constant worry to her that she would have to wait for Miriam, the oldest, to marry first, as propriety dictated, for Miriam showed little interest in becoming anyone's wife. Time and again she had rejected the suitors that Yudel the *shadchan*, the matchmaker, had proposed for her. All were Hasidim of their father, Reb Mordche, the Dubnitzer *rebbe*. Miriam complained that they were like peas in a pod, all with the same appearance—pale, slightly stooped young men with dark wispy beards and glinting spectacles, who stood with averted eyes, blushing, when pointed out to her in the synagogue courtyard on holidays.

"Who are you waiting for," Dina would ask, "the Angel Gabriel?"

Dina was secretly pleased about one particular would-be suitor rejected by Miriam. Leibel Parnes was a young Hasid with black curly hair and the beginnings of a beard who appealed to Dina, for they had almost had an "adventure" together on the last *Purim* holiday, walking to the synagogue. She had passed a group of Hasidim on their way to morning services when suddenly a great gust of wind carried off the black hat belonging to one of them and deposited it at Dina's feet. Picking it up, she hurried over to hand it to the hatless young man, his head now covered only by a black velvet yarmulke, which he held down with his hand while his sidelocks flew about in the wind. As the Hasid took the hat, their eyes met for a brief moment, and he muttered, "Thank you" before hurrying away, a deep flush spreading to his ears.

That had been Leibel Parnes. Since then, six months ago, Dina had thought often of Leibel while going about her daily tasks. She hoped he would not become betrothed to another before she had her chance. If only Miriam would hurry up and choose someone! Everyone knew that Miriam could not hold out much longer. It was very unusual for the daughter of a rabbinic household to disobey her father, rejecting suitors he himself had deemed appropriate. People were already gossiping about Miriam's behavior, and more of the same would bring embarrassment to Reb Mordche.

"Thanks, Dina," said Miriam as Dina finished buttoning her dress and pushed a few stray hairs into Miriam's braided coils. "I'm going out now for a while. Tell Mama I'll be home in time to pick up Shloimeh at *cheder*, at school."

"Where are you going?"

"Oh, just to Chaya Moskowitz's house to return a book."

Miriam picked her way carefully along the dusty main road of the village. She passed a group of four young women whom she had known since childhood. All four were now married, their hair covered with light-colored kerchiefs. Two of them pushed children in shabby carriages. They greeted her perfunctorily with nods or waves and quickly resumed their talk of recipes and childbearing. The sight of these young matrons reminded Miriam of Dina's words of the night before.

"I saw Bleema Goldschatz today. She looked wonderful, Miriam! So happy, and she's already expecting. She was in your class. Just think, Miriam, it could be you! Imagine what it would be like, your own husband, and maybe a baby already!"

How could Miriam explain her feelings to her sister, who fantasized constantly about marriage? For years Dina had been describing her future wedding in intricate detail; how her gown would flow out behind her in a shimmering wave as she glided down the aisle of Kuneh's Inn, smiling behind her veil, while a handsome Hasid, the best-looking of all the young Dubnitzers, waited for her beneath the flower-decked *chupa*.

When they were younger, Miriam had enjoyed sharing in these daydreams with her sister. During the lonely times of her childhood, Dina had been her closest friend and ally. Like Miriam, Dina was a chubby child, with plump limbs and rounded cheeks, but she did not share Miriam's tendencies toward brooding over her weight, nor was she ever the victim of taunts. Instead, her buoyant good spirits and deep-throated chuckle endeared her to everyone in the village. How could Miriam tell her sister that for the last year, while this or that match was being proposed, the sight of the young Hasidim in her father's courtyard had filled her with dread? She could not bear the thought of leaving the warm sanctuary of her home to live with a virtual stranger. Would Dina understand why she felt that way, when Miriam herself could not explain it? And what would Dina think of her self-contained older sister if she knew who really filled Miriam's thoughts these days?

Avoiding the marketplace, she hurried toward the outskirts of town and slipped into the woods that bordered the river. Treading softly over the carpet of dried brown leaves and pine needles that covered the narrow path, she approached a large dead pine tree whose trunk had been split by lightning many years before. The resulting fire had burned upward through the tree trunk, leaving it hollow, and a hole near its base had been enlarged so that a person could stand inside it and look straight up at the sky. The tree was known locally as "the chimney."

Miriam stood inside the tree trunk and waited. After five minutes, she heard a soft crunching sound. Someone was approaching. Her heart leaped and she smiled in anticipation. In a moment he was there—tall, broad-shouldered Tadeusz, his blond, straight hair catching the rays of sunlight that shone through the leaves and pine needles above him. Miriam stepped out of the tree trunk, laughing up at him.

"Have you been waiting long?" asked Tadeusz with a smile, as he bent to kiss her.

"No, no," murmured Miriam. She put her arms around his strong neck and held tight, eyes shut and legs weakening in a rush of desire. Then she released her grip and turned her head away. Always, when they touched or kissed, she felt the desire, and always, immediately, the guilt and shame. It was a sin, a terrible sin, to touch a boy before marriage, even your betrothed. But a gentile boy, a *goy*—you weren't allowed to even *speak* to them. Yet ever since she had first consented to meet Tadeusz in the woods three months ago, she had found it increasingly difficult to resist his hungry kisses, and his strong, insistent hands. She had not succumbed to his wishes—passionate kissing and embracing was all she allowed—but at each meeting she wondered how much longer she could continue like this.

After all, she had loved Tadeusz seven long months, ever since the afternoon she had walked into the kitchen and found him there showing his artwork to Katya, his older sister. Katya was the Rutner family's cook and maid and had been with them for four years. Until that day, Miriam had heard about but never seen Katya's younger brother Tadeusz, who, like herself, was eighteen. His family, who had always lived in the village of Sanomir, ten kilometers distant, had just moved to Dubnitz, and Tadeusz would now meet his sister and walk her home on Monday afternoons when he finished his carpentry work.

Miriam had looked with awe at the sketches of birds, flowers, and animals that he spread over the rustic pine table. Could it be that this strong, rough, *goyishe* carpenter had drawn such fine and delicate images?

"Do you like them?" he asked, smiling at her with his bright blue eyes.

"Yes, they're so beautiful. Did you draw them?"

"Yes, I did. Would you like to see some more?" And he had opened a sketchbook to show her numerous drawings of local people and natural scenes from the surrounding countryside.

Miriam was fascinated. She also loved to draw, but her parents and teachers discouraged the pastime because of the biblical commandment against graven images. In the homes of her more "modern" friends, she had seen lovely paintings hanging on the walls, but her own house contained nothing more artistic than a few lace doilies and several embroidered pillowcases made by her mother or Dina, along with some faded photographs of severe-looking relatives. These were hidden away in a drawer; Miriam had come across them by accident one day as she was searching for some stockings.

"I can show you my paintings and drawings every week, if you like," Tadeusz told her.

Thus began their friendship, the two of them looking at drawings together each Monday afternoon before Tadeusz walked Katya home across the river. Mama was always out at that time shopping in the marketplace, with little Shloimeh tagging after her. Dina usually accompanied them as well. Father would be in the *beis medrash*, the study house. So no one knew she was talking to Tadeusz except for Katya, and if Katya disapproved, she said nothing to Miriam.

After a few meetings, Miriam began to catch herself thinking about Tadeusz often, especially at inappropriate moments such as while saying her prayers before bedtime, or when sitting in the synagogue on the Sabbath during the reading of the *Torah*. It seemed that whenever it was particularly sinful to think of such things as young men, her thoughts would stray to Tadeusz. She felt guilty, but found herself looking forward to his visits more and more. Resolving never to see him again, she would catch herself planning what to wear at their next meeting. She was increasingly terrified that someone in the family would come home and discover them together in the kitchen.

Then, one day, after they had been looking at Tadeusz's drawings together every week for three months, he put his hand over hers while Katya's back was turned. It was only for a second, but in that second, a violent shock coursed through Miriam's body. She quickly withdrew her hand and left the room. During the following days Miriam lived in a state of torment unlike anything she'd ever known. She vowed to forget Tadeusz; still, she relived the moment his hand had covered hers over and over in her mind, each time re-experiencing the thrilling, tingling sensation. Finally it was Monday afternoon again, and Miriam hid in her room, peering through her bedroom window in an agony of conflicting feelings as Tadeusz entered the house, then left with Katya shortly afterward.

Did he ask for me? Did he wonder where I was? Will he stop coming to the house? Questions raced through her mind as she watched them walk up the narrow street toward the river. She strained to see his face—did he look disappointed perhaps, or hurt because of her absence? Was there something in the set of his shoulders that suggested dejection? But no, Tadeusz strode along jauntily until Miriam could no longer see him. The rest of that week, she tried to busy herself in myriad ways, playing with Shloimeh, rereading the faded Yiddish books her religious tutor had once assigned, even taking up her long-forgotten needlework. But it was no use. Monday afternoon found her back in the kitchen, making smalltalk with Katya, all the while stealing little glances from the clock to the door and back.

Suddenly, he was there. Miriam's heart jumped when she saw his broad shoulders and blond hair edging through the heavy door. But something was wrong. Tadeusz barely acknowledged her shy greeting, nor did he have his portfolio of paintings.

"Hurry, Katya, get your hat. We have to go," he told his sister, avoiding Miriam's eyes. Katya went into the pantry to get her hat, coat, and bag. Tadeusz quickly leaned toward Miriam and dropped a small piece of folded paper into her lap. Then, without a word,

9

he hurried outside. Miriam waited until she heard the click of the garden gate. With trembling fingers she unfolded the note. It was written in simple Polish, which Miriam had been taught at home by Mr. Berkowitz, her tutor:

> Dear Miriam:
>
> My sister says it is not proper for me to spend time with you anymore in your kitchen. She is afraid she will lose her position if someone sees us. But you know we are innocent of any wrongdoing. If you trust me, meet me tomorrow evening in the woods on your side of the river, at the tree they call "the chimney." I will wait there at five o'clock.
>
> Yours,
>
> Tadeusz

Miriam's first reaction was to throw the note into the fire. The next morning, after a sleepless night, she had convinced herself to meet him, but only to tell him that they must not see each other again.

Since no one in her family was in the house, Miriam was able to sneak off to the woods without using any of the excuses she had already invented. Tadeusz was there, waiting. He showed her his latest sketches, all drawings of his family members, telling her about each one in turn. Miriam listened, entranced. Katya rarely talked about her family. Yet here was Tadeusz, describing them affectionately as if they were characters in a favorite story: Vladek, with his love of sports; Anton, who played practical jokes; little Yadwiga, who liked to eat sour things like lemons.

The sunshine played hide-and-seek through the branches, warming the young couple as they sat on the bed of needles at the base of the chimney tree. Miriam laughed and talked more freely than in her kitchen, since people rarely walked to this spot during the week and the Jews of her village almost never came here. She found it impossible to tell Tadeusz that she couldn't meet him again. And so, week after week, they met on Tuesday evenings at the chimney tree, with Tadeusz showing Miriam his paintings and sometimes sketching her face as she gazed up at him. Soon she no longer withdrew her hand from his, and when he first kissed her, she surprised both of them by kissing him back. That had been in May. As summer waxed and waned, their feelings for each other grew stronger. When fall came, each clung to the other with a desperation that told of their concern for the coming winter, when it would be too cold and snowy to meet in the woods. Miriam was tortured both by guilt over their relationship and fear that it might end.

"Look, Miriam," said Tadeusz, interrupting her troubled thoughts one day. He unfurled a small, rolled-up piece of paper. Miriam gasped. It was a small painting of herself, unmistakable, with her red hair coiled about her ears. Yet the figure wore no clothes at all. This naked, painted Miriam stood with uplifted arms, fastening her hair. While Miriam tried to recover from the shock of seeing herself so painfully exposed, Tadeusz unrolled two more paintings. With delicate brush strokes and warm-toned pigments, each showed a naked Miriam in a graceful pose; her face expressed no shame at her body being revealed in a way no one had ever seen, not even Dina. Each painting bore his signature: Tadeusz Zbirka.

Tears sprang to Miriam's eyes and she blushed to the roots of her hair. "Tadeusz, how… why…what is this?" she gasped. "What do you mean?" Never very fluent in Polish, she could barely choke the words out.

"Don't cry, Miriam. Oh, please, I didn't mean to upset you. All great artists paint this way. Their models pose for them in the nude. But I knew you'd never do that. So I imagined how you would look. You should be proud of your beauty. In art the body of a woman isn't shameful." He put his arms around her trembling shoulders. But Miriam would not be consoled. She pulled away from him and began rushing blindly through the woods.

Tadeusz quickly gathered up his paintings and began racing after her, tripping over the tangled bracken along the path, but soon gave up because of the lengthening shadows and rising wind. Tucking his paintings back into his worn leather portfolio, he started for home. He would visit Miriam's house next Monday afternoon, as he used to, and perhaps leave her a note.

He made his way quickly through the woods to the river,

hunching his shoulders against the chill autumn wind. His eyes did not catch the flutter of the small, rolled-up paper that lay at the foot of the chimney tree. Nor did he see the slim blonde figure slipping silently through the pines as she bent to retrieve it from its bed of twigs and dried pine needles.

Chapter two

Reb Mordche Rutner swayed over the heavy, dog-eared volume of Talmud that lay open on the long oaken table before him. Nine of his Hasidim sat along the table, peering into their own copies, waiting expectantly for his next question.

"And if you'll say a person *can* buy something which has not yet come into existence, I'll tell you that it's so only in the case of a palm tree, which is certain to come into existence. But here," he chanted, "it's different. First of all, who says the object that the man is guarding will be stolen? And if you'll say it will, then who says the thief will be found? And even if the thief is found, who says he will pay the fine? All this is clear," said Reb Mordche emphatically, "but let's go over it again anyway." His thumb traced an arabesque through the air above the sacred tome.

The rhythmic chanting of the *rebbe* and his Hasidim prevented them from hearing the knocking on the door of the study house until it grew loud and insistent. Reb Mordche signaled for Feivel, his *gabbai*, or personal attendant, to open it. But Feivel had barely risen from his bench when the door burst open, revealing a slim young woman whose straight, pale blonde hair, snub nose, and rough peasant garb identified her as a Polish girl from the nearby countryside. Feivel approached her while the other Hasidim, recovering from their initial shock at seeing a young gentile woman enter the study house, turned their heads back to the *rebbe* and their holy books.

"What is it?" asked Feivel in Yiddish-accented Polish.

"I want to give this to the rabbi," replied the girl, a sly smirk playing about her mouth. She thrust the paper at Feivel and edged quickly out the door. Once outside, Stefa hurried to the back of the low, wooden building, where a pile of firewood was heaped beneath a window. Climbing to the top of the pile, she gripped the sill with one hand and brushed away the frost and dirt from a corner of the grimy, cracked window-pane with the other. From this vantage point, Stefa was able to observe the reaction of the rabbi and his Hasidim.

Feivel shamefully brought the furled paper to the *rebbe*'s table. Should he have allowed her to shove the paper at him that way? Perhaps he should have let it drop and then picked it up, rather than take it directly from the hand of a young *shikse*.

"*Nu, vus iss?* What is it?" asked the *rebbe*.

Feivel looked at the men seated around the table. All of the bearded faces reflected the same nameless foreboding that had gripped him as he slowly handed the paper to the *rebbe*. What would a Polish girl who smiled so strangely want with their *rebbe*? Could the paper be a warning about an impending pogrom, God forbid? There hadn't been one in Dubnitz, thank God, in over fifteen years.

Reb Mordche reached out, took the paper from Feivel, and closed his Talmud. His Hasidim leaned forward anxiously, watching as their *rebbe* unrolled the little scroll. Their anxiety turned to dismay as his face flushed a deep crimson, replaced almost immediately by a ghastly pallor as he slumped senselessly in his chair. The paper slid to the floor, and the Hasidim, with cries of concern, sprang to the stricken *rebbe*'s side, fanning him with their broad-brimmed black hats. One of them loosened Reb Mordche's collar; another rushed to fetch water from a chipped porcelain cistern at the far end of the room.

Avram Hersch, a young Hasid with a curly brown beard, had been sitting at the end of the table farthest from the *rebbe*. He had removed himself from his customary spot closer to the center of the table shortly after *Purim*, when Miriam had turned him down as a prospective suitor. Thus shamed by the *rebbe's* daughter, he no longer felt comfortable sitting near Reb Mordche. Now Avram Hersch walked to the head of the table, where most of the Hasidim were still hovering about the unconscious *rebbe*. Bending down, he nearly collided with Feivel, who apparently had the same purpose in mind. Avram, the more dexterous of the two, quickly stood up and opened the curled paper. "*Oy vay!*" he cried. The other Hasidim immediately turned from ministering to Reb Mordche and gaped in horror at the picture that Avram Hersch had spread out.

It was a painting of Miriam, Reb Mordche's eldest daughter, standing completely unclothed, displaying her body in a way that no woman should, not even for her husband. Not only that, but the smile on her face showed a total lack of concern for such shameful immodesty. After a moment of shocked silence, the Hasidim, finding their tongues, began murmuring amongst themselves and resumed their ministrations to Reb Mordche, who, with a drawn out moan, was returning to consciousness. His eyes opened and he looked around, first at his disciples and then at the table before him, as though he wished to continue the Talmudic discourse abruptly broken off for reasons he no longer remembered. Again he flushed as his eyes fell on the offensive painting, but this time the flush deepened to one of anger as he noticed the signature in the right-hand corner. Written in small Polish characters was the name Tadeusz Zbirka.

Zbirka, Zbirka, thought Reb Mordche. *I've heard that name somewhere. This needs a thorough investigation.* Quickly folding the paper in quarters, he thrust it into his breast pocket and without a word, rose from the table and left the study house for home, leaning heavily on Feivel's arm. The remainder of the group clustered together, talking in low tones as they closed their sacred books and prepared to leave.

Stefa, witnessing the entire scene from her post atop the woodpile, waited until the men's voices and footsteps faded from the courtyard. She then climbed carefully down, smiling inwardly as she brushed the soot from her hands and shirt. So she had gotten dirty and even torn her stocking into the bargain. It was well worth it. Now that stuck-up little Jewish girl with her fancy ways and ridiculous red braids would be in plenty of trouble. Her father would never again let her out of his sight. And as for Tadeusz, he'd soon come back to his Stefa, whose kisses and passionate caresses would make him forget that the Jewess had ever existed. How lucky Stefa had been today. On more than one occasion she had followed Tadeusz through the woods, hiding herself in order to observe his trysts. But never before had she been fortunate enough to come upon evidence as incriminating as an actual painting. Surely the saints favored her this day by putting the picture in her path. Happiness quickened Stefa's nimble steps, and soon she had crossed the narrow bridge traversing the river and was skipping down the winding, rutted dirt road leading to the outer village, where the peasants dwelt in rustic cottages with earthen floors.

"Where have you been, you good-for-nothing whore?" Her brother Piotr's rough voice rudely shook her out of her pleasant reverie as she entered the little cottage they shared with her younger brother Grisha, and their father, who now snored in a corner. His heavy, rattling breaths gave notice to all that he was well satiated with vodka and would not be disturbed. Stefa peered about the dim room, which served as kitchen, bedroom, and family room for her father and Piotr. Stefa and Grisha slept up in the tiny loft, accessible only by a rickety, wooden ladder that creaked, for which they were both thankful, since the noise frightened the mice back into their holes. Pirogi, the old cat, rarely bothered to chase mice anymore, preferring to doze near the fire, stretching out a paw now and then to snare whatever hapless rodent chanced across her path in the gloom.

"Get a move on and make a man some dinner," snarled Piotr. "Worked like an ox all day in the fields, and I come home to find you out whoring, with nothing on the table for us men to eat. Try it again and I'll break both your arms."

Who'd cook your dinner then, thought Stefa contemptuously, but she said nothing. She knew well that Piotr often accompanied his threats with actual blows, and she had no wish for a black eye or swollen purple nose, especially since she planned to accost Tadeusz on his way to work the next morning. Silently, she began peeling potatoes while Grisha, who had just turned ten, set down the tiny wooden pig he had been carving and began to set the table.

Let Piotr yell, she thought. *Someday, he'll eat his words. When Tadeusz goes to Paris and becomes a famous artist, it's me he'll send for. I'll be a rich, fancy woman of the world, married to a great artist, and then I'll send for Grisha. Father and Piotr can rot in hell, for all I'll care.* Her blue eyes shone as cold as the stars in the black autumn sky. Looking out the window, she could see curls of smoke wafting upward from the row of squat thatched huts, filling the night air with the scent of burnt pine.

Breathing with some difficulty, his soul heavy with anguish, Reb Mordche allowed Feivel to open the door for him. They entered the foyer of the comfortable, two-story house that the Hasidim had provided for their *rebbe* and his family. Reb Mordche felt hurt that given his present suffering, only Feivel had seen fit to accompany him home. The others had all remained behind in the study house, presumably discussing the calamity that had befallen their leader. *Already I have fallen in their eyes,* sighed Reb Mordche to himself. *My daughter Miriam has heaped shame upon me, upon my household, and upon the names of my ancestors, may their memories be blessed.*

As the two men walked past the kitchen toward the *rebbe*'s study, Reb Mordche's bitter thoughts were interrupted by the sight of Katya, who was busy scouring one of the heavy, cast-iron pots that had recently contained the family's dinner. At the sudden appearance of two severe-looking, black-garbed Jews, Katya quickly ceased humming the Polish melody she frequently sang to make her work go faster. Wiping her hands on the embroidered cotton apron that had been a birthday gift from Dina, Katya stared at the men, wondering what they could possibly want of her, for in all the years she had worked in his house, Reb Mordche had barely acknowledged her presence, never speaking directly to her, and thanking her with only the merest of grunts when she set his food on the table before him. Nor did Feivel or any of the other Hasidim ever speak more than a word or two to her. Katya took no umbrage at their behavior; it was only to be expected from a holy man and his disciples. Besides, she had always enjoyed a very cordial relationship with the *rebbetzin*, or rabbi's wife, and a joking, almost sisterly one with all of the children.

"Feivel, ask the woman what her last name is," said Reb Mordche, taking Feivel's arm for support as he stood.

"Excuse me, miss, please, the *rebbe* wishes to know your last name," stammered Feivel in labored Polish. This made it twice today that he'd had to address a pretty Polish maiden, and he felt exceedingly embarrassed.

"Zbirka. My name is Katya Zbirka," she replied in Yiddish, which she had learned to speak fluently while in the family's employ. She looked from the face of the *gabbai* to that of the *rebbe* in confusion.

"And ask her now, who is Tadeusz Zbirka?" said Reb Mordche, his hand gripping Feivel's arm more tightly.

"He is my brother, my younger brother," replied Katya, without waiting for Feivel to repeat the *rebbe*'s question. A cold chill ran through her. Tadeusz used to talk to Miriam for hours, here in this kitchen. Could the *rebbe* have found out? But Tadeusz hadn't been at the house in months. Surely the whole business had been harmless anyway and was by this time certainly forgotten. So why was the *rebbe* asking about Tadeusz now?

"I see." Reb Mordche turned and left the room without another word, his loyal *gabbai* following behind. Katya was left alone in the kitchen to ponder the *rebbe*'s words.

Reb Mordche entered his book-lined study and eased himself into the soft green leather chair that stood at the head of the table, upon which a few Hebrew books of various sizes were strewn. Feivel hurried to light the fire, happy to have something to do.

"Feivel, call my son Shloimeh and ask him to come in here," commanded Reb Mordche.

Feivel hurried out and knocked on the door of the small bedroom opposite the rabbi's study. After a moment a small boy of five appeared, looking like a miniature, albeit beardless, Hasid in his black suit, white shirt, and black velvet skullcap. Like Miriam, he, too, was a redhead, and his bright copper-colored side curls bounced gaily as he walked quickly into his father's study.

Reb Mordche's face softened into a smile at the sight of his young son, the child of his old age. Despite the grief today's events had brought, he would not forego his evening ritual of spending time with Shloimeh before the boy went to bed.

"Feivel, you may go home now. I'll see you in the morning," said the *rebbe*, tenderly encircling Shloimeh's thin shoulders with his arms.

Feivel, bowing his head slightly, backed out of the room, only too glad to be on his way after such an exhausting, emotion-filled day.

"Why are you still dressed, my little friend?" asked Reb Mordche, bending his head toward Shloimeh.

"Mama said if I ate my dinner, I could play with my armies," Shloimeh replied in a soft, high-pitched voice. On Shloimeh's fifth birthday, Feivel had presented the boy with twenty wooden soldiers, each wearing the tall "fur" hat of a Cossack and armed with a tiny wooden sword. These soldiers differed in one respect from those owned by Polish children: each soldier was maimed in some way. Several had their noses or ears chipped off, others were missing an arm, and one had lost a leg. These "wounds" had been deliberately and painstakingly inflicted by Feivel in accordance with the Hasidic belief that possession of a representational human figure, if intact and perfect, would violate the biblical prohibition against idol worship. Shloimeh cared not at all that his beloved soldiers were flawed, for each missing feature or limb represented to him a battle scar earned on the field of combat.

"All right, Shloimele, but now you must tell what you learned in *cheder* today. And then, off to bed, because it's very late," said his father.

"*Tati*, Father, I don't like Reb Yossi's *cheder*. I want to go to Reb Shmuel's."

"And why don't you like Reb Yossi's?"

"Because he coughs all the time. And when a boy doesn't know the answer, he pinches him hard, like this." The boy reached out and mischievously pinched his father's cheek lightly.

"*Oy*! And does he ever pinch you?"

"No. The others say it's because I'm Reb Mordche's son. And Dovid'l spits at me."

"*Nu*, enough. When you are older, you can learn in Reb Shmuel's *cheder*. Till then you will stay with Reb Yossi. Know the answers, and no one will think you deserve a pinch. Now, what did you learn today?"

Even before he answered, Shloimeh began rocking back and forth, as if building up a momentum that would propel him forward and carry him through his recitation. In a singsong chant whose rhythm matched the movements of his body, Shloimeh began.

"All the people spoke in one language and they went to a place in Shinnar, I think, and they took bricks and stones and they started building a big tower to reach up to heaven and then God came down to look at this tower and Rashi says He didn't have to come down but He did it to teach the judges that they shouldn't say anybody did a bad thing until they saw and understood what he did."

Breaking suddenly out of the traditional singsong chant he had assumed, Shloimeh exclaimed, "But Reb Yossi always punishes us, even if he didn't see what we did. Even when we didn't do anything! Yesterday he pulled Avramele's ear and it turned all red and Avramele hadn't done anything; only Chaim was laughing because the cat was trying to climb into the window and it kept meowing and—"

"Enough," cut in his father. "Probably Avramele did something, too. Anyway, it's now time for bed. Before you go in, please go upstairs and tell Mama and Miriam to come down to talk to me. Then go right in and say *Kriyas Shma*, the bedtime prayer." He kissed the boy's cheek and sent him on his way with a sigh. *I am*, he thought, *fifty-five years old and I feel like a man of eighty. Who knows if God will spare me and I'll live to see this boy under the marriage canopy? I've yet to have real* nachas*, real pleasure, from my children. And now this new trouble with Miriam. Only God knows where it will lead.* He listened to the clatter of Shloimeh's feet running up the stairs and then to the muffled sound of voices on the floor above.

Miriam lay atop her warm featherbed in the darkened back bedroom. Dina was already asleep. It was only nine o'clock, but Dina had suffered agonizing cramps that evening, as she often did during her time of the month, and so she had gone to bed very early, her pain dulled by the small glass of brandy that Mama always administered for colds and "women's troubles."

When Miriam heard Shloimeh's knock on the door and his whispered "Miriam, *Tati* wants you," her eyes, which had been gazing blankly at the gray dots dancing about in the darkness above her, widened in surprise. *What could* Tati *want me for?* she wondered. *I hope it's not another* shidduch, *another proposed wedding match. That's all I need right now.* She found it difficult to rise from the bed. She had walked Shloimeh home almost in a stupor, unable to shake the feeling of numbness that had enveloped her after she fled the forest. Barely speaking to her mother, sister, and brother, she had picked at the boiled meat, potatoes, and carrots that Katya had set before her, then gone upstairs and, ignoring her sister's moans of pain, lain down on her bed, still and wordless, trying to make some sense of what had happened that afternoon. But she was unable to come to terms with what Tadeusz had done. It was too shameful. All she could conclude was that her teachers, her parents, and her girlfriends had been correct—one must stay as far away as possible from the *goy*im. A Jewish girl was supposed to view herself as the daughter of a king and to behave with the utmost modesty and dignity. She had broken that rule, and obviously Tadeusz did not respect her or he could not have depicted her as he had. *He might as well have seen me naked,* she thought as hot tears rushed to her eyes. *Thank God I never really sinned with him. Well, almost, that day before Succoth....*

"Miriam," Shloimeh called again.

"All right, I'm coming," she answered, and slowly groped her way to the door, not wanting to light the lamp and wake Dina.

Reb Mordche's study had always been an inviting place for Miriam, with its many bookshelves and special smell of old papers, leather bindings, and ink. Even now the room was suffused with the warmth of a small fire that danced merrily on the grate. Both the *rebbe* and his wife, seated nearby on the easy chair, looked up as

Miriam entered. Reb Mordche, motioning for Miriam to be seated, began speaking softly but with great intensity.

"Miriam, you are no longer a child. Your mother and I have been looking forward to the day when you will be a mother in Israel. You have, up till now, turned down all suitors proposed to you. I went along with your wishes, but tell me, Miriam, were none of the Hasidim who came here suitable as a marriage partner? What kind of a husband are you looking for?"

Miriam sighed. So that was it after all. Another *shidduch*. Yet the glint in her father's eye disturbed her. And why, when she looked at Mama, did Mama turn away, avoiding her quick glance?

"I don't know, *Tati*. I don't know what I'm looking for. I just knew I wouldn't be happy with any of these men. They just weren't for me. Perhaps I'm simply not ready."

"Maybe you are ready for something different, then," retorted Reb Mordche, his voice rising. "A more modern man, an unbeliever."

Miriam stared at her father in alarm. Why was he speaking this way? And why was his face darkening in anger, while Mama seemed to be fighting tears?

"No, no, *Tati*. God forbid. Why would you say such a thing?"

"Maybe you want something unusual—an art student, perhaps?"

Miriam's face turned white. She gripped the edge of her chair with damp, trembling hands.

"What do you mean, *Tati*? What are you talking about?"

"This, this I am talking about!" thundered Reb Mordche, thrusting a paper at Miriam. Her eyes caught a glimpse of warm colors—russet, rose, and gold—on the paper as it landed by her feet.

Miriam swallowed hard as tears rose again in her eyes and began to spill down onto her pale cheeks. *My only hope is to lie*, she thought, *to deny everything. How true is the Talmudic saying, "One sin begets another."*

"I don't know what that is. I don't know!" she cried as she snatched the paper and threw it into the fire. The three of them stared silently as the flames licked at the edges of the painting, browning them into a scalloped frame. In a moment, the graceful feminine figure was in flames, too, turning almost instantly to ashes.

"Miriam, you must not lie to us. I know who this Tadeusz Zbirka is. I have spoken to Katya, who will be leaving this house tomorrow. What you must tell us now, what we must know, is whether you have lived with this man as husband and wife. You must tell the truth, for we can have Devorah, the midwife, examine you anyway."

Miriam flushed furiously. Her father had never spoken to her of such personal matters. Even Mama avoided these topics, and when she discussed them, they were couched in biblical terms and presented as circumlocutions. And to be subjected to an examination by Devorah! She'd die first.

"*Tati*, please believe me," she blurted. "I never sinned with Tadeusz that way. I talked with him. He showed me his sketches and he drew pictures of my face, but that was all. You must believe me." Her voice cracked, and she put her head down on her arms and sobbed uncontrollably, vaguely conscious that her mother had begun stroking her hair.

"Well," said her father, "the *Torah* tells us to judge every person as though they were worthy. I believe you, but you must realize what you have done by allowing this *sheygitz*, this gentile, to draw your picture. A young Polish woman brought it to the *beis medrash*, and several of my Hasidim have seen it. Who knows what they thought and what they told others? Do you think it will be easy to find a husband for you now?"

Miriam's sobbing increased. She could well imagine what kind of thoughts the Hasidim, many of whom had known her since childhood, would have about her now. She had sinned and led others to sin, the worst kind of transgressor. How could she ever leave her house, knowing that any Hasid she passed on the street might carry a mental image of her as naked and wanton? What scorn they'd have for her, she who had considered herself too good for any of them to marry. Mama walked around to the back of the chair, nervously patting her daughter's arm. "Don't cry, Miriam. With God's help we'll find you a good *shidduch*, someone from far away who doesn't know anything about this business, and it will all be forgotten. *Tati* already has someone in mind."

"That's true," interjected Reb Mordche. "God willing, you will be a bride after Chanukah."

Miriam shuddered but held her tongue. It would only make matters worse to protest at this point. *Wait until things calm down*, she thought. Quietly, she rose and left the room, feeling her mother's anxious eyes following her as she ascended the narrow staircase. When Miriam's footsteps could no longer be heard, Chaya Rochel looked across the table at her husband.

"My poor Miriam, the little dove," she sighed. "I can't believe that she willfully sinned. She was always such a proud girl. She even walked like a princess. All the women commented on it. And now?"

"Now God will judge," said Reb Mordche as he reached for his Talmud and opened it, a sign to his wife that their conversation was over.

Chapter three

All day and on through the evening, the snow swirled through the village, the bright flakes twisting and turning in the light of the street lamp as the relentless wind tossed them about. *They dance like the demons from Gehenna*, thought Dina as she watched from her window and shivered. What could have caused such a morbid thought to enter my mind, she wondered. She peered at the street below, straining to see as far as possible. Two Hasidim hurried past, huddling into their heavy overcoats to protect themselves from the fierce wind. From the opposite direction, a peasant drove his horse and wagon, leaving a pile of steaming dung in his wake. Suddenly, his wheel became caught in a thick snowdrift, and Dina imagined the man's curses as he climbed down to help his horse pull the wagon out again. But where were Mama, Miriam, and Aunt Sara? Surely they should be on their way back from the *mikveh* by now. Dina sighed as she wiped her breath off the frosty windowpane for what seemed like the hundredth time. Poor Miriam, to have to go to the bathhouse on a freezing night like this.

All at once she saw them—three swaddled figures, arms linked to keep from falling in the snow. She thought about Miriam's strange behavior and her prolonged silences these last few months, ever since *Tati* had returned from Pavlitz and announced that Miriam was betrothed and would be married on the twenty-seventh day of the Jewish month of *Teveth*. The entire household had rejoiced. Even Marika, the new maid, smiled happily, making plans to knit a special sweater as a wedding gift for Miriam.

But Miriam had not rejoiced. She had not even asked about her bridegroom and had barely shown interest when *Tati* described him as a learned scholar. Dina found it difficult to understand Miriam's reaction. She herself, as well as her friends, thought Miriam very lucky to have found a husband so soon after the "portrait scandal," as the women called it. Many of them had predicted that Miriam would remain an old maid, since knowledge of the scandal had reached all of the surrounding villages and even some outlying areas. The stories were no doubt exaggerated, especially when recounted by members of rival Hasidic sects who gleefully predicted the downfall of the Dubnitzer dynasty. Dina was worried about Miriam's lack of interest in her own wedding preparations. Chaya Rochel tried to dispel Dina's anxieties, saying, "Miriam is grown up now. She knows that marriage and children are serious business." But the little nerve that twitched at the corner of Chaya Rochel's mouth betrayed her concern. And Mama did not know about the incident at the river.

One day last month Marika had failed to appear for work at her usual time. Worried, Mama had asked Dina to make inquiries in the village. Together, Dina and Miriam had gone to Marika's cottage and found her in bed, too ill even to come to the door. After giving her a cup of tea, the sisters wished her a quick recovery and left. On their way home they heard laughter as they were crossing the bridge. Looking down at the riverbank, they saw a young Polish couple throwing snowballs at each other. The young man was tall and blond; the girl appeared fair, too, though her head was covered by a wool scarf. The sisters watched as the girl ran toward a nearby stand of trees, with the young fellow in hot pursuit. She turned quickly and shouted, "Try and catch me, Tadeusz!" The young lad quickened his pace. Within seconds, he reached her. Grabbing the girl by the arms, he whirled her around, exclaiming triumphantly, "I've got you now, Stefa!"

Dina shrugged. She was halfway across the bridge when she noticed that Miriam was not following, but standing motionless, her face white as the surrounding snowdrifts. Tears coursed down her cheeks, leaving frosty trails on her pale skin. Dina understood then what had happened. *So that was Tadeusz, the one who signed the portrait.*

The door to the house opened and closed, letting in a blast of icy air as Dina hurried downstairs. The older women were fussing over Miriam, removing her wet outer clothing.

"*Oy*, her hair is still wet," cried Aunt Sara, running her fingers through Miriam's shorn auburn locks, cut earlier that day in preparation for the *sheitel*, the wig that Miriam would put on shortly before the wedding. It would be part of her Sabbath and holiday attire from then on. During the week, she would modestly cover her hair with a kerchief, like all "good religious" married women.

The *sheitel* had been brought all the way from Warsaw by Aunt Leah and Uncle Gershon and now sat proudly in its tall black leather box on the girls' dressing table. "But it's not red," Dina had protested as she took note of its light brown color, with only the faintest of reddish highlights.

"Never mind," Mama had said. "She's had enough of red hair. They hardly make red *sheitel*s anyway."

After the women had finished attending to her, Miriam went upstairs, declining an offer of hot tea. Dina followed close behind.

"What was it like, Miriam?" asked Dina eagerly as her sister undressed and climbed under the featherbed.

"Cold," said Miriam. "I want to sleep."

"But what did Chava say to you? What did she do? Is it true that she pokes you with her finger if you don't go in fast enough?" Dina had heard snatches of stories about Chava, the *mikveh* lady, from her friends, whose older sisters had gotten married.

"No," murmured Miriam and, feigning sleep, ignored her sister's prattle until Dina, too, fell asleep. Miriam had gone through the ritual numbly, as she had all of the other wedding preparations. Chava had examined every inch of her naked body, searching for stray hairs or lint or anything else that would have to be removed before Miriam immersed herself in the murky water. When satisfied that Miriam was completely clean, that her teeth held no particles of food, and that her toenails and fingernails were sufficiently short and free of dirt, Chava led Miriam to the water.

Miriam had descended the slippery steps into the cold water following her mother's instructions—arms and legs spread, mouth and eyes slightly open, up and down two times, making sure her head was completely submerged each time. Then, prompted by Chava, who placed a washcloth on Miriam's head, she intoned the blessing: "Blessed art Thou, O Lord, King of the Universe, who has sanctified us with His commandments and has commanded us regarding the ritual cleansing." Miriam also recited the traditional prayer of thanks to God for allowing her to live to experience the event and then dunked herself a third time. Emerging from the water, she was enveloped in a towel and, amid cries of *"Mazel tov! Mazel tov!"* helped back into her clothes.

Chava had rarely seen a bride so composed, so accepting. She knew about the portrait incident and had expected Miriam to be a rebellious young woman who might have to be forced. She was pleasantly surprised and told the *rebbetzin* that she could be proud of her daughter, who would make a true mother in Israel.

The next day dawned gray and cold, with occasional flurries of snow blowing around the villagers of Dubnitz as they hurried about their various early morning tasks—the Hasidim to the synagogue, the shopkeepers to their stalls, the small boys in their heavy coats and caps running off to *cheder*. Here and there a servant girl scurried through the snowdrifts on some errand for her mistress, the bright patterns of scarf and shawl adding color to the gray and white vista of the street. Soon small groups of women could be seen making their way toward Reb Kuneh's inn, each carrying a steaming bucket or wrapped parcel. These were the wives of the Dubnitzer Hasidim, who were involved in the wedding preparations. The wedding feast would be held at the inn, not far from the synagogue.

Reb Kuneh himself, as always when he hosted a wedding, was full of conflicting emotions. On the one hand, he was happy to be a participant in the *simcha*, the joyous occasion, which would bestow on him a *mitzvah*, not to mention a handsome fee for use of the inn. On the other hand, every wedding caused him great anxiety. Would the food be well prepared? Would there be enough to accommodate the guests? Would the servants get drunk and refuse to cooperate, or even, God forbid, insult the guests? Would the revelries result in damage to his property?

On this particular day he was even more nervous than usual, and, eyebrows bristling, red beard and black coattails flying, he had spent the morning running about the large kitchen, shouting at the cooks and sometimes even at the Dubnitzer wives. After all, he, too, was a Dubnitzer Hasid, and therefore he felt obligated to make a good impression on his *rebbe*. In addition, he would only be able to charge for the food and drinks, not for the musicians, hired help in the kitchen, and other services. Still, as he told his wife, Fruma Yentl, "It isn't every day that the *tzaddik*, our saintly leader, marries off a daughter."

"Especially not *that* daughter," Fruma Yentl had sniffed.

Like Reb Kuneh, Dina Rutner awoke early on the morning of the wedding. She, too, was filled with joy and foreboding. Looking over at the adjacent bed, she marveled at how peacefully Miriam still slept. *How pretty she looks, even with her hair so short*, thought Dina. *This is the very last time I'll ever see her in that bed. No more whispered conversations late at night, no more giggling in the dark over friends, teachers, suitors.* The thought of her sister leaving so soon to go so far from home, and with a young man whom she had never even seen, filled her with despair. *Who knows when she'll come back? It will never be the same again.*

Nonetheless, Dina was looking forward to the evening's festivities, when she herself, dressed like a princess in a blue satin dress, would command much attention as the only sister of the bride, and therefore next in line to be married. She leaned over and gently shook Miriam's shoulder. "Wake up, wake up, Miriam! How can you sleep today? You're a *kalla*, a bride. Aren't you excited? Today you meet your *chusen*, your groom. Soon his mother and sister will be here. You have to be dressed to meet them. Get up already."

Miriam rolled over and burrowed her head deeper into the feather pillows and comforters, trying to shut out Dina's babbling. She had no desire to get up, having had a bad night during which periods of nervous wakefulness had alternated with frighteningly vivid nightmares. Even worse, now that she was awake, the numbness that had sheltered her these past few months was receding and in its place came intense feelings of dread. She was afraid of all the tumult downstairs, clearly audible through the floorboards. She thought of how her doting female relatives would gush over her when all she wanted was to be left alone. The prospect of meeting the groom's mother and sister filled her with anxiety. What would she say to them, these strangers who were about to become her close relatives?

Miriam feared the wedding itself—the crowds, the singing and the dancing, the gaiety that she could never feel. But most of all she feared the bridegroom, Berish, a shadowy figure whose face she had not yet seen, the man to whom she was soon to be bound, spiritually and physically, for the rest of her life. This very night she would be required to submit her body, the body that she had withheld even from Tadeusz, whom she had loved and desired, to an unknown bearded scholar. These and other thoughts that she had previously barred from her consciousness now began to plague her. Horrid images tortured the distraught girl, images of white bony fingers fumbling at her soft pink breasts while a sharp knee forced her legs apart and then…she refused to think anymore and sprang from her bed just as her mother entered the room to help her dress.

Later, as Miriam, clad in a demure, navy blue wool suit, her hair arranged in short curls, walked downstairs with her mother and sister, they passed Marika, who was going upstairs, her arms so laden with sheets and pillows that she could barely squeeze by on the narrow staircase. Marika caught Miriam's eye, blushed, and looked away. It was her job to prepare the girls' back bedroom, which would become the bridal suite for one week; during this time, Dina would sleep on a cot in Shloimeh's room.

The first week of a newlywed couple's marriage was called the

Week of the Seven Benedictions. Each night a small dinner party was held to cheer the bride and groom and to recite appropriate blessings for them. The cheering was necessary because upon consummation of the marriage, the bride became ritually unclean due to the blood she had shed in losing her virginity. She was therefore forbidden to her husband until she immersed herself in the *mikveh* eleven days later. The nightly celebrations were intended to lift the couple's spirits, as well as to tire them out so they would not feel depressed or, worse yet, submit to lust.

Miriam's entrance into the parlor occasioned a noisy outburst of greetings from the numerous aunts, cousins, and female friends who had gathered there.

"Look, here's the *kalla*! *Mazel tov*! What a beauty! *Ken eyne horeh*, may no evil eye befall her! *Oy*, how pale! What a lovely suit! A Paris design! Sit down, sit down!" The ladies bustled about, now leaning over to kiss Miriam or pinch her cheek, then running into the kitchen or out to the privy and back into the parlor again.

During all this time, little Shloimeh, who had already suffered his share of pinches, darted back and forth from the window to the table, where cakes and cookies were artfully laid out, surrounding the silver samovar.

Like every Orthodox Jewish bride or groom, Miriam was required to spend her wedding day in fasting and prayer so that all previous sins would be forgiven. She was only too happy not to eat; her stomach contracted violently at the very sight of food.

"They're here," Shloimeh's voice rang out suddenly, just as the sound of carriage wheels squeaking and horses snorting could be heard from outside.

Moments later the door opened and two women were ushered into the parlor. The other women ran to help them remove their heavy wraps and to inquire after their health and comfort.

"Come in, sit down," cried Chaya Rochel, their hostess until tonight, when they would stay at Kuneh's Inn. "Have some tea and cake," she exhorted. "How was the train ride?"

"The train ride?" grunted Malka, the older woman. "May my enemies have no worse train rides! Four times we had to stop because of the snow. And the wind blew through a crack in the window of our compartment till my ears rang with cold."

At the sound of Malka's hoarse voice, Miriam looked up curiously at the two guests. Malka, the *chusen's* mother, was short and fat, with a double chin and a shapeless, gray-brown marriage wig that rested somewhat askew on her head. She wore a tired-looking gray wool suit and thick, lumpy brown boots. *I wonder that she doesn't take greater pains to dress well, especially on this day*, thought Miriam. *You'd think she'd want to make a good impression on her future daughter-in-law's family.*

Miriam's gaze moved to Malka's daughter, Fayge, who stood silently behind her mother. A bit taller than Malka, Fayge was slight of build and extremely thin. She appeared to be in her mid-twenties and had a small, pinched face with a sharp pointed nose and chin, thin lips, and bright black eyes that took in everything at once. Her dark brown, frizzled hair was knotted clumsily at the nape of her neck in a bun from which numerous curly strands had escaped, standing out about her head like a crinkly halo. In her loose, heavy brown wool dress with its white collar and cuffs, she reminded Miriam of a scrawny bird. The thought brought a slight smile to the young bride's lips when she realized how appropriately the girl was named; *fayge* is the Yiddish word for bird.

"And here is the *kalla*!" bubbled Chaya Rochel, proudly leading the two women to Miriam's chair while Dina nudged her sister to stand up and greet her guests. For a moment Malka stared at Miriam wordlessly as her eyes swept over the girl's comely face and figure. Then, finding her tongue, she sputtered, "Hello, how do you do? I'm so happy to meet you at last," and gave Miriam a brief embrace, tilting her head so Miriam could kiss her cheek.

Fayge extended a delicately boned hand. "How do you do?" she murmured, giving Miriam a piercing glance before quickly turning away. Miriam shivered slightly, despite the warmth from the fireplace.

Miriam found herself barely able to make conversation with her aunts and cousins, who attributed her reticence to a bride's nervousness. Cousin Gina, who with Uncle Zev had arrived yesterday by train from Cracow, gave an animated account of their journey.

"Why didn't you come in your motorcar?" demanded Aunt Hindy. Uncle Zev was the only member of the clan who owned an automobile and was considered a bit "modern" as a result.

"What? In this snow? It could never make the trip," explained Aunt Gina.

At the same time, Cousin Hadassah whispered to some of the other women that she could wait no longer and was going to the study house in the hope of catching a glimpse of the *chusen*. Two other cousins hastily put on their overcoats and accompanied her into the frosty afternoon. Lunch was just about to be served when they returned, complaining that the windows of the *beis medrash* were so dirty they could barely see anything, including the groom. Miriam watched listlessly as the women sat down to a meal of stuffed cabbage, calves' feet jelly, and fruit preserves. Someone had placed a book of psalms in her lap earlier, as she was supposed to recite them off and on during the day. She looked down at the pages, but the black letters swam before her eyes, a meaningless jumble. Instead, she moved her lips quietly in an imitation of prayer so as to dispel any doubts about her piety. Toward evening the parlor emptied as everyone hurried home to dress for the wedding. Miriam was escorted to her room, for a bride on her wedding day is considered especially vulnerable, not only to the evil eye, but to various malevolent spirits eager to pounce on a newlywed.

In the bedroom, Dina unwrapped the wedding dress that had hung on the wall these past two weeks, swathed in paper, since its return from the shop of Itche the tailor. The wedding gown had belonged to the girls' beloved Aunt Shifra, Chaya Rochel's youngest sister. Her body had been racked and ultimately claimed by tuberculosis four years earlier, but her soul was presumably looking down from heaven with joy at the day's festivities.

Once dressed in the heavy satin gown, Miriam sat gingerly in the blue velvet chair that faced her bedroom mirror and table. At that point, Chaya Rochel carefully lifted the marriage wig out of the box, shaking it gently to release the flattened light brown tendrils. Then, with Dina's help, she set it on Miriam's head. It was Dubnitzer tradition for brides to wear their *sheitels* during the wedding as well as afterward.

"So, Miriam," asked Dina. "How do you like it? You won't be *'Miriam Rote'* anymore."

Miriam smiled, but said nothing as her mother put a white satin cap with a long, heavy veil atop the *sheitel.*

"*Nu!*" cried Aunt Sara's voice from downstairs. "Are you all dressed yet? We must leave for the inn."

Marika helped Miriam into her heavy overcoat. Although she had only worked for the family a few months, Marika had quickly replaced Katya as the girls' friend and confidante. Now Miriam squeezed the young woman's hand, for she had seen the tears fill Marika's eyes and knew that the maid was remembering her own wedding day and the strong young man who had died so soon after in a hunting accident.

Outside, an imposing, gilt-trimmed brown brougham stood waiting. Two chestnut mares hitched to the carriage stamped impatiently, breathing clouds of steam into the cold twilight. It was Kuneh's best carriage, reserved for special occasions, even funerals. "But never to carry the casket, only the mourners," Kuneh would explain whenever people questioned the propriety of using the same carriage for two such different events.

Antek, the Polish wagon driver, climbed down from his seat but did not offer to help the Hasidic women into the carriage, knowing they would not touch the hand of any man but their husband or son. Antek watched in amusement as Aunt Sarah, Aunt Hindy, Chaya Rochel, and Dina clambered awkwardly into the coach. But Miriam looked regal, assisted by the others as she climbed daintily in and slid easily into a narrow space. The rest of the family would walk to the inn, where the men, including Shloimeh, were already waiting.

Cousin Gina, trudging in the snow behind the brougham, complained to her sister Esther, "In the snow we have to walk? They couldn't provide a few more carriages? Even a wagon would have been better."

"*Feh*!" retorted Esther. "Who wants to ride in an open wagon and arrive all full of straw and smelling like God knows what? Better to walk."

"And why did she have to pick the winter for her wedding? If it were in spring, summer, or even fall, they could have had the ceremony at the *shul*, with the *chupa*, the canopy, outside."

"Well, you'd still have to walk to the inn after the ceremony," responded Esther. "And you'd be walking in the mud probably, like at Raizel's wedding in Zhamotsk. Remember how you ruined the new suede shoes that Zev bought you in Lemberg? Anyway, Kuneh's has a special window over the *chupa*, and when they open it, they're under the stars, so it's just as good. And besides, once you're there, you're there. Look, here it is already." Esther pointed at the whitewashed stucco two-story building with its gray slate roof, a short distance away. An air of gaiety radiated from the house, due perhaps to the bright yellow light shining from the windows onto the snow and to the strains of Hasidic music emanating from within.

Esther and Gina stepped into the inn's warm, brightly lit anteroom, where their heavy winter wraps were taken away by a robust peasant woman. They were then ushered into a larger room to the right, where golden ribbons were wrapped around the oak support beams that crisscrossed the wide ceiling. The ribbons had been supplied by Gitele, an elderly woman who sold notions and trimmings. Gitele's husband was a Dubnitzer Hasid. The ribbons had been promised by Gitele's husband the very day he had received the news, almost nineteen years ago, that the *rebbe*'s wife had given birth to a daughter. Soon the room was filled with noise as more and more women crowded in. Miriam was ensconced in a tall, gilded armchair whose wooden trim was decorated with ornate flowers, leaves, and assorted curlicues designed to give it the appearance of a queen's throne. Small tables had been set up around the perimeter of the room, holding plates laden with tidbits of herring, slices of sponge and honey cake, and small glasses of brandy. These were merely to stimulate the guests' appetites in anticipation of the feast to come. A similar room had been set aside across the hall for the groom and his retinue. Most of the male guests, after a brief venture into the bride's room, retired to the groom's chamber, where things were quieter. There they could enjoy a piece of schmaltz herring and a glass of schnapps while talking about business or the holy scriptures.

While no wedding could be considered complete without the services of the *klezmerim*, or musicians, Itzik Yankel, the *badchen*, was indispensable. He resembled a large crow as he fluttered about among the guests, swinging the tails of his black frock coat, now announcing the names of several distinguished parties, now introducing relatives from opposite sides to each other, but mostly making speeches and singing songs that aroused the guests either to laughter or tears. Itzik Yankel spent most of his time in the bride's room—he was something of a ladies' man—where he entertained himself royally among the chattering throng of women, whose emotions were more easily manipulated. Walking up to Miriam, he sang in his strong baritone:

> *Lovely Miriam, Miriam red,*
> *A blessing on thy covered head.*
> *No more for you the girlish laughter;*
> *Well you know what follows after.*
> *Once you're saddled with a groom,*
> *Say hello to mop and broom.*
> *Scrub the floors on hands and knees,*
> *Forget the flowers and the trees.*
> *With children coming, one, two, three,*
> *You'll soon forget you were ever free.*
> *The years will bring both joy and woe;*
> *Since Adam and Eve it has been so.*
> *But dry your eyes and fret no more-*
> *A cheerful thought is yet in store.*
> *The best of all you've yet to see:*
> *A mother-in-law yourself you'll be.*

The last line brought laughter and winks from the assembly, some of whom nudged each other and glanced furtively at Malka, the groom's mother, who smiled and nodded in acknowledgment of

Itzik Yankel's words. Fayge, her daughter, did not smile, but bit her lower lip and looked about nervously. Weddings were an ordeal for Fayge; she was certain everyone was talking about her or staring at her pityingly because she had years ago missed her chance at a husband and was now a *farsetzhene*, or one who is left sitting.

After exchanging a few pleasantries with several women, Itzik returned to the groom's chamber, where the men awaited the *badchen's toyreh*, his words of satirical wisdom, much more eagerly than they did the groom's speech, which would come between the ceremony and the dinner. It was the custom of the *badchen* to recite broad parodies of Talmudic *pilpul*, discourse. This was not considered sacrilegious at a wedding, but rather, good clean fun. He bowed low before the groom and Reb Mordche, who were seated next to one another at a long table strewn with pieces of herring, crumbs of cake, and empty or partially filled shot glasses and bottles of brandy. Waving his arms and gesticulating wildly with both thumbs, Itzik Yankel began chanting in the traditional, singsong Talmudic melody.

"Wha-at if a chicken lays an egg on the property of a neighbor? If the chicken is a speckled chicken and the egg is a speckled egg, does it go to the owner of the chicken? Reb *Simcha* Yossel," here Itzik Yankel began his practice of incorporating the names of guests present into the parody, "says, 'Only if the owner has freckles.' And what if he only has one freckle? Then you must count the owner's wife's freckles, according to Reb Kuneh of Dubnitz.

"If, however, the egg is white and the neighbor has a white beard, the egg belongs to the neighbor, according to Reb Leibele. But what if both have white beards, the neighbor and the chicken's owner? Then you divide the white and the yolk, but if one of them has a blond wife, she gets the yolk, which is yellow. If there is no blond wife, then the yolk goes to the one suffering from jaundice, God forbid, according to Reb Anshel Chaim. And if no one has jaundice, then may the good Lord be praised and thanked, who spares us from illness. And if the chicken is a rooster…"

And so it went, with Itzik Yankel posing and answering questions while the Hasidim grinned and at times chortled with laughter.

The moment he finished, to a round of applause and shouts of "*Yasher koach*, may you have strength!" the musicians struck up a familiar tune which signaled that the time for the veiling had come. Immediately, thirty of the younger Hasidim formed a line, and three abreast, faced the groom and began dancing backward in the direction of the main room where the women waited. "Once again," they sang, "there shall be heard in the cities of Judah and on the outskirts of Jerusalem the sound of joy and the sound of happiness, the voice of the groom and the voice of the bride."

Berish, the groom, walked behind the dancers, flanked by his uncle and Reb Mordche, while the rest of the men followed, singing and clapping. The women, hearing the music and the stomping of men's feet, quickly took their places behind the bride, jostling each other for spots that would give them a good view of the groom without bringing them too close to the men. Now the wedding had truly begun.

Chapter four

Dina reached down and squeezed Miriam's hand tightly. Miriam looked up at her little sister, and suddenly the tears that had been dammed up for so long began to fall down her cheeks. She tightened her grip on Dina's hand while reaching for her mother with the other. The assembled women, seeing Miriam's tears, wiped their own eyes and nodded approvingly, as it was customary and more than appropriate for a bride to weep at her wedding.

The noisy, black-garbed throng of men entered, veering suddenly to one side. This was the moment the women had all been waiting for. Berish stood before Miriam for the first time. Through a film of tears Miriam looked up and caught a brief glimpse of burning black eyes in a thin white face upon which sprouted the beginnings of a dark brown beard. Then the heavy veil was lowered, obliterating her vision. She vaguely heard her father recite the traditional speech to the new bride, recounting what her virtues should be—"like the mothers Sarah, Rivke, Rachel, and Leah, dutiful, pious, devoted to husband, home and children." The men then danced out again, and everyone prepared to enter the large back parlor of the inn, where the *chupa*, the wedding canopy, had been set up under a special opening in the roof.

As the three musicians played the traditional solemn tunes reserved for wedding ceremonies, the men sat down on one side of the room while the women found seats across from them. Separating the two groups, a long aisle, covered with a dark red strip of carpet, which led to the embroidered canopy held aloft by four gilded poles wrapped in gold velvet ribbons. The large anteroom where the veiling had taken place was now empty, save for Miriam, Dina, Chaya Rochel, and Reb Mordche.

The musicians struck up the Dubnitzer bridal march as Miriam was propelled along by her mother on one side and her father on the other. She felt her legs moving woodenly down the aisle, then up the two steps leading to the *chupa*. She became dimly aware of the music, and then of the cantor's voice rising in a benediction of welcome to the bride.

Suddenly she felt a firm push against her shoulder blades. "Walk, Miriam!" her mother whispered. Where do I go? she wondered, then remembered that she must circle the groom seven times, once for each of the seven days of creation. Holding her mother's hand, she walked around and around blindly, growing dizzy from the effects of fasting, and from her own disjointed thoughts. Unable to keep count, she would have continued circling had her mother not restrained her after the seventh orbit.

She heard the sound of Uncle Yaacov's voice as he chanted the blessing over the wine, followed by the Marriage Blessing. At that moment, her veil was lifted and a goblet of wine was thrust at her. "Drink, Miriam," Chaya Rochel said softly. "Drink the wine."

Miriam took a sip, then coughed as the warm, sweet wine seared her dry throat. It was the first liquid she had tasted since the night before. Looking up from the cup, she blinked in the light as a mass of dark-bearded faces swam before her eyes. In front of her, a short, thin young man with black eyes was holding out a small ring.

"Behold," he recited in a quavering voice, as Chaya Rochel lifted Miriam's hand towad him.

"Put out your finger," she hissed, pulling at Miriam's index finger.

"Thou art consecrated unto me, according to the laws of Moses and Israel," continued the young man, whom Miriam realized was Berish.

At once she drew her hand back, and the ring slipped to the floor. A gasp rose from the audience as everyone but Miriam and Berish quickly bent to search for the tiny gold band. Miriam stared at Berish over the backs of the others who scrambled about in the narrow space beneath the canopy. *He's thin and pale, like most Hasidic grooms*, she thought. *And also short, at least two inches shorter than me. We will look foolish together.*

Berish, aware of her scrutiny, flushed red and lowered his eyes. Just then Dina stood up, triumphantly brandishing the ring on her pinkie.

"Give it to Berish, you fool," hissed Chaya Rochel, thoroughly embarrassed. She had noticed her machteniste, the groom's mother, and Fayge, his sister, standing near the *chupa* and glaring at the proceedings while she and the others searched for the ring. Once again Berish recited the traditional marriage oath of consecration as he slipped the ring onto Miriam's finger, now tightly enclosed by Chaya Rochel's own two fingers to prevent another mishap.

Now Uncle Yaacov began reading the marriage contract, a lengthy document written in Aramaic, which specified the terms of the marriage, the dowry, and other details, none of which Miriam understood.

Then for what seemed to her like an eternity, the voices of one rabbi after another droned on and on, reciting the many wedding benedictions. Once again, Miriam was given a sip of wine.

Wrapped in a white linen napkin, the wine goblet, which had been placed on the floor, was now to be shattered in memory of the destruction of Jerusalem and the Holy Temple. Berish stamped on it, and it bounced to the left, but the familiar "crack" was not heard. Reb Mordche nudged the goblet back toward Berish with his foot, wondering what else would go wrong, as a few titters were heard from the ladies' section. Berish stamped on the glass again, and this time the glass shattered with a muffled pop. Cries of "*Mazel tov*! *Mazel tov*!" rose from the crowd, and the guests began kissing and embracing one another as the musicians struck up a merry tune.

Miriam and Berish were escorted down the aisle and through the hall to a small room off to one side, where for the first time, they would spend a few minutes alone while the wedding guests took their seats in the dining room. Miriam entered first and Berish followed. The room was cramped and chilly. A table and two chairs had been set up, with two cups of brandy and a few slices of cake laid out so the couple could break their fast.

Miriam eased herself into one of the hard-backed wooden chairs, smoothing the folds of her gown and arranging it neatly about her legs. She felt embarrassed and afraid to look at her new husband, who still hovered near the door. She broke off a small piece of honey cake, but it was dry as dust and crumbled to small fragments in her fingers. She felt no desire to eat or drink, only a mounting tension at the silence in the room. In a few minutes someone would knock on the door and call the couple to the dining room. Yet not a word had passed between the two. Finally, Miriam spoke. Looking up at Berish, she ventured timidly, "Perhaps you'd like a piece of cake?"

Berish, still standing against the closed door, jumped. "What? Cake? She offers cake, they offer cake. Cake and schnapps, schnapps and cake, honey cake, sponge cake," he muttered in an undertone, all the while rubbing his sparse beard with his fingers.

Miriam stared up at him as a cold chill ran through her. Surely this was not a normal way for a groom to act. He hadn't even looked at her, hadn't sat down, certainly had touched no food or drink, and now his muttering had given way to whispered words she could not hear but which seemed to be a repetitive chant of some sort.

Heavy knocking on the door startled both of them. Berish, who had been leaning against it, jumped away as the door swung open, revealing the faces of Reb Mordche and Chaya Rochel. "*Nu*, children," called the *rebbetzin*. "*Mazel tov*! Come out now, it's almost time for Berish's speech, and for the dinner. Miriam, everyone is waiting to dance with you."

Miriam rose quickly and followed her parents, eager to escape the little room and the strange young man who had now stopped chanting but continued to rub his chin with pointed, yellowish-white fingers whose nails, she saw, were bitten to the quick.

Loud and merry dance music greeted the couple as they entered the dining room, which had been divided by a five-foot-high wooden barrier into two separate areas, one group of tables for men and one group for women. On either side of the tables was an open space for dancing. Some girls were already doing a graceful circle dance on the ladies' side of the room, while a group of young men, arms and legs flying, began a frenzied *kazatzka* on the other.

In the center of the room, facing the two groups of tables, was the head table, with the musicians in front. Miriam felt herself being swept into the circle of dancers. Round and round she was pulled, her feet barely touching the ground, as first her mother, then Dina, followed by aunts, cousins, mother-in-law, sister-in-law, and finally all the friends and neighbors, each took their turn. Everyone wanted to dance with the bride. She was conscious only of the music, playing louder and faster, swirling above her head, reaching crescendos and breaking over her like waves as her feet carried her in ever widening circles. A kaleidoscope of faces, lights, and sound whirled about her, the colors and shapes spinning and merging into one another, when suddenly, everything went black and Miriam slumped senseless to the floor, the folds of her satin gown curling about her like the stiff petals of some huge white blossom.

A waiter was dispatched to bring a glass of water, into which Chaya Rochel quickly dipped her fingers, sprinkling the cool droplets onto Miriam's pallid face. The other women clustered about, shouting words of advice over the music, which continued playing as loudly as before, as the men went on dancing, knowing nothing of what transpired on the other side of the barrier.

Miriam opened and closed her eyes, trying to blink away the gray haze that obscured the sea of faces bending over her. "Mama," she begged, "please take me out, take me out, take me away, just for a minute, Mama."

Chaya Rochel and Dina helped Miriam stand up. With her arms around their shoulders, she walked unsteadily between them as

Cousin Gina tried to straighten the wrinkled folds of the bridal gown. Dina and Chaya Rochel led Miriam to the small room where, just a short while before, she had first been alone with Berish. Lowering Miriam onto a chair, Chaya Rochel wiped her daughter's brow with a handkerchief. "Miriam, what is it?" she queried. "Are you feeling better? It must be the fasting. Didn't you eat anything in here?"

"No, Mama. The cake was too dry."

"*Nu*, so you haven't eaten at all. Even last night you pecked at the food like a bird. Are you all right? I myself ate almost nothing for three days before I married your father. I'd look at the food and become dizzy. But maybe a little tea? Dina, go and tell Shloimeh to ask Itzikel for a cup of tea. Or maybe ask a waiter, if you see one."

"Yes, Mama, but I can't go to the men's section now, because I think Berish is giving his speech. I'll try to find a waiter."

Dina left the room. Miriam leaned back in her chair and sighed softly. It was a relief to be away from the crowd of women; the mingled smells of food, stale perfume, and sweat; the loud, insistent music; and the pounding of dancing feet on the hard parquet floor. From this room, with its thick plaster walls and heavy oak door, the noise sounded like a muffled roar, punctuated now and then by the whine of Mendel's violin.

She gazed at her mother's face, with its smooth plump cheeks, its tiny crow's feet radiating from the corners of her warm brown eyes, and the creases near her mouth, whose lips pressed together in concern for her daughter's health. A feeling of love and longing swelled in Miriam's chest, bringing hot tears to her eyes. "Oh, Mama, I want to stay with you forever. Don't make me go away with Berish. I'll always be a good daughter, and I'll take care of you and *Tati*. You won't need Marika anymore. Oh, let me stay with you, Mama," she pleaded.

"Nonsense, Miriam," Chaya Rochel exclaimed as tears filled her own eyes. "Of course you will go with Berish, and be a good Jewish wife. How could you think of staying home and being like a maid? Why, you can't even cook an egg." She forced a laugh, trying to sound cheerful and thereby raise both her daughter's spirits and her own.

Just then Dina entered, holding a steaming glass of tea wrapped in a napkin. "Here, Miriam," she said, putting the glass on the table, whose cloth was still littered with crumbs from the sponge and honey cake. "Drink some tea. It will settle your stomach."

"Oh, you should hear," she went on eagerly. "Berish is giving his speech. It's so profound I couldn't understand a word. Nobody could, I'll bet, except maybe *Tati*. Something about the number seven—seven windows, seven circles, I don't know. What a *talmid chachem*, a learned scholar. I was so proud for you."

Miriam smiled wanly and sipped at the tea, which burned her lips and tongue. There was a soft knock, and Cousin Gina's face, still flushed from dancing, appeared in the doorway. "How are you, Miriam? Are you feeling better?" Without waiting for a reply, she continued. "It's not uncommon at all. It happens all the time, in fact. Remember the wedding of Dvoyreh, the daughter of the Pinsker *Rebbe*? Twice, she fainted dead away, once under the *chupa*, and once during the meal. I'll never forget it. There she was, standing under the canopy, when suddenly bang! Down on the floor."

"No," interrupted Dina, "her mother caught her as she fell. I saw it, too. There was no room under the *chupa* for her to land on the floor."

"What's the difference? She fell, anyway," Gina went on. "They revived her with drops of wine. So stupid. The drops sprinkled on her gown and veil. Wine doesn't come out so easily. Probably her dress was ruined."

"Maybe she could dye it pink," suggested Dina.

"Pink, shmink! I'm sure it was ruined. Then during the meal, one minute she's sitting up talking, then bang! Her head practically in the soup. Speaking of soup, they're starting to serve dinner. If you can get up, Miriam, you should come. Everyone is worrying."

Dina and Chaya Rochel helped Miriam out of her chair, smoothing the folds of her gown and holding her elbows lest, like the famous Dvoyreh, she faint again. Gina flitted alongside them, clucking solicitously and reaching out every so often to touch Miriam's sleeve or the edge of her veil.

As they entered the large, hot dining room, a hush fell over the women, and only the strains of Mendel's violin and the murmuring of the men, seated at their tables on the other side of the room, could be heard. Miriam, Dina, and Chaya Rochel sat down at the women's head table, next to the wooden barrier that separated them from the men. Dina glared at the divider bitterly. Except for when she had walked down the aisle, Leibel Parnes could not see her, nor she him. Not all Hasidic weddings had dividers between the men's and women's tables, but all Dubnitzer weddings did. *It's ridiculous*, thought Dina. *Husbands and wives and sisters and brothers eat at the same table at home. The husbands and wives sleep together at night. So why can't they sit together at a wedding?* She sighed deeply, the knowledge that her own wedding would undoubtedly be exactly the same momentarily dampening her high spirits.

Miriam picked at the chicken and potato pudding on her plate. She had forced herself to down some of the steaming chicken soup, with its golden circles of fat, since that task required only swallowing; chewing took more energy than she could muster. Between each course the musicians intensified their efforts, and the dancing began anew. Miriam sat back, relieved that no one pressed her to join in for fear that she might faint again. One or another friend or relative sat beside her during the dances and tried to make conversation but soon gave up, bored by Miriam's lackluster responses.

"What's wrong with Miriam?" Cousin Esther collared Cousin Roiza as the latter stepped out of the circle of dancers, her breasts heaving in a tight black satin bodice whose tiny rhinestone buttons threatened to escape their moorings for destinations unknown.

"Who knows?" gasped Roiza, sinking into a small folding chair that barely contained her ample behind. She mopped her brow and upper lip with a yellowed lace handkerchief. "Maybe she's not so pleased with the *chusen*. I'll tell you, he looks like a strange duck to me. Did you hear his speech?"

"No, I was talking to Zippoyreh. What did he say, anyway? Everybody said he was such a learned fellow. He certainly looks it. Pale as a ghost."

"Who knows what he said? None of us understood it. Even Chava, who learned in the Beth Jacob school in Warsaw, said it was all gibberish to her. Couldn't make head or tail of it."

"And what's this about Miriam leaving Dubnitz? I thought they would live here, near her mother. Who ever heard of the rabbi's daughter moving so far away, to some little village at the end of the world? What will she do there?"

"Well, from what I heard, it seems the *chusen*'s mother has a bakery. Maybe she needs Miriam to bake the bread and the egg cookies, or punch down the *challah* dough." Roiza shrugged her shoulders.

"Why does she need Miriam to do that? How did she manage all those years without her? Besides, she has a daughter to help her." Esther jerked her head in the direction of Fayge, who stood off to the side as she had all evening, watching the dancers with a slight smirk on her thin lips.

"That plucked chicken?" Roiza shook her head. "You think the likes of her would stand over a hot oven? No. Poor Miriam will have her arms up to the elbows in flour. I tell you, it's not proper for the Dubnitzer's daughter."

"True, but it's better than her being an old maid, like that Fayge, isn't it? And after the whole incident—you know what I'm talking about—who knows who would have married her? So now she'll go away and live in Berish's village, and maybe after a while it will all be forgotten, and then perhaps they'll come back, please God, with a wagonload of children."

"*Oy*, I hope so." Roiza sighed and pushed a few hairs under her heavy marriage wig, whose black shiny curls bore little resemblance to the thin gray wisps that had managed to escape. She knew about the incident that Esther alluded to, although none of the women were familiar with any details. Something about a Polish boy; it was too shameful to discuss, except in hushed tones.

The musicians began packing up their instruments as soon as the dessert dishes were cleared away. It was time for the Seven Benedictions, which accompanied the Grace after Meals. The Dubnitzer and his brother, along with other important Hasidim, intoned the blessings. A hard knot formed in the pit of Miriam's stomach. The wedding was over. Although she would be returning to her mother's house, and even to her own bedroom, everything would be changed. She would be sharing that room not with Dina, as she had every night for the past sixteen years, but with Berish, the specterlike individual who now sat on the other side of the wooden barrier.

As the wedding party left Kuneh's Inn, Miriam's elbow brushed against Berish's. He hurriedly snatched his arm away. Miriam climbed into Reb Kuneh's coach, the same one that had brought her to the wedding. Although Berish was seated beside her, they did not look at each other. Reb Mordche and Chaya Rochel sat opposite the couple. An embarrassed silence that seemed to emanate from the bride and groom affected the bride's parents as well, so that all four sat dumbly, staring out of the coach's windows for the duration of the ride.

When they arrived at the house, Miriam rushed upstairs, while Berish stayed below, in Reb Mordche's study. Chaya Rochel crept off to her own bedroom. Dina and Shloimeh, who had come home in a separate carriage crowded with aunts, uncles, and cousins, went to sleep in Shloimeh's tiny bedroom, barely big enough to accommodate the cot that had been set up for Dina.

The bedroom was so cold that Miriam could see her own breath as she lit the lamp. She turned toward the beds, which were heaped with quilts and counterpanes, gifts from Aunt Sima and Uncle Yaakov, and topped with white featherbeds. They looked like two snow-covered mountains. Miriam wished she were already under the covers, on her way to sleep. Shivering both with cold and nerves, she could barely undo the tiny buttons of her gown. She could not keep her teeth from chattering.

Eventually, she stepped out of her wedding gown and laid it across the chair. Then she took off her marriage wig and set it back in its box on the dresser. In the dim lamplight the wig looked like a small, furry animal in its burrow. Miriam covered the wig box and glanced at herself in the tall, gilt-edged mirror. In her silken slip and short reddish curls she looked like a small child. Removing the slip, she glanced at her smooth naked limbs, then quickly knelt and raised the lid of the carved oak hope chest that stood at the foot of her bed. Reaching in among the tablecloths, napkins, underwear, and nightclothes, she pulled out a white flannel gown and slipped it over her head, enjoying its softness and warmth. Miriam looked in the mirror again. The nightgown's high neck and long sleeves were trimmed with ivory satin ribbon. *It would look so much better if my hair were long, like before,* she thought, giving her curls a shake.

Suddenly, Miriam dove under the bedcovers as a floorboard on the steps creaked softly. Someone was coming upstairs. Since early childhood, whenever she had lain awake at night waiting for her parents to return from a wedding, a condolence call, or some other social obligation, Miriam had been able to identify the footsteps of her family members. *Tati*'s were heavy and decisive, Mama's also heavy but more hesitant. Dina's were light and quick, and Shloimeh's loud and clattering. The footsteps she now heard were soft and slow, like Marika's, but Marika had left for home shortly after the wedding. Miriam huddled down under the covers. Panic rose in her chest. She hugged her knees and stared, wide-eyed, as the brass door handle turned.

Berish's slight, stooped figure stood in the doorway. With the light of the hall lamp shining behind him, he was a black silhouette in a frame. Miriam watched as he entered the room and set his battered leather suitcase inside the closet. His dark eyes flitted about, taking in the gilded armchair, the heavy dresser, the hope chest, the vanity table and bench, and last, the two beds, one of which held her own curled-up form. Without acknowledging Miriam, he began undressing, first removing his black wide-brimmed hat and placing it on the dresser next to Miriam's wig box. Moving from the dresser to the vanity table, Berish reached a bony hand under the fringed linen shade and turned off the lamp, plunging the room into darkness.

For a few moments Miriam, seeing nothing, tracked Berish's movements by the sound of his breathing. Then gradually, her eyes became accustomed to the dark, aided by a thin shaft of moonlight that slanted between the heavy drapes and lent a faint luminescence to objects in the room. Berish sat on the other bed with his back to her. He had removed his black gabardine and white shirt and now wore his ritual fringed garment, the tzitzis, over a flannel undershirt. She could not see the lower part of his body. As she watched him in the pale moonlight, she became aware of a whispering, disembodied voice that seemed to hover above her head, somewhere between the bed and the ceiling. It took several seconds before she realized that the voice was Berish's, and that the words were Hebrew.

49

He must be chanting the Prayers-Upon-Going-to-Bed, she thought in wonder. *Now he won't be allowed to speak until morning. When, then, will he perform the marital duties? Are you supposed to pray first and then do it? Without talking?* Miriam couldn't remember anyone telling her where the bedtime prayers fit in all this. She stopped pondering this dilemma when Berish, in one abrupt, arcing motion, thrust two spindly legs clad in long white underpants across the bed. His feet landed on the floor between the beds, and he stood up and faced her. He was still whispering, but now Miriam could make out a few of the words. *It's not the bedtime prayers*, she realized. After several minutes Berish stopped chanting. Miriam sat up and looked at him. The planes of his face held a faint glow and the whites of his eyes shone coldly.

"Berish?" she whispered.

"I am not Berish."

"Not Berish?" His unexpected remark, combined with the pent-up tension Miriam had been feeling, brought nervous laughter to her lips. "Who are you then, the *tzaddik* of Pilsk?"

Berish's bony hand shot out and clutched Miriam's shoulder. She gasped, both from shock and the pain of his pincerlike grip. "You dare to laugh? Maybe you will laugh again when you know who I am. Our matriarch Sarah laughed when God's angel told her she would bear a son. 'Therefore they called his name Isaac.' Laugh and rejoice, Daughter of Zion. God has chosen you, Miriam of Dubnitz, to accompany me on my sacred mission." He relaxed his grip, but his hand remained on her shoulder.

"Sacred mission?" she whispered. She felt a vague fear. Could this be the same pale *yeshiva* student who had been too shy even to look at her, let alone speak, when they had previously been alone together?

"Yes, you will soon know. But not now. The time is not yet ripe. First I must perform, ah, the other mission."

His hand slowly slid from her shoulder, and he lightly touched the point of her breast, then held the nipple between his two fingers. Through the cloth of her nightgown, his sharp fingers felt like the beak of a predatory bird. An image flashed through her mind—black, greasy-feathered crows perching at the garbage pile outside the village marketplace. Despite her mother's admonitions regarding a good wife's duty, her body froze. She clamped her legs together and stiffened her back, but she had no leverage against Berish, who now leaned over her and pressed her shoulders down onto the soft, fluffy pillows that were part of her dowry.

Miriam was amazed at the strength in his frail-looking body. She felt her nightgown being pushed up above her waist. As in her premarital nightmares, her legs were pried apart by a bony knee. *What's the use of resisting*, she thought. *Give in and have it over with*. She opened her legs weakly, then gasped with pain as she felt something hard ramming into her most secret parts, tearing her open, slamming into her again and again while she bit her lip to keep from crying out. When it was over, Miriam lay numbly on the bed, listening as Berish washed at the pink and white porcelain washstand she and Dina had always used. She, too, would have to wash, but she felt too miserable to get up. Her body was sore, within and without, and she felt defiled, both physically and spiritually. A sticky fluid oozed from her; she felt it seep slowly across her thigh. *Well, at least I'm forbidden to him now*, she thought, *until I go back to the* mikveh. *Maybe I'll never go.*

As if he read her thoughts, Berish spoke. "Now you are truly consecrated unto me. I must now wait for the next sign. When it is revealed, you will know. You will know whom you have married and for what I have been created."

He then climbed into the other bed, and soon she heard his whispered voice again muttering unfamiliar Hebrew and Aramaic words. She listened, and after a while was able to make out a few words of the Prayers-Upon-Going-to-Bed, which soon gave way to soft snoring. *He's asleep. I'll never be able to fall asleep*, thought Miriam. But even then, her thoughts began to drift, and soon she, too, was breathing the light breaths of the dreamer.

Chapter five

The first day of Miriam's married life dawned bright with sunlight. The snow that lay piled on the streets sparkled like millions of diamonds, causing the little boys to squint as they hurried along the narrow pathways on their way to *cheder*. Standing by the bedroom window, Miriam shaded her eyes with her hand as she watched her brother Shloimeh join his friends. Slipping and sliding, the ragtag group of black-garbed children made their way to the study house, their metal lunch pails flashing in the sun and snow.

Miriam's heart swelled with love for the little figure in the long black overcoat. She thought of the times she had cradled him in her arms when he was a baby, and of the many games they'd played as he grew bigger and more talkative. She and Dina had always vied for his affection, competing over who could make him laugh more with her jokes or tell him more interesting stories. Shloimeh had delighted in all the attention. Though he enjoyed playing one against the other, he adored them both. Miriam pictured Shloimeh in the *cheder*. She could almost hear his childish voice reciting his daily lesson. Tears filled her eyes and her throat ached. *How I'll miss him*, she thought, *and Mama, and* Tati, *and Dina. All of this*. She looked around at the familiar room, with its flowered wallpaper and rumpled beds. Her gaze fell on the sleeve of a satin nightdress protruding from beneath the lid of her trousseau chest, and she sighed. *How odd it is*, she thought, *to live in the same house day after day, and sleep in the same bed night after night, for almost nineteen years. You feel as if it will go on forever, and then, one day, everything changes, and you must leave it all behind you. Whether you want to or not.* She moved from the window and sat down on her bed.

The soreness between her legs reminded her of last night's experience. Reaching under her shirt, she adjusted the cotton padding she had placed there to absorb the slight flow of blood that had resulted from her union with Berish. The flow would soon abate, she knew, but until she had seven "clean" days and went to the *mikveh*, Berish could not touch her again, and for that she was thankful. Someone knocked, making Miriam jump. Berish, she knew, would be at the study house all day. He had left even before it was completely light, taking with him his phylacteries and his new *talis*, the striped prayer shawl her father had given him.

Dina entered, blushing deeply. "Miriam, Mama wants you to come down for breakfast. But if you don't want to eat, that's okay, too. A *kalla* can do whatever she wants. Everyone will understand." She looked away.

Miriam rose and washed her hands at the washstand. "What's to eat?" she asked listlessly, drying her hands on the embroidered linen towel that hung on a hook by the door.

"Oh, herring, potatoes, some kasha, coffee—you know." She gave Miriam a sidelong glance, then looked down. "So, how are you, Miri?"

"How should I be?"

"Well, was it, you know, I mean, did he, are you…" Dina bit her lip self-consciously.

Miriam stared at her sister. It wasn't often that Dina was at a loss for words. Still, she had no intention of discussing the intimate details of last night with anyone. As much as she loved her younger sister, she had never confided in Dina before, and she wasn't about to begin now. Dina had too big a mouth. She was apt to blurt out the wrong thing at the worst possible time.

The small, hot kitchen bustled with noise and movement as the two sisters entered. Both Marika and Chaya Rochel were embarrassed at confronting the new bride now that she was, presumably, no longer a virgin. To ease her own discomfort, Marika moved busily about, bringing steaming plates of food to the table with much clattering of crockery and tinkling of glasses and silverware. Chaya Rochel occupied herself with refolding the soft muslin napkins that Marika had already placed at each setting.

When Miriam was seated, Chaya Rochel glanced at her, noting the dark wine-tinged circles under the soft green eyes, and the pallor of her cheeks, with their prominent cheekbones. *She has lost weight*, thought the *rebbetzin. Truly, with all the excitement of the past few weeks, she has eaten almost nothing. Her nerves have always been too delicate. But she'll soon start to fill out again. And with God's help, after the children come, she'll wish she had her girlish figure back.* She put her hands on her own plump hips and smiled, remembering herself as a new bride.

The Week of the Seven Benedictions passed uneventfully. Miriam spent her days going through her belongings, carefully folding her treasured dresses and shawls and placing them in her trunk along with her new nightgowns and robes. Each evening a different group of Hasidim and their wives, along with a few cousins, came to have dinner with the family and to recite the Seven Benedictions after the meal. Berish and Miriam sat at the head of the long table. They exchanged no words, nor any loving looks or smiles, as new brides and grooms sometimes do. But this was not unusual in Hasidic circles, where newly married couples were often strangers to each other and embarrassed by the new intimacy that they had shared on their wedding night.

After the meal, Berish went back to the study house, returning late in the night, after Miriam had gone to bed. She would listen in frozen silence to his chanting and mumbling until she fell into a heavy slumber, full of confused, fragmented dreams. At dawn, he was off again. The day before their departure, Miriam appeared early at the breakfast table. She stabbed wearily at a few pieces of herring on her plate and tasted a bit of boiled potato, which clung like thick paste to her dry mouth. She tried to join in the conversation around her but could not concentrate on talk of the cold weather, the quality of the raisin cake, and the health of Yoizel, the ancient carthorse who occupied the flimsy stable at the other side of the courtyard.

Abruptly, she rose from her chair, which bumped against the table, spilling some of her untouched coffee on the yellow linen cloth. "I'm sorry, Mama," Miriam exclaimed as she clumsily tried to blot the spreading stain with her napkin.

"It's nothing, Miriam. Marika, bring her more coffee," exhorted her mother.

"No, Mama, I'm going out, I want to go to the shops."

"I'll come with you," offered Dina, eagerly rising from her own chair and spilling more coffee as she did so.

Although she had wanted to be alone with her sorrowful thoughts, Miriam could think of no excuse to offer Dina, so the two girls went into the foyer together to put on their heavy coats and shawls and overshoes. The sharp wind and the sunlight reflected by the snowdrifts brought tears to the girls' eyes.

"Miriam, listen." Dina smiled conspiratorially, oblivious to her older sister's drawn face and tight lips. The wind that brought a rosy glow to Dina's full cheeks reddened only the tip of Miriam's delicate nose, making her cheeks appear even whiter than usual. "Mama told me that Yudel the *shadchan* spoke to Papa about me. Oh, let's sit down, my toes are frozen." Dina indicated a weathered wooden bench that stood outside the bakery.

The two sisters gathered the skirts of their long woolen overcoats and sat. Miriam wrapped her shawl more tightly about her thin shoulders and squinted at Dina, who babbled on joyously, her breath forming frosty clouds about her bright face. "I told Mama she must tell Papa to tell Yudel that he should speak to… guess who?"

"What? Who?" murmured Miriam distractedly.

"Leibel! Leibel Parnes. Oh, Miriam, you're not even listening to me. You know I've always liked Leibel. And I know he likes me, too."

"Leibel? He likes you?"

"Yes, I can tell by the way he looks at me, after *shul*, when he walks past. I was standing outside with Leah Freilich and Gitty Posen, and they noticed it, too. He looks right at me, all the time. At first Leah thought it was her that he was looking at, and she got so excited. But Gitty and I showed her the next *Shabbes* that it was really me. Boy was she burnt up. As if Leibel would look at Leah, anyway, with her long horse face."

Dina paused and pulled down the corners of her mouth in imitation of the hapless Leah, but Miriam did not laugh. She gazed at Dina, her face immobile, her body as rigid and motionless as the iron fence palings that jutted out of the sooty snow beside them.

"So," continued Dina, "Mama said that if Papa consented—and I know he will, he's always spoken well of Leibel—and if Leibel agrees—and oh, I hope he will…What if he doesn't? But of course he must. Everyone can see he likes me." She clasped her hands and smiled dreamily, consciously emulating the beautiful noblewoman seated in a rose-covered bower in the painting that hung in her friend Gitty's parlor.

"So, Mama said maybe I could get engaged right after *Purim*, and maybe even get married right after *Shavuos*! And she's so excited. 'To think,' she said, 'two weddings in one year.' Oh, I hope Papa will agree. And Leibel, too, of course." She looked hopefully at Miriam, awaiting a sign of approval or even interest.

"Miriam, what is it? What's wrong?" Dina reached out to her sister, who was staring at her in horror. Bright teardrops left icy streaks in their wake as they coursed slowly down Miriam's cheeks to her chin.

"Oh, Dina," Miriam exclaimed in a choking voice. "Don't do it! Don't throw away your life like that. Don't rush to be a *kalla*. You're so young, only just sixteen. You still have years to enjoy being home, talking with your friends, playing with Shloimeh, helping Mama and Marika."

"But I could still do those things," interjected Dina. "I wouldn't want to stop. I'm not going far away, I'll be here—" She clapped her hand to her mouth, painfully aware of the words she had just blurted out. "Oh Miri, I'm sorry. I forgot you'll be leaving home. It's just so hard to imagine it." She put her arms around her sister and they clung to each other on the hard wooden bench, ignoring the curious glances of the peasants and laborers who stomped past on their way to work.

The warmth of her sister's embrace opened a floodgate, and Miriam sobbed bitterly against Dina's shoulder. "It's not fun to be a *kalla*, Dina. It's horrible, it's awful. Everyone thinks I'm lucky to have gotten a husband, especially a *talmid chachem*, after what happened, you know." A fresh flood of tears poured down her face, leaving a wine-colored stain on Dina's red shawl. "But they don't know what it's like. Berish, he's a stranger, a stranger, and that first night when we—oh, I can't speak of it!" She bit her lower lip and shook her head. "And the rest of the week, of course, he's not allowed to touch me. I'm glad for that, but not even to say one word?"

"You mean he never talks to you at all?" asked Dina, her eyes round.

"Almost never. At first he said I'd soon know who or what he was, or something. I thought he meant because he was a *talmid chachem*, that he intended to become a great sage. But now I don't know. He's always chanting and praying at night, and reading books I don't understand."

"What kind of books?"

"From the *Kabbala*, I think. Mystical works. One time he saw me looking at one, and he just grabbed it away and slammed it shut. He gave me the weirdest look and walked out. Weird, that's just what he is, Dina. He's weird. He scares me."

"But Miriam, maybe you should tell *Tati*. Or at least Mama. You should mention it to her. Maybe it's normal for a *talmid chachem* to act that way. And if it's not normal, well, shouldn't they know about it?"

Miriam looked at Dina. *She's growing up*, she thought. *She has more in her head than bridal gowns and trousseaux.*

"You're right. Maybe I should say something to Mama." *Not to Tati*, she thought with regret. He had avoided her ever since the incident with Tadeusz, refusing to believe that she was innocent of any wrongdoing. She had brought shame upon them, and Miriam had seen that shame reflected in his eyes on the rare occasions when he looked at her.

"Yes, I'll speak to Mama. Let's go home." The two sisters adjusted their heavy shawls and made their way back.

Several times that afternoon, Miriam tried to approach her mother, to talk with her alone. Each time, Chaya Rochel dismissed her, rushing about the kitchen helping Marika prepare a basket of food for the newlyweds to eat on the train.

"Mama, I must speak to you."

"Yes? In a moment, I'm coming."

But that moment never came, and as Chaya Rochel constantly busied herself with chores related to her daughter's departure, Miriam began to suspect that her mother was avoiding the opportunity to talk.

That evening, immediately after dinner, Chaya Rochel rose, bade her guests good night, and retired to her bedroom, announcing, "We must be up very early to see them off tomorrow morning."

Miriam tried to follow her but was intercepted by several female cousins and friends who hugged and kissed her as they made their tearful farewells. Cousin Gina threw her arms about Miriam and exclaimed, "*Oy*, Miriam, Miriam, what did they do to you, sending you off to the ends of the earth! Who knows when we'll see you again? You couldn't find yourself a nice *chusen* here in Dubnitz?" The other women looked away in embarrassment.

Miriam smiled and pressed Gina's hand. *A bride doesn't have to say a word*, she thought. *It's a bride's prerogative to stand quietly, smiling like an idiot, for hours. What does it matter that she's miserable inside, that she hates being married, that she can't stand her new groom and will certainly never 'learn to love him,' as the saying goes? No, none of it matters, just smile, smile like a moron*, thought Miriam bitterly.

Later, as she lay in her bed after tossing about for what must have been hours, Miriam heard Berish enter the room. As usual, she pretended to be asleep. Soon she heard him chanting, as he always did, but this time the words were in Yiddish, as opposed to his usual Hebrew or Aramaic prayers. A chill, like icy fingers, rippled along Miriam's spine as she strained to listen.

Berish rocked back and forth as he chanted:

Small is the cat,
smaller the rat,
smaller the mouse,
smallest the louse.
At the base of the mountain
lies a dark tunnel.
How does one reach it?
Only through a funnel.
What does one find
deep down in the cave?
Darkness of night,
darkness of the grave.

Berish's body rocked rhythmically back and forth as he chanted. Miriam opened one eye and squinted at him in the dark. He sat hunched forward in a chair, his back to her. Now and then, he raised his hands upward, fingers splayed, as in supplication, then lowered them again. She could no longer decipher his words but could still hear the rasping whisper of his voice.

Finally, he rose, walked to the window, cleared his throat, and said, "Blessed art Thou, O Lord, King of the Universe, who hath chosen me, Berish, the son of David, thy servant, as the Lord's anointed." With that, Berish pulled off his boots, removed his clothes, and climbed into bed.

Miriam listened as he began to snore, then she got up, taking care not to make a sound. She dressed hastily, hardly knowing which dress she chose in the blackness of her closet. She then felt under her bed for the small brocaded carpetbag she had packed that afternoon. It contained only one change of clothing, for the train journey. Holding it tightly in one hand, she softly pushed open the bedroom door.

She stiffened as the hook latch fell, clicking against the wooden door frame. But no sound followed, save Berish's throaty snores. Barely breathing, Miriam made her way down the stairs, avoiding the eighth step, which always creaked.

"Sixth step, fifth step, four, three, two, one," murmured Miriam as she descended. "Now if only I can get my shawl on quietly, then out the door and no one—"

"Miriam! What are you doing up so early? And dressed already. And why that old dress, anyway? That's not what we picked out for the trip."

Chaya Rochel smiled up at Miriam from the stairwell, her white nightdress billowing like a ghost in the dim lamplight.

"Oh, Mama, I couldn't sleep; I thought it was morning already. What time is it?"

"Why, it's about four. I couldn't sleep myself, and I came down to drink some tea. I was just going up."

"Four? Oh, isn't that funny, I thought it was five-thirty, and that it was time to get up, so I got dressed. Look, I even started bringing down the suitcases."

Miriam smiled brightly, hoping her mother was convinced.

"And did you wake Berish, too?"

"I tried, but he was fast asleep—oh, Mama, about Berish, please, I must talk to you."

"What is it?" asked Chaya Rochel, alarmed by Miriam's sudden shift in facial expression. Her daughter's smile had vanished, replaced by a look of wide-eyed anguish.

But even as she looked at her mother and tried to formulate her words, Miriam realized it was no use. What could she say? That her new husband chanted and prayed all night? That he barely spoke to her? That he had hurt her on their wedding night? Her mother had always been such a simple person, such an optimist, always dismissing problems with a wave of the hand and a trite Yiddish expression. She would surely do the same even now.

"Go back to sleep, Mama. It's too early."

"Ach, once I'm up I stay up. Is that Shloimeh? *Oy,* how he coughs. I'd better give him some honey." Her slippered feet padded into the kitchen.

Miriam set her bag down in the foyer and trudged wearily back upstairs. Without removing her clothes, she climbed under the eiderdown and curled her body into the still-warm hollow she had vacated moments before. Glancing over at Berish, she was just able to make out his features in the early morning dimness. Sunken cheeks like those of a much older man. Eyebrows drawn together in a frown. Thin lips, slightly parted, revealing the dull luster of a tooth. *He isn't really ugly*, thought Miriam. She closed her eyes and tried to picture herself walking with him down the main road of an unknown Polish village, Berish smiling at her as she slipped along the icy paths. But even as she gazed at him, in her mind's eye, Berish's face began to flicker and waver like a candle flame. Now he was growing taller, broader, and his face and hair were shining in the moonlight. It was no longer Berish but Tadeusz, in black caftan and broad-brimmed black hat, who smiled down at her. She reached out to touch his face and drifted off with him in a swirl of snowflakes and stars.

The morning dawned gray and chill, with a wind like a steel blade whipping along the twisted paths that led up from the river. A small black-clad crowd of relatives and friends huddled together outside the Rutner house to see the newlyweds off on their long journey. As the coach rounded the turn and made its way past Kuneh's Inn, those who had run after it fell away, until only the shrill voice of little Shloimeh was carried on the wind. "Goodbye Miriam, goodbye Berish, goodbye Miriam, goodbye Berish, goodbye, goodbye."

Beside a nearby stand of pines, a slim Polish woman in a red scarf smiled up at her handsome husband as she handed him his lunch pail. The tall blond Pole put down his load of wood and reached for the pail with one hand, encircling his wife's waist with the other. "Until this evening, Stefa," he murmured. He caressed her stomach, already slightly swollen with budding life.

"This evening, Tadeusz," replied his young wife.

Then both stood still and gazed at the dark coach that rounded the bend and rolled on under a leaden sky into the cold morning.

Chapter six

Pavlitz, Poland, 1936

Miriam!" Fayge's shrill voice sounded in her ear. "Six weeks you're here, and still you can't knead dough properly. Pretend it's me you're punching." Fayge's little black eyes twinkled at Miriam maliciously. "I know you think you're too good for us, too good for this work." She wiped a bit of dough from the tip of her sharp nose with a bony finger, leaving a smudge of flour. "The rabbi's daughter! I suppose you thought you'd sit home all day eating our cake while Berish sat and learned in the *beis medrash*." She shook her frizzled head. "What did you expect us to live on, your piddling dowry? Should we eat featherbeds and nightgowns? Times are hard, young lady; this is not Dubnitz. Things are bad here for Jews, and they're not going to get better, either. Have you been reading about that madman in Germany, Hitler? Do you think we'll be safe here, if he starts a war? One way or the other they're all after us, and one way or the other they'll get us. At least you've got a husband, you've enjoyed life a little. But what about me? Who will I ever find, stuck away in this miserable hole? Not like that, you dummy. Like this." She shoved Miriam to one side and began pounding the thick white dough viciously.

Miriam watched her sister-in-law silently. Angry words formed in her head, sharp retorts to Fayge's taunts, but as always she kept them to herself. She had learned from the first day that replying to Fayge in kind only brought on a fresh torrent of abuse. No, it did not pay to further antagonize this frustrated and bitter young woman. *Let her rant and rave*, thought Miriam. Her mind was already elsewhere. Ever since she had decided upon a solution to her problems, Miriam had been much calmer. Her eyes no longer filled with tears at Fayge's insults, and she had ceased to mind her mother-in-law's cold indifference, which alternated with fawning flattery. Besides, nothing she suffered at the hands of those two could compare with what she went through at night, when Berish came home.

For six weeks she had been forced to listen for hours each night as Berish expounded to her on biblical sources and commentaries, all of which were supposed to prove that he, Berish, son of David, was God's chosen and anointed Messiah, soon to reveal himself and deliver his people from the Diaspora to the Promised Land. If after a day of dull, grinding labor in the stifling bakery, Miriam's eyelids drooped or her head nodded during one of his lectures, Berish would rudely yank her arm or poke her in the chest to prevent her from falling asleep before he finished.

Miriam's head swam as he recited; she could see no connection between any of the biblical phrases and the gaunt, bearded figure swaying before her in the dim gaslight that illuminated the cold, cramped room they shared. After the biblical reading, the "ceremonies" began. These varied somewhat from night to night, but all involved one central theme—that of Berish as the Messiah, God's anointed. On some nights, Berish would light seven candles and then, gesturing at Miriam to follow, would march about the room, weaving in and out among the candles, chanting prayers and hymns of his own making. Miriam feared the house would be set afire. Once she singed the hem of her nightdress as she tripped past the dancing yellow flames. On other nights, he forced her to come outside with him so that he could roll naked in the banked snowdrifts. Miriam huddled against the wall of the house, shivering as she watched. When he finished, drenched and icy from head to foot, she wrapped a heavy blanket about him and followed him back to their room, where he dried himself with flannels from her hope chest, muttering incantations as he did so.

During the first weeks, his religious frenzy often aroused him sexually, and he would push Miriam down upon her bed and mount her clumsily, only to lose his erection. Since the night of their wedding, he had become impotent. One night, after removing his clothing, he had commanded Miriam to anoint his head and body with olive oil. When she demurred, he had pinched her cruelly on the arm, whispering, "You are my wife, you must be worthy of me, God's chosen Messiah. You must do my bidding or be driven out to the four winds." Choked with misery, she began spreading oil over his wispy black hair and then down over his thin, white body.

"More, more," he hissed.

"No!" she cried. "I cannot do this."

"What? You dare defy me?" Berish rasped. He reached out to take the bottle from her hand, but it slipped from his fingers and shattered on the floor, splashing the hem of Miriam's nightdress. The sight of the broken shards momentarily inflamed Berish. He leaped upon Miriam, shoving her against the hard wall. Miriam shut her eyes, fearing what would come next, but he shuddered violently and turned away from her. After that he never attempted to mount her again, rationalizing his impotence as a sign from God. According to the Scriptures, the Messiah was not to sire children. Miriam hid the soiled nightdress under a pile of rags behind the house and began planning her escape.

Escape. The very thought had become an obsession, filling her days and nights, giving her hope as she cut hundreds of sugar cookies or kneaded dough for the fragrant *challahs*, the Sabbath bread. Simple tasks in the bakery took on new meaning. While she performed the ritual of the separation of the *challah* dough, as was incumbent upon Jewish women, she related it to her own life. Pinching off a piece of the thick, fluffy dough, she rolled it into a little ball and placed it in the oven, watching as it became crisp and blackened. *That's me,* she thought ruefully. *That's the Miriam I was, the young single girl, happy at home with her family and her foolish dreams of romance. There I am, burnt to a crisp. The girl that I was no longer exists.*

During the first weeks, Miriam had suffered from a wretched loneliness that lay like a stone in her breast. Worse than the bizarre behavior of Berish, worse even than the exhausting, humiliating work in the bakery under Fayge's cruel tutelage, was the feeling of isolation that beset her hour after hour. Here she was, stranded in a tiny village, miles from a home that she had disgraced, and to which, therefore, she could not return.

She tried at first to approach her mother-in-law, who had seemed friendly at the beginning. "*Shvige* Malka," she began, tentatively touching the frayed brown ruffle that edged Malka's sleeve.

"Yes, my dear?" Malka gazed up at her from a pile of bakery receipts and ledgers and smiled, showing large, yellow teeth.

"I have to talk to you. About Berish."

"About Berish? Why should you talk to me about Berish? Talk to Berish about Berish! He's your husband, not mine. My husband is dead." She snapped the ledger book shut with a bang.

Miriam stared at the older woman, who had turned back to her dog-eared receipts. Could it be that Malka, too, like her daughter, begrudged Miriam her husband? What kind of people were these?

She began again. "I don't understand Berish's behavior." She flushed under Malka's piercing gaze.

"Of course not," retorted Malka. "What should you, a woman, a young girl, a child, know of Berish's behavior? What do any of us know of Berish? Who can understand him? He is an *ilui*, a genius. Why, at the age of three he was already reciting scriptures and commentaries by heart—by heart, I'm telling you! And didn't he know the entire tractate of *Nezikin* at the age of seven? *Oy*, how his father, of blessed memory, swelled with pride when he heard him recite it. Berish was always different from the other children. Always learning, always with his head in the holy books. "*Nu*, it's not for you to understand him. It's for you to serve him, and take care of him, and provide him, God willing, with children to delight him in his old age. You should be honored to be the wife of a scholar and sage like Berish! Why, he could have married the daughter of the Yodgeva *tzaddik*."

Miriam had heard the allusion to the daughter of the Yodgeva before from Fayge. It seemed that such a marriage had been in the offing a year earlier but had fallen through for some reason. She had first begun to suspect the reason while sitting in the rickety women's balcony under the pointed eaves of the wooden synagogue of Pavlitz. There, desperately lonely on her first *Shabbes* in Pavlitz, she had smiled at one or two of the young married women, only to be bitterly hurt by their response. Clad like Miriam in black or blue velvet dresses and stiff, brown marriage wigs, the women had given her the barest of smiles before turning their heads and whispering amongst each other. Later, while descending the steep wooden staircase, Miriam heard a whisper above her, "That's her. She married Berish the *meshuggene*, the lunatic."

So that's it, Miriam had thought. *That explains why everyone stares at me wherever I go, and why no one talks to me. That's why Sara Baila, the* mikveh *lady, looked at me so intently last week and asked such queer questions—"So, eh, how is your, ah, husband? So, ah, how does he feel? What is he, ah, doing?' They all know he's crazy, and they all think I'm crazy, too. Who else would marry Berish? They're almost right, anyway. If I stay here much longer, I'll soon be as crazy as he is.*

On Saturday night, after the blessing for the new moon marking the beginning of the month of *Shevat*, Berish stayed later than usual in the study house. Hunched over a tattered volume of Talmud, he swayed back and forth, murmuring hoarsely until his was the only figure left in the pine-paneled room. It was not Talmud that he recited, but one of the many incantations with which he implored God to send him a sign, a portent that it was time for him to finally reveal himself to his people. Had he not dreamed, just last night, that tonight his identity would be made known through the seven symbols that he, Berish, had discovered hidden in his prayer-book binding? The *siddur* had belonged to his saintly father, Reb David Sonnenblatt. Just last Wednesday, while praying the afternoon service, Berish had allowed his fingers to wander over the *siddur's* cracked and faded leather cover, and there, among the whorls and wrinkles, he had seen them: the ram, the stone, the star, the horse, the fish, the scale, and the sword—the same seven symbols that had appeared to him in his dream on Monday night, after he had immersed himself in the snow. And had not two of those symbols, the scale and the fish, appeared before him in the flame of the braided yellow *havdalah* candle when Yoinah the shammes had chanted the *havdalah* service, separating the Holy Sabbath from the profane week?

I must go home now, thought Berish, gathering up his books, *and wake Miriam. She will light the candles for me and help me look for the other five symbols. Last time she said that she, too, could see how the candle wax had formed itself into the ram and the stone.* Warmed by anticipation, Berish barely felt the icy wind as he walked through the deep snow that lay like a quilt on the sleeping village. Once inside his house, he hurried up the stairs and into the dank bedroom he shared with his wife. Leaning over her bed, he whispered, "Wake, woman, to the work of the Creator and His chosen Messiah." Hearing no murmur of response nor protest, Berish reached down to shake Miriam's shoulder. His groping fingers found only the soft white eiderdown that Miriam had brought with her from Dubnitz. Beneath its plump, goose down cover, the narrow bed was empty.

Chapter seven

The wagon wheels creaked and groaned, as if protesting the weight of their load and the slickness of the compacted snow covering the road. Miriam stared out at the two long, gray tracks that trailed behind, framing the horse's hoofprints. A coarse burlap blanket, smelling of horse and mildew, covered her where she lay nestled among sacks of potatoes. The morning star had just risen, and faint streaks of pink penetrated the charcoal haze on the horizon. In the distance, a cock crowed. Exhausted by her long walk and lulled by the rumbling of the wagon, Miriam closed her eyes and slept.

The jolt of the wagon as it pulled to a stop awakened her. The sun shone brightly, glinting off the snowy fields and the tops of the tall pines growing alongside the road. Miriam sat up and reached for the package that lay beneath her legs. The two fluted silver candlesticks that Mama had given her as part of her dowry were still there. Only hours ago, she had hastily wrapped them in a wool traveling dress, along with a few kerchiefs, a blouse, a shawl, a heavy black skirt, and a nightgown, all of which she had thrust into a pillowcase before stealing from the house. Relieved at finding her bundle intact, she stretched her arms and legs and straightened her kerchief. A familiar chanting reached her ears from the other side of the wagon.

"*Boruch atah Adonai, mechayeh hamaysim*, Blessed art Thou, O Lord, who resurrects the dead." It was Yossl, the wagon driver, reciting the morning service. His deep, resonant voice filled her with longing for her home in Dubnitz and the sound of her father at prayer.

The events of the last few weeks seemed unreal to her as she sat among the potatoes and watched Yossl swaying under the tree, his stout body loosely draped in a striped, black-and-white prayer shawl. *God must have sent this kind Jew to me*, she thought. *Who knows what would have happened if he hadn't come along when he did?* After wandering for hours along the snowy road from Pavlitz to the main highway leading to Warsaw, she had come upon a band of peasant boys who began chasing her, jeering and throwing snowballs until she fell into a ditch, losing her marriage wig. Soaked and trembling, she had crouched in the frozen snow until the boys gave up the chase and moved on, shouting, "Jewish whore, we'll catch you yet!" With stiff, red fingers she had scraped about in the snow, searching for the wig, but had been unable to find it in the mud and dead leaves. Still clutching the precious bundle that contained her candlesticks and clothes, she had removed a pale blue kerchief to cover her hair, now grown long enough to touch the top of her lace collar.

She had begun to cry then, fearing that she would freeze to death, when suddenly there came the sound of hoofbeats and the squeak of wagon wheels. Squinting in the dark, she could barely discern the squat, bearded driver. Then, a poignant melody wafted to her across the snowy road: "*There was a Hasid, without food or sustenance.*" It was the song that Hasidim always sang at a *melaveh malkeh*, the Saturday-night party held to send off the Holy Sabbath. Waving her shawl and shouting wildly, Miriam had clambered out of the ditch to flag down the wagon.

Yossl Hecht, as he explained once Miriam had arranged herself in the back of the wagon, had a small hotel in Pilsk, forty kilometers from Warsaw. For the past week he had been staying in the village of Kredmer, near Pavlitz, visiting his *rebbe*. On Thursday afternoon he had bought a week's worth of produce from the local peasants and was now bringing it back to Pilsk.

"But what," he had asked, his deep-set hazel eyes searching her face, "is a pious young woman like you doing, wandering alone on the road in the freezing night?"

Miriam had already prepared her story. "I've come from Kretchtow," she began. "My husband died last week. My mother-in-law hated me because I was from a poor family." Miriam paused to dab at her eyes with the corner of her kerchief. "After the seven days of mourning, she drove me out of the house. I had no one in Kretchtow. My parents are dead and my only sister lives in Warsaw. I'm trying to get there, to stay with her."

Yossl shifted on his seat and scratched his curly gray beard. "*Oy, nebbich*, a pity. I have a daughter just about your age. If such a thing were to happen to her, God forbid—" he shook his head. "Here's what we'll do. I'll take you as far as Pilsk. There, I'll send you to Arye Leib and Menashe, my two brothers, who drive to Warsaw every Monday, where they work all week."

After completing his morning prayers, Yossl removed his prayer shawl and unwound his phylacteries, the leather straps that an observant Jewish man is required to wear on his head and arm while praying on weekday mornings. These he deposited in a worn and faded velvet bag, which he gently stowed behind his wooden seat in the wagon. Then, opening a leather pouch that had been lying under the seat, he offered Miriam half of his meager breakfast. "Here, eat. You must keep up your strength."

Miriam gratefully devoured the hard-boiled egg and boiled potato, washing it down with a tin cup of water.

The drive to Pilsk was uneventful. Miriam spent it gazing at the scenery: flat, snow-covered fields dotted with small peasant farmhouses from whose chimneys smoke curled invitingly; dark, bristling pine forests; and frozen rivers resembling silver ribbons. Here and there a church steeple rose high above the distant rooftops, its black cross stark against the white sky. As the shadows lengthened across the white fields, Miriam tucked her blanket tighter about her and slept again.

71

"Wake up, Ma'am. We're here, in Pilsk."

Miriam opened her eyes and looked about in the fading light. A flurry of activity surrounded her. In front of the wagon a young man in a leather overcoat was unhitching the horse. At the back, children of various ages and heights scampered about, laughing and chattering. Yossl meanwhile, was walking to the house, a whitewashed square building made of wood. A young girl of about sixteen trotted alongside him, talking animatedly and picking bits of straw off his clothing. A few moments later, the girl emerged from the house, accompanied by a heavy woman in a white kerchief who rushed toward the wagon.

"A guest! Come, let me help you down. Children, where are your manners? Zeesy, leave Mirel alone. Arele, get away from there." She plowed into the cluster of children, dispensing slaps and pinches, tweaks and kisses until she reached the wagon, from which Miriam was stiffly descending, her package clutched in one hand.

"Come, darling, take my arm." She offered Miriam a stout right arm encased in a quilted blue jacket. "I'm Hadassah, Yossl's wife. This is our oldest daughter, Yocheved." The young girl smiled, showing dimples in her round, freckled cheeks.

"You'll meet the rest of us later," Hadassah added as she and Yocheved propelled Miriam up the path and into the warm, brightly lit cottage. The rest of the children followed behind, giggling and jostling one another.

Miriam was led to a sagging green sofa and made to sit. A steaming glass of tea and a plate of egg cookies were brought to her on a tray by one of the older daughters, a black-haired, solemn child of twelve. Miriam sipped the tea, feeling its warmth spread through her body. "Thank you so much," she murmured, smiling up at Hadassah.

"It's nothing, nothing. Soon you'll have supper. You must be starved, poor thing. Yossl told me all about it. *Oy*, may God have mercy. You're hardly more than a child. Well, they say we mustn't question God's ways. *Nu, Nu.*" She clucked her tongue sympathetically and stroked Miriam's cheek. The rest of the children stood about, staring quietly at Miriam as she ate and drank.

"Don't stare at our guest! It's not polite," admonished Yossl as he emerged from a back room, his face shining and his beard and earlocks freshly combed. He wore a clean white shirt.

His appearance made Miriam conscious of her own. *I must look a wreck*, she thought, and excused herself to go wash. Yocheved handed her a towel and a bar of yellow soap and directed her to the washroom, which had a sink, a tub, and a toilet with a pull-chain. *How modern*, thought Miriam. *But then, Pilsk is near Warsaw, not out in the backwoods like Dubnitz and Pavlitz.*

Quickly removing her kerchief, shawl, and blouse, she washed her face and hands and the upper part of her body. She glanced in the cracked oval mirror at her face, which was rosy from her long ride in the frosty air. Rivulets of soapy water ran down her neck and between her firm breasts. *I'm still pretty*, she thought. *But what good does it do me? Better to be ugly and single like Fayge than pretty and married like me. Well, I suppose I deserve it for falling in love with Tadeusz. Now I'll have to remain alone forever. Still, I'd rather be alone than with Berish.* When she returned from the bathroom, the family was already seated at the table, except for Yocheved and Hadassah, who were bringing in large pots of meat, potatoes, and beans.

"Thit here," lisped a plump, blond child of about five, indicating the seat next to her with a dimpled finger.

Miriam sat down. Though the high-backed mahogany chair with its purple velvet cushion was not as comfortable as the sofa, it was still a welcome change from the lumpy potatoes she had lain on in the wagon. Her back and legs still ached from the long, rough ride.

"Eat something, darling," urged Hadassah, heaping a steaming mound of stew onto Miriam's plate. "You need strength. So thin, too. *Oy*, what you've been through! But don't think about it now. Here you don't have to worry. Nobody is sending you out into the cold."

"Who thent her out in the cold?" asked the little blond girl on Miriam's left.

"Never mind, Esty, just eat your dinner. Look, you haven't even touched your meat." Hadassah frowned at her youngest daughter.

"Who thent you out?" continued Esty, ignoring her mother,

who had moved on down the table to help two-year-old Motke with his food.

Miriam smiled at Esty. "My mother-in-law."

"Why? Was she a witch?"

"Esty, shush! Leave Miriam alone. She's tired. Here, eat." Yocheved leaned over and began spooning beans into Esty's open mouth, preventing her from asking more questions.

As the meal progressed, the children began to relax, almost forgetting that a stranger sat among them. Ignoring Miriam, they began telling their parents about their day, constantly correcting and interrupting one another. When a noisy argument broke out over which brother hadn't finished his lessons, Yossl, who until then had been eating quietly, sat up in his chair and cleared his throat. The children immediately fell silent and looked at him expectantly.

"This past *Shabbes*," he began, "the *rebbe* gave an excellent vort, talk. 'Why is it,' he asked us, 'that in the beginning of the Book of Leviticus, the letter *aleph* is so small, much smaller than the other letters?'" Yossl paused dramatically, looked around the table, and continued. "It is to show us the great modesty of Moses, our teacher, of whom it is written, 'Moses was the most modest of all people....'"

The slight singsong of Yossl's voice, the heat in the room, and the heavy meal that Miriam had just consumed all combined to numb her senses, and her head began to nod. Noticing this, Hadassah signalled to Yocheved, who helped Miriam out of her chair and led her from the warm room.

"Come, you will sleep with Esty. She doesn't take up much room. Motke is smaller, but he still wets at night."

"I hate to be so much trouble," sighed Miriam.

"Nonsense, it's no trouble at all. You should have seen it on *Shabbes* Chanukah, when my fiance and his parents and two sisters were here. Papa had thought to put them in the inn, but at the last minute there was no room. So we squeezed them in. What fun we had. Mama always says, 'The more the merrier.' Do you come from a big family?"

"Not so big." Miriam smiled to herself, thinking, *She really is just like Dina, with her chattering. They'd make great friends.*

When Yocheved had left the room, Miriam opened her bundle, which had been placed next to the bed. She removed a flannel nightgown and fingered the tiny pink flowers embroidered on its yoke. *I wonder what will happen to all the clothes I left in Pavlitz? Maybe Fayge will keep them.* She laughed silently at the thought of Fayge's scrawny frame enveloped in one of her own woolen frocks. The white bed was soft and inviting. Miriam lay down and was soon so sound asleep that Esty's hopeful whispers and proddings failed to wake her. Disappointed, Esty gave up and snuggled against the sleeping guest. She had wanted to know more about the cruel mother-in-law, who reminded her of characters in the fairy tales she heard from Ninka, the cook in her father's inn. But it would have to wait till morning.

The pale winter sun had just risen when Miriam opened her eyes. The room was cold and she curled herself deeper under the quilts. She was alone in the bed. Where was Esty? The door opened and little Motke entered, trailing a tattered yellow blanket. He peered at Miriam, rubbed his eyes, then toddled out again, leaving behind him the faint, sweetish odor of urine. Miriam climbed out of bed. Reaching into the pillowcase that contained her things, she removed a black shawl, which she wrapped about her. The clink of glasses and silverware and the clatter of dishes reached her ears, along with muffled voices, punctuated now and then by peals of laughter—the sounds of a large, happy family at breakfast. By the time she had washed and dressed, only three children remained at the table—Esty, Motke, and Adina, the solemn-faced twelve-year-old. A red-checked flannel rag, smelling of wintergreen, was wrapped around Adina's face.

"She hath a toothache," explained Esty as she jumped up and took Miriam's hand. "Tell me now."

"Tell you what?" Miriam looked down at the round face with its bright doll-like blue eyes.

"About the witch. The one who threw you out."

"The witch, the witch! Out! Out!" chanted Motke, swaying in his high chair until it threatened to topple over.

"Quiet now!" Hadassah warned, bringing a china teapot and a thick white mug, which she set down in front of Miriam. "What did

I tell you, Esty? Don't you remember?" She reached out and steadied Motke's high chair, then handed him a piece of bread.

"Here, dear, eat some breakfast." Hadassah began smearing a piece of bread with thick, yellow jam. She passed it to Miriam, along with a plate of herring. "Adina, pass the potatoes to Miriam. Eat, Miriam. I didn't want to wake you, but there isn't much time. The uncles will be here any minute."

"Why are they coming?" asked Esty, her mouth full of potatoes.

"To take Miriam to Warsaw, busybody," answered her mother as she swept the crumbs from the table into a napkin.

"Why are you going away? Don't go to Warthaw. Thtay here in Pilthk. You could live here." The child slid off her seat and put her arm up on Miriam's shoulder.

Miriam fingered a wisp of Esty's straight, golden hair. "I can't stay here. I'm going to stay with my sister in Warsaw." She drained her teacup and began stacking the breakfast dishes. As she did so, the door opened and two men in modern, vested business suits walked in.

"Uncle Arye! Uncle Menashe!" Esty flew from her seat and danced around the two men. Menashe, the taller of the two, reached into his pocket and pulled out a gaily dressed rubber doll, which he placed in Esty's outstretched arms. Her delighted squeals brought a broad smile to his dark, bearded face.

Miriam glanced shyly at the men as she continued clearing the table. Menashe was tall and broad-shouldered, with an olive complexion. His neatly trimmed black beard was sprinkled with gray. With his genial smile and twinkling hazel eyes, he resembled his brother Yossl but was clearly several years younger. Miriam guessed he was about forty. Arye Leib looked nothing like his older brothers. He was short and compact, with a curly blond beard and pale blue eyes. He glanced at Miriam and looked away, nervously fingering his gold watch chain.

Such well-dressed men. They must be rich, thought Miriam as she carried a pile of dirty dishes into the kitchen, where Hadassah and Adina were up to their elbows in a sink full of foaming suds.

"Here, Adina, you finish. Achh, Miriam, you are our guest, why are you working?" Hadassah dried her hands on a damp, blue-striped linen towel that hung on a hook over the sink. It was the same type of towel that hung in Miriam's kitchen at home: blue stripes for dairy dishes, red stripes for meat. Taking Miriam by the elbow, she led her back to the dining room, where the uncles had seated themselves. Both stood again as the two women entered.

"*Nu*, Menashe and Arye. My two favorite brothers-in-law. In fact, my only brothers-in-law," joked Hadassah. "Some tea? A piece of cake?"

The brothers shook their heads in unison.

"Thank you, we've already eaten," said Menashe, gesturing at the pale green cake plate, which now held a small piece of yellow sponge cake nestled in a mound of crumbs.

"Some tea, maybe," Hadassah urged, "to wash it down?"

"Nah, it's better not to drink too much tea before a journey," replied Menashe.

Arye Leib cleared his throat and lowered his eyes.

"Let me introduce our guest, so you'll know whom you're driving with." Hadassah touched Miriam's arm lightly. "This is Miriam Friedman, from Kretchtow. Did Yossl tell you anything?"

"Yes, yes," answered Menashe. "He told us everything. We're sorry, Mrs. Friedman, about your trouble. May you be comforted among the mourners of Zion and Jerusalem."

"God gives and God takes away," put in Hadassah. "So, Menashe, how is Fruma? Anything happening yet?"

"No, not really. Last night she had a few pains, but then it all stopped. She was the same last time, with Mordechai."

"Yes, I remember. Well, it was the same with me, too, when I had my fourth. Chayele took her time. Anyway, it should be in a lucky hour. And you, Arye Leib, when will we hear some good news about you?"

Arye gave his sister-in-law a thin smile. "Also in a lucky hour," he muttered, then rose abruptly, letting a shower of crumbs fall from his vest to table and floor.

"All right, time to go," announced Menashe.

Miriam gathered her small bundle with its treasured belongings. The pillowcase had become stained and slightly torn during the journey, and Miriam wished she had had time to wash and mend it. Now she put it under the shawl to hide it from view. *I must look like a beggar next to these two fine gentlemen*, she thought. She had rarely seen observant men dressed in modern clothes. The Jews in Dubnitz and Pavlitz had worn either Hasidic garb or rough workmen's clothing. She had always associated modern dress with freethinkers, yet here were these two, despite their business suits and neatly trimmed beards, reciting the Prayer Upon Sustenance after eating the cake. *Who knows what kind of Jews I'll see in Warsaw?* she wondered.

As she kissed Hadassah and the girls, Miriam wished she could run upstairs and hide in Esty's bedroom. These kind people had been so good to her, they had made her feel like one of them. Now she was about to travel to a large city where she knew no one. Actually, she did have cousins there, but she didn't have their address. Besides, would they take her in? Surely they would soon find out that she'd run off and left her husband, and they'd lose no time in sending her back. No, better to go it alone in Warsaw, find work and a place to live. Sell the candlesticks if necessary, and look for a… Her thoughts were interrupted midsentence as she stepped out the door behind Menashe and Arye Leib. There in the front yard stood a gleaming black motorcar, its polished fender sparkling in the morning sunshine.

Miriam gazed at it in awe, then backed away. "Oh, I can't ride in that."

"Why not? Are you afraid?" Menashe opened the back door and waved his arm toward the plush velvet seat inside.

"I've never ridden in an automobile before." Miriam moved a bit closer to the beautiful machine.

"So what? Oh, you mean because you're in mourning, so maybe you're not allowed to do something new? Arye, do you think that applies to riding in a motorcar? She's never been in one."

Arye scratched his beard. "I really don't know. We could ask the Pilsker *tzaddik*, but there's no time. I doubt if it's really a problem. Of course, if she's concerned, maybe she could wait for a wagon."

"It's all right, I'll ride with you." Miriam quickly climbed into the backseat and placed her package beside her. She wasn't about to be left behind to ride in a cold, bumpy wagon instead of a fancy new motorcar all because of a possible violation of the mourning laws. Especially when she wasn't even a mourner. The two brothers slid into the front seat, and Menashe started the car, which sputtered once or twice, then lurched forward, launching them on their journey.

Miriam settled back in her seat. The car had a wonderful smell, a blend of leather, velvet, pipe tobacco, and something she couldn't identify, petrol perhaps. How smooth and fast the ride was, compared to a horse and wagon. Even the best coach couldn't match it. Only a train was faster, but then you had to put up with all the people—peasants who ate garlicky sausage, crying children, old men hawking and spitting—not to mention the smoke and cinders. No, this really was the way to travel.

Menashe and Arye conversed in the front seat. When bored with the scenery, Miriam tried to listen above the noise of the engine but could only hear bits and pieces:

"…sold him two liters of vodka in advance of the…"

"…delayed shipment for seven weeks while Mendel delivered the rest of the goods to Cracow."

Business. Miriam knew nothing of business transactions and soon gave up listening. She was not tired, so she gazed at the scenery until she became aware that Arye Leib was watching her. Turning from the window, she looked at him.

"You're, ah, all right back there?"

"Oh, yes, it's very comfortable."

He faced front for a while, then craned his neck to look at her, turning away when she met his eyes. After a while she ignored him, not bothering to look up when she sensed him staring at her. She'd had this experience many times in Dubnitz, after synagogue, when some would-be suitor would stare at her over and over again. Berish, too, had done it at times, but for different reasons. Still, it made her want to laugh, for Arye Leib seemed to spend half the time facing forward and half the time gazing back at her. *He'll get a kink in his neck by the time we reach Warsaw*, she thought.

Presently, Miriam noticed that the scenery had changed. The flat farmland outside of Pilsk had given way to clusters of villages, which now seemed to merge into one crowded city. Even as she watched, the streets grew broader, the buildings taller, and the people more numerous. The clean country air, with its scents of pine and occasional wood fires and the pungent smells of the barnyards they had passed, had been replaced by soot, factory smoke, and odors she couldn't identify.

The resulting combination both repelled and excited Miriam, and she leaned forward in her seat, nearly colliding with Arye Leib, who had chosen just that moment to turn around again. He recovered quickly and announced, "Well, this is it; this is Warsaw. Have you been here before?"

"No, never. I was once in Cracow." *What a stupid thing to say,* Miriam reproached herself. *What has Cracow to do with Warsaw, except that they're both big cities. They'll think I'm such a bumpkin.* She felt ashamed before these two worldly men in their well-made, modern clothes and fancy motorcar.

"Where does your sister live? On which street?" Menashe asked, slowing the car so that buildings, houses, and people came into sharper focus.

Under her blue kerchief, Miriam felt her scalp prickle. Street? She knew the names of no streets in Warsaw. Why hadn't she prepared for this? Surely a person is expected to know her sister's address. How could she have sat like a golem all the way from Pilsk, with only the vaguest thoughts of where she was actually going, and what she'd do when she got there?

"Ah, I have her address on a paper, here." She fumbled in her sack.

"Never mind. We'll take you to the Jewish quarter, and from there you can ask for the street when you find the paper," Menashe said. "What do you think of the city?"

Miriam stared out the window. So many sights met her eyes that she couldn't take them all in at once. On both sides were towering brick buildings. Black smoke poured from their thin iron chimneys. The streets were filled with cars, wagons, horses, and people rushing in all directions. The clamor filled her ears. They passed a huge church, its graceful spires and arches pointing heavenward, at odds with the massive gray stones that made up its imposing facade.

Menashe turned left into a street filled with elegant stores whose large windowpanes shone in the afternoon sunlight. In some of them Miriam glimpsed vividly colored clothes, dresses of red, deep blue, and purple. Here and there women could be seen emerging from the shops, their arms filled with gaily wrapped parcels. Sometimes a servant carried the packages for his mistress and led her to a waiting car. Miriam stared in wonder and delight at the clothes these women wore: sleek, dark furs that flattered the body; pale, fluffy furs that billowed about soft leather boots; spotted furs from exotic jungle animals that Miriam could not name. And all with hats to match, and even muffs. Other women wore no furs but instead sported well-tailored coats of soft, rich wool.

Miriam looked down at her heavy shawl and gray wool skirt and sighed. In Dubnitz she had always taken pains with her wardrobe and had been considered among the best-dressed young girls. *Tati* had reproached her on occasion, saying it was not fitting for a rabbi's daughter to be so concerned about her appearance. "Charm is deceitful and beauty is vain; a woman who feareth the Lord, *she* shall be praised," he would quote from King Solomon's Book of Proverbs. She and Dina had laughed, and so had Mama, who had been known as a beauty in her own youth.

Now Menashe steered the car into another street. Here, in the midst of the city, were towering trees—deep green pines, and bare-branched oaks and chestnuts that threw their sparse winter shade over stone statues and snow-covered grass. Plump toddlers in bright scarves and mittens ran squealing through the snow, climbing on statues and ignoring the admonitions of the dark-coated women who walked sedately along the paths, pushing chrome-trimmed baby carriages.

"The Saxon Gardens," explained Menashe. They drove on past a heavy iron gate and entered another neighborhood. The streets had narrowed, and the pedestrians looked different. Jews in traditional Hasidic dress walked up and down the sidewalks, talking and gesticulating. Miriam no longer felt ashamed of her coarse, old-fashioned clothes. Here and there one saw a stylishly dressed matron or a smart-looking businessman, dressed much as Menashe and Arye Leib, but for the most part, the people in this neighborhood resembled those of Dubnitz or Pavlitz. The streets, however, were quite different. *Take the marketplace of Dubnitz*, thought Miriam, *and multiply it by twenty—no, fifty—add a thousand more people, and perhaps you would have the City Market of Warsaw.*

The streets were lined with stores and outdoor stalls. Signs in Yiddish and Polish announced the goods available. Here were row upon row of dusty brown potatoes and shining yellow onions, boxes of bright red and green apples, even oranges and lemons imported from warm countries far away. Women in scarves, knitted hats, and marriage wigs walked among the stalls, pinching the fruit and haggling with the merchants. Farther down were stores selling china—anything from the finest Bavarian porcelain to cheap domestic crockery. Then came the cloth merchants, whose stores were filled with colorful bolts of cotton, linen, muslin, wool, silk, and gabardine. As they passed these, Miriam felt a faint tingle of excitement. She remembered the delightful experience of choosing material for a new holiday outfit. Now they went by the notion stores, and Miriam thought of old Gitele, who sold notions in Dubnitz and had supplied the velvet ribbons for Miriam's wedding.

"Mrs. Friedman," Menashe's voice interrupted her reverie. "If it's all right with you, this is where we are stopping. We are now on Gesia Street, the textile center. Yossl said your brother-in-law, Shmuel Binder, was in the textile business. Here someone will surely know him." He pulled the car over to the side of the road. "Please wait here just a moment, all right? Arye and I have to go inside for a moment, to speak to someone. We'll be right back."

Miriam nodded in assent, wondering why they didn't just let her out and say goodbye. Maybe they were going to make some inquiries on her behalf. No matter. Even if there *were* a Shmuel Binder who worked in textiles, he was no kin to her, simply a made-up name. Menashe soon returned, gallantly opening the door for her and bowing slightly as she slid out, her shabby bundle under her arm. He held a small, folded piece of white paper out to her.

"What is that? You found my sister's address?"

"I thought you had their address."

"Oh, yes, I do. I have it here in my bag."

"No, actually, I, ah…" He cleared his throat and looked off somewhere past Miriam's right ear. "This is Arye Leib's phone number, actually. In case you need anything."

"Oh, thank you so much. You've been so kind already. I'm sure I'll be fine at my sister's." Miriam took the paper and put it inside the pillowcase.

"Well, the truth is, my brother, Arye Leib, you see, ah, he'd like to see you again. I mean, not now. I know it's not proper, so soon after your, ah, tragedy." He coughed softly and looked down. "But maybe in a while—you know, after a few months or so—maybe you could call him, just say hello, to let him know how you are doing."

Miriam stifled a smile. *A few months*, she thought. *Just to make sure I'm not pregnant by my previous husband.* She vaguely remembered a proscription against widows remarrying until three months after their husband's death, for just that reason.

Menashe continued, "My brother Arye, you know…forgive me, but he earns a very good living. So, ah, maybe you'll get in touch later on. Well, good luck to you. May you know of no more sorrow." He touched his hat briefly and hurried into the large warehouse.

Miriam watched with a mixture of relief and dread as Menashe disappeared into the building. She was glad to be spared any further questions about her "sister" and "brother-in-law" for the time being. Yet as she gazed at the busy streets thronged with shoppers, workers, and businessmen scurrying about in all directions, she felt more alone than she could ever remember.

Chapter eight

The afternoon was growing colder, and Miriam had nothing but the clothes she wore and the few items she had stuffed into the pillowcase. Already the sun was sinking and the clouds were tinged with pink. Worse yet, she was beginning to feel hungry, and all she had were a few kopeks in her bag. If only Menashe and Arye Leib had offered her a meal. But, of course, she probably would have refused. Fighting a rising tide of panic, Miriam began walking. I must find work, she resolved. But how did one go about it? A newspaper. One bought a newspaper and consulted the employment listings. Hurriedly, she began to look for a newsstand. Hadn't she seen one a few blocks back? She turned and retraced her steps, anxiety propelling her until she was almost running. There it was, a little kiosk, painted green, where a shrivelled man with an eye patch sold papers and chewing gum.

She removed some kopeks from her bag and chose a Yiddish newspaper. She tried to read it as she walked, but the wind had sprung up, whipping at the pages and causing her eyes to tear. *This is impossible. I must sit down somewhere*, thought Miriam. She scanned the streets, looking for a bench or even a box. Finding none, she tucked the paper under her arm and, clutching her bag with both hands, began walking. Despite the cold, beads of sweat formed on her brow, and her stomach contracted with fear and hunger. She remembered feeling this way whenever she had tarried too long with Tadeusz. After one last kiss, she would rush homeward, unable to stand the thought that Mama would be worried about her. But now there was no warm kitchen to run to, only unfamiliar streets filled with strangers, all hurrying toward some destination. And Mama would surely be frantic with worry as soon as she heard that Miriam had run off. *I'll write her as soon as I find work*, Miriam vowed. *But what does one do first? I need a job, food, and a place to sleep. It's getting dark, and if I don't find shelter, where will I spend the night? Without a decent place to sleep, to freshen up in the morning and change my clothes, how can I look for a job? Who will hire me if I look like a beggar woman? Also, if I don't eat, I'll have no strength...*

Suddenly, a metal sign caught her eye as it swung to and fro in the wind: Friedlander's Pawn Shop. Miriam looked through the smeared windowpane. There on a platform of faded black velvet lay a treasure trove of gold and silver watches, signet rings and brooches shining with colored stones, and necklaces of amber, pearl, and carnelian beads. Above them, on a dusty wooden shelf, were spice boxes made of silver or carved olive wood, and beside them, an array of silver and brass boxes, some round and some oblong. These were containers for the etrog or citron, the lemonlike fruit that men were required to purchase for the Succoth holiday. Behind these were two rows of engraved silver goblets, the *kiddush* cups used for wine on the Sabbath and holidays. Finally, Miriam's eye caught what she had been looking for. There on the highest shelf stood a little thicket of candlesticks. There were pairs of tall and short candlesticks in silver and brass, graceful, multi-armed candelabra, and eight-branched Chanukah menorahs for either candles or olive oil, all bearing witness to joyous holidays and Sabbaths of the past, and hard times of the present. Miriam sighed and entered the dimly lit shop. When she emerged a few minutes later, her pillowcase was considerably lighter, but it also contained four hundred and fifty zlotys and a blue pawn ticket. She paused again at the window, gazed for a moment at the pair of fluted silver candlesticks that had just joined the others on the shelf, then turned and walked in the direction that the pawnbroker had indicated.

When she arrived at the address, 14 Rymarska Street, Miriam looked up at the large brick building before her. In front was a muddy courtyard where a few boys in caftans and earlocks chased each other with sticks. A dirty gray cat slunk along the walls and disappeared into a cellar window. Miriam crossed the courtyard, avoiding the band of children who reminded her of Shloimeh, and opened the door of the building. The halls smelled of boiled potatoes and fried onions. She felt both hungry and nauseated as she climbed the stone steps, each of which had a depression in its center, where numerous feet had trod. At the third landing, Miriam saw the name "Grunwald" that the pawnbroker had given her. She turned the small iron key that protruded from the center of the door, and a bell rang inside. A shuffling sound was heard and the door opened. A stout woman in a white kerchief and flowered apron stood in the doorway, holding a large wooden spoon. The smell of fresh bread wafted from behind her. Miriam shuddered, remembering the bakery in Pavlitz.

"I was told you had a room to rent," she ventured. "David Friedlander sent me."

"Yes, come in. I'm Mrs. Grunwald. My daughter, Baila, got married last week, so now I have an empty room. I told everyone I only wanted a nice young girl to rent it, like my Baila. You look like a nice young girl to me. Where are you from?"

Miriam smiled. "From Kretchtow." She had decided to stay with the story she had used in Pilsk.

"Kretchtow? Really? I have a cousin there. Surely you know her—Miriam Fassbinder?"

Miriam's heart sank. The more questions she was asked, the more details she'd be forced to supply. She would surely trap herself in her own lies. Better to say as little as possible. "Miriam Fassbinder? No, I don't remember the name."

Mrs. Grunwald looked at Miriam strangely. Her eyes wandered from the blue kerchief down to the slim gold wedding band that Miriam wore. "Not know her? How could you not know her? She's the *mikveh* lady. She knows every married woman in Kretchtow."

Miriam flushed scarlet. What bad luck, to meet the cousin of the *mikveh* lady, the caretaker of the ritual bath. "Oh, ah, yes, of course," she stammered. "I forgot her name. You see, I was married in, ah, Varemsk, and when we moved to Kretchtow, I was already pregnant." Miriam paused. Her legs and back ached. Nearby were a small wooden table and four chipped chairs. "May I sit down?" she asked.

"Of course. Forgive me." Mrs. Grunwald pointed to a chair, and Miriam sank into it, feeling exhaustion and despair close over her like a great black cloak.

Mrs. Grunwald sat heavily in the opposite chair and looked at Miriam expectantly. "Yes? And what happened?"

"Oh, a terrible thing. My husband got sick and died, and from the shock I lost the baby."

Miriam lowered her head to the table and buried her face in her hands. It was not hard to cause tears to flow; they came on their own. It seemed to her that she had been fighting tears for months, and now she sobbed with abandon as Mrs. Grunwald awkwardly patted her shaking shoulders. Soon her tears began to ebb, but she kept her face hidden on the table while she took stock of her situation. *What a liar I've become,* she thought. *Of course, I had a lot of practice in Dubnitz, sneaking off to be with* Tadeusz. *It's like* Tati *always said, "One sin leads to another." But if this woman checks with her cousin, she'll know I'm a fraud and she'll certainly turn me out of her house. Well, I can't worry about that now. I've nowhere else to go.*

The tears still swimming in her large green eyes, she looked up at Mrs. Grunwald. "I'm so sorry to burden you with my troubles."

"Oh, my dear, please don't apologize. You've been through so much. But where are your parents? Do you have people here in Warsaw?"

"My parents passed away years ago. I have no one. I came to Warsaw to find work, to start over." *More lies,* she thought. *I've got to change the subject.* "Can I see the room now?" Miriam stood up.

"Certainly. Come this way."

The room was plain but very clean. A narrow iron bed covered with a dotted pink and blue quilt, tattered at the edges, stood along the wall. Opposite was a cardboard bureau painted to look like wood and a chair similar to the one Miriam had sat on in the foyer. A few metal hooks had been nailed into one pale blue wall, next to a print of a vase full of pink and white tulips. A frayed white curtain covered the narrow window that overlooked the courtyard.

Mrs. Grunwald indicated a door across the hall. "The bathroom is over there."

"It's fine. It's lovely." Miriam swallowed, dreading what had to come next. She knew nothing about the prices of rooms and cursed herself for not having asked Mr. Friedlander in the pawnshop what a fair rental would be. "How much?"

"Fifty zlotys a month. It's a very fair price. You won't find a nicer, quieter room. And with a toilet. In some places you'd have to go in a hall bathroom, or even in an outhouse."

"Fine. I'll take it." Miriam had neither the will nor the energy to bargain, though she vaguely felt she was expected to.

"Very good. I'm sure you'll be so happy here. You'll forget all your troubles. I'll treat you like my own daughter. Ah, there's just one thing." Mrs. Grunwald shifted her weight from her left foot to her right. "You must pay the first month's rent in advance. We all have to ask for security, you know."

Miriam took fifty zlotys from her pillowcase and handed it to Mrs. Grunwald, who thanked her and shuffled out.

After a few moments, she knocked on the door. "Would you like something to eat? The rent doesn't include food, but I'm happy to share with you whenever and whatever. Some rolls and coffee, maybe?"

Miriam sighed. She was ravenous, yet she feared that sitting down with Mrs. Grunwald would bring more questions, more deceitful answers. The woman was obviously lonely. But her hunger won out, and she sat down again at Mrs. Grunwald's table, where two places had been set. Warm buttered rolls and steaming coffee soon eased her stomach and settled her nerves. Her landlady, sensing Miriam's reticence, refrained from asking any more questions, urging her instead to "have a nice hot bath and go to bed early," advice that Miriam gladly took. In the narrow bed with its thin hard mattress, Miriam slept the dreamless sleep of a child.

During the next few days, Miriam was driven by one concern only—to find work. The four hundred zlotys she had would soon disappear on food and other odds and ends, and without a job she would have no way to replace it. The newspaper proved useless. Most of the jobs advertised required skills she did not possess, or were located in distant parts of the city. Miriam feared leaving the more secure confines of the Jewish quarter for the strange and unfamiliar avenues of greater Warsaw. Surely, she reasoned, among the many factories and clothing stores in Gesia Street, one could find work.

The first morning, she set out hopefully for the textile center, but after tramping up and down countless stairs and walking in and out of one office after another, she returned home exhausted and discouraged. It was the same in the fur center on Swientojerska Street and the millinery center in Zabia. There was no work to be had for an unskilled woman from the backwoods of Poland. Worse, she discovered that she was only one of a huge army of unemployed who filled the streets daily, indistinguishable from their more fortunate compatriots who were hurrying to their jobs. On the third evening, Miriam consented to have dinner with Mrs. Grunwald instead of a hasty meal in one of the small cafes she frequented while looking for work. Her money supply was dwindling, and besides, the loneliness and depression she felt each evening after a fruitless day in the streets made her crave the warmth of another human being. Mrs. Grunwald, although nosy, was basically kind. Miriam sat down gratefully to a large bowl of boiled noodles and lima beans, which warmed her tired body and uplifted her sagging spirits. Mama had often prepared the same meal on cold winter evenings.

"*Nu?* Any luck?" asked Mrs. Grunwald, her mouth full of noodles.

"No. I haven't been able to find anything. Nothing at all. Everywhere it's the same story. If they advertise a job, by the time I get there, it's already filled. Or else I don't have the skills they need. I'm not very good with a sewing machine, and I don't know how to type at all."

"Ah, what a pity." Mrs. Grunwald continued chewing, then suddenly clapped a hand to her head.

"*Oy!* How stupid of me. Why didn't I think of it before?"

"What is it?" Miriam put down her spoon and leaned forward eagerly.

"Baila's job! Baila worked in a bookstore right here on Rymarska Street before she got married and moved to Lodz. You know, her husband, Zanvl, is from Lodz; his parents have a furniture factory there, very well to do, thank God. Have you ever been to Lodz?"

"Lodz? No. But what were you saying? A bookstore?"

"Oh, yes. Baila worked there. She helped keep the shop clean, you know. She didn't earn much, but still, it was a nice job. Mr. Zwillinger is a very fine man. A bit stern at times, perhaps, but a good man. Such a pity about his wife."

"His wife?" Miriam was becoming impatient. If there were a job in the offing, she wanted the details as fast as possible, without all this extraneous information. But she couldn't risk offending Mrs. Grunwald, her only link in Warsaw to shelter, food, and now, perhaps, steady work.

"She died. She had the 'real thing.'" She sighed heavily and poured the coffee for Miriam and herself. "So young, she was, maybe twenty-six, twenty-seven. She was always such a frail little thing. Never had any children. Finally, she became pregnant. Baila was so happy for them. But then, it wasn't a pregnancy at all. It was the 'sickness,' you know. In the stomach. A few months, and she was gone."

Miriam nodded sadly. There had been a similar case some years ago in Dubnitz. There, too, no one ever mentioned cancer by name, referring to it instead by euphemisms, like Mrs. Grunwald. She began to clear the table while her landlady continued.

"It happened about a year, year and a half ago. Baila said he was never the same after. Always so serious. Anyway, Baila left the week before her wedding; that would be almost two weeks ago. So stupid that I didn't think of it right away. Surely by now the position is taken."

Having seen firsthand how quickly jobs were filled in Warsaw, Miriam agreed but felt compelled to pursue the matter. Here at least she had a name, a connection. Just as the pawnbroker's name had helped her find a room, perhaps Mrs. Grunwald's name could help her land this job. That night she washed and pressed the white linen blouse, trimmed with lace, that she had brought with her from Pavlitz. With a damp cloth she carefully brushed the lint and dust from her black wool skirt and polished her worn boots. Early the next morning, after a light breakfast, she wrapped her black shawl about her shoulders and tied her hair with a white silk scarf. "Wish me luck," she called to Mrs. Grunwald, who answered gaily, "May you have the best of luck!" Then Miriam walked out into the crisp morning, new hope lending bounce to her steps as she picked her way over patches of snow and slush.

The bookshop was only two blocks down and so undistinguished that she nearly passed it by. A yellow sign with dark brown letters that had once been black hung above the door: Zwillinger Books—New and Used. A smaller sign was affixed to the door itself: Closed. Yet someone was inside, for the light was on and Miriam could see movement toward the back of the store. Peering through the book-filled window, she made out rows of bookcases lining the walls of the shop from floor to ceiling; another row ran down the center of the store, creating two narrow aisles. Hesitantly, Miriam tried the door, but it was locked. She rattled the handle, at first softly, then a bit more forcefully, until she saw someone approaching from within. A tall, thin man of about thirty in wire-rimmed spectacles opened the door. Miriam noticed that he was clean-shaven and wore no skullcap. Somehow she had pictured him differently.

Reuben Zwillinger's annoyance at having been disturbed so early dissipated rapidly as he looked at Miriam. In her demure black and white clothing and the posture of a supplicant, she looked almost nunlike, yet there was something bold and worldly in those huge green eyes. The burnished auburn hair that fell across her clear forehead escaping from her head scarf added a warm touch of color, as did the flush in Miriam's cheeks.

"Yes, can I help you? We're not quite open yet, but if you need something special…" He motioned her into the store, which smelled pleasantly of books, ink, and furniture polish. A little brass bell hanging over the door tinkled as she entered. "What kind of book were you looking for?"

"I'm not really looking for a book." Miriam cast about, searching her mind for the right words. Her eyes lit upon a small stepladder near the front of the store. Perched upon it were an open bottle of furniture polish and a crumpled rag. On the counter next to her sat a pile of cardboard-bound books, a few scattered receipts, and a glass that contained the remains of some light coffee. The rim of the glass bore traces of red lipstick.

"No? What then?" He looked at his watch, then at the door, before looking back at Miriam's face.

"I'm sorry to be taking up your time," she apologized.

"That's all right. I'm waiting for my clerk."

Miriam felt a wave of disappointment. Of course. Mrs. Grunwald had been right. The position was filled.

Reuben, noticing her suddenly downcast look, became curious. "What is it you want, if not a book?" he persisted.

"I was recommended by Mrs. Grunwald. I'm renting a room with her. Baila's room. The girl who used to work here." Reuben nodded.

"Mrs. Grunwald thought Baila's job might still be available. But I see it isn't."

"That's true. I filled it the day after Baila left."

Miriam lowered her head and leaned against the counter. The thought of going back out to comb the icy streets again, the humiliation of being constantly turned away, and the horror of being left alone with no money or prospects made her feel weak and ill. This job had been her only hope, however unjustified.

Reuben looked at his watch again. Elka was late, as she had been for the past few days. It was time to open. Moreover, the mess on the counter disgusted him, as did the dust on the shelves. He had started dusting and polishing the bookcases himself, a job Elka should have done yesterday. He was sure he had reminded her. But now there was no time to finish, as customers would soon be entering and he couldn't afford to have furniture oil on his fingers for fear of staining the books. And what was he to do with this young woman here, who looked as if she were about to cry? He reached out to touch her shoulder, then drew his hand back, noticing her wedding band.

So her head scarf was worn for religious reasons, not just against the cold. Wondering why a religious married woman would be boarding with Mrs. Grunwald and looking for work, he decided to question her further.

"Are you alone in Warsaw?" he asked gently. The kindness in his voice and his intelligent blue eyes behind the thick glass lenses gave Miriam new hope. Even if he had no job for her, he might know of someone who did.

She straightened her shoulders and answered, "Yes. I'm all alone. My husband died, and I have no parents. I thought I could make a life for myself here in Warsaw. I was sure I could find work. But nobody will hire me. Everywhere it's the same story, 'The position is filled.' Either that or they won't hire someone with no experience at a sewing machine, or typewriter, or something else. I'm willing to learn. I've always learned quickly, but no one will give me a chance." She paused, surprised at her own torrent of words, then plunged on. "I've even tried taking a job as a maid, but no one wants a Jewish woman for that. They all hire *goyishe* girls. They say I don't look strong enough, or that I won't want to do the work. But I am strong, I never get sick—" She stopped midsentence, and her face flushed scarlet, remembering what Mrs. Grunwald had said about Mr. Zwillinger's wife. But when he continued looking at her expectantly, she went on. "I'm willing to do anything. Any decent work, I mean. If I don't find a job, I'll have nowhere to go. Maybe you know someone who could hire me?" She looked at him imploringly, her eyes a mixture of hope and embarrassment.

Reuben scratched the back of his neck and adjusted his blue silk tie. A strange combination of feelings left him at a loss for words: annoyance at Elka, who still hadn't arrived, mingled with compassion for this pretty young woman. *She claims to be strong, but she looks so thin, like my Pola was,* he thought. *Obviously, she knows something about me, and about Pola, from Mrs. Grunwald. Well, I know what it is to be widowed and alone.* Something about Miriam's figure and the way she held her head awakened another feeling deep within Reuben, a feeling that had lain dormant these many months, and one that he barely acknowledged. He took a deep breath. "You know," he said,

"I do have a clerk. But as you see, it's eight-thirty and she still hasn't arrived. Not only that, she's left a mess from yesterday. In other words, I'm not really satisfied with her work at all. I'll give it another day, and if she's no better, then…Why don't you come back tomorrow morning, at the same time, and we'll talk about it."

Miriam looked up at him with a radiant smile, unable to conceal her excitement. "Oh, thank you so much, Mr. Zwillinger, for even considering me. If your clerk doesn't work out, I'm sure I can be of help to you. I'll be back tomorrow morning."

Reuben watched as she left the store, her shawl and skirt swinging gracefully. The little bell jingled and the door closed softly behind her.

Miriam walked back up Rymarska Street, her mind full of plans. Just in case the job did not work out, she wouldn't waste this day. Rather, she would continue looking for work as she had done before. If she found something, well, she could always weigh it against the job in the bookstore. And if Mr. Zwillinger didn't hire her after all…Miriam's thoughts were rudely interrupted when a young woman, her arms full of books, crashed right into her, almost knocking her down. The woman gave a shriek and began picking up the books, some of which had fallen into a slushy puddle. "Sorry," she sputtered. "Guess I wasn't watching where I was going. I'm late for work."

Miriam bent down and began gathering up some of the damp volumes. "Oh, thanks so much," said the girl. As the two stood together and brushed off the books, she continued. "I work in that bookstore. My boss will murder me, I bet. I was supposed to glue these bindings in place yesterday, in the store, but I didn't finish in time, so I took them home. I'm not really supposed to do that. I thought I'd get in early today and put them away, but I woke up too late." She rolled her large black eyes.

So this is his clerk, thought Miriam. She watched the young shop girl dab furiously at a wet stain on the binding of a book with the hem of her blue serge skirt. Despite the cold, Elka wore a thin, tight-fitting red jacket that emphasized her full bosom, and a matching red hat perched atop stiff black curls. Her cheeks and lips were brightly rouged, and Miriam remembered the soiled coffee glass.

Elka shrugged. "Well, bye." She turned and rushed off in the direction of Mr. Zwillinger's store, her pile of books teetering precariously.

Miriam stared after her. *He'll surely fire her now*, she thought. Immediately, she reproached herself. *One mustn't rejoice at another's misfortune.* Tati *always told us that. But I can't help it.* She was about to walk on when a bit of color in the muddy street caught her eye. Stooping down, she lifted a slim book out of a mud puddle. The volume had a black cover, but the bright green bookmark protruding from its pages had attracted Miriam's eye. Holding the book gingerly between thumb and forefinger, she brushed the slush and mud from its cover with her other hand. *The Love Poems of Nikolaj Myczistrovic.* Should she return it now? No. It would be too forward of her to go back to the bookstore, especially with the clerk there. Better wait and bring it along tomorrow morning. She tucked the wet volume inside the newspaper she carried and made her way to Nalewki Street, where an office job had been advertised.

That evening, cold, hungry, and bone tired, she returned to Mrs. Grunwald's flat. As on every other day, the jobs advertised had been filled, or else she was judged unsuitable. Her landlady was out, but some herring and potatoes, along with cold borscht, had been left on the table, and Miriam fell upon them greedily. Later, as she undressed for bed, she noticed the little book, lying in its wrapping of newspaper, on her dresser. It was still damp, and Miriam began to ruffle through the pages, trying to air it out a bit. Some lines of poetry caught her eye:

> *The fire that burns within your eyes*
> *Kindles in me a deeper flame.*
> *Release to me, with arms and thighs*
> *A love that knows no bounds of shame.*

She turned a few pages and read on:

> *In a darkened glen*
> *In a leafy wood*

96

I drank the beauty of your face.
The curse of men
Our love withstood
Born and lost in a secret place.

The room was growing colder, and Miriam climbed into her narrow bed and drew the pink-and-blue coverlet up to her chest. Leaning on one elbow, she continued reading, shocked at the sentiments some of the poetry revealed. All this talk of lips and thighs. What would Mama think?

Slowly, her eyelids grew heavy, and she closed the book and turned off the small lamp that hung over the bed. Yet she was unable to sleep. Something about that poem…She rose, turned on the lamp, and thumbed through the pages until she found it again: "In a leafy wood…The curse of men…Our love…Born and lost in a secret place." Why, it was as if it had been written about her and Tadeusz. She put the book down, turned off the light, and settled back among the covers, but the words kept echoing through her thoughts, along with memories of Tadeusz in the woods, in the chimney tree. She could feel his arms about her, his strong hands on her breasts, trying to undo her blouse as she giggled and resisted, then gave in to his kisses. Alone in the dark bedroom, she gave herself up to the memories that had so long been buried. Soon warm waves of desire began to spread throughout her body. Imagining Tadeusz in her arms, she hugged her pillow close, until the heat of her arousal abated, leaving a throbbing pain in her fingertips and between her thighs. Still clinging to the pillow, she fell asleep to a frustrating dream in which she frantically chased Tadeusz through a snowy forest, unable to catch him.

Early the next morning, Miriam rose, bathed, and brushed out her gray wool dress with its pearl buttons. Putting it on, she looked at herself in the hall mirror. She had lost some weight, and the dress flattered her small waist and the soft curves of her hips. *As soon as I earn some money, I'll buy new clothes*, she vowed. *I can't get by for long on two outfits.* Too nervous to eat, she planned to skip breakfast and perhaps have a cup of coffee after her meeting with Mr. Zwillinger. If she didn't get the job, she'd have plenty of time, and if she did, well, she had no idea when he'd expect her to begin working.

As Miriam was leaving the house, Mrs. Grunwald shuffled up and pressed something into her hand. "Here, Miriam. This was Baila's, but she hardly used any. Why don't you take it. I don't use this kind."

Miriam held up the tiny glass cube, which was filled with an inch of golden fluid and capped with a silver ball. A black label with silver letters read *Love at Dawn.* Real perfume! Miriam smiled with delight and kissed Mrs. Grunwald's soft cheek, which smelled faintly of cinnamon.

"Thank you so much. It's been so long since I've worn anything but rosewater." She opened the bottle and dabbed a bit of the golden liquid on her wrists and neck. A sweet, citrus fragrance rose up about her face. Suddenly, she remembered.

"The book! How lucky that you reminded me." Turning from the puzzled Mrs. Grunwald, she rushed to her room, set the perfume on the dresser, and picked up the volume of love poems.

"I've got to return this book to Mr. Zwillinger. His clerk dropped it on the street," she explained to Mrs. Grunwald as she unlocked the apartment door.

"Oh, has he a clerk already?"

"Yes, but she may not be staying on."

"Well, good luck to you, then. It's a nice job. Baila always said so."

Miriam hurried out into the hall, her perfume mingling with the early morning smells of eggs, coffee, and pickled herring. When she reached the bookstore, Miriam found that like yesterday, it was still closed. She knocked twice, three times, her stomach gripped by anxiety. *Why isn't he answering? The light is on, but I don't see him. Has he forgotten about me and gone out for breakfast?* She scanned the street, then knocked again. This time she heard movement inside, and soon the door was opened. Mr. Zwillinger's smile as he let her in, coupled with the gay tinkling of the little brass bell, gave Miriam new hope.

"Yes, Mrs. ah—pardon me, I've forgotten your name."

"Friedman, Miriam Friedman. Maybe I didn't tell you yesterday."

"No, I don't think you did, actually. I should have asked. Anyway, you are in luck. Won't you sit down?" He indicated a small stool. Miriam sat lightly on its edge and looked up at Reuben Zwillinger expectantly.

As he spoke, he wiped a spot off the counter with a piece of chamois. "I believe I told you that I wasn't happy with my clerk. That was an understatement. In the few weeks she worked here, she was nearly always late. Punctuality is very important to me." He fixed Miriam with a sharp stare.

She was about to interject about her own punctual habits when he continued. "Not only that, she was sloppy. She left things lying around—books, magazines, coffee cups. Sometimes she'd smudge the pages of a book with lipstick or whatever. That was intolerable. Worse, she misplaced important books and receipts. She once put a book back on the shelf without looking at the author's name carefully, and I couldn't find it for weeks. She'd filed it under the first name instead of the last."

He shook his head in exasperation, then went on. "I was already thinking of giving her notice, but yesterday was the last straw. I had to fire her on the spot."

"What had she done?" asked Miriam innocently, knowing full well what would come next.

"She ruined a dozen of my books, that's what she did. The other day I asked her to glue the bindings on some of them. She had plenty of time in the afternoon, before the after-work crowd came in. God knows what she spent her time on. I had gone out to the book warehouse on Walowa Street. She was supposed to do it here, in the store, of course, but instead she took the books home behind my back. Well, the next day, not only was she late, but she had dropped the whole pile into a mud puddle, and they were soaked. Expensive volumes! I've been trying to dry them out in the back, but they'll never look the same. What's that?"

Miriam was holding out a thin book. "I found it in the mud when I left the store yesterday. I couldn't come back; I had another, ah, interview. But I made sure to bring it today. I tried to dry it out, too."

Reuben examined the book. "*The Love Poems of Nikolai Myczistrovic.*" He smiled. "He's all the rage among young women today. Fortunately, I have other copies. Did you read it?"

Miriam turned scarlet. "Oh, no. I just opened it to air it out."

Reuben smiled, picturing this religious young woman in her modest clothes and head scarf wading through the turgid sexual imagery of Myczistrovic.

"Well, so much for Elka, my clerk," he announced. "Now that I've unloaded all my complaints about her on you, I'm sure you'll be careful not to follow in her footsteps."

"Oh, I promise I won't. You'll see. When do I start?" Miriam stood up, her heart pounding with excitement.

"You start right now." He handed her some coins. "Go across to the coffee shop and bring me back a roll and some black coffee, no sugar. Get some for yourself, too."

Miriam rushed across the street. *A job! I have a job!* she rejoiced inwardly. As she carefully carried back the tin of coffee and the rolls, avoiding the puddles and patches of ice, her thoughts sobered. Mr. Zwillinger seemed quite demanding. What if she failed to measure up?

For the next few days, as Reuben trained her in the tasks she was to perform as his clerk, Miriam strained to memorize his every word, every instruction. She vowed to herself that she would be the very antithesis of Elka, for she would never be late and never misplace or ruin books. There was so much to remember. Every morning, dust the shelves, make sure the books stood evenly in their rows, wipe off the counter, bring coffee. During the day, memorize the categories and locations of the books: modern fiction on the right, from the front to the middle of the store, followed by classical literature and art, then poetry toward the back. The back wall contained religious books, which also took up some shelves on the left side, then philosophy, history, politics, science, and mathematics. Next came the school textbooks, with their colorful bindings. The center rows were for more practical matters: books on gardening, home repairs, cooking, and brightly illustrated children's stories. Finally, to the left of the shop's entrance was a section reserved for rare books. These were Reuben's special treasures, and he combed the city for prize acquisitions, spending hours at libraries, warehouses, and auctions. In these difficult times many people were forced to sell their possessions, and among the first things to go were old and sometimes valuable books. Often Reuben entered the store late in the afternoon, covered with dust and grime from some attic or basement, proudly bearing a tattered volume that he proclaimed was worth "a small fortune—at least twenty zlotys."

The hours Miriam spent in the bookstore were the happiest she had known in a long time. Every morning she rose early, full of energy, and at night she fell into bed exhausted but at peace. How different it was from working in the hot, steamy bakery, with Fayge leaning over her, constantly criticizing and nagging. There, she had never been left alone, yet all the while bitter loneliness had engulfed her like a thick fog. Here, in the shop, it was so different. Reuben Zwillinger proved to be a kind, patient employer who was quick to praise Miriam when her work pleased him. Once satisfied that she could wait on customers, use the adding machine, and file the receipts, he often left the shop for hours at a time. Yet Miriam never felt lonely. She loved walking up and down the narrow aisles, reading the titles of the books and making sure everything was clean and tidy. The smell of the shop and its air of peace and solitude reminded her of the time she had spent alone in *Tati*'s study, preparing her lessons as a little girl.

She also enjoyed meeting the people who came in to browse or to buy. She welcomed the tinkling of the bell above the door as a chance to see a new or familiar face and to enjoy a few words of pleasant conversation. It was such fun to look at a customer and try to guess from his or her appearance and dress what kind of book would be chosen. So many times Miriam was mistaken, yet she never tired of the game. *This fat Polish woman with the chapped face and soiled apron. Surely she's buying a romantic novel for her mistress, or maybe for herself. What!* Principles of Mathematics? Miriam would stifle a laugh. Then there were the prim librarian types, both male and female, who surprised Miriam with their requests for love poetry or marriage manuals. Her favorites were some of the steady customers: Professor Weisbrot, for example, who was writing a *History of the World*, and who groaned with displeasure at all the history books on the shelves. "Ach! Such garbage! Where do they get the nerve to think they are historians?" Rarely did he purchase anything, and when he did, it was invariably a cookbook for his wife. There was also the pretty, blond Mrs. Hirsch, a teacher who often came in after school to buy used children's books for her class library. Like a child herself, she giggled over the stories and pictures, often pointing out the funniest ones to Miriam before leaving with an armful of fairy tales and animal stories. There was one customer whose visits Miriam dreaded. Pinny Cracover was a short, stout man of about thirty with a shock of coarse black hair and a bristling mustache, who worked as a bookkeeper down the street. Several times a week he would burst into the store, setting the bell ringing wildly. If Reuben were out, he merely leafed through some of the rare books, grunted, and left. If Reuben happened to be in the store, he would immediately begin a variation of the same argument:

"Have you read today's paper? Did you see what he's doing now? How could a ridiculous paperhanger like that get into this position? Why, when I was in Cologne in 1927, we jeered at him. Have you heard what he's saying about us? The papers and the radio are blaring it everywhere. As if the Poles need any more encouragement for their own anti-Semitism. But if a civilized Germany," he sneered as he pronounced the words, "can proclaim that we are subhuman parasites, what do you think will happen *here*? Well, I'm leaving, I tell you. And you'd better do the same. Sell your goddamn store and get out!"

Yet as the weeks went by, he did not leave but continued to argue with Reuben on the topic, always with the same result. Reuben listened silently to the harangue and shook his head until Pinny slammed his way out the door. Then, for the remainder of the day, Reuben paced about the store, white-faced, saying little to the customers and almost nothing to Miriam. If she dared to ask a question, he answered coldly in monosyllables before turning his back.

Seeing him like that filled Miriam with icy dread. The peaceful silence of the shop became fraught with tension that hung over her like a tightly pulled cord, ready to snap at any wrong word or deed on her part. On other days, however, Reuben was so calm, so reassuring in his quiet presence, that she felt secure in her position and thought she would be happy working in the shop forever. She still tried hard to please him in her work, no longer from fear of being fired, but because she enjoyed seeing his gentle smile. His words of praise—"Very good, Miriam. Excellent! What a capable girl you are!"—filled her with a warm glow.

Alone in her room at night, Miriam found herself thinking more and more about Reuben. Combing her hair in the mirror as she prepared for bed, she imagined him leaning against the doorframe, watching her. Later, as she pressed her cheek into her pillow and closed her eyes, her usual nighttime fantasy of being held in Tadeusz's arms began to fade. Instead, more and more frequently, it was Reuben's face she saw behind her eyelids, or Reuben's long, tapered fingers reaching for a book. *What's wrong with me?* She asked herself. *I must stop this. I'm still a married woman. I must not get involved with yet another man. Worst of all, these thoughts will make me get careless at work, unable to concentrate. I'll lose my job.* The memory of wandering up and down unfamiliar streets in a desperate search for work was enough to erase romantic reveries from her mind.

At the shop she tried to avoid standing close to Reuben, or engaging in long conversations, especially if they were not work-related. But, as the days passed, it became increasingly more difficult. With the coming of winter, business declined. Customers, eager to rush home after a long day in a poorly heated office, were less likely to stop for a book on the way. With few customers coming in, Reuben spent more time alone with Miriam. The more she tried to withdraw from him by going into the storage room or climbing up on a ladder to dust the shelves, the more he seemed to seek her out. Gradually, Miriam found herself both flattered by his attention and thrilled by his proximity.

Sometimes, in the slow afternoon hours, he would read to her. Her favorites were the sonnets of Shakespeare. She loved them not only for the beauty of the couplets, which Reuben said were far more lovely in their original English, and even rhymed, but also for the rich, sonorous tones of his voice as he read aloud. At other times he read from more modern works: Karl Marx, who urged the common workers to unite against their wealthy oppressors, or Sigmund Freud, a Viennese psychiatrist who claimed that people behaved the way they did because of childhood experiences. Why, he even suggested that little children had sexual urges toward their parents! Hearing Reuben read these passages made Miriam blush and turn away. Reuben would laugh and tell her she was too innocent, too sheltered. *If only he knew how "innocent" I really am*, thought Miriam. *I wonder what he, or Dr. Freud, for that matter, would think about Berish, and the olive oil?* The memory made her shudder.

Sometimes they would discuss religion.

"Are you very religious?" Reuben asked her one day.

"Yes, I was brought up in a Hasidic home."

"Yes, I'm sure you were. Well, so was I, for that matter."

"What? You?" Miriam looked up in surprise at his wavy black hair, trying to imagine him in side locks and skullcap.

"Oh, yes. I was a regular *yeshiva* boy. My father was a Yeremer Hasid. You should have seen me: side locks, caftan, the whole picture. But when I got older, in the *yeshiva*, I found that I had too many questions and not enough answers. So I left the fold, as they say. Since then I've learned there are no answers."

"And are you not at all religious now?"

"Well, actually, I do keep a lot of the traditions. My wife, Pola, was quite religious and she kept me on the right track. So, most of the time I'm a good boy, eating kosher, you know. As for *Shabbes*, well…" He shrugged his shoulders and smiled mischievously.

On another occasion, he asked her, "Why do you cover your hair?"

"Don't you know? A married woman must cover her hair."

"But you're a widow."

Miriam hesitated. She covered her hair because she was a married woman, Mrs. Berish Sonnenblatt, whose husband was alive and well, presumably, in Pavlitz. She quickly thought back to the widows she had known. Did they cover their hair? Yes, her mother-in-law did. So did Fredda Krupnick, a young widow in Dubnitz whose husband had fallen in front of a horse. She strained to remember the rabbinical dictates concerning widows and head coverings and answered him. "A widow should also cover her hair. It's part of the modesty of a woman once she has been married. Unless the head covering would ruin her chances for a future match."

"Ah, yes. The modesty of a woman." Reuben gave her a long look, then turned and slowly walked away, back to his precious collection of rare books. An auction had been rescheduled for that afternoon at two o'clock. A wealthy businessman with even wealthier American backers was one of the fortunate few who would be allowed to emigrate to New York City. His furniture, his violin collection, and his library were to be sold today, and Reuben had planned to be there. Yet two o'clock came and went, and he found himself still in the shop, with no real desire to leave. Lately, this had happened more and more.

At first Reuben attributed his reluctance to leave to the novelty of having a new girl working there. But as time went on, it became clear to him that he was attracted to Miriam as he had not been attracted to any woman before, not even Pola. He loved watching Miriam as she worked, following her graceful fingers as they tripped up and down the keys of the adding machine or catching a glimpse of her shapely calves as she climbed a ladder to reach for a book high on a shelf. The sound of her voice as she conversed with a customer filled him with the keenest pleasure. At night, after work, he generally visited friends to stave off the loneliness that echoed through his silent apartment. Yet lately he found it increasingly difficult to concentrate on their discussions of literature or politics. His attention would wander. One night, while visiting his neighbors Isaac and Bella Fink, he left abruptly, even before tea was served. Bella nodded her head knowingly. "He's still mourning Pola."

"I thought he was over that already," countered Isaac. "After all, it was almost a relief when she died, seeing how she suffered."

"No. Sometimes it hits you later on. Too bad. I had thought of introducing him to Clara Epstein. But I guess he's not ready." She stirred her tea pensively.

In a dark apartment across the street, Reuben lay on the bed that he had shared with his wife and abandoned himself to thoughts of Miriam, thoughts that burned in him like a relentless fever until, unable to sleep and unwilling to give in to the deep urging of his body, he got up and sat at the window, gazing in silent frustration at the quiet street below.

Chapter nine

Spring came, and with the change in the weather, Miriam noticed a change in Reuben. Although he spent more and more time in the shop, he spoke to her less and hardly read to her at all. No matter what she did, he neither praised nor criticized her, yet she knew he wasn't ignoring her, for whenever she turned to ask him a question, his eyes were already there, watching, with an expression that both disturbed and excited her. One afternoon, as Miriam was replacing some art books on the shelves, Reuben walked up and stood next to her, leaning his back against the bookcase.

"Reuben," she said, "please move a bit. You're in my way."

"Am I?" Reuben smiled at her but continued leaning against the shelf.

"Yes, I've got to put these books up there. So you'll have to move." She laughed nervously.

"Make me." Still smiling, he folded his arms but made no attempt to vacate his spot.

"How can I make you?" asked Miriam. She vaguely remembered teasing Shloimeh the way Reuben was teasing her. It seemed like eons ago.

Suddenly, Reuben reached out and encircled Miriam's wrist with his fingers in a light but firm grip. "Push me away," he said, and raised her hand until it touched his chest, which felt warm and alive beneath the smooth fabric of his cotton shirt. His serious blue eyes stared intently into her green ones, which had grown wide with wonder. Just then the bell above the door tinkled. Reuben quickly dropped her hand and walked to the back of the store. Her cheeks flaming, Miriam was left alone to find Mrs. Hirsch a book on snakes and lizards. For the rest of the afternoon, she avoided Reuben's gaze and was glad to leave the shop at closing time.

Alone in bed that night, she wrestled with her thoughts. What was happening? Why couldn't things stay as they were? She considered quitting her job, but the idea filled her with anguish. She loved the work, she loved the shop, she loved—No. She wouldn't think about it anymore. After a restless night she rose early and walked to work through a heavy spring rain that filled the air with the fragrance of new life. With no umbrella, and only a light cotton jacket, she was soon soaked to the skin.

When she entered the store, Reuben stopped her with an uplifted palm. "Stop. Don't take off your wet jacket here. If you hang it on the hook, it will drip on all the magazines. Why don't you go into the storeroom and spread it out near the heater?"

"All right," agreed Miriam. Still dripping, she made her way to the little storeroom at the back of the store, wondering at his request. It had rained before, and he had never paid attention to where she put her wet things. Glancing behind her, she saw him walk to the front of the store.

Miriam rarely spent time in the storeroom. It was small and windowless, crowded with cartons of books and piles of old magazines. In a corner was a gas heater, already glowing, positioned so as not to ignite any of the books or journals. Next to it was a torn leather easy chair. A round, pink-framed mirror hung incongruously on the wall. *A souvenir of Elka, no doubt*, thought Miriam as she glanced at herself. Her silk scarf lay limp on her wet head, and sodden tendrils of auburn hair clung to her forehead and shoulders. Her wet face gleamed in the faint light that came from the heater and the partially open door.

Bending down, she removed her drenched jacket and spread it over the chair, only to find that her white blouse was soaked as well. Suddenly, the room went darker. Miriam gasped. Grabbing her jacket, she clutched its wet fabric to her chest to hide her now transparent blouse and the lacy camisole that showed beneath it. Reuben had entered the storeroom, closing the door behind him. The only light now came from the glowing heater.

"It's all right, Miriam," he said, in a voice that was new to her. "Don't be afraid. I won't hurt you." He walked up to her and gently removed the jacket from her grasp. She immediately crossed her arms over her chest. Reaching up, he untied her silk head scarf and ran his fingers slowly through her wet hair, separating the strands. Then he stood back and looked at her. "How beautiful you are," he whispered. He locked his fingers about her wrists and firmly, but with great gentleness, lowered her hands to her sides. Then, without releasing his grip, he leaned down and rested his lips in the hollow of her neck.

Miriam felt her knees grow weak as desire, long denied, rose up in her. "Someone will come," she forced a choked whisper. "A customer."

"I've locked up the store," murmured Reuben. Taking her in his arms, he sealed her lips with a deep kiss that spoke of his own denial and longing.

In the silent storeroom, with Reuben's strong arms about her and his soft lips on her own, Miriam felt as if she were dreaming. Dimly, she became aware that Reuben was slowly drawing her downward toward the tattered leather easy chair that stood behind them. Still locked in his embrace, she felt his hard maleness surge against her own trembling body. "No," she whispered, turning her head to free her lips from his own. Mustering what strength she could, she locked her knees and pressed her hand hard against his chest to keep from being eased down into the large, deep chair.

Reuben released his grip on her shoulders and stepped back. "I'm sorry, Miriam," he whispered. "I lost my head. It's just that I've waited so long, I've loved you for so long..." Reaching for her again, he kissed her forehead, and she leaned her head against his chest. She could feel his heart pounding, pounding against her cheekbone.

"We musn't do this, we can't do this." She looked up at him, anguish showing in her large eyes. A tear on her cheek glistened in the warm glow of the heater, and Reuben brushed it away with his fingers.

"Is it too soon, my darling?" Miriam nodded her head, grateful for the excuse he had provided her.

"I understand." He stroked her hair, handed her the kerchief, then adjusted his own clothing. "I know how you are feeling. It took me a long time, a very long time, to get over Pola's death. For a while I thought I'd never want another woman. But then you came, and…" He touched her cheek in a light caress, then continued. "I love you, Miriam. Can I dare hope, can I dare ask if you love me?"

Miriam nodded her head and looked into his eyes. The love that shone there brought fresh tears to her own.

Reuben took her hand, fingered the gold wedding ring, and kissed her fingers. "If that's so, then I'll just wait. I'll wait until you are ready. As long as I know that you love me, I can wait for you."

"Like Jacob and Rachel," Miriam said, smiling.

"Fourteen years? God help us!" laughed Reuben as he left the storage room.

Miriam sat down in the leather chair and closed her eyes. What had she done? She had fallen in love with her employer. Not only that, but he had fallen in love with her. Did she love him the way she had loved, or perhaps still loved, Tadeusz? Not really, not yet, perhaps. But then Tadeusz had been the first. She remembered Tzippy Kahn, a friend from Dubnitz who had married a jeweler from Shpelk. Before him she had been engaged to Laizer Braun, a local scholar. How eagerly she had planned her wedding. Although she had barely spoken to Laizer alone, she described her great love for him to all her friends. Then, for some unexplained reason, Laizer broke the engagement and left Dubnitz. How Tzippy had wept, sitting every *Shabbes* in the women's section of the *shul* and sniffling loudly until the cantor's wife frowned at her. Later she had married that jeweler, but even with all her new rings and necklaces, she had confessed to her friends that it wasn't the same. In her heart she longed for Laizer. "He was the first," Tzippy had explained. All the girls had looked at each other, thinking, *How many of us will ever have more than one man, anyway?*

Ah well, thought Miriam, *forget Tadeusz*. But how could she forget Berish? She was still his wife, consecrated to him in soul and body. Sighing heavily, she left the storage room, grateful for the customers browsing in the store, who would take her mind off her difficulties. The days and weeks passed, tinged with a bittersweetness as spring ripened into summer.

Reuben lived for the hours he spent in the store with Miriam. He had resumed reading to her, relishing the quickness with which she grasped the ideas of Freud, Hegel, or Marx. He loved the flush in her cheeks when he read her the sonnets of Shakespeare, or the more explicit love poetry he often chose. Miriam did not work on Saturdays, and on occasion, he would close the store on that day and take her for a stroll in the Saxon Gardens, amidst the fragrant, blossoming trees. On Sundays they often went on picnics or walked the city streets arm in arm. Only the nights were a torment to Reuben, for Miriam would not consent to come to his little apartment. She allowed him up to her place, but only under the watchful eye of Mrs. Grunwald, who beamed at them, and called herself "the *shadchan*," but never left them alone. Late at night, after a good-night kiss and embrace, Reuben would toss in his bed and dream of Miriam and Pola. He did not suspect what tortures Miriam herself went through, alone in her room in the Grunwald apartment.

Lying face down on the narrow cot, Miriam sobbed for hours, her fist shoved into her mouth to prevent Mrs. Grunwald from hearing. Sometimes she felt as if she had spent most of the last two years weeping. Would happiness always be denied her? First it had been Tadeusz. Loving him passionately, she had denied him her body because it was a sin, and now he was lost to her forever. Then she had been married to Berish, a man she feared and loathed. To him she was allowed—no, required—to give her body, with only misery and shame resulting. Now there was Reuben, who loved and wanted her, and whom she loved and wanted in return. Again, she had to deny herself because it was a sin—a far worse sin, even, than sleeping with Tadeusz would have been. What a bitter joke her life was. Yet her days had never been happier. Alone in the store with Reuben, she basked in his love. Even Tadeusz had not loved her as Reuben did. Tadeusz had been more detached, always talking about his paintings, his future. Reuben worshipped her, and she was flattered, and loved him the more in return. Reuben courted her, brought her flowers and little gifts, called her pet names, like Mirele. Once he forgot himself and called her that in front of a customer, causing Miriam to blush beet red and collapse in giggles. Fortunately, it was a new customer who didn't know Miriam and Reuben and took them for man and wife.

Every day at about two o'clock, Reuben would lock the store, and he and Miriam would have sandwiches and coffee. Then they would go back to the storeroom. There, they would kiss and embrace, with Miriam allowing Reuben to run his hands over her body, delicately tracing the outlines of her breasts and hips. Sometimes she would snuggle against him, sitting on his lap in the cozy confines of the easy chair. But always it ended in frustration for both, with Reuben wanting more than Miriam was prepared to give. Finally, one steamy afternoon in late July, Reuben could stand it no longer. He had been watching as Miriam shelved a stack of new children's books. Gracefully, she bent and straightened her body, raising and lowering her arms like a ballet dancer. Walking swiftly up to her, he kicked the pile at her feet so that the brightly colored books scattered in all directions. "Reuben!" Miriam cried, and turned to face him.

He grasped her by the shoulders. "Miriam, marry me."

"Reuben! What are you saying?"

"I'm saying, marry me."

Miriam shook her head wildly. "I can't."

He gripped her shoulders more tightly. "Why can't you?"

"I can't, I … I'm not ready."

"Not ready? Not ready?" he sputtered in anger. "You're ready to spend all your time with me, ready to kiss me, to hold me, to let me feel your body, your breasts, your—"

"Reuben, the door! Someone will come in."

"Let them come in, then. Let them see what a tease you are. You are, you know. You walk around like a pious widow." He reached up and jerked the silk kerchief off her hair, crumpled it into a ball, and tossed it into the air, watching in frustration as it wafted softly to the floor at his feet. "A pious widow, very religious," he went on, kicking at the kerchief, "but you're just a tease. Letting me kiss you, hold you, then pushing me away as if I were some schoolboy. Well, I told you I'd wait, but I've waited long enough. If you wanted to wait until we are married, fine. I want to marry you. I love you. At least I thought I did. But if you won't even consent to that…" He stared at her, anger darkening his keen blue eyes.

Miriam shook her head. "I can't marry you," she said weakly.

Reuben released her. "Well, if you can't marry me, and you won't do anything else for me, there are plenty of women in Warsaw who will!"

He stormed out of the store, slamming the door. The little bell jangled and fell to the floor with a metallic clatter. Miriam walked over and tried to replace it, but the hook had broken. Cradling the bell in her hand, she sat down on the floor and wept. For several long moments, Miriam remained huddled on the floor, Reuben's angry words echoing in her ears. She made no attempt to wipe away the tears that rolled freely down her cheeks, leaving dark, wet spots on the front of her blue silk blouse. Then, hearing footsteps pass near the door, she remembered that customers would soon be entering, and she stood up, wiping her face with her hand. Quickly, she walked to the tiny washroom at the back of the store and splashed cold water on her face and eyes, combed her hair, and straightened her clothes. Returning to the front of the shop, she stopped to pick up her kerchief and replaced it on her hair. Seated behind the counter, she recalled Reuben's words once again. Surely he was right. Things could not go on this way indefinitely. Was she to be punished forever because of her "sin" with Tadeusz? She had suffered enough, had shed enough tears. Passive, she had allowed herself to be manipulated by others. Compelled to give up Tadeusz, forced to marry Berish, would she now have to give up Reuben as well? Clenching her fists and straightening her spine, she resolved to take her life more firmly in hand.

Chapter ten

For the rest of the day, as customers trickled in and out of the shop, Miriam reviewed her options. She could tell Reuben the truth and see if he still wanted her; if so, she would go back to Pavlitz, confront Berish, and ask for a divorce. Or she could forget Berish, continue the deception, and live with Reuben as man and wife, perhaps even go through a wedding ceremony with him. Miriam looked down at her left hand. She no longer wore Berish's ring, but the thought of a false wedding made her shudder. She was, after all, a religious woman, a rabbi's daughter. She had transgressed enough; she would go no further. It was one thing to kiss and hold Reuben while still married to Berish, but to actually commit adultery—no, this she would not do. She had denied Reuben, and herself, these past months; she would continue to do so. There were, of course, two more choices. One, to leave Reuben and go elsewhere. She could do it now. Close the shop, drop the key in the mail slot, pack quickly, and be gone before he even had time to search for her, if he were so inclined. But picturing Reuben—his tall slim body, his black wavy hair and deep-set blue eyes, the touch of his hands, his lips—no, she couldn't leave him. And the last choice, to return to Pavlitz, beg forgiveness, and resume life as Mrs. Berish Sonnenblatt—that was unthinkable. The thought of Berish and his late-night ceremonies made her flesh crawl. So there was, after all, only one option: to tell Reuben the truth.

As the afternoon waned, Miriam waited anxiously for his return. What if he didn't come back? But surely he wouldn't leave his store for long. Evening came, and Miriam did not know what to do. Usually at suppertime, either she or Reuben would stay in the store while the other fetched a light meal and brought it back. They would dine together on the counter before the after-work crowd came in. Although hungry, Miriam didn't want to leave the store. Ignoring her stomach, she waited on customers and mentally prepared herself for her next confrontation with Reuben. It would not be easy to tell him her story, to admit to having deceived him all this time. Once or twice she was tempted to flee, find another job in another city. But instead she sat behind the counter, waiting as the hours ticked by. At closing time, he still hadn't returned. Miriam waited fifteen minutes, half an hour, then closed the shop. Night was falling, and the soft, warm air caressed her as she stepped onto the sidewalk. The street was filled with people heading home after the long, hot day. The languid summer air seemed to slow their pace. Miriam alone walked quickly, peering anxiously at the faces of the passersby. Where was Reuben?

A couple strolled past, arms linked, smiling into each other's eyes. Watching them, Miriam felt a pang and quickened her pace. She had nearly reached her building and could already see several of her neighbors sitting on wooden chairs in the courtyard in an effort to escape their cramped, stifling apartments. Their laughter and voices carried to her. "And so I told her, 'Fayge, that should be your worst problem. Is it a defect that the bride is too beautiful?'"

Abruptly, Miriam turned and began walking in another direction. Barely aware of where she was going, she allowed her feet to carry her down one street and up the next, until she stood before Reuben's building. Ignoring the curious glances of the elderly couples seated on the wooden bench near the door, Miriam climbed the steps and entered. The bulb on the first landing had gone out, and she held tightly onto the railing as she ascended the dark stairway.

Reuben's apartment was on the third floor, at the end of a long hallway. On a few occasions, Miriam had walked him to his door, waiting outside while he retrieved a book or some other needed item. Always she had refused to enter the apartment on the grounds that it wasn't proper, and what would the neighbors think? Now she listened at the door, straining to hear any sound from within. The heavy black door with its round brass knocker exuded a silence louder in her ears than the muted voices and clatter of dishes that came from the other apartments. Softly, she rapped with the knocker, then louder. When no answer came, she rang the bell. For what seemed like an eternity, she waited. Then, with a sinking heart, she turned and walked back down the hall. Reaching the top of the stairs, Miriam heard footsteps. A pair of strong arms grasped her tightly from behind.

"Reuben," she whispered, then closed her eyes as he kissed first her cheekbone, then her neck. She turned and faced him, put her arms about his neck, and met his lips with a kiss that left them both breathless.

The sound of a door opening, then quickly closing again, brought them back to reality.

"Come, Miriam." Reuben took her hand and led her into his apartment.

Miriam looked about with pleasure. "Oh, Reuben! What a lovely flat." Smiling up at him, she suddenly noticed his haggard face and his rumpled clothes, which looked as though they'd been slept in. "But you, Reuben, you look terrible."

"Ah, me." Reuben waved his hand deprecatingly. "Come, I'll show you around." He walked through the rooms, turning on the lamps. The apartment, though small, was spotless. A tiny, well-appointed kitchen led to a small dining area, which contained a round pedestal table and four chairs, all of dark, highly polished wood. Connected to the dining area and slightly larger was the living room, invitingly furnished with a low wooden table piled with books, two sofas, an easy chair, and an oriental rug. The walls were lined with bookshelves. Off to the right was Reuben's bedroom. Miriam glanced shyly at the unmade bed with its deep red comforter, then looked away. Reuben, catching her discomfort, laughed.

"Yes, one bed. Pola had wanted two beds—she was very religious—but I won out. Later she told me she was glad…." His voice trailed off as he stared at a framed picture above the bed. Miriam, following his gaze, saw a portrait of a younger Reuben, in top hat and evening clothes, standing beside a frail young bride with dark eyes and finely etched features. With a sigh, Reuben led Miriam from the room. "Miriam, we must talk. I assume that's why you came. Sit down." He indicated one of the red velvet sofas in the living room, and Miriam sank into it, aware for the first time of how tired she felt. Seating himself in the easy chair on her left, Reuben reached across the arm of the sofa, took her hand, and went on. "I'm sorry about the things I said this afternoon. I felt terrible afterward, that's why I didn't come back. I was planning to stop at your place later tonight."

He drew a deep breath and leaned forward. "Miriam, I'm asking you to marry me, to be my wife. We love each other. Enough time has passed for both of us. Surely it's as frustrating for you as it is for me." His eyes searched hers, begging for an answer.

Miriam sat up and withdrew her hand from his. "Yes, Reuben, of course it's frustrating for me. I do love you. You know I do. Nothing would make me happier than to be your wife."

"If that's true, Miriam darling, then why do you look so unhappy?"

Miriam's lip trembled, but she forced back the tears. She'd had enough of crying. Now was the time to be strong. "Reuben," she reached out and covered his hand with both of hers. Instantly, he raised her hands to his lips and held them there for a moment, then lowered them as he listened.

"Reuben, what I'm about to tell you will shock you. Please don't say anything until I finish. After I tell you, you may be very angry. You may never want to see me again, and if that's so, I'll understand."

Reuben shook his head but said nothing, and Miriam continued.

"When we first met, I told you I was a widow. That was a lie. I'm not Miriam Friedman, widow of Yossi Friedman. I'm Miriam Sonnenblatt, wife of Berish Sonnenblatt of Pavlitz…."

In the apartment across the street, Bella and Isaac Fink,

Reuben's friends, were finishing a game of cards. Bella glanced out the window to the building opposite. "Isaac, I think Reuben has company."

"So?"

"Isaac, I don't mean to be nosy or anything, but there's a woman in his apartment. I can see their shadows on the window shade. Look."

"Maybe you don't *mean* to be nosy, but you are being nosy. It's not our business what Reuben does or who he entertains."

"Well, I think it's nice. It's about time he started seeing someone, a good catch like him. I wonder who she is. Probably that redhead who works in the store. Pretty she is, too."

"Maybe they're discussing business."

"Business, hah!"

Hours later, Bella arose from bed to get a drink of water. Returning, she nudged Isaac, who grunted sleepily.

"Huh? What time is it?"

"Three A.M. And they're still there, discussing 'business.'"

Chapter eleven

The train raced along the tracks, passing fields of yellow buttercups that danced in the breeze. In the distance, a spotted cow suckled a spindly-legged newborn calf. Reuben pointed them out to Miriam, but she continued staring straight ahead, white-faced. He put his arm around her shoulders.

"Miriam, darling, stop worrying. Everything will work out. They can't force you to stay."

"But he can refuse to divorce me."

"He won't. Not after all this time. Obviously, he'll believe you're an adulteress and therefore forbidden to him anyway. We've been through all this so many times." He kissed her cheek, and she leaned her head wearily on his shoulder.

Again, she thought, *I'm branded a sinner without really having sinned. But this time I don't care. I'm only sorry about what my own family will think. But I can explain it all to them later. I wonder if Tati will ever forgive me, though. He never really believed me about Tadeusz.*

She sat up. "If only Berish or Malka had answered my letter. Why do you think they didn't?"

Reuben played with a strand of her hair that had escaped the white kerchief she wore. "Who knows? It's probably a good sign. They want nothing to do with you. He'll be only too happy to divorce you, you'll see. After all, a Messiah's wife shouldn't run away and disappear. It's not proper." He chuckled softly.

"Oh, don't laugh, Reuben. It isn't funny." She nestled against him again.

The train was slowing down. Peering through the window, Miriam could see the platform and the sign, Yankovitz. In this small town was an inn where Miriam and Reuben would stay that night in two separate rooms, or however many nights it took until Berish consented to give her a divorce. It was a short coach ride from the station to Pavlitz. The next morning, after a restless night, Miriam rose early. The sun streamed through the window, creating bright patterns on the polished hardwood floor. She dressed carefully, choosing a sedate, dark blue silk dress and a matching kerchief. Reuben had suggested she go bareheaded to shock Berish and his relatives, but Miriam refused. In spite of everything, she was still a married woman, and she would continue to cover her hair.

At breakfast Miriam toyed with her roll. Her appetite had fled. She touched Reuben's hand gently. "Reuben, I don't want you to come with me today."

"What are you talking about? I must come with you. If he sees me, he'll certainly divorce you. Otherwise, why did I come here? I could have stayed in Warsaw and not closed the store."

Miriam stared at him, her eyes filled with anger and hurt. "I thought you came to give me support, to give me strength. To be with me at the most difficult time of my life. If you're so worried about the store, you can go back."

Reuben flushed. He picked up a small silver spoon and began to stir his tea, then set the spoon down again. "I'm sorry, Miriam. Of course I would have come with you in any case. And I'll stay as long as you want me. I only thought we were following a plan, that I was supposed to come with you to see Berish. We discussed this, even yesterday on the train—"

"No. I changed my mind. I want to face Berish alone. I don't want to go as an adulteress. I'm not an adulteress. You wait for me here at the inn. I'll get a coach back." She sighed wearily.

Reuben looked at her face. She was so pale and drawn, with dark circles under her eyes, yet still so beautiful. Soon she would be his, and all the months of bittersweet torment would be over. He admired her courage in going alone to Pavlitz, although he disagreed with her. He felt her case would be stronger if he were to present himself as her lover. Besides, he was curious to see this Berish, after all Miriam had told him. But for now, he would wait. If she were unsuccessful without him, then he would go along with her. He walked with her to the coach and kissed her as she climbed in.

"Good luck, Miriam darling. Come back as soon as you can."

"I will, Reuben." She waved her hand, then turned away.

As the coach approached Pavlitz, Miriam looked about in surprise. She barely recognized the town. When she had lived here, everything had been shrouded in thick, white snow. How often, at night, had she stared from her window at the bare branches of the trees, pointing heavenward like so many bony fingers. Now the trees proudly stretched their leafy branches toward the warm sun. Birds and insects flew about among the leaves and blossoms. Miriam alighted near the house where she had spent the first months of her marriage. The yard was full of weeds, but a lilac bush, laden with purple plumes, stood near the front door. Who had planted it, and when? Miriam hesitated on the cracked flagstone walk, then went to the door and knocked. No answer. She tried the door, but it was locked. Then she remembered. Of course, how stupid of me. Berish would be at the study house, and Malka and Fayge at the bakery. Well, she would go to the study house and ask Berish to come out. Best to get it over with quickly.

The town seemed strangely quiet as she walked along the dusty main road to the study house. A woman in a white kerchief emerged from her house, carrying a huge tub of laundry. She glanced curiously at Miriam, then looked away. Miriam did not recall her face. The study house looked more ramshackle than she remembered. The paint was chipped and peeling; one of the walls leaned at an odd angle. The door was ajar, and a muffled droning came from within. Miriam was seized with dread as she stood near the open door. Did she dare confront Berish this way? But there could be no turning back.

She peered through the door, blinking her eyes, straining to see into the poorly lit room. Three elderly Hasidim looked up from their yellowed volumes of Talmud. Not recognizing the young intruder, they quickly resumed learning. In the back of the room, a lean figure stood alone, swaying over a lectern. Was it Berish? Miriam stared at the man's narrow shoulders, wondering if she should enter the room or call out his name. Then, as if feeling her gaze, the man turned. Miriam saw with surprise that he had a blond, curly beard. Where was Berish?

She would have to go to the bakery. This was something she had not anticipated. In the preceding weeks, she had rehearsed the scene with Berish over and over in her mind—what she would say to him, what he might answer, what her responses would be. She had expected to see Malka and Fayge at some point, but not before clearing the air with Berish. Now she would have to approach them, if only to find out where Berish was.

The bakery was a short distance from the study house. Miriam walked slowly. She tried to prepare herself for her meeting with her mother-in-law and sister-in-law, but anxiety prevented her from concentrating. Everything distracted her—the white butterfly fluttering above pink roses that climbed a rusted fence; the dirty yellow mongrel trotting along on the other side of the road, followed by a scrawny peasant boy in tattered clothing; the hoarse caw of a crow from the treetops above. Soon she had reached the few shops that made up Pavlitz's center: the shoemaker, the butcher, the dairy, and the bakery. A group of women stood in a cluster, talking. Seeing Miriam, they stopped and stared, then began chattering excitedly. *Perhaps they recognize me*, she thought. Miriam stared at them, trying to pick out a familiar face, but they were all strangers. One by one they averted their eyes.

Miriam continued walking until she stood before the squat brick bakery. Gray smoke billowed from its chimney. The smell of fresh bread, which she had once loved but had quickly grown to hate, filled the air. Miriam looked through the small window. Displayed were a few golden loaves of bread, three Sacher tortes, and several cherry pies. She could not see past the shelves. Then she remembered the back door leading into the work area, where the ovens, tables, and kneading troughs stood. Perhaps Berish was there, forced by her absence to take her place in the bakery. She walked around to the back and pushed the heavy door open. The room was hot and steamy. A thin, dark figure bent at the oven door, removed a pan from within with gloved hands, and turned around.

"Fayge," whispered Miriam.

For a moment the two women stood stock still, staring at each other. Fayge had lost weight. Her frizzled hair stuck out in spiky wisps above her high, narrow forehead. Her black eyes filled with shock and her mouth opened, emitting a shrill screech. The pan she was holding fell from her hands with a loud clatter, spilling a dozen currant buns onto the floor, where they rolled about before coming to rest under the table.

"You!" shrieked Fayge. "How dare you come here! How dare you show your face!"

The door to the outer room opened. Malka, hearing the noise, came rushing in. Seeing Miriam, she stopped short, reeling, and grabbed hold of a chair for support. "What?" she sputtered. "What, you?"

Fayge continued screaming. "What are you doing here? We thought you were dead, we hoped you were dead! How you shamed us! You, you—"

Miriam held up her hand. "Where is Berish?" she asked.

At this, both women began screaming, each one drowning out the other. Miriam strained to make out what they were saying as she backed to the door. Seeing her retreat, Fayge ran ahead and blocked her path, planting her frail body in the doorway. Malka collapsed on a chair and began wailing in a thin, high voice. Miriam stared from one woman to the other in confusion. This was far worse than she had anticipated.

Icy fear gripped her. "Where is Berish?" she repeated. "I must see Berish. Let me pass."

Malka continued her keening cries, but Fayge had stopped

screaming. Now she fixed Miriam with a sharp, piercing glare. She began to whisper hoarsely. "Where is Berish, you ask? Where were you, all this time? Where were you when Berish needed you? Where were you when he ran out in the snow, looking for you? Where were you when he fell into the river and nearly drowned in all the ice? Where were you when he lay sick with pneumonia?" Her voice rose until she was screaming again. "And where were you when he died?"

"Died!" Miriam repeated in shock.

Malka began crying loudly. "My jewel, my angel, my saint, my *tzaddik*!"

Fayge went on, her frizzled curls shaking about her head like so many springs. "Yes, died! He's dead—dead!—because of you. Because you ran away without a word. Where did you go? To another Polish lover? I know all about him, the great artist. Hah, what a bargain we got in you! You should be lying in a grave, not Berish! *You*, you whore!"

Miriam rushed into the front room of the bakery, nearly overturning Malka in her chair. Two red-faced women stood there listening. They turned astonished faces on Miriam as she ran past with Fayge in her wake. Miriam pushed open the front door and rushed out into the sunlight.

Fayge ran after her, screaming, "Whore! Whore!" A currant bun hit Miriam's shoulder as she rushed down the road. Turning, she saw Fayge standing in the doorway, tossing more buns as one of the women tried to restrain her.

A group of little boys coming from *cheder* took up Fayge's chant. "Whore! Whore!" they shouted in their high, sweet voices. Following Fayge's lead, they began pelting Miriam with stones and clods of earth as they raced after her down the main road that led out of Pavlitz. Miriam ran on, panting in the hot sun. Her kerchief blew off, but she didn't stop to retrieve it. A thought suddenly occurred to her as she fled, the word "Whore!" still resounding in her ears. *I'm free! He's dead! I'm free!*

A horse and cart pulled up. "Need a ride, miss?" The driver was an old peasant in a faded blue hat.

"Yes, please. To Yankovitz." Miriam climbed into the wagon.

She was so winded she could hardly breathe. Sharp pains stabbed at her sides. But she could think of only one thing. *Dead!*

As the wagon made its way along the road, she was able to calm down and even rest. She thought of Berish lying in the little cemetery outside of Pavlitz. Poor Berish. He had been so strange, so tormented. She had never loved him, but she hadn't wanted him to die. And now she was free. She sighed. The driver turned his brown, wrinkled face to her. "Why so much running?" he asked.

"Oh, I, ah, had a fight with the lady from the bakery."

"Ah, that one. That skinny one." The old man chuckled. "My wife used to work there not long ago. But she couldn't get along with that one. Like a buzzard, she is. The brother, he was really crazy." He tapped his head with a gnarled finger.

"Really?" asked Miriam.

"Yes, yes. Everyone knew. Thought he was King of the Jews." He laughed again.

"King of the Jews?"

"Yes. You know. The Messiah. Like Jesus Christ. That's why he died. My wife was working there then. The son, he had a wife, but she ran away. So they hired my Maria. But she couldn't work with that buzzard, oh no. The old lady, she wasn't so bad. She's bad now, though, since the son died. She lost her mind. Screaming and hollering all the time."

"How did he die?" Miriam leaned forward to hear better over the rattling wheels and the clatter of the hooves.

"Well, I only know what Maria told me. Like I said, he thought he was the King of the Jews. He went around quiet for a while, even after the wife ran off. Then all of a sudden he started telling everyone he was the Messiah. He ran out naked into the snow. You can just imagine! These are religious people, you know. You are a Jew, yes? So you understand. Well, they chased after him, and he's yelling all the time, 'I am the Messiah!' or whatever. So he ran right into the river. They pulled him out, but he was frozen. So he caught something, in the lungs, you know, and he died. He was crazy. What are you doing in Pavlitz? You from Warsaw? I can tell. Fancy clothes."

"Yes, I'm from Warsaw. I was just passing through."

"Ah, yes. King of the Jews." The old man began chewing on a piece of straw, and Miriam, feeling totally drained, sat back and closed her eyes. She had heard enough.

Reuben sat in the cool parlor of the Yankovitz Inn, reading a newspaper. Suddenly, the door burst open. He stood up in time to catch Miriam as she flew into his arms.

"Oh, Reuben, Reuben!" she exclaimed, laughing and crying at once. "Reuben, you'll never believe it. I'm free!"

"Free? So fast? What do you mean?" Reuben brushed Miriam's glossy hair back from her face with his hand.

"Berish is dead. Oh, God, he's dead! He died of pneumonia. It's terrible. But Reuben, I really was a widow. All that time." She sat down and covered her eyes with her hands as Reuben bent over her, trying to absorb what she was saying through her gasps and sobs.

"Dead! Pneumonia! Poor fellow." Reuben lifted Miriam's chin with his hand. "But Miriam, when did he die?"

Miriam stared into his eyes. "I don't know. He fell into the river, in all the ice. Why, it was in the winter, of course. The ice and snow!"

Reuben stroked her hair. "Even if it happened in March, it's now August. A decent interval. More than enough time." He bent down and put his arms around her shoulders. "Miriam, marry me. Now. Tonight."

Miriam smiled at him through a film of tears. "Not tonight, you silly. We have to make arrangements."

"When, then?"

Miriam hugged him. "Tomorrow," she whispered.

August 12, 1936

Dear Mama,

It is very difficult for me to write this letter to you after all this time. I wanted to write many, many times in the past, but always I was afraid, afraid that you would find me and bring me back to Pavlitz.

Surely you know that I ran away from Berish in February. I wanted to run home to you, but I could not. I felt that I would disgrace you, and especially *Tati* again if I did. I don't know what my mother-in-law told you, but you must believe me and understand that I could not remain with Berish. May God forgive me, but he was not a normal person. Soon after we were married, it became clear that he was very, very sick mentally. I cannot begin to tell you the things he made me do. I will only say that, among other things, he was convinced that he was the Messiah.

You must believe me that I suffered terribly before I was finally forced to leave. Maybe someday I will be able to tell you the things I endured. My heart aches at all the worry you must have felt when you heard I had run away.

After leaving Pavlitz, I traveled to Warsaw, where I found work in a bookstore. I made a good life for myself there, thank God. I rented a room with a very kind and pious widow, Mrs. Grunwald.

You probably know that Berish passed away, of pneumonia, in the winter. I found out when I went back to Pavlitz this month. I was going there to ask for a divorce.

Now I must tell you the most important news, which I hope will make you happy for me. I am married to a wonderful man! He owns the bookstore where I have been working. His wife died a year ago. We were married last week, by the rabbi of the Nowolipki Street synagogue. How I wish you had been with me. My husband, Reuben Zwillinger, is not a Hasid, but he is a good and kind man. He has promised to keep all the *mitzvah*s. You must believe me that in all the time before I married him, I remained a true daughter of Israel, thinking I was still married to Berish.

I hope that you, *Tati*, Dina, and Shloimeh are well, and that you will be glad for me that I have finally found some joy in my life. Reuben and I hope to come and visit you some time soon. Please write to me. I remain as ever your most respectful daughter,

Miriam Zwillinger

August 28, 1936

My Dearest Sister Miriam,

    I have just read the letter you wrote to Mama, and after first dancing around the room with Shloimeh, I ran right home to write to you. Mama says she will also write to you very soon. You cannot know how happy and excited we were to hear from you. Even *Tati* was so pleased, although at first he pretended to be angry. Mama and I cried and cried for joy.

    Why did you wait so long to write to us? When you first left Berish, your mother-in-law wrote us a letter, thinking you had come home. We were so worried and upset! And then, all the months of hearing nothing. Mama and I cried to each other, thinking you may have died, God forbid. And *Tati* locked himself up in his study every night. I know he felt it was all his fault. We tried to keep the news from everyone, even Shloimeh, but he soon overheard our conversations and learned that you were missing. Of course, he cried too, and each night he would look out the window for hours. It was terrible.

    Berish's sister wrote to us when Berish died. We were so sad. We didn't know where you were, so how could you sit *shiva* for your husband, as you must, if you didn't know he had died? We didn't even know what to tell people, since no one in Dubnitz knew you were missing. So in the end we told them nothing. You can imagine how we felt when people would ask us, "How are Miriam and Berish?" And we'd have to say, "Fine, fine" and smile. After a while, we convinced ourselves that you were all right, that you had found a new home somewhere. Thank God it was really true!

    Miriam, I wish you the heartiest *mazel tov* on your marriage to Mr. Zwillinger! How wonderful that you found a nice husband at last! Will it surprise you very much that I am also married? Shortly before we heard that you had run away, I became engaged to Leibel Parnes. I wrote to you, but I suppose you never saw the letter, because you had already left.

Although I was so glad to be marrying Leibel, I was miserable inside with worry over you, and the same was true for all of us. I even wanted to postpone the wedding, but *Tati* said no. So we were married on June 21. Everyone asked where you were, and we told them you were sick. I could tell they all thought you were pregnant. It was awful.

The wedding was very nice, similar to your wedding. Leibel looked very handsome. He knew the truth about you, but no one else did, except us. He is so good and funny. You must come and visit us, with Reuben. Imagine that now we are both married ladies! Leibel and I live on Pilsudskiego, near the box factory. The same street as Leah Halbleiter.

How do you like living in Warsaw? Is it true that everyone is wearing pink and gray this summer? Please write soon. I kiss you a million times,

> Your loving sister,
> Dina (Parnes)

Miriam sat on the edge of her bed, reading and rereading Dina's letter. Her shining auburn hair, still damp from the *mikveh*, hung loosely to her shoulders. She toyed with the pink ribbon at the neck of her white lace-trimmed nightgown.

Reuben emerged from the bathroom, wearing a black silk robe. He smiled at Miriam indulgently. "Are you reading the letter again?"

Miriam laughed, folded the letter, and put it on her night table, tucking it under a pewter-handled hairbrush. "I can't help it. It makes me so happy. I still can't believe everything turned out so wonderfully, for Dina and for me, too."

She held out her arms. Reuben embraced her and kissed her gently. His robe fell open, revealing his strong, lean body. Miriam reached out and turned out the lamp.

"Oh, such modesty," breathed Reuben as he began to undo the tiny buttons on her nightgown. Soon they were lying naked together on Reuben's bed. Miriam had insisted on two beds, dutifully separating them during the time of the month when she was forbidden to her husband. But now the two beds were pushed together, and a large sheet covered both mattresses. Reuben ran his hands slowly over the length of Miriam's smooth, firm body. After twelve days of separation, his desire was strong, but he was a considerate lover who always waited until Miriam was ready. Later, sated with lovemaking, they lay quietly in each other's arms. Miriam soon fell asleep, a blissful smile on her lips. Reuben, however, lay awake.

Above the soft rhythm of Miriam's breathing, he heard the muffled timbre of a neighbor's radio resonating through the wall of the apartment. Although he could not make out the words, the harsh, strident voice was unmistakable. It was the voice of Adolf Hitler—a small man with big plans, a man who vowed not to rest until the likes of Miriam, Reuben, and all others of their kind were exterminated from the face of the earth.

Part Two

Chapter twelve

Warsaw, Poland, 1939

Mama, Mama!" The little boy tugged at his mother's hand and pointed a chubby finger at the swaybacked carriage horse that stood at the side of the street, its head hanging in exhaustion. "Horse! Horse!"

Miriam smiled down at little David and tucked a few coppery curls under his white sun hat. "Yes, darling. A horse. A very tired one. What does a horse say?"

"Neigh, neigh! Buy me candy!"

Laughing at the abrupt transition, Miriam shook her head. "No, sweetheart. We must go home and have supper. Soon Daddy will be home, and he'll want to see you in your nightshirt, ready for bed. And what will he read you?"

"Story!" cried David gleefully.

When they entered their building, David bounced up the stairs with all the speed a twenty-month-old could muster and pounded on the door of their apartment. It was opened by Mariana, the elderly Polish woman Reuben had hired to help with the housework and cooking when Miriam became pregnant with David.

"Good evening, Mariana. Any messages?"

"Only Mr. Zwillinger. He called to say he would be late for dinner."

"Oh. I see. Thank you." Miriam walked slowly into the living room and sank down into a soft chair. Disappointment made her conscious of how tired she was. Now she'd have to wait even longer to share the secret she'd been keeping since morning. She put her feet up on the ottoman and gazed about with satisfaction. This apartment on Sienna Street was much nicer than the one they'd shared previously. The living room was bigger and lighter, and the new gray chairs harmonized with the warm red tones of the couch and carpet. The yellow kitchen was brighter, too, but best of all was the little room that adjoined their own. This was David's nursery, and Reuben had painted it pale blue, with bright blue enamel on the doors and moldings. A hooked rug covered part of the gleaming wood floor, close to David's wooden crib. Miriam had made the rug herself in the late months of her pregnancy when she had been too big and uncomfortable to do much else. From her chair, Miriam could hear David's high-pitched prattle and the deeper tones of Mariana's voice answering him as she served him his supper. Listening to their happy chatter, she forgot her own disappointment over Reuben's message. *How fortunate I am,* she thought. *I have a wonderful husband, an adorable child, a lovely apartment, and even a housekeeper. I have so much to be thankful for, especially in these difficult times, when so many are out of work. And wait till I tell Reuben the news.*

Her thoughts were interrupted by little David, who had finished his dinner and now came galloping into the room, his copper curls bouncing about his head. "Mama! I ate all! I'm a good boy?" He snuggled into her lap.

Miriam hugged him and kissed the top of his head, which still smelled of scented soap from his morning bath. "A very good boy. My best boy. Now come. Mariana will undress you for bed."

"No, you, Mama!" David slid off her lap and stood before her, arms folded across his chest. "You undress David. Not Mariana."

He stamped his foot defiantly.

"Well, all right. Just this once." Miriam got up and walked to the nursery with her son. *Reuben would say I'm spoiling him,* she thought. *But I can't help it. He's so adorable, and he reminds me so much of Shloimeh at this age.*

As she undressed David, she thought back to her last visit to Dubnitz, six months before. *Tati* had been so warm to her and Reuben, so much less uncomfortable than he had been the first time. And Dina's little daughter, Bluma, was so precious, with her huge black eyes and straight dark hair. She was the image of Leibel. And, of course, Dina herself, so huge in her eighth month of pregnancy that Mama wouldn't let her do a thing.

The biggest surprise was Shloimeh, who had shot up like a weed and had become shy and taciturn. He had seemed so old for his nine years. Maybe the knowledge that he would someday be the Dubnitzer *rebbe* had already begun to sink in. She and Reuben had offered to take him back to Warsaw for a brief visit, since he seemed to enjoy playing with little David, but Shloimeh had refused. Shaking his head solemnly, his long side curls swinging, he declared, "I cannot leave. I am in the middle of a very complex portion of the tractate of *Pesachim* and I must not stop in the middle. Besides, my *rebbe* would never allow it. It would be *bitul Torah*, wasting time that should be applied to *Torah* study."

Miriam sighed, remembering the seriousness in Shloimeh's green eyes, which had once sparkled with mischief.

"Tell me a story, Mama." David tugged at her hand.

Miriam sat down on his bed and caressed his soft forehead. Fingering the downy hair on his temples, she began. "Once there was a little little boy named…"

"David!" he broke in gleefully.

"That's right! And this little boy named David lived in a big house with his mommy and his daddy."

David smiled and snuggled down against his pillow. He put his thumb into his mouth, and with the other hand stroked the satin border of his white summer blanket. Soon his eyelids began to lower, and his breathing became more regular. Even when she knew he was fast asleep, Miriam remained sitting on the little bed, gazing at her child's face. How beautiful he was, with his long, golden eyelashes curved against round, rosy cheeks. She leaned over and lightly kissed the top of his head, then smoothed his covers and finally tiptoed out of the room, leaving the door ajar so that the light from the hall would shine in. David was afraid of the dark.

Mariana had just finished setting the table when Miriam entered the kitchen. "So, Mariana. What's new with you today?"

"Oh, the same, the same. Out on the streets, all you hear is war, war, war." She sighed heavily and wiped her brow with a bony hand. "If there's a war, my Tania's Fyodor will be called up. They'll send him God knows where. And she with a new baby." Mariana shook her grizzled head.

"Don't worry, Mariana. Maybe it's just talk." Miriam studied the woman's worn face. Mariana looked particularly tired this evening. It must be the August heat. "Why don't you go home now? I'll serve Mr. Zwillinger when he comes in. And don't worry about the washing up, either."

Mariana protested weakly, then picked up her faded leather pocketbook and left, closing the door gently so as not to disturb David's sleep.

It was after eight when Reuben came home. Miriam ran up to him eagerly as he entered. He kissed her cheek distractedly and looked around. "David asleep?"

Miriam nodded.

"Where's Mariana?" he asked.

"I sent her home early. She looked so tired."

Miriam began serving Reuben his dinner of cold chicken, vegetable salad, and fruit compote. She ate her own portions hungrily, but Reuben only picked at his food.

"What's new in the store today?" Miriam loved hearing about the business. Although she enjoyed the role of housewife and mother, she missed the calm, quiet atmosphere of the bookstore, as well as the friendly give-and-take she'd had with the customers. Naturally shy, she had not made many friends in Warsaw. Except for Mariana and a few local shopkeepers, she often talked to no one but David from the time Reuben left in the morning until he returned in the evening. And Reuben often came home exhausted, especially during the summer, when he rode home on a streetcar crammed with sweaty and ill-humored passengers who jostled him and grumbled at each other all the way down Sienna Street.

"In the store?" Reuben looked up from his plate. "Nothing. Yaacov is turning into a pretty good assistant. Not as good as you were, of course."

Miriam smiled. His words of praise still gave her the deepest pleasure.

When she had cleared away the dishes, Miriam went into the living room, where Reuben sat on the couch, tensely chewing his knuckles as he read the newspaper. Timidly, she sat down next to him.

"Reuben?"

"What is it?" He looked up impatiently. He hated being disturbed when he read the papers.

"I have to tell you something. I've been waiting all day."

She blushed and bit her lip. Reuben put down the paper. "Yes, go on."

"Well, you know how irregular my periods have been since I stopped nursing David. Remember you told me to see Doctor Frisch, and I told you this morning that I was going today?"

"Yes." Reuben swallowed hard, as if he had eaten a dry crust of bread.

"Oh, darling, Doctor Frisch said I'm pregnant! He examined me and said it's very early, but I'm definitely pregnant." She threw her arms around her husband and leaned her face against his chest, then drew back when he failed to respond. Reuben continued to sit stiffly, one hand clutching a corner of the newspaper, which had slid to the floor.

"Reuben, what's the matter? Aren't you pleased? You always said you wanted at least two children."

He sat silently, looking past her at the large windows whose lace curtains stirred feebly in the faint night breeze. Finally, he looked at her face. Her smile had faded, but her eyes were still bright with hope.

"Miriam, Miriam," he sighed, taking her hands in his. "You're such a child yourself. How many times have I told you to read the newspapers, to listen to the radio? You don't even absorb what I tell you about what's going on. Like a child, you live in your happy little world, playing with David and going to the shops. Haven't you understood anything I've been telling you? There's going to be a war, Miriam. A war! No more rumors; it's real and it's imminent. If you'd read yesterday's paper…" He shook his head in exasperation and let go of her hands.

Miriam looked at him in anguish. The threat of war was less upsetting to her than the fact that she and Reuben were having an argument. They rarely quarreled, but when they did, she became terrified, her reaction out of all proportion to the situation. Since she had stopped working in the store, she often worried that Reuben would lose respect for her, would see her as a silly housewife, and would ultimately leave her for a more intelligent and interesting woman. For this reason she had asked him to hire only male assistants, telling Reuben she would feel jealous of any woman who spent so many hours alone with him in the store. Now his angry words seemed to confirm her fears.

"But, but Reuben," she stammered, "I do know what's going on. I do listen. Why, only today Mariana was telling me that everyone is talking about war, and that her son-in-law, Fyodor—"

"Mariana!" Reuben broke in sharply. "You pay more attention to that dull-witted babushka than to me. And now this! And I'm supposed to be glad that you are pregnant! We've got to make plans, figure out what to do. We don't need any more complications than we have already. It's bad enough—" he stopped abruptly.

Miriam's face had taken on a greenish tinge. Suddenly, she dashed to the bathroom. As he followed, Reuben heard the sound of strangled retching, then of water flowing in the sink. He tried the door, but she had locked it. As Reuben stood in the hallway, David gave a faint cry, followed by soft sobbing. He tiptoed to David's room and listened, but the child seemed to have fallen asleep again. When he returned, Miriam had emerged from the bathroom, her ashen face glazed with sweat. Remorse gripped him. It wasn't her fault that she was pregnant, it was more likely his own. And surely she wasn't the only one in Warsaw who didn't like to think about war. She had suffered so much already. Why couldn't she have her sweet dreams and hopes for the future? He stood before her, his head lowered.

"I'm sorry, darling. Are you feeling better?" Tentatively, he touched her wet cheek.

"I don't know. I think I'd better lie down." She swayed slightly, and he held her arm to steady her as they walked to the bedroom. Lying beside her, he stroked her hair and murmured apologies and endearments.

Much later, he made love to her, moving softly and slowly in a gentle rhythm, as if rocking the tiny soul that lay hidden within, until he could no longer control the strength of his passion. He clung to Miriam, burying his face in her hair as she moaned beneath him, her body's deep undulations blending with his own. After a time they lay quietly, resting in each other's arms, until thoughts of war grew as dim and distant as the stars that shone faintly through the gauze curtains.

The summer wore on, with relentless, stifling heat. The heavy, close air seemed at odds with the frenzied talk and animated gestures of Reuben's customers. All day long, people came in and out of the shop, not to buy books—who had the time or patience to read?—but to talk, argue, and ask for and give advice.

One afternoon, Mrs. Hirsch looked in, fanning herself with a printed leaflet, one of many that lay about the streets.

"Mrs. Hirsch!" Reuben exclaimed. "Weren't you away in Otwotsk?"

"No, in Zakopanie. But we had to leave. Avram wouldn't let me stay, he's so nervous with all this." She waved her hands in the air, then began leafing through some botanical textbooks before hurrying out again.

Later, the door opened slowly, and Reuben looked up to see Pinny Cracover, the old firebrand, enter. Reuben was shocked at the change in the man. He had not seen Pinny for several months, had been told that the irritable bookkeeper had finally boarded a boat for Palestine, yet here he was, looking strangely shrunken. The man's black hair was streaked with gray, and his once stout body sagged.

"Pinny! What's happened to you? Didn't you sail to Palestine?"

"Palestine. Agh!" Pinny made a deprecating gesture. "I sailed, I sailed. But did they let us land? The damned British bastards sent us back. Back to our doom, like rats in a trap. Agh," he groaned, then spat into a wrinkled, grayish handkerchief. "And you, Zwillinger? What will you do now, with a wife and child, when they close your shop?"

Reuben scratched his head, gazing about the store. "A wife and child, and another on the way," he said drily.

Pinny frowned at him. "On the way? Get rid of it. Get rid of it, if it's not too late. Don't bring another Jew into a world like this. On the way? We'll soon see what's on the way for us. My own question is, why didn't I jump off the boat? No courage, no courage." He muttered to himself as he lurched out of the store, his body listing to one side like a sinking ship.

That night, for the first time in years, Reuben dreamed about his mother, who had died a decade earlier. In the dream, he sat at the rough plank table in the tiny kitchen where he had spent the first five years of his life. Yet it wasn't a child but the adult Reuben who sat at the table. His mother wore a drab kerchief and a clean but shabby dress that fell shapelessly over her heavy frame.

"Reuben, *tateleh*, dear one," she asked tenderly, "the little goat is out in the rain. Bring it in, please."

What goat? thought Reuben. *Who has a goat in the middle of Warsaw?* But when he walked outside, instead of a crowded street he saw a vast green meadow, and far off, a little white goat romped merrily in the tall grass. As he approached the goat, rain began falling. Huge drops splattered everywhere, yet Reuben remained dry. He walked on, but the goat seemed no nearer. Suddenly, the sky lit up, and a tremendous thunderclap filled the air. He knew he should run to the house, but instead he kept running toward the goat as lightning flashed about him and thunder boomed.

"Reuben! Reuben!" He could hear his mother shrieking at him from the house.

His eyes flew open. It was not his mother but Miriam who

was screaming his name, while all about them came the tremendous fury of explosions and flashing lights. Miriam was sitting up in bed, her eyes wide with terror. Little David huddled between his parents. The child's frightened howls added to the cacophony that filled the room.

Reuben got up and hurriedly pulled on his robe. As he did so, Miriam reached over for the lamp. "No! No lights," admonished Reuben. "Don't you remember the instructions?" For weeks the newspapers and radio had been advising Warsaw residents about the possibility of an air raid. "We must go downstairs, to the basement." He helped Miriam get into her dressing gown, wrapped David in a sheet, and lifted him in his arms.

Out in the hall, they could hear people trooping down the stairs. Someone had turned out the lights on the landings, but several of their neighbors carried carbide lamps, which cast huge flickering shadows on the walls as they passed. David whimpered and pressed his face against Reuben's chest. Miriam was frantically trying to lock the door. She dropped the key and groped about on the floor. "Leave it, Miriam." Reuben took her by the arm.

Suddenly, there was a tremendous crash and they felt the building shudder beneath their feet. The small window above the landing lit up, revealing a sky as bright as day that then went black again. David began screaming.

"Come. Now." Reuben whispered. He pulled Miriam's arm gently, but she did not move. In the darkness he could not see her face. If only he had a light. They had been warned against using candles, so Reuben had purchased a carbide lamp, but in all the confusion it had been left behind on the bedroom shelf.

"Miriam, you must walk. Don't be afraid." He tugged at her arm again.

"I can't." Her voice was a strangled whisper.

"You must."

Heavy footsteps sounded above them as a faint light filled the hall, along with the smell of spicy cologne. Zelig Rubinstein, an elderly bachelor who lived on the fifth floor, was descending the stairs. He was fully dressed in the black suit, white dress shirt, and neat bow tie he always wore, as if he had not been sleeping at all. In addition to his lamp, he carried a newspaper and a small lunch pail.

"Good evening," he called cheerily as he passed, as if he were paying a social call.

In the light of Mr. Rubinstein's lamp, Miriam's face looked ghostly, with round, staring eyes, pinched nostrils, and tight lips. Reuben squeezed her arms, then let go. "I'm taking David down. If we don't go now, we may be killed. Come, we can follow Mr. Rubinstein's lamp."

Miriam grasped his elbow and began moving stiffly behind him down the stairs. Her feet felt like wooden logs, and it was only with the greatest of will that she could move them at all.

Once in the basement, with Reuben's arm about her shoulders and David dozing across their laps, Miriam calmed down, although each new blast left her rigid with fear. A few lights were lit, and in the quiet between explosions, she looked about. The scene was almost funny; she would have laughed out loud had she not been so frightened. Rows of benches had been set up, on which her neighbors had arranged themselves, all in varying states of dress or undress. Mrs. Levy uncovered a large, pendulous breast, stuffed the nipple into the open mouth of her screaming infant, and glared angrily at Mr. Rubinstein, who was ogling her. The latter tried to cover his embarrassment by opening his large newspaper, which refused to cooperate, its pages flapping about with much rustling. A few rows behind them, Mr. Fenster, a wizened old man from the second floor, began coughing, a terrible scraping sound that seemed to come from somewhere far deeper than the wasted lungs of his bent, frail body. As he coughed, the people nearest him slid farther away, with apprehensive glances in his direction, until he seemed to be a little island on the bench, his black eyes darting about even as his body shook with coughing. In front of Miriam sat a young couple whose names she did not know. Like Reuben, the husband had put his right arm around his wife, a pale, blonde girl who was whimpering softly while their fat, black-haired baby slept curled on her lap. Every few minutes the young man gave a slow glance to the left. As Miriam's gaze followed his, she saw the burning brown eyes of Baila Friedberger fluttering coquettishly at the darkly handsome man. Baila, an unmarried secretary who shared a first-floor apartment with two other girls, wore a tight silk dressing gown gaily splotched with bright reddish flowers. Somehow, in the midst of all the chaos, she had managed to put on fresh lipstick. Catching the eye of the young husband once more, Baila leaned forward, displaying her ample cleavage. Miriam smiled to herself as the husband's eyes boggled and he squirmed slightly on his bench.

For quite a while, nobody spoke. Between the bomb blasts, the silence was broken only by coughs, cries, and an occasional hissing whisper. Once, someone broke wind loudly and some of the children tittered. With each explosion, there was a collective gasp followed by a sigh, as if everyone drew breath together as one body. Finally, Mr. Brill, a schoolteacher from the second floor, cleared his throat. "How long do you think it will last?" he called to Mr. Fein, his next-door neighbor.

"Who knows? Could be till morning."

"Maybe longer," ventured Mr. Goldschweig, whose wife was opening a lunch pail. The sulphurous smell of boiled eggs filled the air.

"*Feh*, Mrs. Goldschweig," whined Mrs. Klein, the thin, gray-haired widow who sat behind her. "There's no air as it is. Must you now stink up the place with your eggs?"

"Excuse me, my children must eat," returned Mrs. Goldschweig haughtily, beginning to portion out sandwiches to her fat-faced brood.

"Next she'll serve Limburger cheese," griped the window. "Some people."

"Don't fight!" shouted a voice from the back of the basement. "We have enough problems." Reuben squeezed Miriam's shoulder and they exchanged smiles.

Pale light began filtering through the cracks in the air vent along the wall. Still everyone sat, waiting. Finally, after a long interval of silence during which no planes were heard, a siren went off, the all-clear signal. People began brushing themselves off and getting up. First slowly, and then in hurried groups, they left the dank basement and returned to their apartments.

Miriam walked in front of Reuben, who still held David. The key lay on the floor, glinting dully in the early morning light. Once inside the apartment, Miriam looked at the clock. It was just before six. The apartment felt like a cozy safe haven. Its neatness comforted her. Everything was in order, in place. David was already playing with his toys in the nursery. The only thing that had changed was the smell. Unlike the basement, which had reeked of too many sweaty people crowded in a warm, humid room with stale air, the apartment smelled of smoke, so much so that Miriam's eyes smarted. She walked to the window to open it wider.

"Reuben!" Miriam's scream brought him running from the bedroom, where he had been dressing.

"I know, Miriam," Reuben breathed heavily. "I saw it from the bedroom. God help us."

Together they stood at the window, staring at the devastation below. The streets were full of rubble. In the pale morning light, the sky had a dull, orange-gray cast due to the many fires that burned, some with flames still leaping high in the air, others burning low, letting off thick black smoke. The buildings on their street were all intact, but farther down she could see empty spaces framed by jagged edges, where buildings had been partially or totally destroyed.

Reuben turned away. "Miriam, start packing. We must get out of the city."

"Why? We're safe in the basement." Miriam looked around at her beloved kitchen, with its gleaming counters and copper pots, even as her words rang false in her own ears.

"No we're not. If the building is hit, the basement will become our tomb. I'll pack my things; you pack yours and David's. Take only two changes of clothing for each of you, two of his favorite toys, his blanket…you know. I'll start doing an inventory of what food we need. Go, hurry." He turned away and began opening cabinets.

Miriam felt a pang of hurt. *I should be packing the food,* she thought. *He doesn't trust my judgment, because of how I panicked and froze last night. But I'll show him how strong I can be.* She began gathering up David's things and soon was back in the kitchen with two small suitcases. Reuben stared at them and frowned. "Not suitcases. They're too heavy and bulky. Put the clothes in bags or something—"

"Pillowcases," interjected Miriam, remembering her flight from Pavlitz.

"Yes, go on." Reuben was removing boxes from the pantry and shoving them into a large cloth bag, muttering to himself. "Coffee? Maybe. No. Sugar? Yes, for David. And Miriam. Salt? Yes, some."

Miriam walked up to him. "Reuben," she touched his arm. "What about the store?"

"The store is locked. Then again, who knows if it's still standing?"

"Shouldn't we go and see?"

"No, it's in the wrong direction. We've got to go east. Once things are safe, we can get back to the store."

Miriam stared at him. How could he be so casual about his beloved bookstore, which, next to her and David, had been his life? She went inside to pack. *What does one take when one doesn't know where one is going, or for how long?* Again, Miriam remembered how she had fled from Berish, running madly through the snow. At least now she was not alone. She had Reuben, and David. But how would they travel with little David? Her stomach heaved and she felt faint. *And now I'm pregnant into the bargain*, she thought.

Reuben entered the room. "Brill says the streetcars can't get through. We'll have to walk to the train station."

"Are the trains running?" Miriam turned on the radio, but all it produced was crackling static. She hit it with her fist, then switched it off.

"He didn't know. We'll have to take a chance. Are you almost ready?"

"Yes. Just one more minute." While Reuben and David waited in the hall, Miriam rushed about the apartment, hastily checking every room, as if she were expecting important guests any minute. She couldn't bear to leave it in a disordered state. In their bedroom, her eye was caught by a golden gleam from the top of the dresser. Her earrings. She scooped them up and dropped them into her pocket, then slid the top dresser drawer open and removed a heart-shaped black lacquer box. Inside was her small store of jewelry: the little diamond and sapphire engagement ring that Reuben had given her a day before the wedding, a slim gold bracelet, a pearl necklace, two more pairs of earrings, a coral brooch. Quickly taking a gray wool stocking out of the same drawer, she dropped the contents of the jewelry box into it, rushed out into the hall, and stuffed the stocking into her pillowcase.

Reuben looked at her curiously. "What's that?"

Miriam dropped her voice, lest neighbors should overhear. "My jewelry," she whispered. "I'm afraid to leave it behind."

"You're right. It may come in handy, if we should run out of money. Dubnitz is a long way off."

Dubnitz, thought Miriam as she descended the stairs behind Reuben, holding tight to David's chubby hand. *Who would have thought they'd be going back this way?* Instead of the holiday visit they'd planned for October, they would arrive in early September, unannounced. Refugees fleeing from a bombed city. Even so, it would be wonderful to be home. The thought of seeing her family quickened her steps so that David had to trot as they walked through the vestibule and out of the building.

The streets were crowded with people moving in all directions. Some walked quickly, carrying bags and packages, neat suitcases and clumsily tied parcels. Others went in and out of stores, buying groceries as if it were a normal day. A young Polish nursemaid passed, a child on each arm. The older child, a boy of about seven, wore a blue school uniform and carried a book bag. Miriam stared at them. Could there be school on a day like this? As they walked, they avoided piles of bricks and stones, some still smoldering. A siren went off, and Miriam jumped. Could it be another air raid? But it was an ambulance racing to pick up another unfortunate victim of last night's bombing.

At the railroad station a crowd milled about, shouting and gesticulating. An official-looking man walked out of the office and said something to them. Immediately, the shouting grew louder, the gestures more violent. As the Zwillingers approached, the crowd began breaking up.

"What's going on?" Reuben asked a middle-aged couple laden with hatboxes and imitation wicker valises.

"No trains," grumbled the husband, stopping to shift some of the packages from one hand to the other while his wife set down her own bundles and mopped her brow.

Miriam heard David's piping voice and looked down. "Pee pee, Mama." She took his hand and led him to a patch of weeds behind the ticket office, where he urinated proudly. He had stopped wearing diapers only a month earlier.

When they returned, Reuben said, "We have two choices. Either we go home again and try to hire a car, or we start walking and try our luck catching a ride on a truck or a wagon."

Miriam looked back in the direction from which they had come. Everywhere was evidence of destruction. Whole buildings lay crumbled like David's toy blocks. She thought of her cheerful apartment, then pictured her building collapsing, the walls caving inward like an accordion, crushing all within. She looked up at Reuben, and without a word, he took her arm and they began walking, little David trudging manfully between them. Cars, wagons, and trucks passed them as they went, all laden with people and packages. Often, Reuben raised his arm and hailed them, but no one stopped. When David began to whine, Reuben hoisted him up onto his shoulders, and Miriam handed him a bottle of sugar water, which he drank slowly, gazing down with wonder-filled eyes at the sights about him.

At one point a car approached, honking its horn and trying to force its way through the throng of people and wagons blocking the narrow street. The driver lowered the window and leaned out. "Make way, for God's sake!" he cried. Miriam turned at hearing the loud voice, and met a pair of eyes. A shock of recognition went through her.

"Menashe!" she shouted, rushing toward the car. "Remember me? Miriam. You once drove me here from Pilsk! Can you give us a ride?" Her words were lost in the persistent honking of the horn. Menashe had turned away, and his car was moving slowly forward. Miriam now saw that both the front and back seats were full; a fat blonde woman sat beside the driver, staring at Miriam with a confused expression, while in the back several children of assorted sizes were squeezed together, their faces peering out at her.

"They have no room, anyway," she said to Reuben, as if apologizing for Menashe's having ignored her.

They moved on, stopping only to drink some of the water they had brought. They ate their bread while they walked. As Miriam chewed it slowly, she remembered her great-uncle Mottel's description of the Russian army, into which he had been conscripted and from which he later escaped.

"Marching, marching, eating only bread and water, bread and water, no time even to sit down." She remembered his cracked voice and his pale eyes, dulled by cataracts. It had been difficult to picture Uncle Mottel as a soldier, as difficult as it now was to grasp the reality of her own situation. Was it only twenty-four hours ago that she had sat in her pretty kitchen, spooning eggs into David's mouth, having herself just finished a breakfast of eggs, cheese, and bread with honey?

The sun rose higher in the sky. Miriam felt her clothes sticking to her, clinging to her limbs as she moved. In front of her, a wet stain in the shape of a butterfly had spread across Reuben's back. David had fallen asleep on Reuben's shoulders, his tousled head bobbing against his father's cheek. Out of nowhere came a roaring sound, followed instantly by a terrifying clatter. With one motion, Reuben swung David from his shoulders to his chest, grabbing Miriam's arm with his free hand. Miriam, grasping their bundles, hurried after him. All around them people scattered, their faces anxiously scanning the sky. Miriam and Reuben, along with several other families, ran toward a nearby building, a long, narrow shed with a corrugated tin roof. The shed was locked, and they huddled against its outer walls, trying to squeeze under the roof's narrow overhang.

Miriam looked up. Two planes could be seen, flying low, swooping toward the center of the city. Flashes of light burst from their undersides as black pellets rained down from their bellies. She could hear the bombs exploding, and the rattle of the anti-aircraft guns. Miriam closed her eyes and buried her face in David's soft stomach as they crouched on the ground near the entrance to the shed. She could feel his stomach contract with each explosion, and she hugged him tight. She did not look up until the planes had roared off into the distance and the awful clattering had ceased. Then, walking quickly, their heads bent as if to avoid being hit, they continued on their way. David began crying. Miriam held up a piece of roll, an apple, a jar of water, but he refused each offer, angrily pushing her hand away. Reuben began reciting a children's tale about three goats and an evil troll, yet the boy howled even louder, kicking his feet and demanding to be set down. Finally, Reuben put him down on the ground, insisting that David hold his hand.

Their pace now slowed considerably. Innumerable vehicles, all full, rolled past them, leaving clouds of dust and exhaust fumes that made them cough. The sun shone relentlessly. Miriam felt a burning pain on the back of her right foot. She was not used to long walks, and her shoes were too tight for her swollen feet. When they stopped to rest, she saw that a raw red sore had formed where the shoe rubbed against her skin. She found she could walk more easily if she counted to herself. "One two, one two." She began counting aloud to David, and he joined in, so that it became a game.

"See, David, we are soldiers. We are marching, like the soldiers we saw on Marshalkowska Street. Daddy is our captain. One, two."

All at once there was an enormous crash, followed by a blinding flare of light directly in their path. The child screamed horribly. Breaking away from his father's grasp, he dashed pell-mell across the road and disappeared.

"David!" shrieked Miriam. She ran wildly in the direction her son had taken, dodging jagged chunks of smoldering debris as the bombs and gunfire continued.

"David! David!" Her screams echoed in her ears above the din of the explosions.

Reuben grabbed her arm. "Miriam, stop!" he shouted. She turned to face him. With his dirt-streaked face and blazing eyes, he looked like a madman. A vision flitted through her mind: Berish dancing about the candle flames. She began to laugh hysterically, doubling over, howling with laughter, as tears poured from her eyes. A resounding slap shocked her into silence. Reuben stood over her, his arm still raised, poised to strike again. He watched as reason returned to her eyes, then pulled her under a half-smashed wagon.

"Miriam," he commanded, "stay here, or we'll all be killed. Wait, don't move. I'll find David."

She opened her mouth to protest, but he had already gone. She was left alone to watch in fascination and horror as several nearby buildings splintered into fragments and burst into flames.

They will never come back, she thought. *I'll be left alone, a pregnant widow.* She began to cry, softly at first, then louder, as wave after wave of trembling shook her body. Trying to stop, she bit the back of her hand, leaving wet, puckered tooth marks on the white, blue-veined skin.

Gradually, the noise of the planes receded and the bomb blasts ceased. With the wail of the all-clear siren, people began emerging from their hiding places. She looked off in every direction, fighting the urge to run out and search for Reuben and David. She knew she must stay put so that Reuben could find her. But what about David? What if Reuben hadn't found their baby? What if David were lying somewhere, injured or killed? Surely she, his mother, could find him sooner than anyone. Wasn't there some sort of maternal bond that enabled a mother to find her own child, to choose him from among a hundred other children? She had read of such a thing in some book. Of course, Reuben had pooh-poohed it, had said it was sentimental nonsense. Reuben was always the rationalist, the realist. What good did his realism do now, she asked herself, anger and resentment replacing the terror that had gripped her these last few hours. *He's always right, and I'm always wrong; he always thinks he knows everything. But he didn't let me go after my baby, and now we'll never find him. If he comes back without David*, she vowed, *I'll never live with him again.* Once more she bit her knuckles as the awful trembling in her limbs began anew.

Each person that walked toward her filled her with greater despair. Single people, young couples, old grandparents, families with children all filed by, grateful to be alive after the onslaught. When Miriam could no longer bear to watch them, she rested her head in her hands. *Let them find me*, she thought, as exhaustion numbed her into apathy. Leaning against the wagon with her head buried in her arms, she barely felt the tap on her shoulder. Slowly, she lifted her head.

Reuben stood before her, with David in his arms. Both were filthy, their faces and arms caked with mud and their hair plastered down with water and dirt. But they were safe, both of them. Anger and fear were forgotten as Miriam threw her arms around her husband and son, hugging them close, repeating their names over and over between sobs and kisses.

Reuben stroked her face and hair until she had calmed down enough to listen. "He fell into a ditch behind a storage shed. I nearly fell right over him. I don't even know how I happened to go in the right direction, but somehow I did." His smile shone white in his black-streaked face.

"Thank God," breathed Miriam. Holding each other, they stood quietly for a long time. Finally, they began walking once more. Reuben carried David in his arms while Miriam trudged beside them. The pain in her foot had dulled to a steady throb. After a while she began to feel sleepy. She walked as if in a stupor, concentrating only on the rhythm of her steps. At one point she heard shouting nearby, but neither she nor Reuben paid any attention, for people had shouted at one another all along the way. Others walked in silence, with measured cadence, like mourners following a casket.

The shouting grew louder and closer, forming itself into a name that penetrated their consciousness. "Zwillinger! Zwillinger!" It was Isaac Fink, Reuben's former neighbor, perched atop a mountain of pots, pans, and crates that had been piled helter-skelter into a rickety wagon. Isaac held the reins of a raw-boned brown nag who should have been sent to the glue factory long since.

They rushed over. "Isaac! Where's Bella?"

"She's in the country, in Pludj. We thought it would be safer if she stayed there. I hope we were right. I'm going there now. Can I give you a lift? There's not much room. I've refused everyone else, for fear all my bundles would fall out, but for you…"

He reached down and lifted little David from Reuben's arms, seating the child beside himself while Reuben helped Miriam clamber up into the wagon. There, amid the dishes, brooms, and candlesticks, they made a small place for themselves. Miriam took off her shoes and let her sore feet dangle over the side, where the air could get to the blisters.

"What wonderful luck that you came by, Isaac," said Reuben, smiling up at his friend. "We're on our way to Dubnitz. Miriam is two months pregnant, and no one would pick us up. We were planning to hire a wagon in Bradinska, but if you don't mind us in here, we can just as soon go along to Pludj and catch the train to Dubnitz, if it's running."

"No trouble, don't worry. Want some cheese?" Isaac handed back a wicker basket covered with an orange cloth.

"It's like a picnic," laughed Miriam.

"Yes, some hayride," agreed Isaac, munching on a piece of bread.

They arrived in Pludj at nightfall. Miriam was shocked at the appearance of the village. The pleasant country resort looked like a ghost town. It was completely blacked out, and no one was about except an occasional boy or man running by the neat white cottages that lined the narrow streets.

They pulled up in front of the cottage where Bella was staying, and Isaac helped them all down. Miriam followed as Reuben carried the sleeping David to the door and Isaac knocked softly. The door opened and there stood Bella. At the sight of them, her hands flew to her mouth and her face turned white. Then she threw her arms around Isaac and began crying wildly.

"Oh, Isaac, Isaac, I thought you were dead! I was so worried. Oh, thank God, thank God you're here. But it's not safe. And who are they?" She looked at Reuben and Miriam as if they were strangers.

"Bella, you know Reuben, and Miriam, and this is their little boy." Isaac motioned them inside, where a gas lamp burned on a small oak table. All the windows of the cottage were covered with black paper.

Bella peered at Miriam, then hugged her and kissed her cheek. "Oh, forgive me. I didn't recognize you. So many people, coming and going. Please sit down. Here, you can lay the baby down on the bed." She pointed to a narrow cot in the corner, covered by a dull plaid blanket.

Miriam sank gratefully onto a low wooden chair, its legs and back made of rough, unfinished wood with pieces of bark still clinging to it. She had seen such chairs at the local village fair in Dubnitz, along with brightly embroidered skirts and dresses, colorful cloth dolls, brooms made of twigs, and other simple household items, all handmade by the peasants who lived in and around the town. The memory gladdened her heart and made her forget her fatigue. She was going home.

After laying David down on the bed and covering him with the moth-eaten blanket, Reuben joined them at the table. For a few moments, all sat silent, the stillness broken only by the sound of hoarse wheezing from an adjoining room. Miriam glanced at the room's door, which showed only blackness.

"My mother," explained Bella, noticing Miriam's gaze. "She's eighty-two years old and hasn't been well for the past year. Her lungs are bad. Don't worry, it's not tuberculosis." Miriam had given David a worried look at the mention of the old woman's trouble. A child in their building, a lovely girl of seven, had died of tuberculosis last winter because her mother had refused to send her away to a sanitorium.

"Listen," continued Bella, "don't mention anything about the war in front of my mother. She keeps thinking that it's World War I, when both my cousins were killed. She's very confused, you know. It's no picnic to be old." She scratched at a small mole on her chin and looked toward the bedroom, where the wheezing had gotten louder.

"So, Isaac," said Reuben, placing his hand on his friend's wrist. "What are your plans? Are you staying here, going eastward, or what?"

Isaac shifted in his seat, which was too small and rickety for his wide frame. Bella had risen from the table to make some tea, and he waited until she was busy in the tiny alcove that served as a kitchen before answering.

"If we stay here, we are sitting ducks. We're too close to Warsaw to be safe, and there's really no place to hide. The peasants hate us. They resent it that they have to depend on visitors for their liveli-hood—the way we 'take over' in summer, and then all winter they must scrounge and make do until we show up again. They would never help us. But what can I do? You heard Bella. Her mother is old and sick; she can't travel, and we can't leave her. Not that her mother has long to live anyway, if you call her life living. But Bella says stay. So we stay." He sighed and folded his big, hairy hands.

Bella brought steaming tea in brown earthenware cups, and once more they sat in silence, drinking and listening to the raspy breaths of the old woman in the dark bedroom, who with each wheeze unknowingly sealed the fate of her daughter and son-in-law.

When they finished their tea, Bella spread some quilts on the floor next to David's cot. "I'd give you our room," she said, smiling apologetically, "but Mama sleeps in there with us, and she wakes up every so often."

"Oh, please, Bella, you've done so much for us already. Don't worry about us. Besides, David might wake up, too. It's best if we're near him." Miriam helped her smooth the quilts.

The two couples said goodnight, and Bella and Isaac disap-peared into the blackness of the adjoining room. Despite the hard earth floor under their quilts, Reuben and Miriam slept soundly, exhausted from their journey. The next morning they were awak-ened by the sounds of Bella in the kitchen, preparing breakfast. Her mother already sat at the table, coughing now and then with a dry, rattling sound, like pebbles being shaken in a glass jar.

Reuben and Miriam dressed quickly, and Miriam hurried the drowsy David into his blue knickers and white blouse. The child was eager to go outside and was soon scampering about gleefully among the flowers that grew in profusion all around the yard. "Flowers, Mama!" he called, gaily pointing and clapping his hands. Miriam smiled at him, remembering how he had enjoyed himself in the countryside around Dubnitz on their last visit.

"He takes after your family," Reuben had observed. "Mine were always city folk." Reuben himself always seemed restless when they ventured outside of Warsaw. The Saxon Gardens were country enough for him. Now he was nervously pacing about, anxious to be on the way. They ate a meager breakfast of day-old bread, hard cheese, and coffee, for which Bella again apologized.

"It's so hard to get good food now. The peasants are in such a panic. I think they're hoarding it."

The dusty little railroad depot to which Isaac drove them was crowded with people of all ages walking in and out of the ticket office and scanning the long expanse of track that stretched to the horizon. "Refugees," said Reuben, "like ourselves."

"We Jews have always been refugees," said Isaac, pulling the horse to a stop. "We've been refugees here for seven hundred years, and we'll continue to be refugees here, Germans or no Germans." He helped Miriam and David down and extended his hand to Reuben, who shook it warmly, then embraced him. Tears welled in Miriam's eyes as she watched the two friends say goodbye.

Isaac climbed back up on the wagon, gave David a mock salute, and waved his hand. After turning the reluctant horse around, he drove away without another word. Miriam and David watched as the wagon grew smaller and smaller, then disappeared over a distant ridge. The road was empty. Clouds of grayish-yellow dust billowed above the wagon tracks.

"Where horse, Mama?" David asked, shading his eyes with his hand.

As they watched, a new caravan came over the ridge; more cars, wagons, and even handcarts, full of weary, disheveled Jews traveling eastward in the hope of finding safety and shelter.

Miriam watched the people alight and bid farewell to their loved ones. Some were jolly, clapping each other on the back, shouting, "Take care!" or "Keep in touch!" as though they were parting for a business trip or vacation. Others clung to each other, weeping silently or sobbing loudly, fearful they might not meet again for a long, long time, if ever. The sights and sounds of their anguish frightened and disturbed Miriam. She was glad to be leaving rather than staying behind like Isaac and Bella. At least they had a place to go; her family lived in Dubnitz and she had papers—a wartime measure—sent to her months earlier by her parents, to prove it. Reuben and David, respectively the husband and son of a Dubnitzer, should have no problems either. Thoughts of Dubnitz, and of seeing her family again, made her anxious to go. If only the train would arrive.

Suddenly, the ground began to tremble beneath her feet. The train. People began shouting and scurrying about, lifting their bundles, waving, exchanging names, addresses, embraces, and kisses. But the train did not appear. As far as the eye could see, the tracks were bare, the rails glinting in the sunlight. Then the ground trembled again, and stopped. The crowd stood still, eyes, ears, and feet attuned to each faint tremor of the earth as it came and went. The strange vibrations lasted only a few minutes. Reuben had gone to buy their tickets. When he returned, his face was pale and drawn. "Did you feel it?" he asked.

"Yes, what is it?"

"They're still bombing, probably close to Warsaw. Those are the explosions you are feeling."

Miriam bent down and lifted David in her arms. The earth itself was not safe; it could transmit the evil vibrations of the bombs right to their feet, even when the bombs were not visible. The earth began to rumble again, but this time, instead of stopping, the rumbling grew stronger and more insistent and was soon accompanied by a piercing screech. David began waving his arms and kicking his feet, demanding to be let down. "Train! Mama, train!" he shrieked, pointing at the black locomotive chugging toward them, emitting puffs of gray smoke. Again there were hasty goodbyes as people gathered up their families and belongings and surged toward the train.

The train was already crowded. Nearly all the seats were filled by the time the Zwillingers boarded, but Reuben found Miriam a place in the corner of the car, next to a well-dressed middle-aged couple. She sat David on her lap and Reuben stood above them.

"We'll take turns, Reuben," offered Miriam, "so you won't have to stand so long."

Reuben smiled. "Don't worry, Miriam. People will be getting off before Dubnitz. I won't have to stand for all eight hours."

Once the train began moving, everyone seemed to relax except for the couple next to Miriam. They sat stiffly erect and did not speak to each other, nor to anyone else. When David, always a friendly child, smiled at the woman once or twice, her lips twitched faintly in response, but that was all. Miriam gave them a sidelong glance. They were both in their early fifties, obviously Jewish, and apparently wealthy, judging by the material and cut of their clothes. Despite the heat, they both wore gray wool suits which looked so bulky that Miriam was sure they had on at least one other set of clothing underneath. Several large boxes stood in the aisle near the man's feet. What struck Miriam, however, was neither their clothing nor their bearing, but the grim, tight expressions on their faces. While the other passengers chatted, read, smoked, ate, played cards, and discussed politics and their future plans, this couple said nothing. When Reuben and Miriam opened their food basket and began feeding David and sharing the bread, cheese, and apples they had brought, the woman's eyes flickered in their direction.

Miriam offered an apple, but the woman shook her head, covered her face, and began to cry silently, her body shaking with grief. The husband patted her hand several times, but she shook him off. At this, the man abruptly stood, cleared his throat, and addressed the other passengers in a loud quavering voice.

"We were bombed out. Do you know what this means, to lose your home of thirty years? We have nothing! Nothing but the things we brought to the shelter, nothing else. My wife is a pianist, a composer. She was wonderful, brilliant, and now it's all lost! All her music, her piano, bombed, destroyed. These were our children; we had no other children. My business I had to leave, after thirty-two years. I had a nice small business in my home. I sold linens, all gone. All my inventory gone, gone. Everything, destroyed. Now we are going who knows where, to my wife's cousin that she's never seen; who knows if they'll take us in?"

A young, heavy-set man across the aisle leaned forward. "Why are you so worried? You're alive, thank God for that, at least. So many were killed by the bombs. Thank God you were spared. A house, a factory, so what? Think of the others who were less lucky than you."

"Nonsense!" shouted an old woman, waving a stubby finger at the young man. "You think it's nothing, to lose your home and your livelihood? You think it's easy, when you're not so young anymore, to go running for shelter to a strange place? Where is your heart? You should be ashamed!"

The young man looked shocked and then frightened, as several other people nodded and muttered in assent. He leaned forward again, adjusting his spectacles. "I didn't mean it's nothing, God forbid. I just wanted to give them hope, that's all—that they should see the other side, and be thankful for what they have."

"Thankful, shmankful," scoffed a tall, scholarly-looking man with a thin, pointed beard, who had been standing in the aisle, reading a newspaper. "Thankful to be able to run like a dog from your bombed-out home?"

The argument continued between several of the passengers, but the couple who had started it all were no longer part of it. The composer had fallen asleep, her head bobbing against the windowpane, while her husband stared listlessly into space, folding and unfolding his hands.

It was late in the afternoon when the train pulled into Dubnitz. Reuben, who had found a seat on the other side of the car, made his way past the crates, sacks, valises, and people that filled the aisle, and joined Miriam and David, who were already standing.

"Good luck. I'm sorry about what happened to you," Miriam said to the linen dealer and his wife. "I hope things will be better for you."

The man nodded and rose slightly, extending a hand to shake Reuben's, then sat down again. His wife stared into Miriam's face. "Thank you. You are so sweet. And your darling little boy," she said in a soft voice like that of a young girl. It was the only time she had spoken during the trip.

The Zwillingers were the only ones to get off in Dubnitz. A few *yeshiva* students stood on the platform, bidding farewell to one of their colleagues, who jumped quickly aboard the train just as it was pulling out. Miriam looked about and sighed with relief. *Dubnitz*, she thought. *It never changes. Nothing will happen to this town.*

Chapter thirteen

Standing at the depot was the same faded gray coach with cracked leather upholstery that Miriam remembered from childhood. Even the horse looked the same, a nondescript brown mare who switched her tail at the flies that buzzed about the moist balls of manure between her hooves. The driver was different, but not very. Instead of Meilech Bressler, it was his son Yona, who resembled his father in everything but the color of his beard. He peered at the Zwillingers, flushing a bit when he recognized Miriam. She herself felt embarrassed when confronted with the people of Dubnitz, who still remembered the portrait scandal. Of the subsequent events in her life they knew very little, Pavlitz being so far away. They had been told only that Miriam's husband Berish, the *talmid chachem* of Pavlitz, had died tragically of pneumonia and that Miriam had been married again, not to a Hasid, but to an observant Jew of Hasidic background, which wasn't so bad, considering.

When the coach reached the center of the village, Miriam was surprised at the level of activity, given the time of day. Although it wasn't a market day, people were running in and out of shops in a frenzy of purchasing. She pointed it out to Reuben, who asked Yona what was going on.

"What's going on?" the driver repeated. "Who knows? That's the whole problem. Nobody knows, so everybody is buying food, stocking up. It looks like the Russians are going to take over. If they do, they may grab everything from us. Meanwhile, the peasants are going crazy; they hate the Russians. And when they're nervous, anything can happen—maybe a pogrom, God forbid. Or else maybe the Germans will be here soon. It depends."

"On what?" asked Reuben.

Yona shrugged. "On God. That's who everything depends on in the end. But meanwhile everybody's buying up food, clothing, whatever. Well, here we are. All the best."

He had stopped in front of the Rutner home. A tiny girl in a bright green frock played in the dusty front yard. At the sight of the wagon, she stood still, then dashed into the house.

"Reuben, did you see her?" asked Miriam. "I'll bet that's Bluma. How big she's grown." Eagerly, she opened the door to the coach, jumped out, and ran up the narrow path to the house while Reuben helped David down and paid the driver. Before Miriam even reached the front door, it was flung open and Mama and Dina rushed out, shouting joyfully. Both of them began hugging and kissing Miriam, laughing and crying at the same time.

"It's a miracle, a miracle," Chaya Rochel chanted over and over, lifting David and nuzzling his face and neck. The child twisted his head and struggled.

"Down!" he shouted. He barely remembered his grandmother, his last visit having been six months before.

Reuben hung back, smiling as he watched the women and children. Dina's little girl, Bluma, clung to her mother's dress, sucking her thumb and peering at the visitors with huge, solemn eyes. From inside the house came a loud, squalling cry. Dina exclaimed, "The baby! He's up. Come see him." She hurried into the house, her daughter still clinging to her skirt.

The rest of the family followed. Chaya Rochel bustled about, a broad smile on her face, which appeared to have a few more wrinkles since Miriam had seen her last. "Sit down, sit down," exhorted the *rebbetzin*. "What can I give you? Supper will be ready soon. In the meantime, some tea? Some milk for David?"

They sat down in the hot kitchen. A pile of peeled carrots and potatoes stood on a cutting board next to some chopped onions, whose sharp odor filled the room. Dina entered, holding a fat, dark-haired baby. His black eyes sparkled like two tiny jet beads.

Miriam immediately held out her arms. "Oh, Dina, he's adorable! Another Leibel." She cradled the baby in her arms, gently smoothing his damp curls. David eyed the baby suspiciously, then slid from his chair and climbed onto his father's lap.

"Hey, little man," said Chaya Rochel. "Do you like your baby cousin?"

"No," answered David. "Mama put baby down."

"Oho," laughed Dina. "He's jealous."

"Well, he might as well get used to it," said Miriam, blushing deeply.

Chaya Rochel and Dina looked at her and Reuben, then at each other with a mixture of surprise and delight. "When, darling?" asked Chaya Rochel, while Dina bent over, kissed her sister's cheek, and smiled shyly at Reuben. She and her mother were not yet fully at ease in his presence, behaving with the friendly reserve that Hasidic women used toward men who were not their close relations.

"The end of March, God willing," answered Miriam. It seemed eons away.

"May it be in a fortunate hour," Chaya Rochel and Dina burst out in unison, then laughed.

"Where is Bluma?" asked Miriam.

"Right here," Dina said, pointing downward. The child was standing behind her mother, still clinging to her skirt.

"Is she always this shy?" Miriam asked.

"Pretty much, since Baruch was born. She's having a hard time not being the only baby anymore. They say she'll get over it once he gets a little older and starts to play with her."

"Of course," Chaya Rochel reassured her. "Miriam was the same way."

"And I am sure David will be that way, too, don't you think so, Reuben?" Miriam touched Reuben's hand. He had been sitting quietly, holding David and looking preoccupied. Her touch brought him back, if only momentarily.

"David? Oh, yes. The same," he murmured, then looked off into space again.

Miriam smiled at her mother and sister apologetically. She knew that Reuben felt ill at ease out here in the countryside among her Hasidic relatives, whom he considered provincial and backward. Were it not for the war and the threat to their lives, he would not have come to Dubnitz for anything but short visits. But now here they were, with nowhere to go, and for no one knew how long.

Chaya Rochel leaned forward, deep furrows etching her forehead beneath her white linen kerchief. "So, Miriam, God brought you to us safely. We were so worried, hearing about the bombing in Warsaw. All night I couldn't sleep. I feared the worst, but *Tati* said we must have faith, that God would bring you back to us. And so He did, praised be His name. Was it very bad?"

"Yes, it was terrible. But let's not discuss it now." Miriam eyed David and Bluma meaningfully.

"Of course, you're right. Come, sit in the parlor while Dina and I make supper."

"Where's Marika? Is this her day off?" Miriam looked around at the kitchen, which was clean as ever.

"No, not exactly," said Chaya Rochel. Dina took little Baruch from Miriam and went out to put him in his cradle.

"What do you mean?" Miriam persisted.

"It's complicated. I'll explain later," answered her mother, picking up a carrot and peeling it with fine, swift strokes. "Why don't you go up and lie down in your old room. David can stay and play with Bluma."

At this suggestion, the two children ran to their mothers and stared at each other with hostile eyes.

"It's okay," said Miriam. "I'll take David up with us. He's exhausted, too. I'd like to help you with dinner, though," she offered weakly.

"Nonsense. Dina is here to help. They eat here almost every night. We'll call you when it's ready."

"Thank you, Mama."

Reuben, David, and Miriam climbed the staircase single file, Miriam avoiding the creaky eighth step as she had always done. She envied Dina her closeness with Mama. Because Leibel was the *rebbe's* son-in-law, in addition to being a Dubnitzer Hasid, they ate dinner at the *rebbe's* table all the time. How different life would have been had she married him, Miriam thought. Then she, too, would be eating at her parents' table every evening with her own brood of children. Instead, she had married Berish. But had she not married Berish, she would never have met Reuben. She lay down on her old bed as Reuben and David lay on the other one. Father and son were soon fast asleep, but Miriam let her imagination play at "what if?" What if she had stayed with Berish? What if there were no war? The strangeness she felt at being in her old room began to diminish. The faded, flowered wallpaper, the gilt-edged furniture, were unchanged. Only the occupants of the other bed had altered over time—first Dina, then Berish, and now Reuben, with little David curled beside him. The flowers on the wallpaper grew faint and wavy as Miriam drifted off to sleep.

An hour later they were wakened by a light tapping on the door. Miriam rose sleepily and groped for the lamp, as the room was now dark. Before she could light it, the door opened a crack, letting in a thin shaft of light from the hall. Reuben and David sat up on their bed. David rubbed his eyes and pointed to the door. "Who's that Mama?"

Miriam got up and opened the door, then gave a happy squeal. "Shloimeh!" She reached out and grabbed the boy, planting a kiss on each of his cheeks as he struggled to get away.

His face was still red with embarrassment when Miriam, Reuben, and David came down to dinner a few moments later.

"Shloimeh," teased Miriam, "why so shy? Can't your big sister kiss you anymore?" Shloimeh squirmed in his seat, smiled slightly, and looked down at his plate. As on her last visit, Miriam was surprised by the change in her once bubbly, mischievous little brother, who now looked so slim and serious. His round face had grown thin, and there were dark hollows under his solemn green eyes.

"Sit, sit, Miriam. Reuben, come sit down. Here, David, sit here by *Bubby*, by Grandma." Chaya Rochel pointed out the appropriate chairs around the table while Dina carried in a large tureen of cold borscht.

"Where's *Tati*?" asked Miriam, helping David into the chair beside her own. Bluma sat opposite him, staring with eyes like huge black marbles.

"He'll be here any minute, with Leibel. Then we'll wash and eat."

Miriam looked around the dining room. Something was missing, but she wasn't sure what. She pictured the room as she remembered it, and immediately she realized. "Where are the candlesticks? And all the silver?" she asked, pointing at the heavy wood mantelpiece and sideboard, which, except for a few holy books leaning precariously against one another, were bare.

Chaya Rochel put her fingers to her lips. "Hidden," she whispered. "Everything is put away, buried in a box."

"That's why Marika is gone," broke in Dina.

Miriam looked from her sister to her mother, perplexed, but Reuben nodded his head. "Of course. That was very wise." He looked at Miriam and explained. "Remember what the coach driver said?" Miriam nodded, recalling Yona's words: "The Russians may grab everything from us...anything can happen...a pogrom."

"I understand," she said. "Of course the silver and valuables must be hidden. But what does that have to do with Marika?"

Shloimeh gave her an impatient look. "The Russians are communists. They wouldn't like to see a Polish woman working in the home of a Jewish rabbi."

Miriam looked at Shloimeh in surprise. What did this little *yeshiva* scholar know of communists?

The child sat up straight, proud of the impression he was making on his sister and her husband, and continued. "The Russians will think we are parasites. They don't like religion."

"How do you know this?" asked Miriam.

Shloimeh shrugged his thin shoulders. "Everybody knows." Miriam gave Shloimeh a respectful glance. She remembered the passages from Marx that Reuben used to read to her in the store in the early months of their courtship. She turned to Reuben. "If the Russians hate religion, then why are we safer here, should they take over, than we would be under the Germans?"

Reuben adjusted his tie. "Because," he explained, "the Russians believe in equality. The Germans, or I should say the Nazis, have been persecuting Jews terribly because they believe we are *untermenschen*, subhuman. The Russians—"

His words were interrupted by the entrance of Reb Mordche and his son-in-law, Leibel Parnes. Reuben immediately stood up to show respect for his father-in-law, the Dubnitzer *rebbe*, who, after staring at his daughter and her family in surprise, recovered quickly and extended his hand to Reuben. "*Sholem aleichem*," he said, then motioned for Reuben and Leibel to sit down. He gave Miriam a small smile, which broadened when he looked at little David. Miriam sighed. It would take a bit of time for *Tati* to warm up to her and Reuben again, just as it had on her last visit, but by tomorrow he would be more friendly. Still, she knew there was a rift between her father and herself that could never be completely healed. Reb Mordche had never quite forgiven her for the portrait scandal, even if he truly believed, as he said he did, that she hadn't actually "sinned" with Tadeusz. In addition, he felt guilty about her unfortunate marriage to Berish, for which he was to blame. There was also the fact that Reuben was obviously not a Hasid, although he did seem to be an observant Jew. And yet, any discomfort Reb Mordche felt with his daughter and son-in-law was more than compensated for by the joy he derived from his grandson, David, or Dovid'l, as the *rebbe* preferred to call him. The child was so beautiful, with his coppery curls, chubby, glowing skin, and brilliant, blue-gray eyes. It gave Reb Mordche immense pleasure just to gaze at the boy as he sat at the table, his small fingers toying with the cutlery. Dina's children were beautiful, too, but there was something special about this little boy of Miriam's.

Still smiling at David, Reb Mordche walked to the washstand

by the dining room door. After pushing back his sleeves, he filled the large brass cup with water and poured it first over his right hand, then over his left, repeating the procedure once more before intoning the Hebrew blessing: "Blessed art Thou, O Lord, King of the Universe, who has sanctified us with His commandments and has commanded us regarding the washing of the hands." Wiping his hands on a white linen napkin that hung below the washstand, he returned to his seat at the head of the table. Standing in line, the rest of the family each washed their hands in turn, reciting the blessing quietly.

As Reuben poured the water over his outstretched hands, he felt the anxiety that had been gnawing like a worm at his innards these last few months slowly begin to leave him. *These ancient rituals*, he thought, *have always calmed us and held us together, even in the worst of times*. He remembered reading that during the Middle Ages, Jews had not died of the Black Plague, possibly because they adhered to this very practice of washing the hands before meals, thereby reducing the transmission of germs. He also knew that precisely because Jews didn't die of it in great numbers, they were accused by their gentile neighbors of using witchcraft or poison to cause the plague itself. As a result, thousands of Jews were tortured and murdered. He remembered the words of Pinny Cracover: "They'll get you, one way or the other." He sat down at the table, feeling the anxiety return to his body like a nagging ache.

Miriam stood at the end of the line, holding David's hand. She watched as Leibel washed his hands, dried them, and turned around to hand the towel to Dina. As he held out the towel, Dina gazed up at him, and Miriam saw the look that passed between them, a look as quick and bright as a spark jumping between two cut wires. Their fingers touched briefly beneath the towel, and Dina's cheeks glowed. Miriam looked hastily away as her brother-in-law sat down at the table, but she could not help smiling in wonder as she washed and dried her own hands.

Imagine, she thought. *They really love each other. Just as Reuben and I do*. She looked at her parents. Had they ever loved each other in that way? She had seen evidence of affection between them, looks that bespoke friendship, respect, admiration, and yes, certainly love, but it was old love, comfortable and mellow. Could such love still kindle the kind of spark that had flashed between Leibel and Dina? *What am I thinking about?* Miriam reproached herself, and began chanting the blessing aloud for David's benefit.

The meal was simple—borscht, potatoes, salted herring, slightly dried-out rolls. As in Pludj, it was difficult to get good food. In these last confusing days, the stores had not opened and the peasants had stayed away from town. Reb Mordche finished his borscht, wiped the pink liquid from his beard and mustache with his napkin, and leaned forward.

"So, Reuben, Miriam, thank God you and the child have arrived safely. God has delivered you from the hands of our enemies, the Germans, may their names be blotted out. We do not yet know what fate awaits us, but we must be thankful for what we have escaped. This *Shabbes*, in *shul*, you must say the prayer of *Gomel*."

Reuben nodded. He vaguely recalled the prayer, which is recited on the Sabbath after one has had a narrow escape from any kind of mortal danger. A faint memory came back to him. He, a child of seven or eight in a caftan and round black hat, his arm in a sling, standing with his father in the Gesia Street synagogue reciting the *Gomel*. A few days earlier he had jumped onto a moving streetcar only to be pushed off by a local ruffian, and he had broken his arm. Now he looked at his father-in-law.

"*Rebbe*," he said, using the title by which Leibel always addressed Reb Mordche, "Miriam and I are very grateful to be here, whatever happens. But we do not want to be a burden to you and the *rebbetzin*. If your Hasidim can find us a place to stay, I will be happy to pay whatever is asked. I have some money."

At this point Miriam nudged him gently with her knee. Understanding the gesture, he interjected, "Thank God," then continued. "And, uh, God willing, I will look for work, starting tomorrow."

"Yes," agreed Reb Mordche. "If the Russians come in, we will all be working soon enough. These Cossacks will not appreciate *Torah* study as a vocation. In any case, as it is written in the *Sayings of the Fathers*, 'If there is no flour, there can be no *Torah* study.' But, thank

God, Leibel can help us in this respect. We have already discussed it."

Leibel sat up straight, winked at Bluma, and pushed away his plate. "Yes, the *rebbe* is right. You know I work for a grain distributor in Snietzin. I've already asked him if he can take on several more laborers in his mill. I was thinking of some of the *kollel bochorim*, young married men who study *Torah*. I'm sure there'll be a place for you, too, Reuben."

Reuben smiled gratefully at his brother-in-law, with whom he had always felt a warm rapport. "Thank you, Leibel, that is already a great relief to me. But what about the *rebbe*?"

"Don't worry," admonished Reb Mordche. "For this, too, Leibel has a solution. I, too, will work in the mill."

Miriam gasped. "You, *Tati*? You will work in a gristmill?"

"Of course," answered Reb Mordche. "That is what is meant by the expression I just quoted. What was it, Shloimeh?"

"'If there is no flour, there can be no *Torah* study,'" mumbled Shloimeh absentmindedly.

Miriam rose early the next morning. Reuben and David were still sleeping as she quietly left her bed and tiptoed to the window. She gazed up and down the road as far as she could see. Everything was calm and peaceful in the pale morning light. A cluster of Hasidim, some with black-and-white-striped prayer shawls wrapped about their shoulders, walked toward her father's synagogue. She heard the downstairs door close, and a moment later, Shloimeh walked stiffly down the path, head bent forward, hands clasped behind him, a miniature of their father in his black caftan and knee pants. His wide black hat obscured his face. Watching his funny, headlong gait, she wondered how long it had been since he had stopped streaking from the house, his lunch pail clanging beside him, dashing off to meet his friends on the way to *cheder*. A heavy sadness gripped her as she thought of the little boy who had grown up all too quickly. She turned from the window and began to dress, careful not to wake her husband and son. A distant thrumming brought her back to the window. She had heard that sound before somewhere, but the occasion was buried in her memory and she was unable to identify it. More people were passing their front gate, peasants as well as Hasidim. They talked to each other excitedly, using animated gestures, but Miriam could not make out the words. The vibration grew louder, and Miriam suddenly remembered what it was. On the eve of every major holiday, numerous Dubnitzer Hasidim from the far reaches of Galicia converged on the town in a sea of black as they marched to Reb Mordche's synagogue. The vibrations of their feet could be heard even before their black hats bobbed into view over the top of the hill.

Now she automatically looked to where the road led up the hill. Nothing was visible. Then suddenly, she saw them. But they were soldiers in caps and matching olive uniforms. She watched, frozen, as row upon row of them appeared on the horizon and marched down the road toward her house. They sang as they marched, and one column held aloft a red flag with a yellow emblem that she could not make out. As the soldiers approached, the citizens of Dubnitz began rushing about on the streets in an effort to get out of the way of the advancing troops. They pounded on doors and were quickly admitted to the neighboring houses. A few Hasidim had gained entry to her own home, and she heard their voices in the hall. Reuben came and stood beside her at the window, with David in his arms. Now the soldiers were marching right past their house, singing and carrying banners and large posters bearing the faces of their leaders. Miriam shuddered and edged closer to her husband, who put his arm about her shoulders protectively. She turned and looked up at him, seeking reassurance in his calm, gray-blue eyes. "What will they do to us, Reuben?"

"Nothing, hopefully. We'll all have to find work, I suppose. You heard what Leibel said. But we would have to do that anyway. I certainly have no intention of sponging off your parents."

"What about me? Do you think I'll have to get a job?" Even as she asked, her hand brushed over her slightly swollen abdomen in an unconscious gesture that did not escape Reuben's notice.

"No, Miriam, I think not. You've got a small child to care for, and your pregnancy will soon be obvious as well. I doubt that you'll have to work. Let's go downstairs now and see what's happening."

When they entered the kitchen, Chaya Rochel informed them

that Reb Mordche and his Hasidim had already left for the synagogue. Reuben hastily reached for his prayer shawl and hurried out to catch up with them to find out whatever he could. The women had been instructed not to leave the house until the men returned.

Miriam and her mother spent an anxious morning together, playing with David and venturing guesses as to what would happen to their town and their lives now that the Russians had marched into Dubnitz. It was with a mixture of relief and dread that they greeted Reuben when he returned hours later. He had little information for them, other than that Dubnitz was now under Russian rule, as was most of eastern Poland; that the takeover had been peaceful, and that the soldiers seemed friendly.

The next few days revealed little more, until one afternoon it was announced that there would be a meeting in the village square. The square was filled with Hasidim, peasants, and Russian soldiers when the Zwillingers arrived, together with Miriam's father and Leibel. Miriam could not take her eyes off the soldiers in their neat uniforms with the red stars on their chests. Were they friend or foe? Somehow, they did not look very menacing. They smiled a good deal as they milled about, now and then offering cigarettes and tobacco to the villagers or handing them pamphlets with pictures of Lenin and Stalin on the cover.

A wooden platform had been set up, and a hush descended on the crowd as a middle-aged soldier, resplendent with medals, climbed up and began speaking into a megaphone in Russian-accented Polish.

"Good afternoon, my good people of Dubnitz. My name is General Leonid Antonayevski. I am now the administrator of this town, as an official representative of the Soviet Union. We are here as your friends, to protect you in these troubled times. If you follow the guidelines set down in the literature that you are about to receive, no harm will befall you. On the contrary, your lives will improve one hundred percent. Until now, you have been living in a corrupt society, where a few had much, and many had nothing."

There were some murmurs of assent from the crowd.

"Under Soviet rule, this will all change. For are we not all equal, all citizens under one authority? Each citizen must contribute to society to the best of his capacity, and he will then be rewarded according to his needs, and to the needs of his family. No one need go hungry, for there will be enough for all."

Here the crowd, urged on by the soldiers, began cheering. Miriam and Reuben had inched their way closer to the podium, and from that vantage point they studied the general. He was about forty-two years old, of medium height with broad shoulders. His chest glittered with medals. His wide face with its high cheekbones was impassive. A few strands of light brown hair had escaped from under his hat and lay across his smooth, square brow. His small eyes drifted over the crowd. At one point he seemed to catch Miriam's gaze, and she quickly looked away. When she glanced back, he was looking past her, and she decided she must have imagined it. After all, there were so many people gathered here. He spoke a few moments longer about equality and mutual cooperation, then signaled his underlings to begin distributing more pamphlets and leaflets, which were eagerly snatched up by the peasants, most of whom couldn't read, and more reservedly accepted by the Hasidim, many of whom could.

Within a few days, life became "normal" under Russian rule. The stores, which had been closed, opened again, and brisk business was done between the shopkeepers and the soldiers, who were eager to buy. This delighted the Dubnitzer merchants, who promptly raised prices, causing the local citizens to complain. Long lines began forming at stores stocking basic necessities, and a primitive black market developed, with people hoarding goods and selling them at vastly inflated prices. Within weeks, it was announced that all able-bodied men and women must find work. Those who did not were subject to arrest. But finding a job was no easy task in a provincial town like Dubnitz, with its large Hasidic population, many of whom spent most of their time studying. Many families prepared to leave for the larger cities, where work was easier to come by. There were many tearful farewells as Hasidim and their families came to pay their respects to their *rebbe*, whom they had served all their lives, and at whose table they had spent every Jewish holiday.

Leibel, true to his word, found jobs for Reuben and Reb

Mordche in the gristmill where he worked. The mill had been nationalized in the second week of the takeover. Reb Mordche became a
"foreman." Since his health had become delicate in recent years, and
since the mill's owner could not countenance his *rebbe* working, he
was given a small room with a table and bench where he studied Talmud several hours a day. When the Russian officer who supervised the
mill came upstairs, Leibel knocked surreptitiously on the *rebbe's* door.
Reb Mordche would then leave the little alcove and begin pacing up
and down the floor, observing the workers as they ground the meal
and packed it into burlap sacks. As the men worked, they chanted
the plaintive words of an old Yiddish song:

> Oh Master of the Universe,
> Help, already, all the Jews.
> Oh Master of the Universe,
> Let me be among them.
> Oh bring, already, the redemption.
> Let the Messiah already come!

The slow, sad melody appealed to the Russian overseer, reminding him of the ponderous folk songs of his native village on the Volga
River.

Gradually, the people of Dubnitz adjusted to their new situation. Since Miriam and Dina too were expected to work, it was
decided that Chaya Rochel, who was old enough to be allowed a
work release, would stay at home and care for the children. Dina
quickly got a job in her mother-in-law's small grocery, which had
also been nationalized. Twice a day she rushed home to nurse little
Baruch, then hurried back to the tiny shop to take her place behind
the narrow, glass-topped counter, where she sold milk, eggs, sugar,
kosher sausage, and whatever else was imported from the larger cities
or brought in by the local farmers and peasants.

When Miriam registered for work, she listed her previous
experience in both the Warsaw bookstore and the Pavlitz bakery.
Since Dubnitz had few stores but did have a bakery that was being
expanded to accommodate the needs of the soldiers, Miriam was

given a job there, much to her dismay. The rest of the family rejoiced, for they would now have a steady supply of bread. No longer would Shloimeh spend long, miserable hours on the bread line, sweating in the hot sun, being shoved and elbowed, and more often than not returning home empty-handed.

From her first day in the bakery however, Miriam was miserable. The heat, humidity, and atmosphere of the place brought back the bitter memories of her service in Malka and Fayge's bakery in Pavlitz. The fact that she was now three months pregnant made matters worse, for her sensitive stomach often rebelled at the cloying, doughy smells that permeated the moist air. Several times a day she fought down waves of nausea that threatened to engulf her, and on many occasions she had to run outside behind the building, where she retched violently, sometimes vomiting up her last meal. Still, she told no one at home about her discomfort, for the bread was a vital necessity, as was the job itself. Lately, stories had been told in Dubnitz of arrests taking place in the nearby cities of Miniesz and Chierenska. During the night, it was said, soldiers would come and arrest people—sometimes fathers, sometimes adult sons, and sometimes whole families—for being "parasites," "enemies of the people," or "capitalists." These people were put on trains and shipped far away to the frozen wastes of Siberia, where they were never heard from again. People were arrested for such "crimes" as not showing up for work, not having proper papers, or appearing too prosperous. Such things had not happened in Dubnitz, and many dismissed them as rumors, or even lies, but still they gave the Dubnitzers pause.

There was another reason why Miriam dragged herself to the bakery each morning, a reason she could confide to no one. She was deathly afraid to miss even a day of work, for she knew her absence would be noticed, and no one could cover up for her. The bakery, which had been a small, two-room structure similar to the one in Pavlitz, was now in the process of being expanded, as many more soldiers had arrived in town since the takeover. Walls were smashed in, and the noise of saws and hammers contributed to Miriam's general discomfort, as did the powdery plaster dust that drifted in the air and coated everything, blending with the ever-present flour.

The overseer of the expansion was General Antonayevski, the military administrator of Dubnitz. Bored with this sleepy little village to which he had been assigned, and sorely missing the excitement and bustle of his native Kiev, he found the expansion an interesting diversion and the beautiful baker's assistant even more distracting. From the first time he entered the bakery, he had noticed Miriam's lovely face and slim, graceful figure. Her white apron hid the early signs of her pregnancy, but her face had taken on a glowing fullness that flattered her. The hot damp air in the bakery turned the hair that escaped her crisp white kerchief to soft auburn waves on her forehead. The general made a practice of entering the baking area several times a day to "buy" fresh rolls or cakes for himself and his workers, though he seldom paid. Once there, he would linger, his eyes following Miriam's every move. The original owner of the shop, Reb Shmuel Kalisher, had left Dubnitz to join his family in Lodz several months before, and the nationalized bakery was now run by a newcomer to Dubnitz, a Mrs. Baum, who had fled to Dubnitz from Cracow. A tall, thin, timid woman, she was terrified of the general and consequently found his entry into the bakery the perfect excuse to run to the storeroom or the outhouse—anywhere his piercing gaze could not reach. "Oh, my dear, when he comes in, I get so frightened. I just have to run to the outhouse. I really can't help it, you know. I've always been afraid of soldiers."

Miriam had looked at her contemptuously, knowing she would get no help from this frightened woman. For his part, the general was delighted at the effect his appearance had on Mrs. Baum, as it meant he would be alone with Miriam.

In the beginning, he asked her questions about herself. Was she married? What did her husband do? Did she have children? Miriam told him as little as possible, for she knew he had the power to determine the fate of the family. He himself had indicated as much on more than one occasion: "Oh, your husband, he is working, yes? He is a diligent worker, I hope. Worthy of a wife such as you. Why last week, in Chierenska, they arrested four men. They wouldn't work, wouldn't contribute their share."

So the stories are true, thought Miriam as an icy chill gripped her stomach. One day he entered the store just as Miriam was struggling to overcome a bout of nausea. Seeing him, she fought it with all her might. *If he sees I'm ill, he'll think I'm faking it to avoid working. Even worse, if he believes I'm ill, or finds out I'm pregnant, he'll think I can't work, and he'll give my job away, or blackmail me with it. Who knows what he is capable of doing?* So she turned her back and began forming bagels, her stomach contracting into hard, painful knots as she forced down her nausea. But it was too late. The general came up behind her and grasped her arm, causing her to stiffen. Beads of cold sweat stood on her face as she turned to him.

"What's the matter, little redhead? You look ill today."

"It's nothing," Miriam stammered. "Just the heat."

"Yes, it is very hot, especially in here. Why don't you come outside, where it's cooler?" Without waiting for her answer, he propelled her outdoors, his hand grasping her arm like a vise.

Behind the bakery was a huge pile of brick, stone, and other building materials. The loud hum and clatter of construction machines sounded in their ears as they walked. General Antonayevski led Miriam to the pile of stone and brick and positioned her between it and the bakery wall itself. There, they could not be seen by Mrs. Baum as she left the outhouse, nor by the workmen who busied themselves on the other side of the wall. Their voices, too, were muffled by the noise coming from the expansion project. The general leaned closer to Miriam. Terrified, she closed her eyes and held her breath, repelled by the smell of vodka on his. Mistaking her closed eyes and quick, gasping breaths as a sign of passion, the general removed Miriam's kerchief and began stroking her hair, all the while continuing to grip her arm tightly with his other hand.

"You are a beautiful woman," he murmured as his hand traveled down her cheek to her shoulder. "Far too beautiful for this little one-horse town. You should be an officer's lady, in Kiev. You should be dressed in satin and silk, with diamonds here," he fingered her earlobe, "and here." He touched her throat, where her pulse fluttered. "You must come to my room," he whispered, "where we can talk, and be comfortable. I have some lovely chocolate." He reached into his pocket and removed a red-and-gold-wrapped bonbon, which he shoved into the neck of her dress, pushing it down until his hand was between her breasts. There he deposited the chocolate, then began to roughly fondle her round, full breasts. Miriam held her breath and stood rigidly, fighting tears, until he removed his hand.

"Will you come to my room?" he whispered, breathing vodka fumes into her ashen face.

"I can't. My husband," Miriam gasped. If only he would release her arm, which was growing numb under his pincerlike grasp.

"Your husband. Too bad. Perhaps he could take a little trip…" The general smiled, his eyes narrowing to black slits in his broad face.

Miriam stiffened and drew back. "If you send my husband away, I'll tell everyone. I'll go away myself. I'll go to Moscow, I'll tell your superiors," she sputtered, then stopped, horrified at her own words.

The general's smile widened. "My little green-eyed cat. See how she spits at me. Oh, I love an angry woman. Look how you've excited me."

Just then, the noise of the machines stopped, and the workmen's voices could be heard. It was time for their lunch break. The general cursed volubly in Russian. "The men's break," he exclaimed. "Too bad. And I can't be seen like this. Not proper, in such tight trousers." He laughed loudly, released Miriam, and staggered off toward the outhouse just as Mrs. Baum emerged and sprinted, rabbitlike, to the bakery.

Miriam heard the general laugh again as he entered the outhouse. Suddenly, she bent and vomited violently, splattering the brick and stones at her feet. The brightly wrapped bonbon fell from her shirt, landing in the puddle of vomit, where it glittered incongruously. Weak and reeling, she walked back into the bakery. The hot steam hit her like a furnace blast as she entered the work area, and she sank down on a chair near the door. Mrs. Baum eyed her curiously.

"Aren't you feeling well, dear?" she asked, sprinkling a pan of pale yellow crescent-shaped cookies with confectioner's sugar.

"I'll be all right in a little while," Miriam whispered, wiping her brow with her handkerchief. "It's just the heat."

"I hope you'll feel better soon," said Mrs. Baum. "There's so much work to do today. Any other day I'd tell you to go home, but the soldiers are having some kind of a party this evening, in honor of the general's wife."

"His wife?"

"Yes, General Antonayevski's wife is scheduled to arrive sometime this afternoon. Now maybe he'll spend less time around here. He makes me so nervous, I can't get any work done. Actually, I think he has his eye on you, my dear." Mrs. Baum tittered as she brushed at some powdered sugar that had missed her apron and landed on her black skirt, leaving a constellation of white specks.

"So," she continued, "we still need six dozen sugar cookies, eight poppy-seed cakes, and three dozen rolls, in addition to what we baked this morning. But you rest there until you feel a bit better." She turned and slid a pan of cookies into the large, triple-tiered oven.

Rest, thought Miriam. *How can I rest after she gives me a workload like that?* Wearily, she rose from her chair and walked to the table, where she began rolling out the cookie dough.

As she worked, she reviewed the morning's events. Her legs still shook a bit and her hands trembled slightly as she remembered the general's vodka breath, the odious touch of his hand, and his menacing words. She recalled in horror how he had threatened to send Reuben away, to deport him. *But maybe he was just bluffing. After all, his wife is coming today, so surely he wasn't serious when he invited me to his room. Besides, if he tries anything now, I can threaten to tell her, maybe even actually do it.* Somehow this thought did not comfort Miriam but frightened her even more. If she aroused the general's ire, he could have them all deported, and God only knows what would happen to them then. Her only hope was that he would leave her alone once his wife arrived.

She continued working, rolling out the dough, cutting the cookies, breaking the eggs into a glass one at a time, then holding the glass up to the light to check for blood spots, which would render the egg non-kosher, and therefore unfit for use. As she worked, she noticed a dull ache in her abdomen. She ignored it as she hurried through her work, anxious to complete the requisite baking before closing time. She sprinkled a pan of cookies with the last few poppy seeds from the nearly empty can, then looked about on the shelves for a new one. Not finding it, she called out to Mrs. Baum. "Where are the poppy seeds?"

"There must be some in the storage room, if there aren't any in here," the older woman answered as she brushed a tray of rolls with egg white.

Miriam walked into the storeroom and looked about. Yes, there on a shelf above her was a tall cylinder of poppy seeds. Unfortunately, a large sack of flour lay on the floor, blocking her access to the shelf. Miriam bent and began pulling the sack away, when suddenly she felt a searing pain in her lower abdomen. She stood up slowly, hands clutching her belly, hardly daring to breathe, as the pain gradually receded. She was about to call for Mrs. Baum to help her move the sack when she became aware of a wetness between her legs. Fluid was seeping out of her, slowly trickling down her thighs. Her mind racing in panic, she hurried to the outhouse, a hot, smelly booth that she usually avoided except when absolutely necessary.

She had barely closed the wooden door and removed her undergarments when a great gush of blood poured out of her, splashing onto the slimy wooden planks of the outhouse floor, quickly followed by thick gelatinous clots of shapeless matter that fell between her feet. Rigid with terror, Miriam leaned against the outhouse door, pushing it open a crack, and screamed for Mrs. Baum. It seemed like hours, as Miriam stood screaming, with blood streaming from between her legs, until Mrs. Baum rushed up and pulled open the door of the outhouse. Dimly, Miriam felt herself being carried in the arms of a Russian workman. "Get my husband," she whispered through cracked lips before losing consciousness.

For eight days after the miscarriage, Miriam lay on her bed with the shades drawn. David, despite his tearful protestations, had been moved downstairs to sleep in Shloimeh's room. For one hour each day he was allowed to play in his mother's room, but she was easily exhausted and could barely respond to his constant stream of questions and chatter. Hour after hour, Miriam lay staring at the ceiling, engulfed in a gloom so deep that neither her husband's loving words nor her son's bright smiles could dispel it. Eventually, on the eighth day, her despondency began to lift, and she came downstairs for the first time. She was still bleeding, but only slightly, and she felt stronger. Last week, Devorah the midwife had assured her after much probing and kneading of her sore abdomen that nothing had remained inside and that she would be able to bear children again after a reasonable length of time. "And don't wait too long," the apple-cheeked Devorah had admonished, giving Reuben a sharp look before packing up her instruments and leaving the house. The following day, Reuben brought in Dr. Yablonska, the doctor for the Russian troops, and he reiterated Devorah's prognosis.

When Miriam appeared in the kitchen, pale and wan but dressed in a bright green frock that set off her eyes, Chaya Rochel rushed over to embrace her. "Miriam, darling, how wonderful to see you up and about. We were so worried about you. Reuben, especially; he walked around like a ghost. He'll be so happy to see you out of bed. Can I give you something to eat or drink?" She began bustling about, opening cabinets and removing boxes and tins.

"No, Mama. What you gave me this morning was fine." She began to walk unsteadily toward the door.

"Miriam!" exclaimed her mother, "Where are you going?"

"To work, Mama. I've been away much too long." Miriam adjusted her kerchief and smoothed her skirt. "I'm afraid I'll lose my place. I may have already lost it."

"To work! Are you *meshugge?*" cried Chaya Rochel. "Mrs. Baum said she'd hold your place for you if she could. You're not strong enough to work yet. You'll give yourself an infection, God forbid."

"No, I won't. I'm fine. People go back to work a week after childbirth very often, and I didn't even have a child."

"That's true, but what you had was even worse. The shock, the loss of blood. At least wait another day or so," pleaded Chaya Rochel.

"All right," agreed Miriam. "One more day."

When Reuben returned from work that evening, he was thrilled to see Miriam helping her mother in the kitchen and talking happily to little David, who kept jumping up and hugging his mother's legs in his joy at having her back to normal. Unlike his mother-in-law, Reuben agreed that Miriam should return to work as soon as possible, provided she was careful not to strain herself in any way. He felt sure that the sooner she resumed her normal routine, the better she would feel.

Miriam had her own reasons for wanting to return to the bakery. She was sure that she would not lose her position, for the general would not replace her. Twice this past week, while she had lain upstairs in bed, her brother Shloimeh had brought her messages in sealed envelopes that he said had been given to him by Mrs. Baum. Upon opening them, she found handwritten notes from the general. The first one read:

> My Little Tigress:
> How sorry I am to learn that you are ill.
> I wait eagerly for your return. Do not think of applying for work elsewhere.
> Your Soldier of Fortune

With the second message he had enclosed a sprig of violets. Her throat constricted with revulsion as she read:

> My Green-Eyed Cat:
> The cakes in the bakery have lost their sweetness.
> Come back soon, and enrich my days with your sugar and spice.

Again he had signed it "Your Soldier of Fortune." After reading each message, Miriam had been seized with a sick despair. She was afraid to tell Reuben, knowing that he would confront the general, who could then have him deported. Already, several men in Dubnitz, immigrants from Warsaw like themselves, had been issued passports labeling them as undesirables. It was only a matter of time before they were sent away. She shuddered to think of this happening to her beloved Reuben.

Instead, after much tortured soul-searching, she decided to

confront the general herself. She would threaten to show the notes to his wife. Although he hadn't signed them, surely his wife would recognize his writing. Miriam hoped that she would not actually have to approach this woman, but rather that the threat alone would be enough—what if the general's wife didn't believe her, or worse, didn't care?

As she walked to the bakery, her legs still unsteady from a combination of weakness and fear, she saw a crowd of soldiers in the street. She walked on until she saw a familiar figure seated upon a black horse, reaching down and shaking hands with some of the soldiers. Her body tensed as she recognized General Antonayevski in full dress uniform. She had just slipped behind a tall Hasid who stood surveying the scene when a horse-drawn coach came down the street from the other direction, stopping a few feet from the general. Its driver jumped out, opened the door, and extended his hand to the occupant. Miriam watched in surprise as a woman slowly eased her body out of the coach. She was grossly obese, her huge body encased in an ill-fitting dress of black voile. Great rolls of fat on her neck and arms shook as she descended the steps of the coach. Her smooth yellow hair was pulled tightly into a braided bun that sat directly on top of her head, making her round face look even fatter. As Miriam studied the woman's features—her blue eyes, small upturned nose, and gently curved lips—she realized that this grotesque figure waddling toward the general had once been a beautiful lady. The general dismounted, bowed slightly to the woman, took her elbow, and led her into a nearby building, which Miriam knew was his official headquarters.

"Who is that woman?" Miriam asked a young girl standing near her on the street.

"Don't you know? That's Madame General, his wife. Isn't she something?" The girl laughed and briefly imitated the waddling of the general's wife, before walking away.

Miriam turned down the path leading to the bakery. Mrs. Baum was outside, sweeping the walk. When she saw Miriam, she threw down her broom and rushed to her, waving her arms and exclaiming loudly, "Miriam! Back so soon? How are you? A hundred times I wanted to visit, but your brother said you wouldn't see anyone." Her words tumbled from her lips in a nervous torrent as she hovered about Miriam, who had already taken her accustomed place at the work-table in the back room.

"Yes. I received the messages you sent with him," said Miriam in a flat voice as she began to drop cookie dough onto a floured board.

"Well, I won't ask you what was in them," said Mrs. Baum. Miriam gave her a withering look.

Undaunted, Mrs. Baum continued. "You know about him, don't you? Did anyone tell you?"

"Tell me what?"

"Why, that he is leaving Dubnitz. Today, in fact."

Miriam stared at Mrs. Baum. "Really?" she asked. "Thank God. But how did it happen that he is leaving?"

Mrs. Baum gave Miriam a penetrating look, delighted at having some important information to impart. She had often wished, during the weeks they had worked together, that Miriam were less taciturn and more interested in hearing and exchanging gossip. Now she licked her lips and continued. "It was his wife. Did you see her? Quite a woman. Who would have thought he'd have a wife like that? Anyway, she arrived last week, took one look at Dubnitz and decided she wouldn't stay. He offered to send her back home to Kiev, but she refused and demanded that they transfer to Lvov. Apparently, his superiors have granted the request, because he's leaving today. So!" She flashed Miriam a gap-toothed smile. "I guess we won't miss him around here, will we?"

"No, we certainly won't," agreed Miriam. The knowledge that the general was leaving infused her body with new strength, and she worked happily for the rest of the day, barely noticing the heat and noise.

Life continued peacefully for the Zwillingers under Russian rule. The three men of the family kept their jobs at the gristmill, for the most part unmolested by the Russian authorities. Occasionally, there was a political rally or patriotic parade, during which all workers were called upon to march down Dubnitz's main street, banners and posters in hand. It was a strange sight to see Hasidim and peasants marching together, all carrying large portraits of Lenin and Stalin. Unlike many others, the Rutner, Zwillinger, and Parnes families were spared the annoyance of the bread and sugar lines because of Miriam's job in the bakery and Dina's in the little grocery store. Except when there were general shortages, they were usually able to obtain whatever staples they needed, as well as occasional luxuries like chocolate or sweet cream. Chaya Rochel spent her days happily caring for Bluma and David, who had become inseparable, and little Baruch, who had grown into a clever, mischievous toddler. Only Shloimeh seemed to be suffering. Forced to attend the secular government school during the day, he made up the time away from *Torah* study at night, learning with his father from seven until ten in the evening. Often, after his father retired for the night, Shloimeh would stay on in the study, his thin body swaying over the large, heavy volumes of Talmud. Sometimes Miriam or Chaya Rochel would come down in the early hours of the morning to find him still in the study, sprawled across the open book, his eyes closed and lips parted in sleep. Only then did he resemble the child Miriam remembered. During the day, his drawn, pale face was full of solemnity, and his speech was measured and serious.

Occasionally, Shloimeh's intensity and diligence made Miriam think of Berish, and a pang of fear pierced her heart. Would Shloimeh's obsessive fanaticism push him over the edge of reason, as had happened to Berish? When she voiced these fears to Reuben, he reassured her that Shloimeh was perfectly normal, albeit on the serious side, and his extreme religiosity was a reaction to the tense times in which they all lived. In truth, despite the relative calm of their lives, tension and fear were never far from the surface. Lately there had been many nighttime arrests of so-called "enemies of the people." The Jews of Dubnitz went to sleep at night with a feeling of foreboding, ready to wake at any moment to the dreaded knock at the door. Yet as time went on, even this fear abated as the arrests grew less frequent.

In November 1940, Miriam was delighted to discover that she was pregnant again. Because of her previous miscarriage, she was allowed by the new administrator of the city, a corpulent, balding man named General Kuzinsky, to work a reduced number of hours. This gave her time to rest and to play with the children. David was now a sturdy three-year-old who prattled incessantly about his two favorite subjects, soldiers and horses. The winter passed peacefully. Heavy snows blanketed Dubnitz, muffling sounds and slowing movement. The war seemed farther away, and the people of the town, vaguely apprehensive about relatives in western Poland from whom they got no news, settled in and waited. Spring came late that year, with chilly weather lasting until the end of April.

May Day was a Russian national holiday. A parade was scheduled for the morning hours. Miriam would be allowed to remain in the bakery, but Reuben, Leibel, and even Reb Mordche would have to march. At ten o'clock, little David heard the sound of the bugles and drums in the distance as he played in his Aunt Dina's house. He ran to his grandmother and tugged at her skirt. "*Bubby*! Take me to the parade!"

Chaya Rochel smoothed his red-gold curls and adjusted his blue skullcap. "I would take you, *tateleh*, but you know that Bluma has a fever, and she can't go out. So we'll just have to stay here and listen to the music."

"No!" David stamped his foot in anger. "I go myself!"

He ran to the door and tried the handle, but it was locked. Frustrated and angry, he banged on it with his small fists and howled.

"David, darling, come into the dining room." Chaya Rochel pulled him gently to a standing position as he continued sobbing. "Look out the window, maybe you can watch from there. A little boy cannot go alone to the parade. It's too dangerous. Someone might step on you." She led the whimpering child to the dining room window.

David pressed his nose against the glass, then wailed in disappointment. "Can't see! The trees are in the way!"

Chaya Rochel glanced at the window and sighed. It was true. There were several spindly yew trees blocking the view. "Well then," she suggested, "why don't you go up and get your toy soldiers and make your own parade. But don't wake Bluma and Baruch."

David pondered his grandmother's suggestion, then nodded and ran upstairs to the attic room where the toys were kept. Once there, he heard the drumming and the marching feet very clearly, for the parade was about to pass the corner of the street that intersected his own. David looked about the attic room. In the middle of one wall was a small, round window, like a porthole, that opened outward. He ran to it but could not reach it. On the other side of the room was an old, weather-beaten rush chair that had belonged to the previous occupants of the house. David grasped the chair, pushed it across the floor until it was under the window, and climbed up. There. Now he could see perfectly.

At the corner of the street, soldiers were marching, waving banners and chanting. Suddenly, he saw his own papa marching with a bright red flag. He leaned forward and pressed his face and arms against the glass. As he did so, the window swung open, and David lost his footing when the chair slid back. "Papa!" he screamed, then tumbled headfirst from the attic window.

Chaya Rochel heard the thud as she was dusting the dining room furniture. She knew, even before she reached the still, broken body, that something terrible had happened. When she saw David lying on the little stone patio, his glazed eyes staring blankly as blood oozed from the back of his head, her knees buckled and she grasped the side of the house for support. A scream started in her throat but died there, emerging as a choked whisper. Fighting to control her reeling senses, she began running. Several Dubnitzer Hasidim marching in the procession were startled to see their *rebbetzin* racing toward them, waving her arms and shouting hoarsely. They broke ranks and ran to her, frightened by her wild-eyed look and incoherent cries. Once they understood what she was saying, they sped off, returning with Reuben and Leibel. Messengers were dispatched for the *rebbe* and Dr. Yablonska. Reuben decided that Miriam should not be brought back from work until the doctor had seen the child. Once a diagnosis was given, Reuben himself would fetch Miriam and break the news as gently as possible. Otherwise, the terrible shock might send her into premature labor.

Shortly after the Russian takeover in 1939, a small hospital had been set up in Dubnitz to treat soldiers and their families; local peasants and townspeople were also admitted. Previously, these people had been treated at home by healers until a doctor could be fetched from a distant, larger city. It was to this makeshift hospital that the unconscious David was brought. While Dr. Yablonska examined the boy, Reuben, Leibel, and Reb Mordche waited in the hall, where they were soon joined by a group of Hasidim. Reuben watched silently as the black-clothed, bearded men swayed in unison, chanting psalms in voices filled with entreaty, begging God to heal the sick child. The ancient Hebrew poetry, dimly remembered from his youth, calmed Reuben. Yet he felt he was an outsider among them, and although his lips tried to form the words, he could not pray.

Dr. Yablonska's face was grave when he emerged from David's room. The Hasidim immediately ceased their prayers and turned to him expectantly. He motioned for Reuben to follow him, and the two men walked down the hall together. Reb Mordche, Leibel, and the rest of the Hasidim strained to hear the doctor's muffled, Russian-accented Polish.

Reuben looked into the doctor's solemn gray eyes. "I want the truth," he said in a steady voice that belied his inner turmoil.

The doctor glanced in the direction of David's room before returning Reuben's gaze. "The situation is very serious," he said. "The child has broken his left leg in two places. He also has multiple fractures of the ribs. We are fortunate that his lungs were not punctured, and that his spinal column is intact. That in itself is miraculous, considering the height from which he fell, and the fact that he landed on hard stone. But his skull has been fractured, and there appears to have been some bleeding into the brain. The boy is in a coma. He responds only to gross stimuli. We cannot assess now whether the brain itself has been damaged, nor the extent of the damage. We can try to relieve the pressure on the brain, and then we must wait."

"Wait for what?" Reuben clenched and unclenched his fists.

"To see what happens within the next day or two. To see if

he regains consciousness, or at least becomes more responsive." The doctor's eyes darted about nervously, and he lowered his voice. "In truth, Mr. Zwillinger, I'll do what I can, but I am severely limited here. The hospital receives only what the authorities provide, and that is not much. It is both a blessing and a curse that we are not near the front. There, you would have more doctors and nurses and better supplies. On the other hand, an injured child is not a high priority. I tell you this in the strictest confidence, you understand."

"Yes, I understand," said Reuben. *An injured child*, he thought bitterly. *Better make that a Jewish child.*

Dr. Yablonska cleared his throat and continued. "My best advice to you is to wait a few weeks until the broken bones begin to knit and the pressure on the brain has abated. Then, once the child can travel, you should bring him to Kiev. There, in the general hospital, he will receive the best possible care. Dr. Karnoshvili, the head of neurosurgery, was a professor of mine. I will write to him and forward all the records, if necessary. In the meantime, as I said, we can only wait and…" He gestured toward the Hasidim, who had resumed their chanting. "Though I shouldn't say this and I do not want to be quoted, prayer may help, if only to alleviate your own anxiety." He extended his hand and grasped Reuben's warmly. "You should go home now. There's nothing you can do at this time. And remember, you must watch your wife very carefully now. Let her stay in bed, perhaps. We don't want a repeat of last time. How far along is she?"

"Six months."

"So she must be very careful. You already have one child in danger. Let's not have a second. I will see you here tonight, after nine, if you wish." The doctor bowed slightly as Reuben thanked him, then turned and walked away down the corridor.

Behind Reuben, a door opened, and he watched dazedly as a young, blond nurse in a starched cap and slightly soiled uniform hurried out, carrying a tray filled with tiny vials and bottles that rattled and tinkled as she marched crisply down the hall. She glanced with distaste at the cluster of Hasidim as she passed them, then disappeared through another door.

Reuben walked slowly toward his father-in-law, mentally reviewing Dr. Yablonska's words. Leibel rushed up, took his elbow, and escorted him to the group of Hasidim, who hovered protectively around their *rebbe*. Briefly, Reuben recounted to Reb Mordche what Dr. Yablonska had said about David's condition, and what he had advised. The *rebbe* listened attentively until Reuben finished speaking. Then, rising from the chair that one of his disciples had fetched, he faced his son-in-law.

"With the help of God," he declared in a strong voice, "this child was born. With the help of God, he was saved from the fire and bombs of Warsaw. And with the help of God, he will be saved now. You must do what the doctor says, but always remember, the doctor is only the messenger of the Master of the Universe. "Now," the *rebbe* lowered his voice to a softer tone, "go to Miriam. We will stay here and continue reciting psalms. If you are needed, Leibel will come for you. Do not worry. With God's help," he repeated, "the child will be spared."

Miriam was removing a steaming pan of kaiser rolls from the oven when Reuben entered the bakery. A smile of greeting froze on her lips when she saw the expression on his ashen face. "Reuben!" she exclaimed. "What's wrong?"

Reuben looked into her eyes and struggled to speak. "Where is Mrs. Baum?" he asked, absently clearing away some tins on the counter as Miriam set down the baking pan.

"She's in the back. What is it? Has something happened to David?" she asked in a trembling voice.

Reuben slid behind the counter and put his arms around his wife, drawing her close. "Miriam, darling, you must come home with me. David is all right, but he has been hurt. The doctor says not to worry. He says to look after you, first and foremost."

He forced a smile, but the stricken look on her face tore at his heart.

"David is hurt?" she cried. "Where is he? I must go to him!" She began removing her apron, but her trembling fingers could not undo the knot at the back. Reuben untied it for her and helped her take it off, all the while speaking in what he hoped was a calm, reassuring tone.

"He is in the military hospital. He's in very good hands; Dr. Yablonska assured me that he will look after him himself and see to it that he gets the best of care."

"Let's go!" Miriam was already at the door when Mrs. Baum entered, carrying a large sack of flour. She gave Reuben a surprised smile.

"Mrs. Baum, our son has been hurt. Miriam must go home now."

Mrs. Baum set down the sack of flour and scurried out after them, shouting, "What? Hurt? What happened? The little boy?" Receiving no answer, she shrugged exasperatedly and went back into the bakery.

Miriam walked as quickly as her condition allowed. Although she was six months pregnant and carrying big, her figure was still graceful. She had never developed the arch-backed, waddling gait so common to pregnant women, her sister Dina included. Rather, Miriam seemed to slide forward with a fluid motion that reminded Reuben of a stately ship coming into harbor. He had often joked with Miriam about this, lovingly dubbing her "ss Fecundity" or "ss Uterus." By the time they reached the hospital, Miriam was flushed and breathless. Reuben held her arm tightly as he guided her toward David's room. As they passed the group of Hasidim, Leibel, indicating Miriam with his eyes, shot Reuben a questioning glance, but Reb Mordche nodded his head at Reuben, as if to say, "yes, let her go in."

David's room was tiny, with bare green walls. A metal cot, a small nightstand, and two wooden chairs took up nearly all of the floor space. Still, it was one of only two private rooms that the hospital had to offer, and Dr. Yablonska had assured Reuben that this little room was better for David than a crowded, noisy ward. Reuben's throat constricted at the sight of his son. His bright-haired, merry child, always so lively and full of mischief, now lay motionless on the white bed, his head and body swathed in bandages.

David's eyes were closed, and he looked as if he were sleeping peacefully. The sight of the child's blue-tinged, translucent eyelids and the long golden eyelashes that rested on the rounded cheeks, now so devoid of color, brought tears to Reuben's eyes. He swallowed hard and set his shoulders. He must not show his anguish in front of Miriam. He looked at his wife. Her pallor matched that of her son.

"David? My baby?" she whispered.

"Don't wake him," breathed Reuben. Later, he thought, he would explain to her about the injuries, the coma, the hospital in Kiev.

Ignoring Reuben, she called the child again, this time in a slightly louder voice. As she did so, she slipped her forefinger into David's tiny fist. Often, when David slept at home, Miriam or Reuben would put a finger into the child's hand. Always, no matter how deeply he slept, his small fingers would curl tightly about the adult finger, making it difficult to remove. Miriam stood frozen, waiting for what Reuben had named the David Zwillinger Reflex. David's fingers remained open and motionless. A sob escaped her throat as she withdrew her hand from that of her son. Reuben held Miriam close, and the two stood at the child's bedside, embracing each other and crying quietly. The door opened slightly and Leibel's dark, bearded face looked in. Then it closed again softly, with a muffled click that the three Zwillingers did not hear.

In the days that followed, Miriam felt as if she, too, were in a coma. After the first night of crying, she had been unable to shed any more tears. She felt drained of all emotion and was conscious only of a great heaviness that suffused her limbs, making every movement difficult. It was a chore even to breathe. Only one feeling penetrated her stupor: the compelling need to be with her child. Each morning, after a wretched, sleepless night, she would hurry to the hospital, there to sit all day at David's bedside, helping the nurses spoon liquid between his parched lips, change his bedding, and wash his face. Refusing to heed Dr. Yablonska's orders to stay home and rest, she did not leave her child's side until evening, when Reuben came to the hospital after work. They would eat their dinner together by David's bed, and then Dina or Chaya Rochel would walk Miriam home. Every other day, Dina left work early to watch the children so that her mother could go to the hospital to be with Miriam and David. Chaya Rochel had been consumed by guilt ever since the accident, blaming herself for having sent David up to the attic. The family's protestations that David and Bluma had played up there dozens of times before were to no avail. She feared not only for David, but for Miriam's unborn child. If something should happen to either one, or both, their blood would be upon her head. Hour after hour, when not busy with Bluma and Baruch, she chanted psalms and prayed to God to take pity on an old woman and spare the lives of her injured grandson and the grandchild yet to be born.

After the first week, Reuben applied for permission to bring David to Kiev. Anxiously, they waited for an answer. David's condition did not change. Occasionally, he opened his eyes, but they did not focus, and he stared blankly at his parents without a glimmer of recognition before closing them again. Eventually, sixteen days after the accident, a letter arrived granting Reuben official permission to travel with David to the general hospital in Kiev.

To Reuben's dismay, Miriam received this news with intensified feelings of depression. "Miriam," he argued, "at least now we have some hope. Physically, David is well enough to travel in his cot by train, and in Kiev they'll be able to stimulate him, get him to respond. Dr. Yablonska told me about the sophisticated equipment and techniques they have. You'll see, darling. He'll be all right. In a few weeks he'll be back, all well again, climbing on everything—"

Miriam grasped Reuben's shoulder's, her eyes blazing. "I want to be with him," she whispered through clenched teeth. "I cannot stay here, alone, without you, without David, waiting and worrying."

"Of course, Miriam, I know you want to be with David and me, and that you'll worry, but you must be reasonable. You cannot travel now. It's absolutely forbidden. Something could happen to the baby."

"To hell with the baby!" cried Miriam. Her vehemence, after so many days of apathy, startled Reuben, yet somehow cheered him.

"Miriam, you know you don't mean what you're saying." He put his arms around her, but she pushed him away roughly.

"I do mean it!" she cried. Angry tears stood in her eyes as she went on. "Think how terrible it is for me to be crippled this way, unable to be with you and David because of a child I don't know at all, when it's David who really needs me. What if he wakes up and cries for his mama? Oh, God!" The tears flowed freely now, and this time she did not resist when Reuben took her in his arms and rocked her gently. The curve of her swollen belly pressed along his side. All at once, he felt a faint fluttering against his stomach, and he placed his hand on Miriam's abdomen. Immediately, the movement stopped, as it always did when Reuben tried to feel for it with his hand. Lifting Miriam's chin, he smiled into her eyes. In spite of herself, she returned his smile.

"Such an obedient child," joked Reuben. "I have only to raise my hand and he stops what he's doing." They always referred to the unborn infant as "he" because David had insisted it was a boy; he refused to countenance the idea of a sister. Bluma had a baby brother, he would have a baby brother.

Miriam continued smiling at Reuben, her eyes and cheeks glistening with tears. She fingered his shirt collar, then reached up and touched his cheek. "When will you go?"

"The doctor will let me know in the morning. He's already sent the records to Kiev. He wants us to go as soon as possible."

Once again, they embraced. Miriam leaned her cheek against Reuben's chest, deriving comfort from his calm strength. Who would comfort her in the weeks to come, while he and David were gone? She held him tight, then released him, straightening her spine.

"You must go as soon as you can. The sooner you leave, the sooner you'll both be back. And, of course, you must be back in time for the baby." She looked at Reuben uncertainly. He took her hand and squeezed it lightly, then brought it to his lips before releasing it.

"Of course we'll be back by then. The baby's due in what, ten weeks? Surely, with the good care David will receive in Kiev, he'll have improved enough in less time than that, and we'll both be home. So don't worry. You must take care of yourself, first and foremost. Promise me you'll be careful, that you won't neglect your own health."

Miriam nodded. "I promise, Reuben. I can't promise not to

worry, but I will take good care of myself. Mama will see to that anyhow."

The next morning Miriam and Reuben were both at the hospital before eight o'clock. Reuben should have been at work, but Leibel agreed to cover for him should any questions be asked. Dr. Yablonska arrived shortly after they did, and after examining David, he called them into his tiny office.

Miriam clutched Reuben's hand apprehensively as she entered. Her stomach had clenched itself into a tight, hard knot, and the unborn baby's furious kicking only increased her unease. The doctor's eyes were kind, and as he stood to greet them, he smiled.

"Well, I am glad to say there has been some improvement. It's only a slight improvement, not enough for anyone but me to notice or evaluate, but hopefully it is an indication of progress, with more progress to come. The boy's reflexes have sharpened; he is somewhat more responsive, and his color is better."

Miriam leaned eagerly toward Dr. Yablonska. Hope had heightened the color in her own cheeks, and her eyes had a new luster. "Does this mean he can remain here?" she asked.

The doctor shook his head sadly. "No, I'm afraid the trip must be taken. I know what it means to you at this time, to be separated." His eyes flitted from Miriam's face to her swollen stomach, then back again. "But right now it is more crucial than ever that David receive the best possible care. In fact, if you can leave this afternoon, that would be best. I have already sent the records on ahead, and I will give you the latest medical reports, as well as another letter of introduction to take with you. You will also have the good fortune to be accompanied by one of my nurses, whom I'm sure you know, Mrs. Milgrova. It happens that she herself is being transferred to Kiev, so you can travel together."

Reuben and Miriam nodded in unison. They knew and liked Mrs. Milgrova, or Nelya, as she insisted they call her. A plump, florid-faced bundle of energy, she tended to David with a rare combination of warmth and efficiency that had won the Zwillinger's confidence from the very first day. It was a great relief to both of them that she would be there to tend to David on the eight-hour journey. Yet when the time came for Miriam to say goodbye to Reuben and David, her feelings of hope and relief fled, and she was seized once more by anxiety and despair. Reuben had been her rock, her source of strength and calm in these last troubled weeks of David's illness. Neither her father's pronouncements regarding God's capacities as healer of the sick, nor her mother's guilty solicitude were reassuring. Dina and Leibel were very kind, talking to her about David in a matter-of-fact yet optimistic fashion, but lately she had avoided their home. The lively antics and happy prattle of Bluma and Baruch only underscored the gravity of David's condition.

Now she stood at the train station, watching as Nelya wheeled David toward the platform in a large pram. David should have been too tall for it, but since the accident, he tended to lie curled, almost in a fetal position. Both Dr. Yablonska and Nelya had assured Miriam that David was quite comfortable in the pram, and that it was really the best conveyance for him until he could be put in a berth on the train.

Miriam leaned over and kissed her child's cool, white forehead. His eyes were closed, yet his face held some inner tension, as if he were having a nightmare and might soon waken with a cry. She smoothed his red-gold curls and brushed away her tears from his soft cheek. She turned as Reuben touched her shoulder, and they held each other tight for one long moment, oblivious to the screeching of the train's wheels and its mournful whistle. David's eyelids flickered slightly in response to the noise but remained closed.

Reuben kissed Miriam once more, then helped the nurse lift the carriage up into the railroad car. He turned back, waved to his in-laws, blew Miriam one last kiss, and disappeared into the train. Reb Mordche and Chaya Rochel, along with Dina and Leibel, surrounded Miriam and closed ranks. Quietly, the family group walked back to the waiting coach. The train shuddered twice and lurched forward on the tracks, moving slowly at first, then gathering speed as it continued its long journey east.

Chapter fourteen

May 25, 1941

Dearest Miriam,

I hope this letter reaches you quickly and finds all of you well. I know what the mail is like these days and would have written sooner, but I was so involved in getting myself and David settled that I had hardly a minute to myself.

David is now in Kiev General Hospital. Dr. Karnoshvili seems to be an exceptionally able and sensitive physician, and David is looking better and more responsive already. The doctor feels optimistic, although he will not give me a prognosis at this early stage. Still, I feel confident that our little David will soon be sitting up in bed and chattering away about his hobbyhorse, Jerzy.

My darling Miriam, I think about you constantly. As much as you wish to be with us, I wish it also. But you must take care of your health and that of little "question mark" inside. I must stop writing, as the nurse has asked me to help wash David. You see, I am making myself useful. In addition, I am working hard at improving my Russian, though fortunately Dr. Karnoshvili is fluent in Polish.

Please answer quickly. I love you very much. My best regards to all.

Thinking of you always,

Your Reuben

Miriam sighed and folded the letter, placing it in her night-stand. It had arrived yesterday, June 21, four weeks after having been written. Four weeks of worry about Reuben and David, four weeks of mailing letters to Kiev General Hospital and receiving no response, and now this letter, written on May 25. Anything could have happened in the meantime—an improvement in David's condition, a crisis, or worse. There was no way of knowing. Until she received another letter from Reuben, she must go on as she had for the last month, reading, sewing, and chatting with her mother and Dina, and, less often, with her father, Leibel, and Shloimeh. She looked at the little gilt and porcelain clock on the dresser. Eight o'clock. Today she would continue working on the stuffed bear she was sewing for David out of his old blanket, read a bit, take a short walk.

Time was both her friend and her enemy. Each new day yawned ahead of her like an empty chasm, to be filled with meaningless activity, yet each day also brought Reuben and David's homecoming that much closer. Until then, she could only wait. She was too far advanced in her pregnancy to work, and even simple household chores had become difficult. She worried at times about the effect her constant anxiety was having on her baby. The doctor, as well as Chaya Rochel and Dina, reassured her that the child would be born healthy and happy, perfectly oblivious to its mother's prenatal emotional state, but Miriam was not so sure. A story Marika had once told her returned to haunt her—Marika had owned a pet dog, Chula, who was terribly nervous and irritable during her pregnancies; when her litters were born, some of the pups were so excitable that Marika's father had drowned them in the river.

Loud knocking on the front door interrupted her thoughts, and she hurriedly drew on her voluminous wrapper. Tying her head scarf behind her ears, she started down the stairs. Just then, the door burst open and Leibel rushed in, his brow beaded with sweat and his cheeks flaming.

Looking about wildly, he spied Miriam and shouted, "Where's Mama?"

"Leibel!" Miriam secured her wrapper with a long fringed sash and shoved a stray lock of her hair under her kerchief. "What's wrong?"

Leibel stared at Miriam, then shook his head. He knew he should not upset her, but she had to know the truth, for her own safety. "Come downstairs, Miriam. There's something I must tell you."

Miriam carefully made her way down the narrow stairs and into the dining room, easing her swollen body onto a chair just as her mother entered from the kitchen.

"Leibel!" exclaimed Chaya Rochel in surprise. "What are you doing here? Is Baruch sick again, God forbid? I'm just on my way over." She began removing her apron.

Leibel motioned her to a seat. "Sit down, Mama, please. I must speak to both of you. Something terrible has happened. We had just arrived at the factory when the night watchman, Stavos, ran up to us with his little wireless. He told us that the Ribbentrop-Molotov pact is broken. Germany has declared war on Russia. Even now, cities are being bombed. We could be next."

Chaya Rochel gasped. "Bombs? Here in Dubnitz?"

"Yes," continued Leibel. "We must take shelter at the first sound of a siren. You two must come home with me. Behind our house is the old potato cellar. There's enough room in there for all of us."

Miriam stared at him in disbelief. The thought of Dina's damp, moldering potato cellar made her shudder. She couldn't imagine being crowded in down there, especially in her condition. The whole situation seemed unreal. Until now, life had been relatively calm and quiet for the Jews of Dubnitz. Even the deportations had ceased in the last few months. It had been a long time since she had given much thought to politics. David's illness had taken precedence over everything.

Now, as the reality of these new developments began to sink

in, she sat rigidly in her chair, trying to imagine the implications for herself and her family here in Dubnitz, as well as for Reuben and David in Kiev. Leibel continued talking, but Miriam no longer heard. Over and over, the same terrible thought ran through her mind: *The Nazis are coming. I'll never see Reuben and David again.*

"Miriam, are you all right? My God, she's gone white as chalk." Chaya Rochel leaned forward and peered into Miriam's face, covering her daughter's icy hand with her own warm one.

Miriam turned to her mother and tried to speak calmly. "I'm all right, Mama. It's just the shock." Disordered fragments of plans and ideas churned about in her mind. She slid her chair back and stood up. "I must go out and get some air."

"What? Now?" Her mother and brother-in-law looked at her incredulously.

"Yes, now," insisted Miriam. "I'll go up and dress."

She walked upstairs, deliberately slowing her steps to forestall her mother's usual admonishment, "Don't rush, you could fall." But Chaya Rochel and Leibel had already resumed their conversation; she could hear their voices, although she could no longer make out the words.

Once in her room, she chose a simple, pale cotton smock that matched her kerchief. There were gay pink, white, and yellow rosettes embroidered in the smocking, one of the projects Miriam had set herself in the past month while awaiting word from Reuben. She did not pause to admire her handiwork but quickly pulled the dress on and went downstairs.

"Miriam, don't go out," cried Chaya Rochel as her daughter opened the heavy door, letting in a warm, fragrant breeze.

"I won't go far, Mama," Miriam answered as she stepped into the bright sunshine. "I must have some air. The baby is pressing on me and I can't breathe."

Back straight, belly thrust forward, she walked toward the center of town. The streets were filled with confused and frightened people, and Miriam was reminded of Warsaw in September 1939, and also of Dubnitz in the early days of the Russian Occupation. Unlike those days, however, the faces of the Jews now bespoke not mere uncertainty, but terror. No one had known what to expect from the Russians, but all knew about the Nazis' attitude toward Jews. Although the Russians had tried to suppress them, occasional reports had filtered into Dubnitz from western Poland—reports of mass deportations, forced labor, torture, and worse.

The people thronged in front of the small shops, forming long, disorganized lines as they jostled each other in a desperate attempt to buy food before it became unobtainable. Automatically, Miriam looked toward the bakery. For a moment, she caught a glimpse of Mrs. Baum's confused face in the doorway, her gap-toothed mouth forming words that Miriam couldn't hear. Then the writhing mass of customers filled the entrance, blocking Mrs. Baum from view. It was the same at the butcher's and the greengrocer's: more lines of people, pushing and shouting. Thinking of the probable food shortages to come, Miriam felt grateful for her family's connections. Leibel's mother still worked in the grocery store, and Mrs. Baum always set aside bread, rolls, and even cake for Miriam and her family. In addition, the Dubnitzer Hasidim would never let their *rebbe* and his family starve. During the previous shortages, there was always someone who would bring an offering of food for the *rebbe* and his household—a piece of fish for the Sabbath, a raisin loaf, a dozen eggs. No, food should not be a problem.

Miriam continued walking, making her way slowly past the center of town, following the road that led toward Kuneh's Inn. That gray, imposing structure had long since been taken over as housing for the Russian officers and their families. Now, as she approached, the building hummed with activity. Soldiers hurried in and out of the inn, carrying boxes and parcels of all shapes and sizes, which they proceeded to load onto military trucks parked in the road. Women and children scrambled about among them, helping to load their belongings or just getting underfoot.

Off to the side, under a half-dead oak tree, stood the once proud coach that had carried Miriam away from Dubnitz as a young bride. For a while the Russian officers had used it for Sunday outings, until they were reprimanded by the higher authorities for behaving in such a bourgeois manner. Now it stood in the grass, its windows broken, its chrome trim dull and chipped, the spokes of its large wheels jagged and rusting. The horses were long gone, shot "accidentally on purpose" by a soldier doing target practice during a meat shortage. The tough old horse flesh had been a culinary disappointment, however, and the trigger-happy soldier had been thenceforth known by his fellows as "Josef Horsemeat." Now, barbecued horses and Sunday outings were forgotten, as the Russians prepared to move eastward in a desperate rush to escape the advancing Germans.

A slim, blonde woman emerged from the building. Moving closer, Miriam recognized Tozsia, a nurse from the military hospital who had occasionally cared for David during the night shifts. Although somewhat taciturn, she had been efficient and kindly. Quickly organizing her disjointed thoughts, Miriam walked up to her.

"Toszia."

The woman turned and regarded Miriam with surprised blue eyes. "Mrs. Zwillinger. How is your son?"

"He's doing better, I think. I had a letter this week, one letter." Miriam paused, trying to remain calm, then went on.

"They are in Kiev. I have to get to them. Otherwise, with this new situation, once the Germans get here…" Her voice trailed off and she shook her head, then began again. "I must get to my husband and child, in Kiev. Surely some of you are going in that direction."

Toszia nodded. "Yes. I myself am going to Kiev."

Miriam's eyes brightened with hope. "Please let me come with you. I cannot stay here, when they are so far away. Who knows what will happen?"

As she and Tozsia stood talking, a young Russian corporal leaped from the back of a parked truck and dashed up the steps, nearly colliding with Miriam. His black eyes flashed angrily. "Out of my way, you cow," he muttered as he brushed past her and grabbed Tozsia roughly by the arm. "Come on, Toszia. What is all this chit-chat? There's not a moment to lose." He pulled her along as he ran back down the stairs, two steps at a time. Miriam followed after them carefully, avoiding the people who ran here and there, threatening to bowl over the big pregnant Jewish woman who didn't belong there in any case.

She approached the mud-splattered gray-green truck whose van was now full of the soldiers' families, Toszia among them. "Please," she cried again. "Take me with you. I must get to Kiev."

The passengers stopped talking and stared at her. A few women began tittering. Soon the men and children joined in, and Miriam's words were lost in their mocking laughter. Miriam ignored their taunts. Desperately, she rushed to the opening of the van, trying to catch sight of Toszia. "Please," she repeated, "I can pay you." The laughter grew louder.

"Pay us!" shouted a heavy, black-haired woman as she clutched a chubby child of six or seven to her chest.

"Of course," scoffed her husband, his medals glinting as he loaded more parcels into the van. "Jews can always pay."

"Just what we need," interjected another voice. "A pregnant Jewish bitch, ready to give birth to a Jewish bastard any minute."

Slowly, the great muddy tires of the truck began turning. With the motor's roar, Miriam could hear no more voices, but she caught a fleeting glimpse of Toszia, who stared back, her mouth set in a thin line and her eyes bright, before turning her head away.

Miriam stepped to one side as the convoy rumbled forward. She watched the trucks disappear around the bend, and her hopes of getting to Kiev disappeared with them. If only I weren't pregnant, she thought as tears welled in her eyes and her throat tightened. *I could have jumped on somehow. And why didn't I think to give them a letter for Reuben, at least? Now it's too late.*

She looked once more at the soldiers. They, too, would be leaving soon in another convoy, having received their orders to withdraw. Their hard faces told her to expect no help from them.

Miriam trudged back toward town, stopping every so often to rest. Each step was an ordeal. The baby kicked, squirmed, and pressed its body now against her lungs, then against her stomach and bladder. Sometimes she felt her womb harden with an intense but painless contraction. She did not remember experiencing these during her first pregnancy, but Dr. Yablonska had assured her that they were normal.

Dr. Yablonska! She had not spoken to him in several days,

but surely he, of all the Russians, would be able to help her. Perhaps another of his nurses was returning to Kiev, just as Mrs. Milgrova had done. And if he had arranged for his nurses to travel, he could arrange it for her as well. She began walking to the hospital, eagerly planning what to say to the doctor. Even before she reached her destination, Miriam sensed that something was wrong. The little ambulance wagon was not in the yard, though that could mean it was out on call. Even so, things seemed far too quiet. Where were the patients, who often waited outside rather than sit in the hot, crowded anteroom?

An ominous stillness emanated from the building itself. Miriam tried the front door, but it was locked. She walked to the side of the building and peered through a window, where a shade had been left half open. Squinting, she could barely make out a small room containing two empty beds. The sheets were in disarray, as if the occupants had gotten up to use the bathroom and would soon be returning.

As Miriam moved away from the window, a peasant woman called to her from the street. "Gone. All gone."

"Gone," repeated Miriam. "Gone where?"

The woman shrugged her broad shoulders. "Who knows? Early this morning they took out all the sick ones, sent them home. The ones who couldn't walk they sent in a wagon. My husband came home that way. He was just operated on three days ago. They sewed up his hand for him. He needs medicine. I came before to see if there was any, but it's all closed, locked up."

"Where is Dr. Yablonska?"

"He's gone, too. All of them. My sister told me. She saw them leave a little while ago. What's the matter, your baby coming? My sister can help you. She delivered all my kids."

Miriam thanked the woman and began walking home, despair clouding her thoughts. The streets were still crowded with Hasidim and peasants as Miriam made her way down the main road, past the few shops that made up Dubnitz's center. She heard snatches of conversation as she passed the long queues stretching from the shop doors out into the road.

"Don't worry," said a young Hasid with a crooked leg, which

he supported with the help of a mahogany cane. "The Russians will defend us. They have sworn to fight to the last man."

"Bah," spat a portly black-haired man in a factory worker's uniform. "Where are they now? I haven't seen a soldier since this morning."

A thin woman in a faded housedress asked in a quavering voice, "When do you think the Germans will get here?" Her eyes darted nervously among the crowd, as if searching for Nazis.

"Never, please God," answered a red-faced woman in a black marriage wig.

Miriam grimaced wryly as she continued on her way. She knew that the Russian soldiers had already left.

Leibel and Chaya Rochel were still at the house when she returned, as were Reb Mordche, Dina, her children, and Shloimeh. When she told them that the Russian soldiers had gone, Leibel's face grew dark with anger. He banged his fist hard on the dining room table, setting the teacups rattling. "That's just what the Nazis are waiting for," he declared. "Now we are defenseless. No army, nothing to stop them."

"Leibel," said Miriam, staring into his deep-set black eyes that burned with frustration and bitterness, "we can still follow the Russians. We can go east, before it's too late. We can get a coach; for Reb Mordche and his family—"

"I will not go." Reb Mordche's voice rang out loud and deep. His family members stopped speaking and turned to listen.

"I will not leave my Hasidim," the *rebbe* continued. He rose from his chair and glared at his family, daring them to contradict him. When no one spoke, he went on. "For thousands of years our enemies have driven us from our homes, which were then looted and pillaged while we wandered, starving and homeless, at the mercy of our enemies. My Hasidim look to me now for leadership and strength. I will not leave them. No, we will stay here, where we have lived for so many years. The Highest One helped us when we were ruled by the Russians, so that we were able to remain here in peace, and so will He save us from the Germans."

He remained standing, looking first at his wife, then at his children and son-in-law, and last at his grandchildren, who sat huddled in a corner, frightened by the tone of their *zayde's* voice.

A loud scraping sound broke the silence. Miriam had slid her chair back and now stood facing her father. "*Tati*, you can all stay here, but I must go," she announced. Dina gasped, and Chaya Rochel shook her head slowly from side to side. "I must be with Reuben and David. I cannot remain here another day. God only knows what will happen, and I must be with them. They need me, and I need them…" She broke off, her voice choked with tears.

"I understand how you feel," said Reb Mordche. A range of emotions played over his face: kindness and concern followed by guilt, and finally, despair. "But it is not possible for you, in your condition, to travel. The danger, both for you and for the unborn child, is too great."

Both Dina and Chaya Rochel murmured in assent. Miriam, searching for an ally, cast Leibel a beseeching look, but he looked away, frowning. Only Shloimeh caught her eye, staring at her with an expression she could not fathom, before he rose and left the room.

A great weariness descended upon Miriam, and she, too, left the table. With slow, heavy steps, she climbed the narrow staircase to her room. There she lay down upon her bed and stared up at the ceiling. Exhaustion seemed to spiral up from within her until it filled the room and she felt as if she were drowning in fatigue. She knew she should think, plan, find a way to escape, but she could not free her mind from the terror that gripped it. Finally, she gave herself up to a numbness that receded into sleep.

Loud banging on the front door, accompanied by harsh shouts, awakened her. She glanced at the clock—it was five in the afternoon. She had slept for several hours—she was not sure how many—but still she felt exhausted. The noise continued. Straightening her clothes and kerchief, she went downstairs and was shocked to find the parlor crowded with Hasidim. Others stood in the entrance hall. The knocking on the front door went on and on, yet no one moved to answer it.

"Open up," cried a voice in German-accented Polish.

"Open, please, good people," cried a second voice, which

Miriam recognized as that of Antek, who once worked for Kuneh the innkeeper. Motioning for Miriam and Dina to leave the room, Leibel made his way through the group of Hasidim to unlock the door.

Miriam, Dina, and Chaya Rochel retreated to the kitchen along with Bluma and Baruch, who clung to their mother's skirt and sucked their thumbs, their soft, round faces pale with fright. Shloimeh, too, had been ordered to the kitchen, but he rejoined the Hasidim as soon as Leibel's back was turned. Miriam peered through the kitchen door, which was slightly ajar. She could see her father, surrounded by his Hasidim, making his way to the front door, fending off the protecting arms of his disciples. Now Leibel had opened the door, and Miriam was shocked at how young the entering soldier looked. His face was smooth and pink-cheeked, like that of a teenage boy. Yet he wore the insignia of an officer, similar to that worn by the Russian officers who had ruled Dubnitz only yesterday. Unlike the Russians, however, his uniform was black, and the visored hat perched atop his blond hair bore a white skull and crossbones. On his shoulder were sewn two jagged bolts of lightning. Miriam's throat constricted. She had heard about Hitler's SS, his special forces, although she was unsure of their precise role in Hitler's army. Dina craned her neck to catch a glimpse of the invaders, but Miriam was in the way. Afraid to ask her sister to move for fear her whispers would be heard in the hall, Dina walked instead to the window. She stared out for a few moments, mesmerized, then turned away and sat down heavily on a soft chair.

The courtyard was full of German soldiers. They walked about, laughing and chatting. Some smoked cigarettes. Two of them entered the *beis medrash*. Beyond them, on the street, she had seen row after row of soldiers marching, two by two. How had they gotten here so fast? By plane? Truck? Hearing voices in the hall, she squeezed herself beside Miriam's cumbersome frame in an effort to see what was happening.

Both the Nazi and Antek stood in the front parlor. The young officer looked around the room, a bemused smile on his lips. Miriam had never before seen such a smile. It was at once boyish and sinister. "Which one is he?" he asked Antek.

The peasant scratched his neck with nervous, bony fingers

whose tips were stained brown with tobacco. His pointed Adam's apple moved up and down in his scrawny neck like a mole trapped in its tunnel.

"Which one?" he croaked, looking at the German with red-rimmed, frightened eyes.

Before the officer could answer, loud shouts were heard in the courtyard. The three women rushed to the kitchen window, while the Nazi officer, holding firmly to Antek's shoulder, drew his revolver, pointed it at the Hasidim in the hall, and backed toward the front door.

The shouts were coming from the *beis medrash*. As Miriam watched in horror, a group of German soldiers dragged two Hasidim from the building. Several other Hasidim tried to intercede, but the drawn guns of the soldiers quickly stopped them. With cries of anguish, they stood by, helpless, as their two friends were kicked and punched by the Germans.

Suddenly, the young officer, his left arm still pointing the gun, leaned out the door and shouted at the men in German. Immediately, they released their two bloodied captives, who were helped to their feet by their friends and brought back into the study house. Another command from the officer dispersed the soldiers, who slunk away, muttering angrily. The officer then slid back through the door, turning on his smile like a beam of cold light.

"You see?" he asked. "You have nothing to fear if you behave in a reasonable manner. I am, after all, a reasonable man." He paused, flicking his pointed tongue across his lips. "Now," he said, addressing first Antek and then the assembled Hasidim, "who is your leader? Which of you is the great miracle rabbi?"

No one moved. The Nazi scanned the room, searching. His pale eyes lit upon Shloimeh, who now stood in the hallway, among the men. The officer pointed his gun in the boy's direction. "You, my lad, come over here."

Shloimeh's startled eyes darted back and forth between the gun and the man's face, with its dimpled chin. He began moving forward, pushing past the Hasidim, slowly approaching the officer. The soldier released Antek with a contemptuous shove. The peasant fell against

Moishe Chernowitz, an elderly Hasid who had been standing near the door, and both momentarily lost their footing, shuffling about before standing firm once again.

The soldier smiled. "Thank you for the traditional dancing. I know you are famous for this." Then, turning from Moishe and Antek, he reached out and grasped Shloimeh firmly by the arm.

Chaya Rochel gasped. Miriam put her arm around her mother as the old woman began to whisper the words of a psalm. "I shall not fear the tens of thousands who surround me; rise up my God, and save us…"

The Nazi's tall figure loomed over Shloimeh, who now stood before him, gazing up into the man's face. Miriam looked from the black-uniformed Nazi to the black-clad little Hasid, her beloved Shloimeh, whose thin, frail arm trembled slightly in the officer's grip.

The Nazi smiled down at Shloimeh. Then, his smile fading from his lips, he looked up at the Hasidim. "Move back," he commanded, in a voice cold as steel. "It's too crowded here. Too hot." His lips curled with distaste. "It stinks, too." He turned his gaze back to the child, still gripping Shloimeh's arm tightly. As he did so, several Nazi soldiers peered in through the door, then withdrew, positioning themselves just outside the house. The sun danced across their buttons and medals. Miriam was reminded of David's love of soldiers, especially in their dress uniforms. For the first time since he had left for Kiev, she breathed a prayer of thanks that he was far away, safe in a clean white hospital bed, with his father close by.

The officer leaned forward, bending his upper body stiffly from the hips. He looked directly into Shloimeh's eyes. The room fell silent; no sigh, no intake of breath, no whispered prayers were heard. Everyone stood transfixed, eyes riveted on this incongruous pair. With their eyes, with their thoughts, with their very souls, they willed the officer and his soldiers to disappear, to leave them in peace. Yet neither they nor the Nazis moved.

Slowly and deliberately, the officer raised his gun, pointing it directly at Shloimeh's head. As all eyes watched, the gun barrel moved closer and closer until it touched Shloimeh's temple. The boy flinched slightly as the cold metal met his skin, and the sudden movement set his earlocks swinging. The gentle motion caught the officer's eye. "Look at these corkscrews," he murmured. With the point of the gun, he played a game, first nudging an earlock back, then letting it fall forward again. Miriam watched the soft reddish curl swing back and forth, back and forth, realizing that it had become a pendulum, ticking off the minutes of Shloimeh's life. Near the doorway, the soldiers remained poised, their rifles raised, ready to do battle with the unarmed Hasidim.

"Where is your *rebbe*?" demanded the officer. "Who is he? Which one of these fine gentlemen? Tell me, little one, if you want to live." He cocked his pistol with a metallic click that sent a shock wave through the room. Shloimeh's jaw dropped slightly, but still he kept his eyes fixed on the officer's face.

All at once, there was a flurry of noise and movement from the back of the room. Reb Mordche pushed aside two of his Hasidim, who had been shielding him with their bodies, and forcefully strode forward. His disciples immediately made a path for him in the crowded room, as they did every Sabbath and holiday evening as he entered the synagogue to give a *dvar Torah*, a discussion of the Holy Law. His deep voice rang out in the quiet room. "I am the *rebbe*! I am Reb Mordche of Dubnitz, the leader of these people. Now deal with me, and do not torment an innocent child."

The officer stared as the old man presented himself. He released Shloimeh, who moved back a few steps, then stopped. "So you are the *rebbe*." The officer's lip curled back in a sneer. "A fine figure of a man." He poked the muzzle of his gun into Reb Mordche's stomach, then withdrew it. "Kind of fat, aren't you? Where do you get so much food, eh? This is wartime. My soldiers are going hungry while you vermin are gorging yourselves, eh?" He gazed around the room. The Hasidim stared back, their eyes blazing anger and defiance at this gentile devil who had dared insult their *rebbe*, yet they knew they could do nothing, for the soldiers by the doorway kept their rifles trained on the room, eager to shoot down anyone who made the slightest motion.

The officer reached out and grabbed the *rebbe*'s lapel, jerking him forward. "All right," he barked. "Come with me. We will have a discussion, a Talmudic discourse in more comfortable quarters. The rest of you," his eyes swept the room, "stay where you are. You are forbidden to leave this house until seven P.M., when you will have fifteen minutes to return to your homes. After that, the curfew will be strictly enforced. Anyone found out on the street will be subject to the discipline of the Reich."

Pushing Reb Mordche before him, the Nazi officer left the house. His soldiers formed a double column behind him, two of their number marching backward, guns still trained on the Rutner house.

Inside, the Hasidim rushed to the door and windows, watching their *rebbe* as he was led away. Chaya Rochel began to sob. Dina and Miriam knelt beside her and the three women hugged each other. Shloimeh jumped up and grabbed something from the mantelpiece. Squeezing past the Hasidim clustered at the door, he burst from the house, screaming, "*Tati, Tati!*" His bony legs in their white stockings flashed beneath his gabardine as he ran, his right arm extended before him. Miriam flew to the window. What was Shloimeh doing?

As she watched, a soldier raised his rifle, aimed, and fired. Shloimeh spun around, teetered slightly, and fell to the ground. A dark stain spread slowly beneath his thin, spread-eagled body. Miriam, her screams echoing in her ears, tried to rush to him but was restrained by someone whose face she could not see. Gasping and sobbing, she struggled but could not break loose. In a frenzy she bent and bit deep into the hand that held her. The hand released its grip and she ran forward through the open door of the house.

The soldiers had moved on down the street. Ignoring Miriam, they marched behind their leader, who no longer held onto Reb Mordche. It was not necessary, for the old man had fainted with shock at seeing his son shot. Two soldiers now dragged him along by the arms. But Miriam could not see this, nor did she understand the meaning of the long, jagged stripes his limp feet had engraved in the dirt road.

Miriam's eyes were fixed upon a small object that lay near Shloimeh's bleeding, lifeless body. It was this object that he had been carrying as he ran after his father. There on the ground next to

Shloimeh's outstretched right hand lay Reb Mordche's *tefilin* bag, its blue velvet cover slowly turning darker as it absorbed the lifeblood of the Dubnitzer heir, the future Dubnitzer *rebbe*.

Chapter fifteen

In the cool dewy light of morning, a small group of mourners huddled together beside a newly dug grave. The funeral ceremony had been cut short. Halfway through Leibel's eulogy of Shloimeh, which he delivered in a voice racked with sobs, a troop of soldiers stormed in. Pointing their loaded rifles at the multitude of Hasidim crowding the synagogue, the Germans ordered them to disperse. Those not nimble enough in complying were poked and prodded with rifle butts. Reb Shimshon Anshpitzer, an elderly Hasid who had been the *shames*, the beadle, of Reb Mordche's father some forty years before, was struck across the cheek. The blow left a crescent-shaped cut and an ugly, swelling bruise. Dazed and bleeding, he was led away by his sons.

At first the soldiers would not allow the pallbearers to bring the casket up the hill to the cemetery. They surrounded the small pine box that held Shloimeh's body and declared that they would take care of the Jewish dead. Finally, they demanded several hundred zlotys from Leibel, who immediately dispatched Feivel to collect the sum from the Hasidim who had gone to the study house. The corporal, a short, drab-haired man who looked not at all like Hitler's conception of the Aryan master race, pocketed the money. He then allowed ten men, the minimum number necessary for a quorum at the graveside, to carry the coffin up the hill and bury it there.

Leibel glanced round at the nine men who stood with him beside the open grave. None were relatives of the deceased. In Leibel's eyes, it was a strange funeral. Sometimes when an old person died, there were no direct relatives at the graveside. But here was a child being buried, and he, Leibel, a brother-in-law, was the closest male family member present. Women were not allowed at the cemetery, according to a much disputed but immutable Dubnitzer tradition. The child's own father, the Dubnitzer himself, who unfailingly attended the funerals of his Hasidim and their families, from the most venerable elders to unnamed stillborn infants, was not present to bid farewell to his only son. He was a prisoner somewhere in the old hospital building, which now served as Gestapo headquarters. Perhaps he did not know of Shloimeh's death. Would it be possible to get a message to him, so that he could begin observing the *shiva*, the seven-day mourning period, or should he be spared any more pain?

Such were Leibel's thoughts as Reb Sholem Geldzahler began chanting the Prayer for the Dead in his sweet tenor voice:

> Almighty, full of compassion,
> Thou who dwellest in the highest heights,
> Grant perfect repose
> Beneath the wings of the Divine Presence,
> In the exalted spheres of the holy and pure,
> Who shine like the brightness of the firmament,
> For the soul of Shloimeh ben Harav Mordche Amram
> Who has gone to eternity,
> And for whom charity has been donated
> In remembrance of his soul.
> May Paradise be his resting place.
> Therefore, may the Merciful One bring him under the
> Shelter of His wings forever and may his soul
> Be bound up in the bond of eternal life.
> May God be his inheritance

And may he rest in peace,
And let us say, Amen.

As the men murmured, "Amen" in answer to the ancient prayer, Leibel looked up from the clods of dirt that surrounded the open grave to see three figures approaching. At first he saw only their heads, as they were far down the hill. From his vantage point it looked as if some monstrous three-headed creature was lumbering slowly toward them, so close together did they walk. As they drew nearer, he saw that the three were women. Even before he could discern their faces, he knew who they were; his wife Dina, his sister-in-law Miriam, and his mother-in-law Chaya Rochel. The women had their arms about each other, the sisters supporting their mother between them. As they neared the grave, Reb Dovid Kempner stepped forward. As head of the burial society, it was his duty to turn the women away, in keeping with Dubnitzer custom. He took a few steps toward them, then stopped.

Chaya Rochel stood before him, having shaken free from her daughters' arms. The men were shocked at the *rebbetzin*'s appearance. This plump woman, who always brimmed with vitality and good humor, had turned into a wrinkled, gray-faced crone overnight. Pointing her fingers first at Reb Dovid, then making a sweep of her arm to encompass the rest of the assembled men, she opened her mouth to speak. Several seconds passed before her voice emerged from her throat. Then, in a cracked whisper, she said, "Do you dare turn a mother from her child's grave, a child whom she suckled at the breast?" Some of the men flinched and looked away, but she went on. "Do you dare drive sisters from the grave of their only brother, whom they adored as the apple of their eyes? And do you dare deny the proper mourning ritual to the only son of the Dubnitzer?" Her voice rose to an angry wail. "Woe unto you, any one of you," she gave Leibel a piercing stare, "who dares deny me or my daughters the right to mourn our dead as we see fit. And woe unto me, a mother who cannot bid her only son his final farewell."

The men stepped away from the grave, allowing the three women to approach. One by one they bent over the hole, which now held the spare pine box. Silently, with tears coursing down their cheeks, they drew back as Leibel raised his shovel and threw the first clods of dirt on the coffin. Following an ancient Jewish custom, he then replaced the shovel in the earth rather than passing it to his neighbor, to avoid passing on the "contagion" of death.

Each man present poured dirt into the grave. With every thud of earth upon the casket, a different image of Shloimeh flashed before Miriam's eyes: Shloimeh at his circumcision, squalling with all the rage and pain his tiny body could muster, and later, contentedly sucking on the wine-soaked corner of a napkin, all pain forgotten, as the Hasidim sang and danced around him. She remembered the stink of his soiled diapers and also the sweet cozy baby smell of his skin after the bath that she, at age thirteen, had loved to give him. She saw him as a toddler and could almost feel again the gentle pressure of his chubby hand as she walked with him through the village, his funny little voice incessantly questioning her with words she could barely understand. How quickly the toddler became a schoolboy, attending *cheder* with his friends, his baby curls shorn except for the earlocks of which he was so proud. And finally, Shloimeh at the age of ten, grown thin and serious, talking about the war with an understanding far beyond his years. *Oh, Shloimeh, darling brother, would you have put aside your childhood as quickly as you did, had you known how soon it would end, and in what manner?* Miriam covered her eyes with her hands and wept anew. Beside her, Dina and Chaya Rochel cried quietly as Reb Geldzahler chanted the timeless Aramaic poetry of the burial *Kaddish*. The men then formed two lines so that Chaya Rochel, Miriam, and Dina could pass between them, according to tradition.

Not since the great diphtheria epidemic of 1926, which claimed seventy-two members of Dubnitz's Jewish population, could the Dubnitzer Hasidim recall a *shiva* like the one observed at the Rutner household for Shloimeh. So oppressive was the grief that pervaded the household that even the peasants who entered the door to bring food left quickly, without speaking, chastened by the silence and sorrow within. The profound quiet in the house was broken only by the soft sobs of the mourners and by the whispered voices of those who had come to comfort them and pay their respects. A thick wax candle in a tall glass burned on the mantelpiece, casting fluttering shadows on the opposite wall. All of the mirrors in the house had been covered with sheets to underscore the unseemliness of vanity at a time of death.

Miriam, Dina, and Chaya Rochel sat in the parlor on low stools provided by the burial society, in keeping with the custom that mourners sit close to the earth that had claimed their dead. Unlike their Polish Catholic neighbors, they did not wear black, but rather gray, brown, and dark blue dresses, which they would not change during the seven days of mourning. Below the collar of each dress was a deep rent, a symbol of mourning since Biblical times.

Many years before, when taken by Chaya Rochel to pay a condolence call, Miriam had asked her mother why the widow did not wear a black dress and veil like those in the romance novels she sometimes read at friends' houses. "What a question," Chaya Rochel had snorted. "Is black for us always a sign of mourning? Look at your father, and all his Hasidim. They are always dressed in black. A Jew can mourn in any color."

Because of their status as mourners, the three women were not required to cook or perform household chores. These duties were taken over by two wives of Dubnitzer Hasidim. On the very first day of the *shiva*, even before the funeral had ended, they had rushed to the Rutner home, bringing the traditional round foods—eggs and bagels—to symbolize that life is a cycle and must therefore go on. Quickly, the women draped cloth over the mirrors and set out the food, and just as quickly they hurried away, leaving Sara Presser, a pale, taciturn fifteen-year-old, to minister to the bereaved. The women felt they should have stayed, but it was all too terrible. What would they say to the *rebbetzin*, with her only son murdered and her husband, the revered Dubnitzer Rov, imprisoned God knows where? For even more than the grief at Shloimeh's death, the awful uncertainty surrounding the *rebbe*'s absence cast a pall over the house, raising questions that no one dared ask.

In addition to the tight-lipped Sara, who moved silently through the rooms, serving and removing food, straightening books on the shelves, and washing the kitchen floor countless times although no one had soiled it, Leibel Parnes worked tirelessly from morning till night. He did not, however, confine his activities to the Rutner home, but spent his time running between the German army head-quarters and the Gestapo office. Along with Feivel the *gabbai*, and several other Hasidim, he was determined to locate Reb Mordche, who was last seen being dragged into the Gestapo building. This was the headquarters of the Nazi police. Five times Leibel had tried to gain entry to the building, and each time he was cruelly turned away with threats of bodily harm pursuing him. The last time, he was actually punched and kicked by Gestapo officers at the door. Still, he refused to be deterred.

On the last day of the *shiva*, he went to see Stashek, a Polish boy who occasionally ran errands for the Hasidim. Cautiously, he rapped on the door of Stashek's home, a small, tidy-looking cottage with whitewashed walls and a small vegetable garden in front. He knocked several times. Finally, the frightened face of Stashek's mother appeared in the doorway. Leibel touched his hat and bowed slightly. "Good morning, Panie. May I have a word with your son, Stashek?"

The woman smiled uncertainly. Leibel noticed that many of her teeth were gone, although she was still young. "Stashek is not here."

She began to close the rough wooden door. Leibel reached out and grasped the edge of it. "Please, Panie, I know he is here. May I speak with him?"

The woman's smile disappeared, and furrows creased her bow under its flowered babushka. "Please," she begged. "Go away. We do not need Jews here. Not now. Go away."

As she pulled the door closed, another face appeared behind her. "I'll handle it, Mother."

Stashek, a slightly built youth of seventeen, stepped outside. "Yes, Reb Parnes. How can I help you?"

After nine P.M., the streets of Dubnitz were virtually deserted, save for the occasional rangy dog or cat and a few German soldiers talking and laughing as they patrolled in pairs. Near the Gestapo building, a small figure clad in a peasant kerchief and long black skirt crept silently along the street. Slowly, he approached the building, made his way around back, then walked up to the tall barbed-wire fence that had recently been erected. Removing his skirt, he tossed it upward, where it caught on the barbs atop the fence. Hoisting himself up, he folded the cloth onto the barbs, blunting their sharp points. He then pulled himself over, landing lightly on the other side. Walking stealthily in the soundless, catlike way he had practiced since childhood, Stashek crept to the wall of the building, moving along it until he came to the window he was seeking. It was a small, square opening six inches above the ground. An iron grille had been hammered over it from the inside.

Narrowing his eyes, Stashek peered between the bars until he could see the room's interior, which was lit only by a flickering candle, even though the building had electricity. The room was small, about nine feet square, and devoid of furniture, except for a wooden chair and a narrow metal cot. Beneath the cot, Stashek could discern the dull sheen of a tin pail, probably used as a chamber pot.

In the dim light, Stashek could barely distinguish the figure that lay on the bed, especially because that figure was dressed in dark clothing. As he watched, the prisoner moaned and slowly raised himself, turning his head so that his face became visible in the candlelight. Stashek suppressed a gasp at the sight of that face. From the shape of the head, the set of the eyes, and the angle of the nose, he recognized Reb Mordche.

All of the peasants in Dubnitz knew who the *rebbe* was, but Stashek knew him firsthand. Often he ran errands for the Hasidim and even lit the lamps on Friday night and Saturday evenings in the *beis medrash*, as this activity was forbidden to Jews on the Sabbath. Reb Mordche always insisted that Stashek be paid immediately after the *havdalah* ceremony on Saturday night, reminding his disciples, "Thou shalt not stay the payment of a hired worker overnight." Leibel had translated the saying for Stashek, who was impressed that the Jews' holy *Torah* concerned itself with such everyday matters and was so sensitive to the needs of servants. He pictured Reb Mordche in the study house, surrounded by his Hasidim, raising and lowering his hand as he expounded some biblical passage, his broad gray beard spread out upon his chest like some costly fur piece. Now he felt sickened as he looked at the *rebbe*'s face, for that proud beard was no more. Instead, the rabbi's jaws and upper lip were covered with deep cuts, scratches, and matted tufts of bloody hair. His shirtfront, always so immaculately white, was full of dark bloodstains. Stashek shuddered. Obviously, the *rebbe*'s beard had been forcibly ripped out. His forehead, too, was bruised, and a great jagged gash ran diagonally from his hairline to his left eyebrow.

If they did that to him, what will they do to me if they find me here? Stashek slipped away from the window and made his way back to the fence, scaling it where the black skirt still padded the sharp points. Once on the ground, he pulled at the skirt until it hung down toward him. With his knife, he sliced off the little strip that held fast to the barbs, wrapped the remaining material around his waist, secured his babushka, and hurried home. He knew the black fabric could not be traced to him: nearly every peasant woman owned a skirt made from it. The news about the *rebbe* would have to wait till morning. He had risked enough for one night.

Even before Stashek knocked the next morning, Leibel was at the door waiting. The door to a house of mourning was customarily left unlocked once the family had risen, so that people could come and go without creating a disturbance. In this special situation, with Nazi soldiers everywhere, it had been suggested that the Rutners make an exception and lock the door, but Chaya Rochel had refused. "My door will be open," she insisted. "Those Nazi murderers don't need locks to get in anyhow. Let them see we are not afraid of them, that our tradition and our faith are stronger than they." Moved by her display of bravery in the face of tragedy, the Hasidim respectfully acceded to her wishes.

When Stashek entered the house, Chaya Rochel, Dina, and Miriam looked up expectantly, but he motioned for Leibel to come outside.

Leibel pulled the door almost closed behind him and began questioning the youth. "Yes, what did you find out?"

"The rabbi is alive."

"God be praised. Where is he?"

"In a basement room at the Gestapo headquarters."

"Is he all right? Did you see him?"

"I saw him."

"Well, how is he? How did he look?"

Stashek shifted his weight from one foot to the other and looked away.

"Well?" Leibel moved closer to him, holding him captive with his eyes.

"He, the *rebbe*, he is in pain. He is bleeding. They have beaten him and torn off his beard."

From behind the door came a piercing shriek, followed by prolonged wailing. The three women had been standing just inside to hear what Stashek had to say. Unnerved, the boy shook his head and turned to go. He had already been paid; there was no use staying longer.

The news about Reb Mordche drove his Hasidim into a frenzy. Day after day Leibel and his emissaries went to Gestapo headquarters, offering gifts of money, jewels, and silver artifacts. Generally, these were confiscated, but no news regarding the *rebbe* was forthcoming. Finally, on the sixth day, the Nazi officer greeted them with a broad smile.

"Again you seek your rabbi? What persistence! Jesus Christ himself didn't have such faithful followers. You people should know all about it. Remember Judas?" He laughed. "Well, you can satisfy yourself that the rabbi is not here."

Leibel stepped forward as the Hasidim murmured to each other, digesting this frightening information. "Not here? Where then, have you taken him?"

Feivel, the *gabbai*, edged Leibel aside. "He is a very important man," he shouted. "Our rabbi has hundreds of followers all over Poland. Terrible things will happen to you if you mistreat our rabbi."

Leibel squeezed Feivel's arm hard, and the man flushed and stopped speaking. The rest of the Hasidim looked at each other. It was impossible to know how to act toward these Nazis. If you were an important prisoner, perhaps they would treat you better. On the other hand, they might single out the important ones for special punishment. Hadn't they already done so with the *rebbe?* Better for Feivel to have kept quiet. Now the damage was done.

The officer smiled again. "Yes. We know he is very important. That's why we sent him away. To do some very important work for us. After all, a rabbi must also work with his hands. Jesus was a rabbi, but he was also a carpenter." He rubbed his own long-fingered hands together, scanning the faces of the Hasidim.

"You seem to be skeptical. Do you want proof that your rabbi isn't here?" He stared at each man in turn, waiting for an answer. When none came, he spoke again. "One of you may come inside and inspect the premises, if you like. You will see how we treat our guests. Which of you men volunteers to enter our modest little guest house?"

The men hung back. To enter the Gestapo headquarters could mean instant arrest, deportation, even murder. No one knew what to expect from the Nazis, only that it was certain to be terrible.

The officer leaned against the doorframe, struck a match, and casually lit a cigarette. The obvious agitation he had caused this little group of Jews amused him. Both he and they knew that their fates rested in his hands, but it was fun to play cat and mouse with them, to watch them approach and withdraw as he pulled the strings. He drew deeply on his cigarette, waiting.

Leibel broke the silence, stepping forward and raising his hand. "I do. I volunteer. I wish to inspect the premises, to be sure that the rabbi is gone."

The officer pursed his lips and slowly exhaled smoke directly into Leibel's face. "Very well. Only one of you. Any others?"

Feivel stepped up to Leibel. "I, too, wish to see."

"All right. The rest of you, away from here!"

As the remaining men began hurrying back to the *beis medrash*, the Nazi called to them. "Stop! Where are your badges?"

The men paused and looked at one another in confusion. Badges? What did he mean?

"Oh, yes. They have not yet been issued. You, come over here," The officer pointed to Menachem Block, a young butcher with a bristling red beard. Menachem glanced at his friends, then walked up to the officer, who stood waiting with Leibel and Feivel.

"Wait here, you three." The Nazi disappeared into the building, then returned carrying several small boxes. As if to allay their curiosity, the officer reached into a box and held up a small Star of David made of yellow cloth. In its center was printed the word *Jew* in Polish.

"Here. Take these." He handed out the boxes to Menachem. "Have your women sew these on your clothing. Every person over the age of twelve must wear a star on their clothing whenever they go outside. Anyone who does not will be severely punished."

Menachem nodded, took the boxes, and rejoined the waiting Hasidim. When they were out of earshot, Menachem sneered and said, "Badges? So these are the famous badges we've all heard about!"

"Isn't it strange," put in Mordechai, a frail Hasid with a sparse, pointy gray beard, "that they need badges in order to identify us? If we Jews are the *untermenschen* they say we are, they should be able to spot us right off, badge or no badge."

"Right," said David Lemberg, a short, rotund figure of a man who was a distant cousin of the *rebbe*'s. "As if we Hasidim need badges to mark us off as Jews anyhow. What would they mistake us for, Chinamen?"

The men snickered amongst themselves as they walked on. Mordechai turned around, trying to see what had happened to Leibel and Feivel, but they had already entered the building.

The officer introduced the two Hasidim to a small group of Russian collaborators who lounged in what had been the hospital waiting room.

"These two fellows want to be sure the rabbi is no longer vacationing here." He indicated the Hasidim with his cigarette, then continued, "Ivan, come. Let us show them around."

A tall, gangly soldier stood up. His scraggly blond hair seemed at odds with his olive complexion and dark eyes.

A strange mix, thought Leibel, eyeing the young soldier, who adjusted his clothing and ambled over.

"What are you staring at, Jew?" the young man asked, leaning forward and breathing beery fumes into Leibel's face.

"Nothing at all. I—" Leibel's words were cut off by a fierce jab that caught him just below the breastbone, doubling him over and setting him coughing.

The officer who had escorted the Hasidim stepped between Leibel and the soldier. "Leave him be, you Russian scum!" he commanded. "After all, they will think we are barbarians."

The young soldier smirked and turned away as Leibel and Feivel were led down the corridor.

The officer, whose name was Heinz Dribber, opened a few doors that led to small, bare rooms. "See?" he said. "No rabbi." He led them farther down the hall until they reached a door at the end, which Dribber opened. The Hasidim blinked, staring into the blackness. What was it? Another room?

"Go in," urged Dribber. "I'll strike a light in a moment."

He reached out and gave Feivel a mighty shove, which sent him sprawling forward into Leibel. Leibel lost his footing, and both men, arms and legs scrabbling for footholds, went crashing down the stone staircase they had been unable to see. Dribber laughed, locked the door, and, turning with a smart click of the heels, went back to his office.

When Leibel and Feivel failed to return home that night, Dina and Temerl, Feivel's wife, decided to go together to the Gestapo headquarters. Hearing of this plan, the Hasidim put the women under guard, declaring that it was a "danger unto death" for them to go. Instead, several Hasidim, including Feivel's brother, Zalman, defied the curfew and set out for the Gestapo building at eleven P.M.

At the gate, a moon-faced young soldier raised his bayonet and pointed at them. "Go away," he said, in the cold, guttural tones of his native Bavaria. "Go now, or you will all be arrested. You have no business here."

Zalman stepped forward. "Where are the Jews you have arrested—my brother and his friend, and our rabbi, who has been here for two weeks already?"

The German thrust his chin forward and glared at the group. "Who are you to question us? One more step and I'll cut you open from your funny beard right down to there." He pointed the bayonet downward, toward Zalman's crotch.

The sound of his voice attracted several White Russian "police," who crowded the doorway, staring at the little group of Jews clustered together just beyond the gate. "Do they want to join the party?" asked one, evoking laughter in the others.

Zalman looked at his fellow Hasidim. "We had better go back," he said. Turning again to face the soldiers, he drew in a deep breath and declared, "You cannot do this to us, and to our rabbi. We will be back, many more of us. In the meantime, God will judge you for your deeds."

"Yah, God loves all you rotten Jews," shouted one of the soldiers.

"Right," answered another. "He proves it by making them peel their peckers when they're born." He twirled his bayonet suggestively, while the others laughed and jeered. Zalman and his cohorts turned and walked stiffly away in the direction they had come.

During the next two weeks, life became a waking nightmare for the Rutner family. Both Chaya Rochel and Dina were inconsolable, spending their time weeping or staring blankly into space. When they spoke, it was only to discuss the plight of their missing husbands. If the children, Bluma and Baruch, were with them, they tried to control their tears, and even managed to smile, but the underlying tension was always close to the surface.

Miriam, although shattered by the death of her brother and gravely worried about Leibel and especially her father, was better able to maintain her composure. It was she who took over the care of the children, dressing and feeding them, reading them stories about the fools of Chelm, and inventing simple games. She was grateful for the children, whose bright faces cheered her and prevented her from sinking into the depression that had claimed her mother and sister. Occasionally, she felt that Dina was giving her angry looks, but she was not sure, since Dina was quite often sullen and brooding these days. *Perhaps*, thought Miriam, *Dina resents me because my husband and child are far away from the clutches of the Nazis.* This kindled a deep anger in Miriam. *After all*, she told herself, *it's not as if we know that all is well with Reuben and David, either. And David was so sick when he left. Who knows if he ever came out of the coma, if he's even still alive?* At times, when she was alone, Miriam's worry and anguish over her husband and child threatened to engulf her, and she fought to keep from crying out. Holding her swollen belly as silent tears coursed down her face, she cursed the world into which this new baby would be born, a world in which the baby's father and brother were so far out of reach, in which its ten-year-old uncle had just been murdered, while another uncle was now in the murderers' clutches, not to mention the baby's *zayde*, who might not even be alive anymore, God forbid. Then the baby would kick and squirm within her, and she would recall momentarily the joyous hope she had felt just a few months before when the baby had first quickened, hope that had since turned to ashes in her heart.

On the fifteenth day since Leibel's arrest, and the twenty-eighth since Reb Mordche had been seized, Miriam was woken during the night by a soft but insistent tapping at the front door. She rolled heavily onto her side and was about to swing her legs off the bed, when she heard Dina's running feet and the click of the door being unlocked. A loud shriek pierced the quiet of the night, followed by a heavy thud and the murmur of deep voices. Miriam threw on her tentlike wrapper and hurried downstairs in her bare feet.

In the dim light on the staircase, she saw three figures standing over a fourth, who was lying on the floor. When she reached the bottom step, she stood still, gripping her throat in shock. Dina stood with her arms around Leibel while Chaya Rochel bent over Reb Mordche, who lay prone on the polished wood floor of the hallway.

The rabbi was barely recognizable. His beard was a mass of short prickly white hair with scabby patches showing through. A deep scar creased his forehead under his snowy hair. His hat and skullcap were gone. It was the first time in her life that Miriam had seen her father bareheaded, but she scarcely noticed, so ghastly was his appearance. His cheeks were hollow and sunken, as were his eyes, and his body had shrunk to half its usual size. She moved forward to offer her assistance as Leibel, Dina, and Chaya Rochel began to lift the *rebbe*, but her mother waved her away. Of course. She had forgotten that she was forbidden to lift things. Instead, she watched as her father was carried to a couch in the parlor. Her mother brought in a thick quilt and covered him; although it was August, he was shivering uncontrollably.

It was only when Reb Mordche stopped shaking and lay quietly on the couch that Miriam turned and looked at Leibel. She was shocked by what she saw, for he, too, had changed drastically. He was thin and wasted, looking as if he had lost at least twenty pounds. His usually florid face was gray and pinched. Only his eyes blazed with their usual fire. Dina hovered over him, offering food, which he declined, then tea, which he accepted and drank with trembling hands. When he finished, he spoke for the first time since entering the house. "I must rest."

Dina led him into Shloimeh's old bedroom, which was the closest room to the parlor, and closed the door behind them. Chaya Rochel looked up at Miriam with weary eyes.

"Go back to bed, Miriam. You need your sleep."

"I want to stay here with you and *Tati*. What if you need something?"

"Nonsense. I'll take care of *Tati*." She gazed down at her husband and sighed. "What have they done to him? The big heroes, torturing an old man."

"Thank God he's alive," said Miriam. Her voice sounded oddly flat to her own ears.

"Alive," Chaya Rochel repeated. She leaned back in her chair. "Go to bed," she commanded, and set her lips in a thin, bitter line.

Miriam sighed and slowly ascended the stairs. *What has happened to us,* she asked herself. *In Warsaw before the war, I used to get upset if a cake I baked fell flat or I couldn't find shoes to match a new purse. I thought life would go on as it had. Reuben and I were happy, the store was doing well, David was so adorable.* A sob caught in her throat as she thought of David. She lay down in the fetal position she had adopted since the sixth month of her pregnancy and tried not to think of all the things that had occurred in the months since David's accident. If she did, anxiety would overwhelm her, and she would writhe on the mattress in an agony of real and imagined horrors. Finally, Miriam drifted off into semiconsciousness. She was about to fall asleep when loud banging on the front door brought her sharply awake. She dressed quickly, making sure to choose a smock with a yellow star. Loud pounding these days could only mean Nazis.

Three times in the last few days, they had come here, menacing the women and demanding valuables. Chaya Rochel had protested, but they threatened to take Dina and the children, and once to "cut open that one's belly," pointing their bayoneted rifles at Miriam, who had not had time to hide with Baruch and Bluma.

Chaya Rochel had unearthed their silver and jewelry, parceling it out each time the Nazis came. Now there was nothing left but Reb Mordche and Shloimeh's *kiddush* cups and the silver candlesticks that had belonged to Aunt Shifra. These were hidden under the grate of the fireplace in the rabbi's study.

"Open up!" The accents were German, not White Russian.

So these are officers, thought Miriam. *To what do we owe this honor?*

She took the sleepy-eyed Bluma and Baruch from their cots, which had been squeezed between the two beds in her room, and hid them behind a panel in the closet, offering them a few toys and some stale rolls that were kept in the bedroom for just such an eventuality. The children were used to it; even little Baruch hardly ever cried in there, but played contentedly with his sister.

Before Miriam reached the stairway, she heard the men speaking in broken Polish. "Your men have been released, yes? They are returned safely. So now you must pay. Give us your gold. Now!"

Chaya Rochel answered in an angry whisper, "I have nothing. I've given you everything. Please, my husband is sick. Do not wake him."

The officer's voice rose. "Sick? He'll wish he were dead if you don't give us what we want."

"I have nothing," Chaya Rochel whispered, her voice as dry as the rustling of dead leaves.

"Search the house," commanded the officer.

Miriam quickly slipped back into her bedroom and joined the

children in the tiny cubicle behind the closet. Leibel had built the partition there early in the Russian occupation; there was another just like it in her parents' closet. She lowered her body to the floor, but it was nearly impossible to sit comfortably. She was too big. The children climbed on her, giggling and whispering. "Shhh!" she hissed. From downstairs came the noise of glass breaking, of scraping, pounding, then of wood splintering. Miriam could not stand it. Her mother and Dina were down there with no protection. Leibel was too weak and ill to do anything, and her father…sliding the partition aside, she motioned the children to stay silent with a finger to her lips. Then, straightening her dress and kerchief, she went downstairs.

Chaya Rochel stood in the parlor next to Reb Mordche, who still lay on the couch. His eyes were open, but they did not seem to see Miriam as she entered the room. Chaya Rochel shook her head at Miriam and pointed frantically upstairs, but it was too late. The three soldiers came back into the room, one of them holding the polished wooden box containing the silver goblets and candlesticks.

Seeing Miriam, they exchanged smiles. "What have we here?" bellowed the tallest of the three.

"A fat cow about to calve," answered the one who held the silver.

"A lying bitch, you mean," said the third. "Did you hear the old one there? 'We have nothing, we have nothing,'" he mimicked in a high, whining voice. Turning toward the door of Shloimeh's room, he shouted. "Come out, I told you!"

Dina emerged, still dressed in yesterday's clothing, her eyes heavy from lack of sleep, followed by Leibel, who looked too ill to stand. Yet stand he did, staunchly placing himself before the three women and glaring at the Nazis.

"Look at him, such a hero," said the tall officer. "Well, you can sit here a while. We will decide what to do with you later. Lying, thieving filth, hiding your silver like that. Johannes! Stay here and watch these pigs; we'll be back later." He walked out the door, followed by his companion, who cradled the wooden box. Johannes, with a disgusted look at his charges, sat down beside the door and began smoking a foul-smelling cigar. Presently, he fell asleep, his hands clasping the rifle that stood between his knees.

Leibel motioned for the women to follow him into the kitchen. Once there, Dina began to cry. "The children are still upstairs. Any minute they'll come out. They're hungry. Who knows what that animal will do to them?"

Leibel nodded. "We'll have to escape. That slob has fallen asleep, but how can we carry the *rebbe* out of here without waking him? If we could all manage to get out the back window…"

Chaya Rochel set a tray of dry rolls and a cup of tea, along with a piece of salted herring, in front of Leibel. He rose stiffly, washed his hands, and blessed the bread, which he fell upon ravenously while Dina went upstairs to feed the children. The *rebbetzin* prepared a thin gruel of barley, milk, and water, which she brought to the parlor to spoon-feed her husband.

Miriam and Leibel were alone in the kitchen. She watched silently as he devoured his food, and waited while he mumbled the benediction. By then, Dina and Chaya Rochel had returned. "He cannot eat," complained the *rebbetzin*, her eyes full of tears. "What did they do to him?"

"Better you shouldn't ask, Mama," said Dina. "Leibel told me enough during the night. Better you shouldn't know." She got up to see to her children, afraid to leave them alone. She wished Miriam would go to them, as she had these past weeks, so that she could minister to poor Leibel, but Miriam seemed rooted to her chair.

Ah well, thought Dina. *She has her own problems, about to give birth, and Reuben and David so far away. At least I have Leibel back now, and my children are with me.* She sighed, glanced warily at the sleeping soldier and tiptoed upstairs.

A low moan from Reb Mordche caused the soldier to stir. Dina froze in her tracks, staring at him, but presently a rattling snore escaped his lips, and she continued up the stairs. In the kitchen, Chaya Rochel washed the few dishes that they had used, then sat down next to Miriam, so that both women faced Leibel across the old oaken table with its grooved and pitted surface. "So, Leibel," the *rebbetzin* asked, "what happened to you, and to the *rebbe?* And where is Feivel? Tell us what you have told Dina. I'm stronger than she is, I've been through plenty; I have to know." Then, glancing at Miriam, she nervously fingered the nicks in the tabletop, running her hand over the familiar flaws. "Miriam," she urged, "go upstairs. Maybe Dina needs help. Anyway, this is not for you."

Miriam leaned back in her chair, so that her body seemed to grow even larger and rounder. "Mama, I'm not a child," she retorted. "Like you, I've also been through plenty, and I'll probably go through a lot more yet. I have a right to know what happened to *Tati*, and to Leibel and Feivel." She looked at Leibel expectantly.

Leibel folded his hands on the table and hung his head. It was several moments before he spoke, and then his voice was barely audible. "Feivel and I went to the headquarters with the others. The officer allowed the two of us to enter. He said he would show us that the *rebbe* was not there." He sighed deeply, a ragged, broken breath that seemed to come from his very soul. "I don't know why we went in. We knew it was dangerous. But somehow I felt—we felt—that maybe the *rebbe* was there, and if we saw him, maybe we could help him. And I thought, well, if they arrest me as well at least we'll all be together, and we'll think of a plan to get out, and in the meantime I'll be with my *rebbe*. So Feivel and I walked with him—the officer, the *scharfuhrer*—down the corridors, and he opened up doors and said, 'See? Your rabbi is not here.'

"Well, at the end of the hall there was a door. He opened it, it was pitch dark, and he pushed us forward. Feivel fell into me and we both fell down the stairs that we hadn't been able to see. They were very hard, made of stone, and while I was only bruised, Feivel hit his head on the bottom step. He must have gotten a concussion; I couldn't wake him. It was dark, but I could feel that he was breathing. I also felt the blood on my hand from his head wound, and I tried to bandage him with my handkerchief, but it was so dark I could hardly tell what I was doing.

"In the morning they came in—the officer, his name is Dribber, and two White Russian policemen—and told us to get up. I was already up, I had even *davened* in the dark there, but Feivel didn't move. They had lanterns, and I could see that he was still breathing, but he had lost a lot of blood. Well, one of the men went down and nudged Feivel with his boot. 'Get up, you filthy swine,' or whatever—you know the usual blessings they bestow on us." Leibel wiped his brow with the back of his hand, stared off toward the window for a few seconds, then resumed his narrative.

"Feivel still didn't respond. The man kicked him hard, with his boot. Well, I'm no hero, far from it, but I stepped forward. I stood over Feivel and said, 'Stop, he's wounded, you know.' And the man... the man slammed his rifle butt into my stomach. I fell back from the pain, I couldn't breathe. I couldn't stop him." Leibel stopped speaking and lowered his eyes, but not before Miriam caught the gleam of a tear that he brushed away with his fingertips.

"God have mercy on us," whispered Chaya Rochel.

Leibel swallowed his tears and went on. "The man, the Russian Nazi, he lifted his rifle butt over Feivel and said again, 'Get up. I command you to get up.' And when Feivel didn't, he slammed the gun butt down into Feivel's head again and again." Leibel lowered his head to the table and buried it in his arms. His body shook with great choking sobs that he fought to suppress, for fear they would waken the soldier who snored in the hallway. Finally, he sat up and began speaking again, in a surprisingly calm voice. "He struck him until his head was smashed; I knew he was dead. Then they carried him out. They said to me as they were going back up the stairs, dragging Feivel with them, 'You will be next,' or something like that. Then they left me there in the dark, for I don't know how long, in this little corridor. I couldn't sit on the ground, it was covered with blood, so I sat on the stairs. I said the *Kel Moleh Rachamim*, God Full of Mercy, for Feivel, may his memory be blessed.

"Much later, they came for me. They brought me upstairs and gave me some water and some bread and told me I was going to work. You can imagine, I was in no condition even to stand. I was all stiff from sitting on the stone steps and in shock because of Feivel. Also, I was bruised myself from the fall. Anyhow, they put me on a truck with twelve other men, mostly Jews: Yehuda Lifshitz and Berel Adelson, Mendel Itzkowitz and some others, and a few Poles.

"We rode all day in this closed truck, and it was hot, I can't tell you how hot it was. Finally, we arrived at some kind of camp; there were tents. They unloaded us and gave us shovels and picks. They said we had to dig trenches. I don't even know where it was."

His voice faded and he closed his eyes. Miriam gazed at the deep lines that creased his cheeks, running down to his beard. Had they been there before? She remembered his having dimples.

Dina came in, sat down beside Leibel, and took his hand. "The children are asleep. You should sleep too, *tateleh*," she said, her eyes full of love and concern. "He didn't sleep all night," she explained to her mother and sister.

Leibel gave her the semblance of a smile and shook his head. "Now is not the time for sleeping. Soon they'll be back, and who knows what will happen then? We must be prepared."

Miriam sat up with a start. "Why are we sitting here talking? We can escape before they get back," she whispered. "One of us can hand the children out to the rest. We'll go out the back window—"

"Having a coffee klatsch?" came a voice from the doorway. Miriam's heart sank. The soldier stood there, smiling at them. "Thank God he doesn't understand Yiddish," she said, avoiding his arrogant stare.

"Keep talking, I don't care. Just give me some food. Got any bacon?" he sneered.

Chaya Rochel rose and prepared a tray of rolls, herring, and tea. "There's little enough to eat these days," she muttered in Yiddish. "They take it all anyway. But to have to serve them in my own house!" She handed the tray to the soldier and quickly turned away, holding her hands out before her as if they had touched something unclean.

The soldier took the tray back to his post at the door, where he balanced it on his knees and began eating. Miriam glanced at him from time to time, a quick look from beneath her lowered lashes so that he would not notice. He was a fastidious eater, neatly removing the tiny bones from the herring and laying them on the side of the blue-and-white plate, gathering the many crumbs that fell from the dry roll into his napkin. There was a strange fascination in watching him eat his food; Miriam found herself almost staring at times, until Leibel spoke again.

"We worked very hard," he said, extending his hands, which were full of blisters and cuts and blackened with dirt that no amount of washing would remove. "We dug ditches. We had to take the rocks out of the earth and pile them on the side. I don't know which was worse—the big heavy ones that nearly broke my back, or the small ones, of which there were so many, you had to stop constantly to clear them away. They didn't give us anything to put the rocks in—no wheelbarrow, nothing—so you had to use your hands. You dug out a handful of rocks, carried them to the pile on the side, dropped them, came back, dug some more."

Chaya Rochel got up to check on her husband. Satisfied that he still slept soundly, she returned, nodding at Leibel to go on.

"For me it wasn't so bad; after all, I'm young and fairly strong, although I can't say I'm used to such work."

"Who is, from us?" interjected Dina.

"We worked all day. Morning and evening they gave us a thin soup, watery, with no taste, and water to drink. At first we wouldn't eat it, because we thought surely it couldn't be kosher, but soon we did, or we would have starved."

"*Pikuach nefesh*, a life in danger," murmured Chaya Rochel, referring to the law that states that a Jew may violate religious precepts if doing so might save his life or that of someone else.

"At night we slept in tents, on straw pallets that were lumpy, full of bedbugs. Still, you were tired, you slept. On the third day, we were moved to another location. When we started working, I saw Yerucham Bistritsky, from Dronovarskov. He said to me, 'Come with me, I'll show you something.' We had to sneak around the work crew—you didn't want the guards to see you walking anywhere. He took me to a place behind the pile of rocks; there was a little cavern they had hollowed out, and in it was our *rebbe*, lying on the ground.

"The men took turns bringing him water and wiping his face. God will reward them. They took their lives in their hands, because of the danger from the guards. I became the main guardian of our *rebbe*; whenever I had a minute to spare, I was with him. He was supposed to be working, and on the first few days he tried to work, but of course he was too weak from being jailed, beaten, and starved. We were afraid that he would die. At night I was supposed to go back to my own tent, but I traded places with someone, a Bilgiver Hasid, so I could sleep in the *rebbe*'s tent. And there at night, you really saw his righteousness, his greatness. He would not accept any food unless he was shown that everyone had enough for himself. He said, 'I am an old man, it doesn't matter. Save the others.'"

Chaya Rochel stifled a sob, nervously glancing at the soldier, who had finished eating and now sat idly in the doorway, leaning back in his chair with his black-booted feet stretched out before him. Abruptly, he shifted in his seat, rubbed his crotch, rose, and stepped just outside the open door, where he relieved himself in the scraggly yew trees, splashing noisily before coming back inside. Dina and her mother exchanged disgusted glances, and Leibel continued.

"After everyone was in bed and the guards had counted us, the *rebbe* would give a *dvar Torah*. One night one of the men asked him, 'Why does God allow this brutality?' I'll never forget what he answered. He said, "The whale is the largest mammal, and all the creatures fear it, but when it dies and is washed up onshore, it produces a terrible stench, worse than any other living thing. So too, with the Germans. They were considered the most highly cultured, the most civilized of humans. The whole world looked up to them. But when they became too powerful, they became corrupt, and now their deeds stink to heaven, both in the eyes of man and in the eyes of God. Such is God's way to teach us, "Do not put your trust in mankind." Just as they rose, so they will fall, and be washed up onshore; for their downfall will be greater than that of any nation, and their name will be synonymous with brutality and murder forever, like the nation of Amalek.'"

Leibel's eyes flashed and his hands shook as he related these words, but his voice was strong and clear. Something in its tone roused the German soldier, who sat up in his chair and glared at Leibel. Then, kicking aside his tray so that the dishes and cups fell away with a clatter, he strode into the dining room.

"Enough of this chitchat," he snarled. "You think I don't

understand your filthy gutter language? I'm German, not one of the Russian morons who work here in this shit hole. I can understand Jew-talk." He leaned forward on his rifle, staring at them menacingly.

Miriam and Leibel exchanged glances. Who knows how much he had understood? Much of Yiddish was derived from German, but it was still different enough that Yiddish-speaking Jews had less difficulty comprehending German than the other way around.

The soldier looked at his watch with an angry scowl. "Where are they?" he grumbled. He spat on the ground and returned to his seat, but his composure was gone. Nervously, he glanced from the Jews in his charge to the road before the house, then down to his watch. He did not have to wait long. Not more than ten minutes had passed when Officer Dribber appeared in the doorway.

"Good morning, Johannes. Have you had a pleasant night? Now we are here to liven up the proceedings." Johannes started up eagerly, his black mood immediately dispelled.

Dribber looked from one family member to another, his gaze lingering on the sleeping *rebbe* for a moment before it came back to Dina. "Who else is in the house?" he demanded, speaking in clipped tones around the cigarette that dangled from his teeth.

Dina's large round eyes stared up at him. "No one," she answered.

Miriam looked at the floor, lest by the flicker of an eyelid, the twitch of a lip, she betray the whereabouts of the little ones who still napped upstairs.

"Search the house," drawled Dribber, as if bored by the whole matter.

Dina stared straight ahead, but her cheeks went white. Leibel reached out his hand and took hers.

Two soldiers started up the stairs. "Never mind," called Dribber. "It won't be necessary." The soldiers returned to the hallway, awaiting further instructions.

Dina and Leibel exchanged the briefest of glances, but Miriam caught the sparkle of relief in Dina's eye. Her children would be spared, at least for now. Chaya Rochel whispered something, which Miriam assumed was a prayer of thanks.

Dribber bent over Reb Mordche, who had opened his eyes and seemed more alert than he had been since being brought home. "Get up, old man," Dribber said, his voice surprisingly gentle.

Leibel let go his wife's hand and moved toward Reb Mordche.

"Stay back!" commanded Dribber as Johannes hoisted his rifle, aimed it at Leibel, then lowered it again.

The rabbi slowly sat up on the couch and moved aside the bedclothes. Dribber leaned down, took Reb Mordche's arm, and helped him rise. Two of the soldiers exchanged smirks.

"All right," barked Dribber, once Reb Mordche was on his feet. "Everyone outside! March!"

He jerked his rifle at the door, motioning for his hostages to exit. Leibel and Dina went first, followed by Miriam, while Chaya Rochel supported her husband, who could barely walk. At once Leibel left Dina's side and took the *rebbe*'s other arm, half carrying him as they began walking down the road in the direction the officer indicated. They had gone but a few yards when a crackling noise behind them made them instinctively turn around. Dina clutched at her kerchief, then began screaming. She and Leibel ran toward the house but were blocked by a phalanx of soldiers who crossed their rifles before them.

"Walk, or we'll shoot you all, every one of you."

"Shoot me, then!" shrieked Dina. With all of her strength she pushed aside the rifles and ran toward the house. Flames were leaping from the parlor window, where the curtains had been set alight. Like the tongues of ravenous demons, they licked upward toward the second floor, where Bluma and Baruch had been left sleeping. Leibel tried to run after his wife but was caught and held by the soldiers. Though he struggled violently, he could not break free. Miriam stared, half uncomprehending, as Dina's body was silhouetted against the flaming doorway. Suddenly, a shot rang out, and Dina crumpled to the ground, her white kerchief darkening with blood. Leibel gave a soft moan and stopped struggling. With vacant eyes, he turned, and once again supporting his father-in-law, resumed walking toward the woods.

The little party with its military escort was taken across the wooden plank bridge, over the river, and into the stand of trees that bordered the gentile section of Dubnitz. There they were marched deeper into the woods, treading over brown, summer-scorched pine needles and dry twigs that snapped underfoot. Presently, they came to a clearing, a meadow where Pan Vorny, an elderly peasant with seven brawny sons, tended a small flock of dusty sheep. Today however, neither sheep nor shepherds were to be seen. Instead, a crowd of about sixty Jews, some still in their nightclothes, stood huddled together while soldiers walked among them, handing out objects that Miriam soon saw were shovels. A groan of dismay came from the group when they recognized their *rebbe* as he was led closer. The crowd surged forward as numerous Dubnitzer Hasidim pushed to get near him, to protect him or offer assistance in some way.

The sudden movement enraged the German guards, who screamed at their charges, "Get back! Get back!" The men had barely begun to respond when four shots rang out in quick succession. Like duck pins, four Hasidim dropped to the ground, to the accompaniment of loud wails from their family members.

"Dig! Dig, I say!" shrieked the officer in charge, brandishing his rifle as if it were a shovel. The other soldiers raised their rifles to shoulder height, keeping them trained on the crowd.

Miriam looked at her father. He was staring at the four fallen Hasidim, whose blood now seeped slowly into the meadow grass. Sensing her gaze, he turned to her. An expression of indescribable pain filled his eyes. Miriam could not bear it and looked away at her mother. Chaya Rochel's face was buried in her hands and she wept softly, moaning "Dina, Dina, my treasure, my dove, and the babies, oh, God, the babies, the babies…" Her voice trailed off as she shook with anguished sobs. Miriam turned to Leibel, who met her gaze. Gone was the vacant look she had seen before in his black eyes. Now they burned with helpless fury.

Just then a Nazi officer approached and roughly thrust a shovel at Miriam. "Dig, you fat cow," he commanded. Miriam stared at him, uncomprehending. How could she dig? She was not even allowed to lift anything. Infuriated by her lack of response, the soldier reared back. Leibel stepped quickly in front of her, and in so doing caught the full force of the soldier's vicious jackboot, which had been meant for Miriam's swollen belly. With a grunt, Leibel doubled over, clutching his abdomen. The soldier then raised the shovel and brought it down with all his might squarely on the crown of Leibel's head. Miriam stared in horrified disbelief as a gaping wound appeared in Leibel's skull. Blood poured from the gash, along with bone fragments and bits of wrinkled, claylike matter that she realized, with terrible certainty, was brain tissue. After kicking at Leibel's fallen body, the soldier wiped his shovel on the grass and walked away.

All around them, people were digging, and a huge, open ditch was being formed. Chaya Rochel, too, had been given a shovel, and Miriam stared as her bent and broken mother pretended to dig. Reb Mordche, too weak and ill to stand, was being supported by two of his Hasidim, whose faces Miriam vaguely remembered. *What are their names?* she asked herself, then wondered why it should matter, when they were all surely about to die. They dug through the morning, the afternoon and on into the soft summer evening. A light breeze ruffled the hair of the children, who had long since stopped whining for food and water and now watched the adults with great, staring eyes. There were no babies here, Miriam noticed, only children over the age of six or so. Where were the little ones? In a group of people to her left, she recognized Leah Moskowitz, who had given birth to a son just three weeks earlier. The circumcision had been performed in secret, with none of the traditional gaiety. The baby's father, a Dubnitzer Hasid, had allowed no levity while his *rebbe*'s heir was lying murdered in his grave, and the *rebbe* himself held captive.

The awful, stricken look on Leah's face made Miriam wonder if the infant had not met a fate similar to that of Bluma and Baruch. She lifted her eyes to the sky, which looked strangely red. Just then, the pungent smell of smoke was carried to her nostrils by the evening breeze. From the reactions of those around her, she realized they had noticed it, too. Several people broke rhythm, setting their shovels down and pointing at the sky. At once, a collective knowledge spread through the crowd. "The village is burning!" screamed Frumet Geldzahler. A shot meant to silence her missed its mark, and her aged father crumpled to the ground.

"Dig! Dig!" shouted the soldiers, taking aim.

A profound sense of unreality gripped Miriam as she watched her fellow townspeople resume their digging. She closed her eyes, shutting out the scene. *I am back in Warsaw,* she told herself. *Reuben is at work and David is playing in the next room. We will soon go visit my family in Dubnitz. Dina will be sewing a colorful quilt with Bluma and Baruch's names stitched on it in blue and yellow letters. Shloimeh will be starting a new tractate of Talmud,* Baitza. Tati *and Mama will entertain a guest from Cracow, Reb Zalman Singer. Mama will serve stuffed cabbage, beef stew, and roasted potatoes, with fruit compote and apple strudel for dessert.* Tati *will tell the story of the Miracle Worker of Kreznikov.*

"Halt!" came a loud shout, followed by other cries of "Stop digging! Shovels down!" Miriam opened her eyes, blinking in the smoky air. The soldiers, their guns drawn, moved quickly among the crowd, collecting the shovels. Before them loomed a yawning cavern, some fifty feet deep. Had they actually dug all this in one day? It was hard to believe.

"Forward!" came a shout. The crowd was pushed closer to the edge of the pit. Miriam nearly tripped on a soft bundle that lay beneath her feet. With horror she realized it was Leibel's body. A great wave of revulsion swept over her. Gasping and crying, she backed away blindly, forcing her large body between the people moving past in the opposite direction. She soon found herself near the edge of the crowd. What had she done? She had left Mama and *Tati* alone! She must get back to them. Behind her was a line of people, and behind them the soldiers. She tried to push forward but could no longer force her way through. Nor could she see what was happening up front, at the edge of the pit. Only the sounds of gunfire and the voices of the people around her, many of whom were whispering the *Shema Yisrael*, the prayer traditionally said by Jews about to die, gave her an inkling of what was happening.

Soon she no longer had to guess. The people before her were told to undress. Miriam tried not to look as these Hasidim, whose lives were a tribute to modesty in behavior, both public and private, now shed their clothes before the eyes of all.

"Get in," the soldiers commanded the row of Jews closest to the pit. Miriam focused on one young woman, Regina Silber, with whom she had gone to school. Her hair, never uncovered in public since her marriage, was short and curly. Her body was thin, with a sharply protruding spinal column. On her left shoulder blade was a large brown birthmark shaped like a mouse. Regina had once told Miriam that this mark appeared because her mother had been frightened by a mouse shortly before Regina's birth. Now Miriam could not keep her eyes off it as Regina slowly bent down and lowered herself into the pit.

"Lie down! Across!" Miriam kept her eyes on the little brown mouse as Regina and the others in her row lay themselves crosswise atop the bodies of those who had gone before. A volley of shots rang out, and the birthmark disappeared under someone's flailing arm, which was soon still.

"Quickly!" came the order. Miriam realized she had not obeyed the command to undress. She removed her head scarf and let it fall, then unbuttoned her smock and stepped out of it. Finally, she took off her underclothes, made specially for pregnant women by Sara Gitel, the seamstress. She glanced at her clothing as it lay in a heap at her feet. In the fading sunlight, the yellow star resembled a fallen autumn leaf. *I will say the Shema*, thought Miriam, but her tongue felt thick and lifeless as a stone, nor could she remember the words.

"Lie down!" She lowered herself into the ditch and lay across someone's warm flesh. *Sorry*, she thought. Her body tensed as a volley of shots was fired. A blinding flash seemed to split her head from ear to ear; she saw and heard no more.

The soldiers fired several more rounds into the pit, then watched and waited, smoking cigarettes and talking softly. When all movement and sound, all twitching and flailing of limbs, had ceased, they emptied their rifle chambers of spent shells and prepared to leave. A special contingent had sorted the clothes, first checking carefully for jewels and money; now they, too, had finished. Night had fallen. In the moonlight the soldiers formed ranks and walked double-file back through the woods. Two soldiers were left behind to stand guard. At first they stood at opposite sides of the pit, but when the sounds of the platoon had faded away, one joined the other. Removing a pack of cards from his breast pocket, he sat down on a pile of wood.

"When will they bring the gasoline?" asked his comrade.

"Tomorrow, I expect. Can't leave them too long. Not in this heat."

"Phew, they stink already," agreed his friend. "Why not tonight? Makes a nice bonfire."

"That's just it. They used it all in the village, burning the Jews' homes, and their synagogue. Some stupid ass forgot to set some aside for tonight."

"His head will roll."

They turned their attention to the cards. "One quick game. Soon the girls will be here."

"Hah, you really arranged it! And what if we get caught?"

"Who's to tell? Dead men don't tell tales. And if *you* talk, you're a dead man, too." He sliced his finger across his throat.

Presently, there came the sound of footsteps from the trees behind them. The men turned around slowly, guns drawn, then lowered them as two Polish girls in peasant garb appeared, giggling. Glancing about, the men slipped off between the trees, following them.

Miriam slowly raised her head, straining to see movement in the woods where the soldiers had disappeared. A searing pain tore at her scalp. She felt the spot with her fingers, and they came away wet and shining in the moonlight. The bullet that had grazed her skull had torn the flesh. *Get up*, she told herself, though she wondered why she should not just lie down again and let death claim her as it had the rest of them—her parents, Leibel, Dina, the children. She, too, should be dead. She lay under the weight of a great weariness, a terrible lassitude that drained her of all will to move, to think, to do anything but sink deeper into the pit until she would be truly joined with her townspeople.

Something moved beneath her. Shocked out of her stupor, Miriam slid sideways, feeling the body that lay under her for any sign of life. She saw a face with round staring eyes, mouth slightly open—an expression of surprise, but not of horror. Again the movement, a flutter, which Miriam now realized came not from the poor soul who lay beneath her, but from within herself: a message from the little prisoner in her womb. It came to Miriam as a startling revelation. *It's still alive! The child within me lives!* It was amazing to her that through all she had suffered, the tiny life inside her still fought for survival, still expected—demanded—to have its share of the world. If she were to die, then this child, too, would die. This little being whom she had harbored and sheltered for nine months and who was almost ready to be born would never know what it meant to open its smoky-blue eyes and feel its mother's love. And this baby had not only a mother, but a father and a brother who were alive in Kiev and would, please God, return someday, looking for mother and baby.

She pictured Reuben, tall and slightly stooped, his dark hair graying. David, too, would be older, taller certainly, and probably thinner. She saw them walking toward her, stepping on bodies as they approached, coming nearer, nearer—but when she reached out her hand, they vanished. Now she saw them wandering through the streets of Dubnitz, weaving in and out among the narrow lanes and twisting alleyways, shouting, "Miriam! Mama!" Raising herself on her elbow, she held out a hand and tried to call to them, but no sound came. Instead, a great wrenching pain seized her abdomen, and she gasped, doubling over. When the pain subsided, she opened her eyes. Reuben and David were gone, and she found herself once more alone with the dead, and with her pain. *Where are they? I must find them.* She tried to get up, but the corpses under and around her were slippery with blood and body fluids, and she kept falling and sliding upon them. With all her strength, she dragged herself over stiffly contorted arms and legs, shrunken chests, and swollen bellies. Finally, retching and crying, she reached the edge of the pit.

As she struggled to pull herself out, another great spasm gripped her stomach, and she slid downward once more. When the pain had spent itself, she clawed her way up the side of the pit again and lay on the ground, heaving and shaking with exhaustion. She remained there for what seemed like hours, motionless except when gripped by another terrible contraction. Finally, when she had regained some strength in her trembling limbs, she began crawling. Dragging her great, naked belly over prickly twigs, rocks, and pinecones until she was covered with cuts and scratches, she made her way into the woods. There she stopped to rest, huddled under a clump of trees. The woods were eerily silent. *Why?* she wondered.

In her shock-imposed, dreamlike state, she did not realize that the sounds she had made—the panting and gasping, the crackling of the twigs—had silenced the forest creatures. Slowly, they resumed their noises: crickets chirping, tree frogs singing. A pale moth bobbed in the air before her face like a lost spirit. As she rested, she realized that a long time had elapsed since her last pain. She tried to sleep but became conscious that she was very, very cold. It had been warm in the pit, with the heat given off by already decomposing bodies, but now her wet, naked body shivered. Wrapping her arms around herself for warmth, she listened to the night noises until her ears picked up a different sound. Her whole body tensed with fear as she strained to hear. There it was again: a faint snore, such as she had occasionally heard Reuben make when she lay awake at night, nestled in the warm concavity of his body.

She sat rigid against the tree, the cold and discomfort forgotten. Someone was asleep nearby, but the slightest sound from her could change that. It was too dark to judge how well she was hidden; she couldn't see much of her surroundings. But if she stayed where she was, she could be found and killed. She would have to get away, as quietly as possible. Again, she began to crawl, slowly, slowly, trying not to rustle the twigs beneath her, trying to stifle her own labored breathing. After a short distance, she felt something under her fingertips. Groping about among the leaves and twigs, she realized it was a piece of fabric, some article of clothing, which upon further examination proved to be a skirt made of the dark, coarse material that peasant girls wore every day. How had it come to be here? She remembered the two girls who had approached the sentries. Surely all four were lying nearby; it was their breathing she had heard. She must get away, but she would take the skirt with her. What good fortune to have found it. She wrapped it around her shoulders and inched along, not stopping until she was a reasonable distance from the sleeping couples. Then, after careful listening brought no sounds of breathing to her ears, she stood up cautiously and pulled the skirt over her head. Even had she not been pregnant, it would have been too small; as it was, she could barely get it below her shoulders. She fastened it so that it hung from an inch above her breasts to an inch below her knees. With her nakedness covered, she felt much less vulnerable and even dared walk upright, tiptoeing carefully through the trees, her hands extended before her like a blind person. She did not want a tree limb to catch her in the stomach.

She walked on and on until she heard the sound of rushing water. *Oh no,* she asked herself in despair, *have I gone back to where I started?* She moved toward the sound, and gradually the trees thinned and she found herself at the riverbank. But this was not the place where Jewish and gentile Dubnitz were separated by a narrow stream. Instead, the moonlight revealed a wide, rushing river full of shining boulders and broken tree limbs that glistened whitely before disappearing into the froth. On the other side was a broad meadow, and beyond that, the great dark forest of her childhood nightmares. Surely there must be a way to cross the river—a bridge, perhaps? She could not remember. She started walking along the riverbank, but now the lack of food and water, combined with shock and loss of blood, began to exact their toll. Her head throbbed angrily. Gingerly, she touched the wound on her scalp. It was caked with dried blood. She felt so dizzy she could hardly stand. The river, meadow, and trees spun before her, forming a monstrous whirlpool that threatened to suck her into its vortex. At the same time, her abdomen contracted once again; the awful spasms had returned.

Miriam sank to her knees in the soft clay beside the river. *Water,* she thought. *I must have water.* She inched her way down toward the shining water that would quench her thirst and soothe her burning face. Soon, soon she would feel the icy liquid between her lips. She leaned toward the river, and the clay bank gave way under her weight, sending her tumbling into the roiling water.

Chapter sixteen

Silence. Warmth. Then a terrible pain that sank like giant shark's teeth into her belly. She cried out, writhing, twisting her sweat-slicked body. The pain did not stop. Someone gripped her hand. Reuben? But the fingers were crooked and gnarled, the hand itself weightless as a pinecone. The pain rolled away, leaving her breathless for a moment before returning with twice its previous fury. Miriam screamed and screamed. She felt as if her insides were being torn from her; she wished they would be torn from her, if that would make the pain stop.

A voice murmured something, in a language she barely understood. It was rich country-peasant Polish, which she had not heard in years. The word was repeated. "Push!"

Miriam pushed, bearing down with all her might as a burning pain ripped her from groin to chest.

"Again," croaked the voice, and Miriam pushed with all the strength she could summon in her exhausted state. Again the awful burning, and suddenly a feeling of release, followed by less intense but still painful cramps.

"Oh, let me rest," murmured Miriam through parched lips. The horrible pains were subsiding, and she wanted only to sleep, to sleep and wake up far away, with Reuben and David beside her. But she was not allowed to rest. Instead, someone was shaking her shoulder and trying to raise her head, which still ached dully. She heard a strange, strangled coughing that gave way to a series of wails. Her eyes opened just as a warm, moist, squirming creature was placed upon her belly.

"Look," said the hoarse voice she had been listening to for what seemed like an eternity. Miriam slowly raised her head. There, lying across her stomach, was a naked, bloody infant squalling for all it was worth. Standing beside it, her head hovering just above the baby, was a withered, ancient woman who gave Miriam a wide, toothless grin.

"You have a daughter," she lisped in a voice dry as cobwebs. "God has spared you and your child." Miriam managed a weak smile in return. Who was this woman? And who else was in the room, rattling crockery somewhere behind Miriam's head? It did not matter. She was too tired to care.

"Drink this now." The crone held a cup of tepid liquid to her lips, supporting Miriam's head with her arm.

Miriam drank. The taste was bitter, but she drained the cup and asked for more to ease her burning thirst. Again, the cup was offered, and as she drank, she felt her limbs becoming heavy and numb, and her mind begin drifting. She was vaguely aware of someone removing the baby from where it rested on her abdomen, but she did not protest. She wanted only to sleep, and sleep she did, a black, drugged, and dreamless sleep from which she awoke many hours later, her body racked with pain.

The sun streamed through the two square windows of the hut, and thin shafts of light full of dancing dust motes entered through chinks in the wall. Raising herself on one elbow, Miriam slowly surveyed her surroundings. She was in the bedroom of a two-room peasant hut. From the little she could see through the open doorway, the front room served as both kitchen and sitting room. She did not recall being in the bedroom before, and in fact she had not—the birth had taken place in the kitchen, on the planked pine table, which had been covered with clean straw. Now she lay on a low wooden bed, covered with several layers of threadbare but clean cotton blankets. Close by was a rush-basket such as peasants made and sold on market days. Inside the basket, swaddled in clean, faded scraps of cloth, slept a dark-haired infant. Miriam raised herself higher and stared at the tiny face. She saw dark eyelashes, wispy brows, a slightly flattened baby nose, and delicate pink lips.

"Reuben," she whispered. "She looks just like you." Miriam reached out to hold the baby, but the room went dark before her eyes and she fell back upon the tattered sheets.

For days Miriam hovered between sleep and wakefulness, occasionally opening her mouth to swallow strange liquids, both bitter and sweet, now and then opening her eyes and trying to focus on her infant, or on the two women who brought her drinks and washed her body with wet rags. Then, exhausted, she drifted off again. At times she was aware of a third person in the room, a stranger who did not tend to her but seemed somehow connected with the baby. As the days passed, Miriam grew stronger, and the thick fog-like stupor that had dulled her mind gradually lifted. When the old women entered Miriam's room on the tenth morning since the birth, they were surprised and pleased to find her holding the tiny baby in her arms. Elvedchka, who was in her seventies but looked much older, hurried to the bed with short, scuttling steps. "Be careful," she warned. "You are still weak. Call me when you want me to take the baby."

The elder sister Lyuba smiled and nodded, her mouth a wide, black cavern in the brown face with its fine tracery of lines and wrinkles. Ninety years old, she was well versed in the wisdom of the forest, and though she could no longer walk without the aid of a cane, she continued to supervise her younger sister in the preparation of herbal teas and medicines, for which the pair were famous throughout the countryside. Miriam returned the sisters' smiles.

"I don't know who you are," she said, "or why you have done this for me. I can only thank you. I know that you saved me, and my baby. I remember when I was about to be shot." She leaned back, tired from the exertion of speaking, took a deep breath, and continued. "How did you find me? How did you get me away from the Germans?"

She was amazed when Elvedchka told of seeing her fall into the river, and of how she had dragged Miriam from the shallow but turbulent waters. Once Miriam was on the riverbank, Elvedchka had brought Lyuba to watch over her and had gone to fetch her son, Mirko. It was he who had carried Miriam back to the sisters' hut.

The baby gave a sharp cry, startling Miriam. She looked down at the child, then lifted the edge of the blanket to conceal herself from the women's gaze and offered the child her breast. The baby sucked violently for a few seconds, then began to scream, its tiny face turning a deep vermilion. Miriam looked at the women in helpless confusion.

Lyuba laughed with a soundless cackle that shook her frail body, and Elvedchka pursed her lips, waggling a crooked finger at Miriam. "You trying to nurse that baby? How can you nurse that baby? You've got no milk! You haven't nursed since she was born, your milk is dried up."

Miriam stared at them, wide-eyed. Of course. "Then, how..." Her eyes darted around the room. Had they boiled milk and water with some sugar and fed her baby with a bottle, as was the fashion in Warsaw?

Just then the ragged brown blanket that served as a partition between the two rooms was pushed aside. A young girl of about seventeen entered and without a word, walked up to Miriam and swept the child from her arms. Lifting aside her coarse shirt, she exposed the large white globe of her breast. Eagerly, the baby clamped onto the rosy nipple and began sucking with satisfied grunts and little smacking noises. As Elvedchka and Lyuba left the room, the girl sat down heavily on a low stool, stared at Miriam, and, after a few minutes, shifted the baby to her other breast.

Miriam smiled tentatively as a rush of confused feelings washed over her, a mixture of curiosity, jealousy, and gratitude. The girl smiled back, revealing strong, widely spaced white teeth. Her face was round and smooth, with the bright pink cheeks common to peasant girls who worked out-of-doors. Her large blue eyes had a slight slant, and her nose was wide and upturned, with perfectly round nostrils. Two thick, golden brown plaits hung to her ample waist. Ample, too, were her well-padded arms and legs. A warm, animal smell came from her body.

"What is your name?" asked Miriam hesitantly. She felt like an intruder, watching her own baby so happily taking nourishment from this stranger. The girl's mouth opened wider, and a thin string of saliva dribbled from the corner of her lips down to her chin. Rocking back and forth on her wide haunches, she made a few inarticulate sounds. Then, with a low-pitched chuckle, she bent her head and gave the baby a moist kiss on its tiny cheek before removing her breast from its mouth, which had now stopped sucking. Miriam sat frozen, staring first at the distended nipple that the girl was attempting to cover, then at her own infant, who closed her eyes and was now dozing contentedly, nestled in the girl's arms.

Just then Elvedchka entered the room. Seeing the look of revulsion on Miriam's face, she frowned. "You don't like it, eh?" she asked, smoothing the bedclothes with quick, angry movements. "You don't like it that she nurses your baby?"

Miriam swallowed hard and shook her head rapidly. "Oh, no, it's just that she's, I mean she is..." Miriam faltered. Embarrassment at being confronted prevented her from expressing her thoughts coherently.

"I know, I know," Elvedchka muttered as she plumped up the old misshapen feather pillow that lay behind Miriam's back. Then, straightening her spine as much as her arthritis allowed, she clenched her fists against her hips and faced Miriam, her tiny eyes in their wrinkled sockets flashing with anger. "You think you are better than Marya."

Miriam shook her head desperately, but Elvedchka went on, her hoarse voice dry and cold in the warm room. "What makes you better than Marya? That you can speak? You are but a Jew who denies our Savior. I know very well that you are a Jew. Don't worry, I won't turn you in to the Nazi butchers. I have nothing to do with them, nor they with me. I kill no one and nothing. I did not save your life to give it away to them. Better to have left you to drown than to hand you to them. But now you, you listen to me." She pointed a gnarled finger, first at Miriam, then at Marya, who smiled her wide, gap-toothed smile as the baby slept in her lap. "You are a Jew who sins with every breath. Marya is an innocent, an innocent who has never sinned in her life. Some may think she has, but I tell you she has not. She is merely an instrument, a vessel that others have used as a means to sin. But that is also because of her innocence, because she doesn't know."

Sensing Miriam's confusion, she went on. "The women wanted to kill her, because of the men. Ever since she was twelve years old, the men in the village wouldn't stay away from her. Three babies she has had. Two of them are with her—you'll see them when you get strong enough to go out. The last one is dead. It died one night in its sleep, the night before you came. The father's wife had put a curse on it. And then you came, and had your baby. God sent your baby to Marya, and Marya to your baby."

Miriam lay back weakly on the pillow. "Does she think the baby is hers?" she asked, staring at her infant as it lay cradled in Marya's round arms.

Elvedchka gave a barklike laugh. "No! She gives it back to you, doesn't she?"

"How did she come to you?" Miriam asked, to keep the conversation away from herself and the fact that she was a "sinful Jew."

"Why shouldn't she? She is my granddaughter." Elvedchka finished straightening the numerous icons and candles that stood on a narrow wooden table near the window. She patted Marya's golden hair lightly and shuffled out of the room.

Day by day, Miriam grew stronger. When the cramped hut became too confining, she took the baby in her arms and sat outside in the shade of the maple tree. She never ventured farther than a few feet from the hut for fear of being seen by some peasant coming for a cure, or far worse, by one of the small bands of German soldiers who sometimes roamed the woods and tramped about the little hamlets looking for food, women, and hidden Jews. When anyone appeared beyond the stand of trees marking the edge of the forest, the sisters' rangy mongrel, Luk, would begin barking and straining at his chain.

Immediately, Miriam would slip into the hut, hand the baby to Marya, and hide herself in the large linen chest that stood next to the bed in the back room. Miriam was now strong enough to lift the heavy lid and climb in unassisted.

Among yellowed moldering sheets and tablecloths that had last been used twenty years before, when Elvedchka's husband had been alive, Miriam waited, sweating in the dark heat of the coffinlike chest, which had been punctured with air holes to keep the linen fresh. She emerged only when Elvedchka gave her the all-clear signal: four knocks on the side of the box. Sometimes she was hidden for what seemed like hours while Elvedchka and Lyuba prepared poultices and dressed a peasant's gashed thumb or advised a young bride on fertility-enhancing foods. Miriam would shift her weight painfully from one knee to the other, clenching her teeth and wiping the sweat from her brow. Certain they had forgotten about her, she would start to emerge, only to hear the dog barking again or a strange voice in the kitchen, forcing her to lower the lid and resume her crouched position. When not concealed, Miriam tried to make herself useful, but the women didn't want or need her help, waving her away if she started to peel a potato or wash a plate. She had sensed a cold hostility from Elvedchka ever since their conversation about Marya. No matter how many smiles Miriam gave Marya or how many kindnesses she showed her, the old woman perceived her true feelings about the idiot peasant girl.

As the weeks went by, Miriam began to feel more and more uneasy. The women fed her, and even washed her clothing, but barely spoke to her. The pleasantries they used to exchange about the baby had dwindled to almost nothing. They had even stopped using the name Miriam had given the baby—Rebecca, which Reuben had chosen in honor of his mother. Instead, they now called her Anzia, after Marya's dead baby. Miriam shuddered whenever she heard it.

At night, Miriam lay awake for hours. Sometimes she heard the sisters whispering in the kitchen, where they slept. Marya no longer stayed overnight in the hut, since Rebecca, now three months old, had stopped nursing at night. Instead she left a cup of breast milk, which the women placed in a cool spot under the window. Should the baby awaken, Miriam was to soak a piece of cotton in the milk and give it to Rebecca to suck on. When Miriam suggested that perhaps they could begin weaning the baby to cow's milk, Elvedchka gave her a sly look and shook her head. "No cow's milk is as rich as Marya's own. See how she thrives?" And it was true. Miriam had to admit that Rebecca brimmed with health. But at night, listening to the hiss of their whispers, Miriam went cold with fear. Surely they were plotting against her; she had become a millstone around their necks. They hated her, she could see it plainly enough, and they loved Rebecca. They would not turn her in, for that would bring reprisals upon themselves. Instead they would kill her and no one would be any the wiser. Then little "Anzia" would be theirs forever. Already she was like a baby sister to Marya's two toddlers, who came daily to the hut to play with her, delighting in her coos and smiles. They had been told that Miriam was an auntie from Britska, and they accepted this, showing no more interest in her than they would in any other stranger who avoided their gaze and left the room when they approached.

Yes, the old ladies would certainly get rid of her, thought Miriam. But how? Poison probably, since they knew the properties of every berry and tree root; every mushroom in the forest yielded to them its healthful or deadly secrets. She knew how they would dispose of her; the only question was when. She would have to get away. Her one hope was to take the baby and make her way somehow to the Russian border, and from there to Kiev, where she would find Reuben and David. Barely able to sleep or eat, Miriam lost the weight she had put on since the sisters had begun caring for her. Pale and gaunt, she lived on the brink of hysteria, unable to think clearly enough to plan an escape. Whenever she thought of leaving, she pictured herself as a young bride fleeing from Pavlitz in the snow, or again, walking away from bomb-blasted Warsaw with Reuben and David. These images would then be replaced by a clouded vision of herself climbing out of the slimy, foul-smelling ditch. If she were alone, she could perhaps run away, but with a three-month-old infant? And now it was cold, the woods were full of dead leaves that crunched and whispered underfoot, and the night wind left traces of frost on the rooftops and windows. The sisters had already stuffed up their own broken windows with rags and straw, making the hut secure against the onslaught of winter.

If she were to leave the baby…but no, it was unthinkable, though the child seemed to belong more to Marya than herself. Marya meant smiles, warmth, and food, while Miriam's hands were cold and tense, her knees hard, and her smile tight and twisted.

Late one evening, as Marya nursed Rebecca, Luk barked sharply, twice. Miriam prepared to climb into the chest, but the dog did not bark again. Miriam opened the door a crack and peered at the crest of the hill. Luk was reclining quietly. Everything was peaceful. The sisters began to undress for bed while Marya set the baby in its cot and made ready to go home. She listened at the door, as was her habit, then went out into the cold. Miriam watched her large frame moving across the yard. The moon was veiled in silvery mist and the air had a crystalline tingle. Snow would fall soon.

Miriam closed and latched the door. There was a heaviness in her limbs as she made her way into the little back room. Perhaps tonight she would sleep, free of the fearful thoughts that pursued her, hour after hour, day and night. Rebecca slept soundlessly, the sisters snored in the front room. No one would harm or disturb her, at least until morning. A few hours of dreamless sleep was all she asked. Or if she had to dream, let it be about before, about Reuben or little David, when he was healthy and full of life. Let her not see again in her tortured slumber the sight of Dina falling to the ground before her flaming house, or the image of Leibel's smashed skull beneath the German soldier's shovel. She lay her head on the rough pillow, closed her eyes, and dozed. Suddenly, she was wide-awake. Something was happening in the front room. She heard the sound of breaking crockery, followed by a strange choking noise that was accompanied by banging and thrashing. Miriam sat up in panic. Her first impulse was to grab the child and climb into the linen chest. But what if Rebecca should cry out? Instead she slid the cradle under the bed. As she did so, the wooden runner caught, scraping loudly on the hard floor.

Instantly, the door flew open. In the pale light that shone

through the tattered window curtain, Miriam saw him—a German soldier, his uniform torn, his face and hands covered with a dark, shining liquid that Miriam knew could only be blood. Her mouth opened in terror, but even as she thought to scream, she stopped, remembering the baby who miraculously was still sleeping, hidden beneath the bulky bed.

The German squinted at Miriam, then struck a match and held it aloft. "Where is she?" he asked. His voice was thick and his words slurred.

Drunk, thought Miriam. *That might make it easier to escape.* "I don't understand," she whispered in Polish, trying her best to imitate the peasant accent. God forbid he should detect any Yiddish inflection in her speech.

"Where is she?" he repeated. "Where is that filthy Polish whore? She took my money." He held up the match, shining its feeble flame into Miriam's face. "Where is my money? Give me back my money, filthy Polish whore, slimy Polish pig!"

Miriam backed away toward the window. Her hands groped behind her for a weapon. Where were the icons? She couldn't reach them. The soldier lurched toward her, moving around the side of the bed. The match burned down and went out. Cursing, he reached into his pocket for another. At that moment, Miriam's hand found one of the icons and she swung it high, but the soldier caught her hand in midair and held her pinned against the wall. The icon fell to the floor with a heavy thud. Immediately, another sound filled the room; Rebecca wailing, haven been woken by the noise.

The soldier, confused, reeled around, and then stood stock still, his face contorted in horror. Framed in the doorway stood Marya, the moon shining white on her fair hair and flowing clothes. In her hand a silver sickle gleamed. Instinctively, Miriam dropped to the floor. With her hands over her face, she peered between the cracks in her fingers as Marya and the soldier began a bizarre dance, the rumpled bed between them. He moved to the left and Marya followed, he stepped to the right, and she followed. From side to side they stepped, facing each other across the bed while the sickle shone like a crescent moon. For a few moments, Miriam cowered behind the soldier. Then a thought flashed in her head, and when the soldier once more stepped sideways, she grabbed his ankle and pulled. With a scream the soldier fell forward on the bed, and Miriam saw the bright metal tool swoop downward in a glinting curve once, only once, and the scream stopped. Again there came a heavy thud, and again the sounds of Rebecca wailing. Had she been crying the whole time? Miriam scarcely knew.

Together, she and Marya dragged the German's bleeding, headless body off the bed and pulled it into the front room. As she passed it, Marya kicked his severed head away as if it were no more than a turnip. Finally, they were able to remove the cradle from beneath the bed. Marya immediately sat down and offered her nipple to Rebecca, who was soon calmly sucking. Miriam, shaking, looked for a place to sit down, but the bed was drenched in blood. She went into the front room, lit a candle, and looked about, seeing the decapitated figure at her feet and the two sisters lying stabbed and strangled in their beds. Broken dishes and bedclothes were strewn everywhere. On the table, intact among the shards, was a cup of milk. Miriam recognized the cup. It was Marya's milk. She had forgotten to leave it for Rebecca and had come back with it, expecting to run home to her children. Instead, she had found her grandmother and great-aunt dead. She had probably taken the sickle from the shed outside the door and gone into the bedroom to save Miriam and Rebecca. Of course, Miriam realized, she would never know for sure what had happened. Dazed and trembling, she lifted the cup of Marya's milk to her lips, drank it, and fell to the floor in a faint.

Chapter seventeen

Despite the wind that howled outside and piled the snow in thick, sloping drifts against the side of the barn, Miriam felt hot, so hot that she awoke to find herself drenched in sweat, as she had every night for the past four days. It had been that long since a grim-faced Mirko had washed and buried the twisted, bloody bodies of his mother and aunt in the little family graveyard, amid the fallen headstones and weather-beaten crosses. Alone in the dawn hours, he had dug their graves and lowered in the bodies, not even summoning the village priest. The soldier's body had been disposed of, but how and where Mirko would not say. Even the dog, Luk, was now lying beneath the earth. Marya's children had found him with his skull smashed, probably by the rifle butt of the now dead German. As for the sisters' hut, Mirko had burned it to the ground, destroying the evidence.

After the burials, Mirko had tramped back to his own hut, where Marya and Miriam sat waiting as the children played with Rebecca. Miriam shuddered with fear as she heard his heavy tread at the door. She knew what was coming. Always sullen in her presence, disapproving of the fact that his mother had sheltered a Jew,

Mirko had now seen his misgivings justified. Obviously, he believed the soldier had come looking for her, had killed the old women for hiding her, and was in turn killed by poor Marya, who no more understood the implications of her act than would a three-year-old child. When Miriam had described to him what had happened, he spat on the floor and glared at her before getting on with his grisly task. Now that the bodies were buried, he would deal with Miriam.

Sure enough, after drinking the broth that Marya offered him, he jerked his head toward Miriam. "Away," he said.

Miriam stared, saying nothing.

"Away," he repeated, pointing at the door. "You get out. It's all your fault. They will come looking for him and they'll find you. Even if you're gone, they may find out what happened. You must leave. Now."

Miriam understood. If he were accused in the death of the German, he would blame it on the Jewess who had passed through, and point them in her direction. If she stayed and they were found out, he would be killed for harboring her.

He pointed at the Rebecca, who was cooing and squealing in Marya's lap. Her dark newborn hair had fallen out, replaced by fluffy ringlets of reddish gold. She could easily pass for Marya's own. "Leave the child," Mirko commanded. "You go."

Miriam rose and faced him. "Where can I go?" she asked. "My people are dead, my village burned. We are surrounded by woods. It's snowing; I have no warm clothes, no boots." Her voice trailed off and she looked at Rebecca, who waved a baby fist in the air. Squaring her shoulders, Miriam continued. "Of course I cannot take the child. But I cannot leave her either. Why don't you just kill me now?" she demanded, her voice rising. "Kill me, and bury me next to the German. I'd rather die now than freeze out in the snow." She walked over to Marya and lifted Rebecca from her lap, cradling the child's downy head under her chin.

Mirko clenched and unclenched his fists. "I am not a murderer," he answered. "I do not kill anyone. But I do not put my life in danger, and the lives of my daughter and grandchildren, for your

sake. You may not stay here any longer. Take some of Marya's things."
He gestured toward the back of the hut, where Marya slept with her
children. "A blanket, a shawl, whatever. Shoes I cannot give you. I
need…wait."

He went into the back, opened a box, and drew out a parcel,
which he handed to Miriam. It was wrapped in tattered, yellowed
newspaper. Giving Rebecca back to Marya, she unwrapped it to find
a pair of ancient boots, the faded leather creased into permanent
cracks and the toes bent up so that they reminded Miriam of the
elves' shoes in the old stories her maid had told David back in Warsaw.
They were a woman's boots; perhaps they had belonged to Mirko's
wife, who had died giving birth to Marya. Surely they would not fit
Marya, who clumped about in an old pair of her father's.

Seating herself on a three-legged milking stool that had long
ago found its way into the house, Miriam squeezed her feet into
the boots. They pinched viciously, but there was no other choice. If
she were to be forced out into the snow without her child and with
nowhere to go, tight boots were not a legitimate worry. She gathered
up a few shawls, wrapped them in a blanket, and bent down to hold
her baby one last time. Rebecca snuggled against her but quickly
reached down to Marya, whose warm softness she preferred. Setting
the baby down, Miriam felt tears swell her throat. When had she last
cried? She could not remember. With dry eyes she opened the door
and stepped out into the snowy yard.

She had not walked more than a few feet when she heard
Marya's low-pitched wails. As Miriam turned, the door flew open
and Marya burst out, running pell-mell at her, blond braids flying.
The heavy girl grabbed Miriam, nearly bowling her over, crying and
grunting so that Miriam's shawl became damp with saliva and tears.
She tried to disengage herself, but the girl was much stronger and
held her fast, her massive body heaving spasmodically as she sobbed.
After a few minutes, Mirko emerged from the hut, followed by one
of Marya's children, who had run barefoot and half-dressed into the
snow to see what the commotion was about. Seeing his mother crying, he added his own screams until Mirko clamped his brawny hand
over the child's mouth and shoved him back toward the hut. Mirko

then began pulling at Marya, but she bit hard into his hand, so that he let her go with a loud stream of curses.

The noise brought several other peasants running from the two or three huts that squatted like mushrooms on the edge of the woods. They stopped in their tracks and gaped at Miriam, their open mouths exhaling steam that swirled away in the wind and snow.

"My cousin," explained Mirko sheepishly, gesturing at Miriam. "She is visiting from Bitemka and was just going out walking. Marya, you know, she didn't understand." He rubbed his hammy hands together in the cold, trying to soothe the area where Marya's teeth had broken the skin.

A wizened peasant stepped forward, leering at Miriam through one blue eye. The other was clouded over with a white membrane. "A cousin, eh? Too bad I don't have such cousins." Addressing Miriam, he said, "Lucky for you he's an old dog, this Mirko. He was quite a rooster in his day." He chuckled to himself and moved off with the others, the brief flurry of excitement over.

Thus Mirko was forced to let Miriam stay. She slept in the barn, there being no room in the hut for another person. Mirko would certainly not give up his bed for a Jew. At first Miriam was allowed to go into the house during the day. After a few weeks however, Mirko said his neighbors were becoming suspicious about her extended visit, and he made her stay in the barn all the time. Marya would bring Rebecca there to visit with her mother while she brought Miriam her potatoes and broth, and an occasional egg.

Miriam lived for her child's brief visits. She craved companionship and could barely recall the last real conversation she'd had. Mirko ignored her, Marya's children rarely came out to the barn, and Marya, though happy enough to listen to Miriam, could not reply except with grunts and excited head jerks. Miriam worried that Rebecca, now more than six months old, would not develop properly, since she heard so little speech. True, Marya's children spoke to her, but their speech was infantile. Between Rebecca's visits, Miriam recited to herself all the little poems and rhymes she used to tell David. She had begged for a pencil to write them down, but Mirko said he had none. So she spent hours singing them to herself, and then to the baby, who responded with delighted squeals and bright-eyed excitement. Another skill Miriam acquired in the barn was the art of milking a cow. This she learned by watching Marya, who soon allowed her to take over. Miriam had to laugh at herself; she who had been so squeamish that the very smell of a barn used to set her retching would now squat on a stool beside the cow's warm flanks and squeeze the silky teats so that they yielded rich white milk that steamed as it landed in the bucket. She happily fed the cows too, bringing them armfuls of fodder stored away for the winter. She talked to them, practicing and perfecting her Polish, stroking their soft bellies, rubbing their heads, and smiling into their dreamy brown eyes. She was grateful for their gentle company, for their body heat that kept the barn warm, and for the creamy milk that sustained her.

When winter waned and the first rains came, turning the yard into thick red-brown mud, Rebecca was weaned, and when the first blades of new green grass poked their way up in the meadow and the cows were turned out into the fresh air, Mirko told Miriam to leave. Marya was not in the hut; she had gone out to the field with the cows and had taken the children with her. Miriam was sitting alone in the barn, mending her coarse brown shawl for the fifth time. She wrapped it about her shoulders and stood up. "My baby!" she exclaimed. "I cannot leave my baby. Let me go and get her, and then we will go. I promise. You'll never see us again."

Mirko ran his fingers through his coarse, graying hair and shook his head. "Don't be a fool," he said. "You'll never survive with the baby. She is noisy. You wouldn't be able to hide, or travel. Leave her, she is safe with us. Later, you will come back and take her. Don't worry, we'll give her back to you. In the meantime she'll be safe and well cared for."

Miriam stared into Mirko's cold black eyes, trying to discern what feelings actually lay within. She knew he didn't care about her, but did he actually care about Rebecca, was he truly concerned for her safety? Had he perhaps grown attached to the child, so that he wouldn't let her go? Or did he fear Marya's reaction when she discovered that Rebecca was gone? Mirko's face was impassive; the flat

planes of his broad features reminded her of a stone statue in the
Saxon Gardens.

Slowly, she gathered up her meager belongings—a tattered
blanket, a threadbare dress many sizes too big, the old boots Mirko
had given her months before. Mirko watched her in silence. Finished
with her packing, she turned to face him. "Thank you," she said, her
eyes filling with tears. "You have been kind to me and to Rebecca."

Mirko continued gazing at her, his face expressionless.

"I don't know how I can leave my baby," she continued, beginning to sob, "but I will come back. I'll come back and find her, no
matter where she is. If I don't, then my husband—someone from
my family—will." She fought back the tears and walked to the barn
door.

Mirko cleared his throat. "Wait," he said. Miriam turned to
him, hoping that he'd changed his mind and would let her stay or
tell her to take the baby. But instead he asked, "Do you know where
to go?"

Miriam gave a short, dry laugh. "Where to go? How could I
know where to go? Where can I go?"

Mirko pointed a thick, stubby finger out the door. "Go east,"
he said. "Go through the woods, go away from the path of the sun.
At the other side of the woods, there is a stone wall, but you can get
over it. Then you'll be in a field on Count Fyedritzki's estate. Maybe
there you can find work. You don't really look like a Jew." Seeing her
hesitation, he went on. "It's not even far away. You can come back,
maybe, and visit the child. At night, or very early, before dawn."
Abruptly, he turned away and began raking at the dirty straw in the
stall beside him. Without looking up, he exhorted, "Go. Go now. It
will be better for you."

Miriam walked out of the barn. She knew that off to her left
in the field, Rebecca crawled in the moist grass on her chubby knees,
following Marya and her children. She wanted to run in that direction, to gather up her child and carry her in her arms to wherever she
was destined to go. Yet her legs propelled her the other way, eastward,
toward the woods. She walked slowly, feeling as if she were being
driven by a force that she could not control. An inner voice told

her that both she and Rebecca would be safer this way. The voice urged her on, into the thick pine woods where the filtered sunlight fell but dimly, making it look like early evening when in fact it was only ten o'clock in the morning. In the stillness, the voice resounded in her head, speaking not in Mirko's hoarse peasant dialect, but in Reuben's scholarly Polish. She was headed east; perhaps, she thought, she could keep going in that direction, cross the border somehow, and make her way to Reuben and David. For a brief moment the old hope quickened her steps, but instantly she thought of Rebecca. How could she leave her so far behind? She walked on, trying not to lose the narrow path the peasants had made long ago as they entered the woods to gather mushrooms and wild berries. Once or twice she strayed into the trees by mistake. Frantic, she would retrace her steps until she found the path again.

Mirko had given her some bread and cheese and a goatskin filled with water, but she did not eat anything until she was light-headed with hunger. At that point she broke off a small piece of cheese and chewed it slowly, washing it down with a swallow of water. She hoarded the rest for fear she would starve before finding her way out of the forest. When exhaustion overtook her, she sank down into the dead leaves and pine needles at her feet, afraid to leave the path, for it was becoming dark, and the air now had a chill that her ragged shawl did little to dispel. After a few moments, she got up again, her fear of spending the night in the woods driving her onward. Always she looked at the jagged little piece of sky above her head, trying to gauge the location of the sun, trying to keep it behind her. Once night fell she would be lost, with no light, no way to see the path. As the last pale shafts of sun fell across her trail, she realized that the trees were thinning out and she could see something up ahead—a clearing, perhaps? She forgot her hunger and fatigue and began jogging briskly along the path, oblivious to the brambles that tore at her skin and clothes, and the broken branches that threatened to trip her.

Finally, she saw it: a wall of large, round stones set one upon the other with no cement between them, held in place only by their weight and the skill with which they had been balanced. The wall was about six feet high. Tying her bundle around her waist, she felt about among the stones for a projection, a handhold she could use to pull herself up and over. But the stones were smooth, and slick with the evening dew. Even when she got a foothold, her hand kept slipping off. Beads of sweat broke out on her brow as she tried again and again to secure a hold on the rocks.

"Need help?" a clear voice rang out behind her, breaking the evening stillness.

With a cry of fright, Miriam spun around. A young man stood behind her, his starched white shirtsleeves glowing in the fading light. Miriam could not help staring. It had been years since she had seen someone dressed that way—not since before the war, certainly. The youth wore tight-fitting breeches and neat, polished black boots. A trim vest of some soft material, suede perhaps, was buttoned over his chest. Across it hung a golden watch chain. A silk scarf tied at the throat completed his wardrobe. But more than his clothing, Miriam stared at his face. He was young, no more than sixteen or seventeen, with wide blue eyes, a straight nose, and thin lips that curved in a gentle smile above a strong jaw. Most striking was his hair, thick and blond. It caught the evening breeze and blew lightly across his forehead. The resemblance was remarkable. *Tadeusz*, she thought. But of course it was not. Tadeusz would be in his mid-twenties by now, and besides, he was a peasant, while this was obviously a nobleman.

"Why do you stare at me that way?" The boy stepped back, smiling. "You look as if you've seen a ghost."

"You look...you remind me of someone I once knew."

"Really? From where?"

Miriam shook her head. She had neither the strength nor the spirit to engage in light banter with this young stranger who had startled her so. "Oh, it was long ago. It doesn't matter."

"What are you doing here? Why were you trying to climb over? It's dangerous. We have dogs, you know."

"I don't hear any."

"Walk with me to the gate. It's not far and I have a key. Are you visiting someone?"

"Yes, no, I—" Miriam tried to collect her thoughts. "I'm looking for work."

"I see. What can you do?"

"Milk the cows. I can milk the cows," she said, eagerly, praying that he would believe her. "And," she added, "I can cook and bake. I'm a wonderful baker."

The youth stepped back and appraised her, noting her ill-fitting, tattered clothes and lumpy boots. Such garb was not uncommon for a peasant girl, yet somehow she didn't seem like one, at least not the ones he had known. "Where are you from?" he asked.

"From Yoldga," Miriam answered without hesitation. She had planned her story carefully while walking through the woods. It was similar to the one she had told her landlady when she first came to Warsaw; a dead husband, unfriendly in-laws.

"But you don't sound as if you're from Yoldga. I've met people from there. You have some kind of an accent."

Miriam was glad of the deepening dusk, which prevented the boy from seeing the color drain from her face. Could he tell she was a Jew? She had tried so hard to lose her accent, but at her age…He continued staring at her, and she felt she must answer him. Her brain racing, she blurted, "Oh, I wasn't born in Yoldga. I was born in Mizhensk, up north, and I also spent some years in Brimmatz, near Germany, as a child." She hoped the reference to Germany might account for the slight Yiddish intonation she was sure he discerned.

"Really," he said in an indifferent tone. She could not tell if he believed her or not. "It's getting late. Come, I'll open the gate."

She followed him along the wall to the heavy iron gate. He drew the chain from his vest pocket. On it hung a round gold watch and a stubby metal key, which he inserted in the lock and turned. The gate swung open and he held it for her, allowing her to precede him onto the grounds. From out of nowhere a silver-furred wolfhound bounded up, nuzzled the boy, sniffed at Miriam, and loped off.

"Not very ferocious," remarked Miriam with relief. Like most Polish Jews, she had been raised to fear and despise dogs, especially since they seemed to take special delight in harassing Jews.

"Oh, he's ferocious enough, but you're with me, so he knows you're okay. What's your name, anyway?"

They walked down a long, gravel-covered path bordered on each side by wide fields. "Bronya. Bronya Borkowska."

He extended his hand. "A pleasure to make your acquaintance. I am Wladislaw Fyedritzki, the second son and heir of Count Wladislaw Fyedritzki."

Miriam, not sure what to say, shook his hand and curtsied awkwardly. She had never met nobility before.

They walked on in silence until a group of long, low buildings came into view. "This is where the farm workers live," explained Wladislaw. "If you are hired, you will live here, too."

"If you are hired," thought Miriam. *And what if I am not?*

Turning to her young companion, she looked at him beseechingly. "Please, I beg you to help me. I must find work here. I have nowhere to go. I'll starve to death."

"Can't you find work on a farm somewhere?"

"It's wartime. No one has enough food. No one wants to share. The Nazis take everything as it is. Please." She touched his sleeve. "Don't send me away. I don't want to die."

Wladislaw looked at her again. The rising moon shone on her smooth brow and firm cheeks, which had filled out, thanks to the rich milk of Mirko's cows. Her baggy dress and worn shawl hid her figure, but she was tall and carried herself well. Even so, she was old. Anyone could see she was at least twenty-two. He preferred his country girls between the ages of fifteen and eighteen, at most twenty. Since his first sexual experience with a buxom sixteen-year-old shepherdess three years before, when he was fourteen, he had formed certain likes and dislikes. Still, he could be flexible, if the girl were good-looking and pliant. Besides, they could always use another milkmaid. He would speak to Lech, the overseer, first thing in the morning. In the meantime she could sleep in the barn.

"Look," he addressed Miriam. "Come into the barn. Zoszia will set you some food and show you where to stay, and tomorrow we'll see what can be done."

Miriam thanked him profusely and followed him to the barn, which amazed her with its size and cleanliness. Young men and women scurried about getting the cows bedded down for the night, sweeping the area around the stalls, filling water troughs, and spreading clean, dry straw on the floor. A few of them glanced at Miriam curiously when she entered, but kept on at their work, afraid to be thought lazy by the young master. He approached a plump woman with faded blond hair and flat features.

"Gina, this is Bronya. Let her sleep here for the night. She's looking for work. I'll speak to Lech in the morning."

Gina glanced at Miriam, then at Wladislaw and lowered her eyes. "Yes, certainly," she murmured.

"All right then. I'll be back tomorrow. Good night." He turned with a wave and walked out of the barn.

At once the girls left their jobs and approached Miriam. The men gazed at her briefly, then returned to their work, but the girls began barraging her with questions. She repeated the story she had told young Fyedritzki, elaborating according to their queries. She was Bronya Borkowska, lately of Yoldga, a war widow who was seeking farm work.

Gina smiled at her, revealing a mouthful of chipped and crooked teeth. "Imagine, Wlad telling you to sleep in the barn. What impudence!"

A large-boned young woman with muscular arms and coppery red hair laughed hoarsely. "That's what he thinks of us. Cows." The others joined in the mocking laughter.

Noticing Miriam's confusion, Gina explained, "Wlad fancies himself a great big bull in the barnyard, trying to have his pleasure with any girl he takes a fancy to. But he's really just a silly calf. Only you have to watch out for him. He's very moody."

"How do you mean, watch out?"

"Well, you have to act very servile, or he will tell Lech you're not doing your job. And if he gets you alone and bothers you, then you must threaten to tell his mother. Sometimes that works, sometimes not. Every month a girl leaves here because of him. Some are forced out for not giving in. But even those that do, he gets angry at for some trifle and has them fired. The best thing is to stay out of his way."

Miriam shook her head in confusion. If he were so capricious and cruel, why had he bothered to help her at all?

"Anyway," interjected a tiny woman with wispy brown hair and a pointed chin, "Wlad is the least of our problems."

"Why is that?"

"Why, you simpleton, where've you been? Who do you think runs this estate now, Fyedritzki? The count lies in bed all day, dead drunk ever since the Nazis took over."

"The Nazis?"

"Of course, who else, the Chinese? The Nazis took over all of the estates. Major Fenstermacher and Colonel Schmidt. All the milk and wool and everything we produce now goes to help the soldiers of the Fatherland," she smirked. "And for them we add a special touch of Poland." The other girls giggled.

"Hush," said Gina. "She'll soon find out."

The women returned to their work as Miriam watched carefully, pleased to see that her experience on Mirko's meager farm could be transferred to this much larger estate. She laughed appreciatively as the girls took turns spitting into the milk buckets once they were filled. "A touch of Poland," she repeated.

When the evening work was finished, Miriam accompanied the workers to a long wooden building with a low ceiling and many narrow wooden tables and benches. An old memory of her father's study house in Dubnitz surfaced, with black-garbed Hasidim seated at similar tables, swaying and chanting. Instantly, she put the picture out of her mind and sat down between Gina and a tiny, thin-haired girl whose name was Fyodora. Steaming soup and thick chunks of bread were served up in wooden bowls. She looked at the pinkish bits of meat that floated in the soup and realized they were pork. With Elvedchka and with Mirko, she had avoided pork, although she had at times eaten broth made from chicken, which, not having been ritually slaughtered, soaked, and salted, was equally unkosher. But they had known she was a Jew from the start. To refuse the soup here, however, would call attention to herself.

Even as she hesitated, someone called out. "You, the new one!

The food not good enough for you? If you don't want it, I'll take it!" All along the table, heads rose from the bowls to stare at Miriam.

Mortified, she began eating. *God will forgive me*, she thought. *After all, my life is in danger.* Nazis ran the estate. She had walked all this way only to find herself in the lion's den. Had Mirko known? After supper Gina led her to another building in the compound. In it were four large rooms, each containing six metal cots, three washstands, and four metal wardrobes. The women stood back, waiting for Miriam's comments, and she realized she was supposed to be enthusiastic. She smiled, clapped her hands, and exclaimed, "What luxury! Am I really to sleep here?"

The young women smiled back. Gina waved at the room and said, "Yes. See, we are well taken care of, even now. There are no more troops here; they moved on to Puldiczewski's estate, so we have our rooms back. The wardrobes are small, though, so we keep our things under the pillows. Imagine, we even have pillows! Of course, they're filled with straw, but it's better than what I had at home. And there are no bedbugs. We keep very clean. The mistress insists on it. No lice either, since we disinfected after the soldiers left."

Miriam was given a cot previously occupied by an unfortunate girl who had teased Wladislaw one time too many and was now presumably walking home to Prymedowa, eight miles west.

The next morning, when it was barely light, Miriam was already in the barn, making her acquaintance with the cows who would be in her charge. Gina felt that she would make a better impression on Lech this way and be allowed to stay. Soon the overseer himself entered. A short, rotund man of about fifty, with red-veined cheeks and a bald crown fringed by pale mouse-colored hair, he spotted Miriam immediately and walked over. "Who is this?" he demanded.

Gina introduced them. "Wlad said he'll speak to you about hiring her." She and Lech both laughed, and Gina turned to Miriam.

"You'll be old and gray before we see Wlad. He sleeps till ten if he can and spends the rest of the day roaming around, avoiding Fenstermacher and Schmidt, who fortunately for us have an eye for young men. Of course, lucky for Wlad, right now they still have eyes only for each other. Schmidt is violently jealous, too. You should hear their arguments." She and Lech laughed again.

And so it was settled. Miriam had a job, nourishing food, and a soft bed. During the day, she worked hard, and the other girls were friendly but not intrusive. By listening to their prayers at night, she soon knew the words as well as anyone. She was gratified that the girls were simple country folk who had had little direct contact with Jewish women and didn't seem suspicious of her. By all rights she should have been satisfied, but instead she walked about consumed by guilt and anxiety. Where were Reuben and David? What was little Rebecca doing? Why had she, Miriam, lived, while the rest of her family lay dead, denied even the dignity of a decent burial place? Such thoughts plagued her at her work, and late at night she sobbed into her pillow before falling into a tortured sleep. The other women nodded knowingly; some of them had also lost husbands and lovers in the war. If Miriam were reserved, even aloof, well, who knows what she'd had to bear under the thumb of a cruel mother-in-law who had finally driven her out? And, of course, she'd left a child behind, with the grandmother. They all knew of similar cases since this terrible war had begun.

And so the months passed, and Miriam gradually became Bronya the country girl. She cried less and less often in the late hours of the night. New girls came and went, but Miriam stayed on. The flaxen-haired Gina became her friend, and to her she confided the imaginary details of her past life, gleaned from stories that Katya the maid had related in Chaya Rochel's cozy kitchen so many years before. Practice had made Miriam an adept liar, and falsehood tripped so easily over her tongue that she barely knew when she was lying and when she was telling the truth. Occasionally, in the rare moments when she was alone, a longing seized her to be with Rebecca. She tried to picture her daughter but was able to envision neither the baby she had left nor the toddler Rebecca had since become. Her memories of David were much sharper. Perhaps it was because Rebecca had never really been her own. *But she will be*, Miriam vowed. *I'll get her back, and I'll care for her myself. And someday, we'll all be together again—Reuben, David, Rebecca, and myself.*

Many times she thought of leaving the estate and going back through the woods, just for a brief visit, even a glimpse of her child. One moonless night she awoke, thinking she had heard a child crying. On impulse she arose and walked as far as the estate wall, only to find it topped with coils of barbed wire. She could not remember having seen them when she last passed there some months before. Sadly, she returned to her cottage, the sleek wolfhound Zik gamboling beside her. Yet she was not a prisoner. She could have asked for a few days' leave and gone to see Rebecca. But each time she resolved to go, a feeling of dread and despair would overtake her. The woods, it seemed, were full of Nazi soldiers searching for partisans. These Nazis liked nothing better than to have their way with the country girls, despite all their pronouncements about "Polish swine" and "Slavic filth." For Miriam the danger was far greater, for if by some chance they discovered she was a Jew…she could not risk it. She had to preserve herself, to stay alive as long as possible, if not for her own sake, then for Rebecca's. What would happen to the child if Miriam were killed? Reuben and David would never find the little girl, who would grow up among backward peasants, doomed to a life of poverty, toil, and ignorance. The farm meant safety and security, at least for now.

Chapter eighteen

One bleak winter evening in 1945, Miriam looked up from the pile of potatoes she was peeling for Christmas dinner and realized with a shock that she had been working on the estate for more than two and a half years. On that same winter evening, a ragged line of men marched two by two in an endless procession, pushing forward into the frozen Siberian night. A wet snow was falling, as it had been for days, and the ground beneath their feet was covered with a blanket of slick frost that made walking nearly impossible. One man clutched his partner's arm and staggered.

"I can't go on," he gasped, his body shaking violently as he struggled to keep up. A spasm of coughing seized him, and he spat, leaving a bloody stain on the gray snow at his feet.

"You must," whispered his companion, who put an arm around him and practically carried him over the snow and slush.

"I'm frozen," the man whispered. "I shall die of the cold. Let me stay here and die."

"No," said his companion. "You've made it this far, you must keep on. Soon we'll have shelter." Removing his ragged jacket, he slipped it over the other's shoulders, wrapping himself in a frayed army blanket. He shivered in the biting wind but kept on marching, holding the other fellow against him to help the man walk and to keep himself warm. They had not gone ten yards when the man fell again. Reuben bent to help him, when he was jabbed cruelly in the back by a rifle butt.

"Keep moving," barked the Russian guard.

Reuben hesitated, but another thrust with the rifle butt propelled him forward, and he was forced to leave his friend behind. Moments later, a shot rang out. Reuben turned but could see nothing in the swirling snow except the haggard faces of his comrades marching behind him. He never found his friend. Hours later, they arrived at the filthy barracks where they were to be incarcerated indefinitely.

"Papers!" Demanded the pig-faced captain. Only then did Reuben discover that his papers had been left behind, in the breast pocket of the jacket he had given to his friend, who lay dead on a Siberian roadside, his body partially covered in a soft, white shroud of snow.

In early spring, the fragile peace of Fyedritzki's estate was finally shattered. The sound of gunfire became increasingly frequent, and each day seemed to bring the fighting closer to the estate walls. At night planes roared overhead, shells exploded in the distance, and the milkmaids cowered in their beds, whispering prayers in the total blackness. Not one candle flame could be left to flicker, lest the Russians see the light and use it to target their bombs. At such times Miriam lay frozen on her cot, thinking of her daughter. Was Rebecca safe? Did Marya know enough to extinguish the lights? Would they keep the child indoors? Everyone said the war would end soon, and she burned with impatience to get back to Rebecca.

One wet March morning the girls were awakened before dawn by frantic pounding on the barracks door. Miriam stared in bleary-eyed wonder as Wladislaw Fyedritzki burst into the room, his hair dishevelled and his clothing askew. He appeared to be wearing his nightclothes beneath his coat and was in a state of great excitement. "Wake up!" He said. "They've gone!"

"Who? Who's gone?" some of the girls shouted, while others rubbed their eyes and looked about in confusion.

"Schmidt and Fenstermacher, those goddamn Nazi faggots."
Wlad's voice bordered on hysteria, and he waved his arms wildly as
he shouted. "I saw them leave. They've packed up and slunk away,
gone who knows where. We're free!" He gave a loud, hoarse laugh,
and ran from the room.

Instantly, the women began chattering as they hastily pulled
on their clothes. The Germans had left! What could it mean? The
voice of Katerina, a beautiful Slavic girl of nineteen, rang out. "The
Russians!" she cried. "They're afraid of the Russian liberators." The
women all agreed. Surely the Russians were on their way, and those
Germans who did not flee would be killed.

Sitting on their beds in the early morning light, the girls began
making plans for the future. Some decided to go home to their native
villages, others to stay on at the estate if they could. For Miriam there
was no question. She would leave as soon as possible. The thought of
the Russian soldiers' onslaught cheered her, yet made her uneasy as
well. She remembered General Antonayevski and shuddered. Without
saying goodbye, she gathered her few belongings and slipped away
while the women were still at breakfast. Fortunately, the gate was open.
Schmidt and Fenstermacher had not bothered to close it.

Once again Miriam was in the woods, but this time she moved
westward, keeping the morning sun at her back. The trails were full
of mud, and Miriam's coarse shoes were soon caked in it. She walked
slowly, always on the lookout for others, German soldiers especially,
yet the only people she saw were two peasant girls who stared at her
curiously before running off along a narrow trail that veered sharply
from her own. She walked all day, without stopping to rest, eat, or
drink. The years of farm work had built her up and given her stamina,
and the wish to see her child pushed all other thoughts from her mind.
Finally, as the moon rose, the trees began to thin out, and the little
village came into view. How silent and poor the little huts looked.
No smoke came from the chimneys, and no movement could be seen
outside, not even a pig or a chicken scratching in the mud. Miriam's
heart began to hammer. She started to run, each step thudding in
her ears as her alarm mounted. Reaching the village, she dashed first
to Mirko's hut, then to all of the others in turn, racing from door to

door, pounding and calling. It was no use. In every hut the furniture was broken, pillows ripped, pots and dishes strewn about, and not a soul was seen. The village had been plundered and abandoned. Miriam threw herself upon the cold earthen floor of the last hut in the village and lay there, too exhausted even to weep. Eventually, she slept.

She awoke at dawn, filthy, and weak from hunger. Going outside, she drew some water from the well, washed her face and hands, and drank deep, until she felt strength rising again within her. Slowly, she began to walk down to the riverbank. The river was swollen with melted snow and early spring rain. Sparkling water lapped at the muddy shore and splashed against the large, polished rocks that protruded from its depths like the knees of a submerged giant. Twigs and broken branches rushed by, tossed about in the swift current. Miriam walked cautiously along the bank. Soon she came to a small plank bridge. Its weathered gray wood was worn smooth by the bare feet and heavy boots of the peasants who had walked from Mirko's tiny nameless village to the deep woods on the opposite bank, to gather berries and mushrooms and hunt the rabbits and deer that lived within. Beyond those woods was Dubnitz, her childhood village, her home. Her feet were drawing her there, although she did not know if anyone, Jewish or gentile, remained. Still, where else could she go?

Wrapping her old shawl about her against the March wind, she made her way across the bridge and into the woods. A crooked path meandered through the trees; she had a vague memory of having followed it on some occasion in the distant past, she could not remember when. She was grateful for it now and walked quickly. Her only thought was to find Rebecca. Someone, somewhere would know of her. Marya should be easy to trace. But what if she couldn't find her? Miriam refused to entertain the thought, just as she refused to countenance the possibility that she might not find Reuben and David. Hope had sustained her these last few years; she would not give it up now.

When Miriam finally emerged from the woods, she came upon a great, grassy mound that rose gently above the surrounding meadow. She paid little attention to it as she rushed on toward the pine trees that bordered the gentile section of Dubnitz. Only later, with horror, did she remember Pan Vorny's meadow, and what that grassy mound actually contained.

The gentile sector looked much as it always had; mean little huts arranged around an open, muddy area where a well had been dug by an ancestor of one of the village elders. Today however, the area bustled with more activity than it ever had in the past. Women and children scurried about in and out of houses, carrying bundles and tattered suitcases. Few men were to be seen. As Miriam approached, some of the women glanced at her curiously but did not cease their frenzied activity. Miriam lowered her shawl over her face. It would not do to be recognized. The peasants in this town had all worked for the Jews, all of them knew who Reb Mordche was, and many were familiar with his family members. Yet she had to ask someone about Mirko's village, or she would never find Rebecca. A young girl of about twelve approached, carrying a chipped china pitcher that looked as though it had once been valuable. Where did she get such a thing? Miriam walked toward the child. Surely the girl was too young to remember her; three and a half years is a long time for someone so young.

"Excuse me," Miriam began in her best peasant Polish. "Do you know the little village there, behind the woods?"

"Yes," replied the girl, gaping at the stranger with round, gray eyes.

"What happened there? Where are the people?"

The girl wiped her nose with the back of her wrist and shrugged. "Gone." She hoisted the pitcher, with its delicate tracing of gold leaves, and darted off. Miriam ran after her.

"Gone where?" she panted as she caught up to the child at the entrance to one of the cottages.

"I don't know. Dead." The girl pointed to one of the nearby cabins, whose door was slightly ajar. "Ask in there," she said. "I have no time to talk. We must hide everything fast, you know."

"Hide everything? Why?"

The child frowned at Miriam, her eyes narrowing. "Who are you, anyway? Don't you know anything? From the Russians, of course.

They'll take everything. They'll take us, too. First we hide the things, then we hide ourselves. Go in there and ask, she knows." She pointed again to the cottage and dashed off.

Miriam, her whole body trembling, approached the cottage. She could barely compose her thoughts. Dead! The girl had said they were dead! Her little Rebecca, whom she had barely known, gone now forever. She entered the cottage and looked about. An elderly woman sat at a table, on which were piled shining cups, trays, and bowls. Even in the dim light, Miriam could see that they were made of silver. The woman looked up and let out a muffled shriek. She walked up to Miriam and stared into her face. Suddenly, her hand shot out and she tore the shawl from Miriam's head and shoulders.

"So it *is* you," she said.

Miriam opened her lips, but several seconds elapsed before she could force the sounds from her throat. "Panie Zbirka," she whispered. Her knees felt weak and she grasped a chair to keep from falling. How had she not recognized the cottage, having been there so many times in her youth to call for Katya or walk her home? Of course she had known Panie Zbirka, Katya's mother. A chill ran through her. This hunched, gray-haired woman was also Tadeusz's mother.

"You remember me?" Miriam asked.

"Of course. Katya was like a sister to you. But you spread an evil story about her, something to make her lose her job. She would not say what it was." The woman sniffed and sat down once more at the table.

"You were killed," she continued. "They saw it. All of you were shot. How did you live?" As she spoke, she began wrapping the silver pieces in rags, which she tied with bits of string. Before Miriam could answer, Panie Zbirka went on. "Katya is not here now. She went to live in Brimpolnya, with her husband."

Miriam nodded her head. The woman seemed half-crazed, the way her eyes darted about. She obviously bore Miriam great hostility, without even knowing why Katya had really been fired. How could she now ask her about Mirko and the village beyond the river?

A terrible groan came from the back room, startling Miriam

out of her thoughts. The old woman rose. "That is my son," she said. "My soldier, my hero." She walked to the rear of the cottage.

Slowly, Miriam rose from her chair. Like one in a nightmare who tries to run but is paralyzed, she found herself following the woman instead of fleeing from the hut. She paused outside the door and looked in. An evil smell emanated from within. The old woman was bending over a figure that lay on a mattress. The figure turned his face toward the door. Miriam gasped. The blond hair still fell across the broad forehead, the left cheekbone was high and smooth, the nose straight, the jaw firm. The left eye stared, bright and blue. But where the right eye should have been was a crude patch, and beneath it the cheekbone was caved in and the lips slit to reveal broken teeth shining in a horrid grin. The right elbow supported the frail body, but the arm ended in a stump, as did the right leg, encased in filthy bandages from which the terrible stench exuded.

Panie Zbirka dipped a rag into a basin of water and laid it across the man's forehead. "Sleep, Tadeusz," she said. "Sleep." He moaned, closed his eye, and lay back on the mattress, no longer interested in his mother, nor in the young visitor whom he could barely see in the shadowy doorway.

The old woman withdrew from the room. Miriam backed out slowly behind her. "What happened to him?" she whispered, fighting the rising nausea that gripped her stomach and chest.

"Tadeusz was a soldier," shrugged the peasant woman, who had resumed wrapping the silver.

"Yes?" prompted Miriam.

"He was hit by a German shell. The doctors cut off his hand and leg there, at the front. That is how he came home to us. His wife took one look at him, and during the night she took their son, Stefan, and disappeared, who knows where."

His wife. So he, too, had married. A terrible pity and despair overwhelmed Miriam. Tears began coursing down her cheeks, and Mrs. Zbirka looked at her in surprise but said nothing.

"Panie Zbirka," called a young voice from outside the hut.

The woman rose and went out.

Miriam remained seated for a moment. Then she got up and walked back into the tiny room where Tadeusz lay. Ignoring the stench as best as she could, she knelt beside the tattered mattress. "Tadeusz," she whispered. "It's Miriam, Miriam Rutner."

He opened his eye and stared hard at her. She could see pain, confusion, and finally remembrance flicker in the feverish blue gaze. His mouth opened, and he produced some garbled sounds, and then shook his head sadly.

"Can't you speak?" Miriam whispered.

Again the slow, sad shake of the head. Miriam reached for his good hand, and a sob escaped her throat. His fingers pressed her own in an icy grip, then relaxed as their strength ebbed.

"Tadeusz," she began, but could not go on. What could she say to him? That she had loved him once, when he was strong and whole, a talented artist who painted lovely pictures with his gifted right hand? She heard the front door open and close. She must leave him now, or his mother would think it strange. Yet she could not leave him that way, without a word, as he lay so close to death.

"Tadeusz," she breathed. "I never forgot you. And I never will."

Once more she felt the tension in his frozen fingers, and once more his eye stared into her own with a fierce intensity that spoke more eloquently than any words he had uttered in the days of their courtship.

She rose then and left him. "He cried out," she explained to Mrs. Zbirka, who was just coming into the room. "But he's all right now, I think."

The old woman peered in at her son. "Yes. He's all right. He's almost smiling. Maybe he thought you were Stefa. He doesn't really understand much. He cannot speak, nothing. They say he won't last the week." She began packing the wrapped silver into a large basket that she had brought in from outside.

"Mrs. Zbirka, I won't keep you any longer. I'm terribly, terribly sorry about your son." The old woman nodded without stopping her work.

"I, too, have a son," continued Miriam. "He was also hurt badly.

But he was just a little boy, and now he's in Kiev, and I have to find him. But first I must know something. They told me you might be able to help."

Mrs. Zbirka gave Miriam a curious look. "Me? How can I help you?" she asked indifferently.

"You know the little village, the hamlet that lies beyond the woods, on the other side of the river?"

"Which? There are many villages."

"The tiny village, just about eight or nine huts, really. Two very old women used to live there; they gave people medicine. A man named Mirko had a small farm. He had a mute daughter."

Mrs. Zbirka nodded her head. "Yes, I know it. What of it?"

"What happened to the people there? Where are they?"

"What happened? There was a battle there. A group of German soldiers were running back. They sought shelter there. They tried to take over the village, but the partisans were waiting. They killed them. All of them."

"Killed who?" Miriam felt blood pounding against her temples.

"Why, the Germans. The partisans shot some and hung the rest." She unwrapped a curved goblet, held it up to the light, and turned it about before rewrapping it. Miriam gaped at it, trying hard to conceal her emotions. She recognized the goblet. It was a silver *kiddush* cup, like any other except for the engraved crown on one side. It had been Shloimeh's. She was sure of it. The crown had been engraved especially for him. It was the symbol of King Solomon, his namesake.

"Why do you ask about the village?" demanded Mrs. Zbirka as she thrust the cup deep among the wrapped parcels in the basket. Something in Miriam's look had disturbed her, and she momentarily regretted that the Jewess had seen all the silver. Still, what could she do, alone in the world as she was? *One word from a Pole like me and she's finished*, thought the old woman.

Miriam hesitated, afraid to tell the truth to this woman whose glance held a dark malevolence. "There was a man there who helped us once. He helped my father, and I promised him that if I could

I would try to…" She realized that her words made no sense; she could not think of a plausible story. Finally, she blurted, "My niece was there," as if concern for a niece was somehow safer than concern for a daughter.

"Your niece?" Mrs. Zbirka again looked at her curiously. Miriam instantly regretted her story. Why had she not simply asked where the people in the village had gone? But there was nothing she could do; she had to go on.

"My sister's child. She left her with a young girl, a mute. Her name was Marya, Mirko's daughter."

The woman raised her head and looked at Miriam sharply. "I don't know who's from there. I know that the few young men who were left went with the partisans. The one or two old ones went with the women and children to Jewish Dubnitz, to the Gestapo head-quarters in the old school. The Germans left there just a few days before. The women didn't want to be alone in that village. It wasn't safe, so few people, all alone."

Miriam nodded and stood up. "Thank you Mrs. Zbirka. Again, I'm so sorry about your son. I hope he will be spared more pain, and you, as well."

Mrs. Zbirka walked to the door and opened it. "Well, goodbye, Miss Miriam."

As Miriam began making her way down the muddy road, the woman called after her, "Wait!" and motioned for her to return. Miriam came and stood at the doorway impatiently. She wanted to rush to the old school building where Rebecca surely was, not spend any more time on this side of town.

Mrs. Zbirka leaned forward and spoke in a whisper. "Listen to me. Get your niece and go away. Don't stay here, where everyone knows you. The people here, well, they don't want to see the Jews back here so fast, you know. Go someplace else. You don't look like a Jew, you can hide it." She paused, opened her mouth as if to say more, then abruptly turned away, closing the door behind her.

Go someplace else. The words echoed in Miriam's head as she walked. Where could she go? She had long dreamed of coming back to Dubnitz with Rebecca and waiting for the war to end. When it did, Reuben would be free to return to her, with David. But if she left Dubnitz, what then? A solution formed itself in her mind as she hurried across the wooden bridge that led to Jewish Dubnitz. She would leave word with someone in town, someone Reuben would remember: Antek the carriage driver. He would tell Reuben where to find her. New hope gave a lightness to her feet as she tripped over the wooden bridge and rushed through the stand of pines that led to her native village. But once she had left the wood, she came to a sudden stop, and the joy that had so quickly sprung up in her heart fled at the sight of the charred mounds of rubble and broken stone foundations, all that was left of the houses she had known so well.

Only a few buildings remained standing, among them several houses, the stores in the marketplace, the box factory, and off in the distance, the old school that had become first a hospital and then Gestapo headquarters. Seeing it, Miriam began walking faster; running would attract too much attention. Even so, the peasants walking in and out of the remaining houses stared after her.

Miriam walked up the stone steps of the building and opened the door. The corridors were just as she remembered. Seeing them brought back the agonizing hours she had spent there, waiting and watching while David lay for so long in his twilight world. Now she had no time to dwell on the past, and she began frantically knocking on doors and calling out. "Is anyone here? Marya! Marya!"

A door opened and a tiny, frail old woman peered out. "What do you want?"

Miriam tried to compose herself. "I am looking for a young woman with three small children. The woman doesn't speak; she cannot. She's heavy, blonde, her name is Marya. She's from the village beyond the river."

The woman nodded her head in a series of rapid jerks. "Downstairs," she said, motioning to a door at the end of the corridor.

As Miriam began descending the stairs, her heavy work shoes clomping dully on the stone, a shiver ran through her. This was the staircase Leibel had described, and down below were the dungeons where both he and her father had been starved and tortured by Nazis. Yet even this knowledge could not quell her eagerness as she reached the lower level and heard the sound of children's laughter. She hurried down the hall, opening doors to the right and left. The dungeons had been hastily converted into makeshift dormitories; each housed a woman or two, and several children. As she opened each door, children stopped their games and stared at Miriam with frightened eyes. Finally, at the fourth door, she heard a familiar voice—it sounded like Yanusch, Marya's little boy. She opened the door and was immediately engulfed in a smothering embrace—Marya. When she freed herself, she glanced about the tiny cubicle, which contained one cot and a few straw pallets crowded together on the floor. Yanusch and Polka, Marya's daughter, both much bigger than Miriam remembered, stood staring and smiling, while there on the cot sat a fragile, doll-like child with red-gold hair and huge, blue-green eyes.

Miriam flew to her and caught her in her arms as tears streamed down her own cheeks. "Rebecca, my Rebecca, my baby," she cried, burying her face in the child's hair. The girl's delicate body stiffened. She began screaming and flailing her bony arms and legs, desperately fighting to get away.

"Mama! Mama!" she shrieked, reaching out to Marya. Polka and Yanusch began wailing, adding to the commotion. Two women opened the door and peered in curiously, then shut it again. Screaming children were no novelty in these times. Marya took the hysterical child from Miriam and began rocking her, making soft, inarticulate sounds in her throat. The child stopped screaming but continued to sob and hiccough, all the while looking at Miriam with suspicious eyes.

Yanusch moved closer and stared into Miriam's face. Miriam bent down and touched his wheat-colored hair. "Yanusch, don't you remember me? You're a big boy now—what are you, six or seven years old?" Yanusch shrugged.

"When you were very small," continued Miriam, "maybe four or so, I lived with you and Polka, and your mama. Your grandfather, Mirko, was there, too."

Polka covered her mouth and giggled. Yanusch shrugged again. "Grandfather is dead," he said.

"Oh. I didn't know. I'm sorry. But Yanusch, and you, Polka,

don't you remember me? I lived in the barn. Rebecca," she pointed at the still-shuddering child, "is my little girl. I am her *mamushka*."

Yanusch squinted his eyes. "I remember you. You sang songs in the barn. But," he pointed at Rebecca, "this is Anzia. She is our sister."

Polka, who had not yet said a word, repeated, "She's our sister."

Miriam looked at Marya in despair. If only she could speak! Marya had been nodding her head and pointing from Rebecca to Miriam all the while, but the children were not convinced. Finally, she thrust the squirming girl at Miriam, and the three children began shrieking anew.

It cannot be helped, thought Miriam. "Goodbye, Marya," she shouted over the wails of the children. "Thank you. I'll repay you soon." And she carried Rebecca from the room.

The child kicked and screamed all the way up the stairs, down the hall, and out of the building. Miriam could barely carry her down the main street of Dubnitz. Worse, peasants on the street were glaring at her suspiciously as she passed, and whispering to one another. Suddenly, one of them, a thin girl with pockmarked cheeks and scraggly braids, rushed up to Miriam as she struggled with her daughter. Miriam recognized her. It was Katrina, who had worked for the Schendler family. Dassy Schendler had been a friend of Miriam's for about three years, until they had an argument over a missing hair ribbon.

Now Katrina planted herself in Miriam's path, and her companions stepped up close behind. "You," said the servant girl, pointing her finger in Miriam's face. Rebecca stopped crying and stared at the woman with huge round eyes. "I know you," she continued. "You're that Miri, Miriam, the rabbi's daughter." The three peasant women who accompanied her all nodded in agreement.

Katrina pointed at Rebecca. "What are you doing with that child?"

Miriam drew herself up and stared angrily at Katrina. How dare this peasant have the impertinence to interrogate her this way, knowing that she was the Dubnitzer's daughter? "She's my child," she said defiantly. "I'm her mother."

"Oh, yes?" Katrina spat on the ground. "Prove it." She poked her face at Rebecca and stared. "She looks like a Christian child to me. How do we know you're not taking her away to kill her?"

"Yes, and use her blood to make *matzoh*," jeered a toothless woman standing behind Katrina. "Isn't your Passover coming soon?"

Fury set Miriam's teeth on edge. "Jews don't kill children," she said, glaring at her accusers. "And we don't use any kind of blood. Ever. It's not even kosher. It's all a lie, an excuse to murder us."

Katrina laughed. "We don't need an excuse to kill Jews. The Germans didn't either. We can kill you right now, and your brat, too. You're supposed to be dead anyhow."

The four peasant women formed a tight circle around Miriam. From somewhere behind came a shout: "The Russians are in Brimpolnya!"

Immediately, the peasants forgot Miriam and raced off to prepare for the arrival of the "liberators," who would surely be in Dubnitz within a day or two. Miriam gripped Rebecca's hand. "Anzia!" she commanded. "Run!"

Miraculously, the child obeyed, and they both sped off down the road to Kuneh's Inn. What a relief to see the familiar gray stones of the old building, still standing. And there, moving about in the front garden, was the hunched figure of Antek, the aged wagon driver.

"Antek," shouted Miriam, gasping for breath as she approached with Rebecca in tow.

The wizened peasant turned around slowly. He stared at Miriam uncomprehending, rubbing his grizzled scalp. After a while, a light seemed to flicker in his pale eyes. "You are the rabbi's eldest. But alive! You were taken away, shot with the rest. How did you…" He suddenly hung his head, shamefully recalling his own role in leading the Nazis to the rabbi's house.

"I lived. It doesn't matter. Now I must get away, stay someplace where I'll be safe with my daughter."

Antek nodded his head. "Yes, safe. Safe," he repeated. "Antek,"

Miriam begged, "you have a wagon still, don't you? Please, drive me to Bitempsk. It's not so far, and nobody knows me there. Unless," she faltered. "Are there still Jews left in Bitempsk?" Her heart pounded hopefully. She'd had cousins there before the war.

Antek shook his head. "I cannot drive you there. The Germans took the horses. There are only a few left, to work the farms. On Wednesday I'll have one, but only to go to Vlashk. And as far as Jews are concerned, they say there are no Jews left anymore. All killed. All."

Miriam hesitated. She had never been to Vlashk. There had not been much of a Jewish community there, only a few isolated farmers, followers of the Scolener *rebbe*. Still, it was as good a place as any. She could probably get farm work there.

"Antek." She stared at him, all the while holding tight to Rebecca, who was beginning to squirm and whimper. "My father and his people were kind to you. Because of us, you and your family always had enough to eat, warm clothing to wear. Your own boss, Kuneh, was a Dubnitzer Hasid. God has helped me survive the war. He will help you, too, for helping me. Nothing bad will happen to you. Help me just this once more. Let me hide somewhere tomorrow, and take me on Wednesday to Vlashk. God will surely reward you."

Antek blinked and scratched his chin. "Hide you?" He shrugged. "You can stay in the inn. There's an empty room no one ever goes into."

"What do you mean, an empty room? Who's staying in the inn now?"

"Well, the Germans used it, but they left, so some of our families, their homes weren't so good, you know, so they moved into the inn."

Miriam felt her scalp prickle with fear. Peasants from Dubnitz living at the inn? How could she stay there and risk being killed?

Antek, sensing her doubts, went on. "There's a little room in back, behind the big hall. The soldiers stored paper and things there, but it's empty now. I can put in a blanket or two. But only for two nights."

Glancing about to make sure no one was watching, he led her

inside, past the big hall and into the little room at the back. Then he left, promising to return shortly with food for her and her child, who lay down on a pile of newspapers and immediately fell asleep. Miriam looked around. A sense of wonder, tinged with irony, filled her. This was the *yichud* room, the tiny room where she and Berish had been alone for the first time after their wedding ceremony. She pictured his pale face and dark whiskers and recalled how he had mumbled so strangely. *"She offers cake, they offer cake."* Not long after, they had ridden out of Dubnitz, with Antek driving the coach. It was only fitting that he should again drive her down the road from the small town of her birth.

Later that evening, when Rebecca awoke in the dark and began crying, Miriam cuddled her in her arms and softly sang the nursery rhymes she had sung to her in the barn three years before. The gentle cadences and foolish words comforted the child, who soon fell asleep again. The next day she seemed more trusting of Miriam and even ate a bit of the bread that Antek brought. But she still refused to speak. From the moment Miriam had taken her from Marya, she had not uttered a word. To Miriam's concerned queries she shook her head no or nodded yes, keeping her lips clamped shut. They spent the day in the tiny room, eating the meager rations that Antek had given them. They used an old bucket as a chamber pot. The room quickly became stuffy and smelly, but there was nothing Miriam could do, for if she walked into the hall, she would surely be recognized.

On Wednesday, Miriam rose before dawn, washed herself and her daughter with the few remaining drops of water, and waited for Antek, who arrived just after eight with some fresh bread, a jar of water, and a few pieces of dried apple, which Rebecca devoured greedily. When they finished their breakfast, he handed Miriam a black shawl. "Put it over your head," he said, "so they won't see the hair. The hair they would remember."

The shawl was none too clean, but Miriam draped it over her head and shoulders. She herself was much in need of a bath and this was no time to be squeamish. She took Rebecca's hand, glanced one last time at the *yichud* room, and followed Antek to the horse and wagon tethered outside. The wagon was actually an ox-cart, and the horse a skinny old nag whose ribs showed through and whose sides were full of ulcers. It did not matter. Nothing mattered but to find safety, somewhere not too far away, until Reuben and David returned.

As the wagon pulled out of Dubnitz, Miriam was reminded of Lot's wife, who she always thought had received an excessive punishment for looking back at the destruction of Sodom. In Miriam's case, it was not God, but she herself who commanded, don't look back. Don't look at the burned houses, the rubble and charred sticks that once housed your own family, the blackened remains of the study house where your father and brother recited the ancient teachings. Don't look at the ruined synagogue, where your people chanted and prayed to a God who turned His face away. Remember only the old Dubnitz, the Dubnitz you knew as a child, before the Nazis, before the Russians, and even before your disgrace. Putting her arm around her silent child, she straightened her back and stared directly ahead as far as her eyes could see down the winding, rutted road that led to Vlashk. They reached the little town in the evening, as the peasants were beginning to drift in from the fields for drinks and fellowship. Antek helped Miriam and Rebecca down from the wagon, doffed his hat, and began tying up the exhausted horse. Miriam touched his arm.

"Antek," she began, "I don't know how to thank you for what you have done for me. Right now I have nothing, but someday I will repay you. I promise you that. Didn't my people always keep their promises to you?" Antek nodded and smiled in embarrassment.

"Now, Antek, I have one more favor to ask. It won't require much of you, but it will be the most important thing in the world for me. My husband, Reuben Zwillinger, is in Kiev with my son. Any day now, they will be coming back, looking for me. As soon as I find a place to stay, I will write to you at the inn, telling you where I am. I'll also leave word here, if I leave Vlashk, as to where I'll be. I know Reuben will come back to Dubnitz, and when he does, he'll look for you for any word about me. Please, please tell him where to find me. He will surely be able to pay you well. Will you do this for me, Antek?"

Again the peasant nodded his head. "Yes, Miss Miriam, I will do it."

"And you will be rewarded, Antek. By God as well as by us. Thank you again."

They waved to each other and walked off in opposite directions, he to a saloon to get water for his horse and whiskey for himself, and she and Rebecca down the main road that led through the town and out to the surrounding farms.

An hour later, Antek emerged from the saloon, a satisfied smile on his face. He had drunk his fill of sharp potato vodka and then joined in a raucous card game. The loser had skulked off, muttering curses, as Antek gleefully pocketed his winnings, thirty-eight rubles. Not much, but enough to pay for his drinks. As he set down a bucket of water for his horse, he felt a heavy hand on his shoulder and turned to face Grigor, the man he had bested moments before.

"Give me back my money," whispered Grigor, breathing whiskey fumes into Antek's face.

"But it's mine. I won it," Antek protested.

The man reached up and clutched the driver's collar, nearly choking him. "You cheated," he growled. "Now hand it over."

"Surely," sputtered Antek as he reached into his pocket and handed the man a crumpled wad of bills. "Here, take it. I meant no harm to you."

He turned to his wagon, but Grigor grabbed his arm. "How much for the nag?" he demanded, jerking his thumb at the mare as she thrust her long muzzle into the water bucket.

"Oh, no, my kind sir." Antek laughed nervously. "She is not for sale."

"No? Then I'll have her for free." Grigor raised his foot and propelled it forward with all his drunken power into Antek's gut. The driver doubled over in agony, gasping. A second kick to the head sent him sprawling into the gutter. The very last thing Antek saw was the soft, shining underbelly of his beloved mare as she raised her hoof and brought it down heavily on his head, placidly obeying her new master as he drove the wagon over Antek's broken, lifeless body.

Panie Poljemie was short and stout, with twinkling blue eyes and deep dimples in each round cheek. When Miriam and Rebecca appeared at her door, Panie Poljemie had to look twice to make sure it wasn't her own child and grandchild she was seeing. Upon determining that they were actually strangers, she decided that God had sent them to her, seeing how sorely she missed her own family.

Her daughter Vinka was a redhead like Miriam and even had a daughter a bit older than Rebecca. But Vinka lived far away, in Przemsk, so Panie Poljemie was alone, having lost her husband the year before. She ran her little farm on the outskirts of Vlashk as best as she could by herself, for she had little money to pay for help. Miriam's offer to work for room and board was most welcome. The arrangement was mutually satisfactory, and Miriam found a measure of contentment for the first time in years. It was late March, the war was ending, and she and her daughter were safe. Soon Reuben and David would return and they would all be reunited. Even when the Russians had marched into Vlashk, they did not bother with the poor, isolated little farm, preferring to stay in town, where there was more choice in food, liquor, women, and household goods. The months passed, each day bringing more news about the Russian advances westward. One freezing January day came wonderful tidings. Warsaw had been liberated by the Red Army. *Should I go there?* wondered Miriam. Instead she waited, safe and close enough to Dubnitz that Reuben could find her quickly.

On May 8, 1945, Panie Poljemie came rushing into the kitchen, her cheeks flaming. Throwing down the bags of flour she had brought back from the marketplace, she jumped about, clapping her hands like a child. "The war is over! The war is over! Germany has surrendered!" Grabbing Miriam by both hands, she danced her around the little kitchen while Rebecca squealed excitedly and raced after them, wheeling and spinning until she fell dizzily to the floor.

The war was over. Miriam had only to wait for word from Reuben. The weeks went by. The trees shed their blossoms and were filled with thick, glossy leaves. Birds and insects filled the humid air with their songs and droning. Rebecca, having long since found her tongue, now chattered incessantly and followed Miriam everywhere, a chubby, sunburned child with red-gold braids that bounced on her shoulders.

Many times Miriam was tempted to return to Dubnitz, but always she stayed away, remembering Katrina's taunting threats. Instead, when she was not working, she wrote letters; letters to Antek in Dubnitz, reminding him of his promise and of her present address in Vlashk, letters to Reuben at the old address—General Hospital, Kiev. Finally, after what seemed like an endless wait, a letter came for Miriam. Her hands trembled as she looked at the Russian characters, the Kiev postmark. It was from the administrator of Kiev General Hospital. Miriam ran with the letter to the Russian military office in Vlashk, where it was translated:

My Dear Mrs. Zwillinger:

It is with great regret that I inform you of bad news regarding your husband, Reuben Zwillinger, and your son, David Zwillinger.

When we received your letter asking of his whereabouts, we made our own investigation, since many of us remembered both him and your son fondly.

Your son David was gravely ill when he arrived at our hospital, but with the help of our devoted staff, he made a full recovery and was released to your husband's custody. Shortly thereafter, your husband left the child with a Russian family and tried to return to Poland, probably in an attempt to reach you, since mail had stopped getting through.

Unfortunately, he was caught by the authorities and deported as a political prisoner to Siberia. He died there in December 1944, and his papers were sent to the military office in Kiev. It was from there that we were given this information. Your husband's papers have been forwarded to you and will arrive under separate cover.

As for your son, it is with great sadness that we must inform you that the family who was caring for him reported that he died of scarlet fever.

We at the Kiev General Hospital are very grieved to have to provide you with this information. We do so because of our warm feelings for your husband and son, and to put your mind at ease regarding their whereabouts.

Respectfully,

Dr. Alexander Raber, Administrator
Kiev General Hospital

The Russian officer finished reading the letter. He folded it and handed it back to Miriam, who sat silently staring at him, her eyes blank with incomprehension. The officer, a lean, dark man in his early forties, was not unsympathetic. He cared little or nothing for Jews, but this was a beautiful woman, and a widow besides. Inclining his head toward Miriam, he asked, "Can I get you some water?" When she shook her head, he went on. "How terrible for you to receive such news. And you are all alone here. I suppose most of your people were killed. Zwillinger…a Jewish name. How did you survive? Anyhow, don't worry. I will keep your secret." He shook his head and sighed. "What a terrible war. Well, if you need anything, anything at all, I am here, at your service." He reached down and touched Miriam's shoulder, then offered his hand to help her up from the chair.

Ignoring him, Miriam rose, and clutching the letter to her chest, slowly left the room. Somehow she managed to walk the two miles back to the farm. Once there, she went into her room and began throwing her meager belongings into a flour sack. Panie Poljemie stood in the doorway and plied her with questions, which Miriam would not answer. Finally, her packing finished, she turned to the old woman. "My husband and son are dead. I have no need to stay here any longer. I thank you for everything you've done for us." She bent and wrapped her arms around Panie Poljemie's plump body. The two women hugged each other and sobbed while Rebecca watched, wide-eyed, hugging a shabby cornhusk doll.

Chapter nineteen

The train sped across the countryside, winding its way through fields and woods, passing towns both bustling and desolate. Some portions of the track were new, hastily laid down by the Germans to speed their retreat, replacing sections destroyed by Allied bombs.

Rebecca stared out the window, her nose pressed against the smudged glass. "Mama, look!" She pointed at whatever caught her eye—a pair of horses, a peasant waving a hoe in rhythmic salute, a flock of creamy sheep. Despite the dusty air that blew in through the windows, the train was hot, and Miriam dabbed at the grimy rivulets of sweat that formed on Rebecca's forehead and neck. The cramped car was filled with people, mostly Polish peasants on their way to Warsaw, where one could buy many things that had been scarce during the war. Without the Jews, many marketplaces in the small towns and villages had closed down, and the Poles had been forced to do without. Now that it was safe to travel, their desire for "quality" big-city merchandise had been rekindled. But Poles were not the only passengers. Here and there sat a different type of traveler, those whose emaciated frames, hunched posture, and burning, haunted eyes marked them as clearly as the yellow star that they had once worn, or perhaps refused to wear.

These were the survivors. These were the Jews who had crawled out of attics, closets, cellars, and barns, Jews who had been liberated from concentration camps, Jews who had been saved by their gentile countrymen or merely overlooked. All possessed one common feature that set them apart from their Polish compatriots: they carried the stamp of despair upon their features and the burden of desolation upon their shoulders. All had struggled for survival, clinging to a fervent hope that kept them alive, only to find, at the end of the war, that they were now alone. The loved ones they sought were, in most cases, never found. Here and there, brothers and cousins were reunited, or perhaps even a mother and child, as in Miriam's case. Sometimes a whole family managed to survive. But most had emerged from hiding and dragged themselves back to their hometowns only to find burnt-out rubble and hostile strangers living in their homes, and no word of their lost husbands, wives, parents, children, siblings, aunts, uncles, and cousins. The Poles shrank from these Jewish passengers, their traditional aversion made even stronger by the deplorable appearance of the survivors. They avoided them as if fearing the contagion of their misery.

Miriam herself was both attracted and repelled by them. They were Jews like herself; they, too, had suffered unspeakable horrors and yet somehow had managed to live. At the same time, she found herself guiltily resenting them, if only because their faces were not the ones she wished to see. The gaunt, hollow-cheeked man with the close-cropped black hair who leaned against the window and moaned occasionally—why had he lived and not Reuben? The frail, blond boy sucking his thumb and clinging to the knee of an elderly man—what right had he to life, when David had none? The elderly man himself, perhaps the child's grandfather, sitting silently with vacant eyes—he was just a simple Jew, whereas her own father, who lay rotting in an unmarked grave, was the Dubnitzer *rebbe*.

She knew her thoughts were horrible, sinful, and selfish—bitter fruits that grew out of the depression clogging her spirit like foul, black mud. Afraid that others would read her feelings, she averted her face from them. Later, when time had assuaged some of the hurt, she would find herself drawn to these people. But for the moment, she was alone in her bereavement, wanting only Rebecca for company, and sometimes not even her. For Rebecca had grown into a gleeful, mischievous child who could neither understand nor tolerate her mother's transformation from an anxious yet hopeful person who played games and sang nursery songs as she did the farm chores, to a silent, tight-lipped stranger who often wept.

"Wake up, Missus, this is the end of the line." The porter prodded her shoulder gently. Miriam opened her eyes. Rebecca still slept, snuggled against her mother's shoulder, but all around, people were gathering up their belongings, stretching their tired muscles, and leaving the train. The little blond boy tottered past on stick-like legs, clutching tightly to the old man's hand.

"Are we home, *Zayde*?"

"Yes, *tateleh*," replied the grandfather. "We are home."

Home, thought Miriam as she alighted from the train with Rebecca. Where was home? Dubnitz had once been her home, but now she could not return without fear of losing her life. Warsaw, too, had been her home, during the happy, early years of her courtship and marriage to Reuben. But what could it mean to her now, alone as she was, with only Rebecca to remind her that she had once been his lover and wife.

The train stopped in a suburb of the city. Beyond, the tracks were still twisted and broken, only partially repaired. There were no streetcars. Tired as they were, Miriam and Rebecca walked the rest of the way. She remembered her departure from Warsaw, fleeing as bombs fell and artillery flared. She recalled the flying bricks, the falling buildings, yet nothing in those memories prepared her for the sight she now beheld as she approached the city.

Warsaw was in ruins. All around her were rubble-filled lots where once tall buildings had stood. Ragged people picked their way about the piles of brick and stone, hoping to find something of value, something that might bring a few kopeks on the black market. The hot breezes were full of dust and ash. Rebecca cried that her feet hurt; the ill-fitting shoes Miriam had bought her in Vlashk were poorly suited for the broken sidewalks of Warsaw. Miriam lifted the child but was soon forced to set her down; she was too heavy. "You'll have to walk," she said. "We'll go slowly." Rebecca whimpered and refused to go on. Miriam was reminded again of her flight from the city; she had had a painful blister on her foot that made walking difficult. Reuben had carried David.

Out of nowhere a man in rusty black clothing appeared. Miriam looked at his face. He returned her gaze suspiciously, then walked away. *He is a Jew*, thought Miriam. *Perhaps he will help us.* Pulling Rebecca by the hand, ignoring her howls, she rushed after the man.

"Sir," she called, "excuse me, can you help me?"

The man stopped and turned slowly. Miriam shuddered inwardly at the sight of his emaciated face and sunken eyes. *"Amcha?"* he asked in a quavering voice.

"What? I beg your pardon?" answered Miriam. Perhaps he thought she was someone he knew.

The man stared into her face again, then turned and shuffled away, ignoring her as she called after him. She had not spoken in Yiddish, nor had she understood the password, which she found out later had been used by Jews in the occupied countries to identify one another. Since she did not respond appropriately, the man assumed she was a gentile and walked away. Pulling Rebecca along, Miriam continued threading her way among the ruins. Suddenly, a grotesquely twisted steel frame loomed up before her. With a shock, she realized that she was facing the remains of the central railroad station, for she had been following the path of the broken tracks.

A horn blared. She jumped, nearly falling over Rebecca, who began to shriek in terror. A car was riding down the debris-strewn street, and she quickly moved out of its path, her heart pounding. The car slowed as it passed her, and a man leaned out. He had dark hair, fair skin, and wore glasses like the kind Reuben used to wear. There was something familiar in his face, and even in his manner as he leaned down toward her from the passenger seat of the car. Miriam felt a surge of hope. Surely he was a Jew. The Yiddish words left her mouth almost before she could form them: "Please, can you help us?" It was the first time she had spoken Yiddish in four years.

The car stopped, and the passenger, whose name was Benjamin Steinberg, got out and opened the back door, motioning for her and Rebecca to get in. He spoke a halting Yiddish that was full of unfamiliar words, which Miriam assumed were English. "Don't be afraid," he said. "I'm an American. I'm with the Joint Distribution Committee. We are here to help you. There are many Jewish refugees here."

He offered to bring her to the committee headquarters, and she gratefully accepted. Miriam did not wish to speak, and Mr. Steinberg respectfully left her alone with her thoughts. Rebecca soon fell asleep, lulled by the rocking of the car, her head in Miriam's lap.

Slowly, the car made its way through the broken streets, and Miriam gazed in wonder and horror at the massive destruction that told of the city's agony. On the once beautiful Francizkana Street, amongst the smashed ruins of stately buildings, many shops had been hastily set up. Miriam caught a glimpse of colorful fruits and vegetables in one, china and crockery in another. Who could afford to buy these rich wares now? The American read the question in her eyes and explained. "Only the privileged few can buy in those shops—high officials, diplomats. The general population is starving."

In the center of town, the streets were filled with peddlers, haggling and shouting, displaying their wares. It resembled the Warsaw Miriam recalled, but for one startling detail. None of the peddlers looked Jewish. All were obviously Poles, who had gladly taken over this traditionally Jewish role. Their appearance, and the cacophony of Polish words they shouted, underscored for Miriam the great change Hitler had wrought.

Soon the Saxon Gardens came into view. Even before the car rolled past, Miriam could see the broken, denuded trees and the headless statues. The earth in the park bristled with crude wooden crosses. "What are those for?" she asked.

"They were put there to mark graves, where Polish fighters fell."

"What about the Jewish graves?"

"Look there." He indicated a vast mound of earth at the park's Iron Gate. "That is the mass grave for Jews."

The old car rode on. Soon a huge, twisted mass of metal could be seen.

"What is that?" Miriam pointed. Even before he answered, she recognized it. Here had been the great city market, once so full of vitality and color. Now, in its ruined state, it resembled a great iron zoo whose metal cages had somehow burst asunder, leaving its inhabitants free to escape. Here and there were charred and splintered placards, some hanging precariously by a single nail, proclaiming in faded half-words the goods that had once been for sale. Finally, the car stopped. They had reached the Joint Distribution Committee. It had been set up in one of the few buildings that remained more or less intact.

The office was filled with people waiting in lines, sitting or standing about, talking to one another. Many clustered about the various lists of names affixed to the walls. Some seemed heartened after perusing them, others turned away crestfallen, but all added their own before walking on. Miriam soon learned that these were lists of survivors, written by the survivors themselves in the hope that some relative would see them. She walked up and scanned the list for people from her section of Galicia, but the names began to swim before her eyes. Still, she forced herself to read on. Not a single name meant anything to her. From Dubnitz and its surrounding villages, not one Jewish name was listed. She lifted the pencil to add her own name and Rebecca's, then stopped. What was the point? No one she loved had survived. Even if some distant relatives had lived, would they care about her, she of the portrait scandal? The last time she had seen any of them was at her wedding to Berish.

She moved away from the list and sat down on the floor. Someone offered her and Rebecca a slice of bread and some tea. They ate, drank, and waited. Hours later, a kindly-looking man with a thin, deeply lined face gave her an address where she could stay until suitable housing was found for her.

"Home" became a cramped, two-room apartment, shared with two other "families," in a partially ruined building. The stairs were improvised—wooden planks erected where stone steps had once been. Rebecca cried often and demanded to leave the hot, crowded flat, but Miriam kept her close. She feared the stairs. One false step and the child could fall to her death. Every day she took the child with her to the Joint to have a nourishing meal, to scan for any new names, and to find out what was to be done.

One day, as she listened in horror to the emaciated survivor of a concentration camp, she felt a tap on her shoulder. Thinking it was Rebecca, whom she had sent to the other side of the room, she turned in annoyance.

An old man stood behind her. "Miriam?" he asked hoarsely.

Miriam stood up and stared at the man. Her eyes took in his frail, stooped frame with its baggy, ill-fitting Joint-issued clothes, his deeply wrinkled cheeks covered with gray stubble, his sunken lips and hollow, red-rimmed eyes. Somehow a name formed itself in her brain, pushing its way upward through layers of forgotten memories. "Isaac," she whispered. "Isaac Fink." Tears sprang to her eyes and she reached out to her old friend from Warsaw. The two clung to each other, sobbing in the crowded room. Around them people looked briefly at this strange pair—the young, healthy woman and the old-looking, wizened man—then turned away. They had seen many such reunions, each one kindling brief hope for themselves, or the bitter reality of being utterly alone.

Life became easier for Miriam and Rebecca because of Isaac. He had been released from Auschwitz months before, one of a small remnant of Polish Jews to have survived that terrible place. All of his family, including Bella, had been murdered. After returning to Warsaw, he had been able to get a job with the Joint because he spoke some English. He even had a decent apartment—one large room in the basement of a half-fallen building. Best of all, he had been put on a list for emigration to America. Soon he would be leaving for Bremerhaven to board a ship that would take him away from Poland forever.

Within two days of their meeting, Isaac asked Miriam and Rebecca to move in with him. Three months later, Mr. Isaac Fink and his new wife, Mrs. Miriam Rutner Sonnenblatt Zwillinger Fink, and her daughter, Rebecca Zwillinger, sailed on a U.S. Army transport ship, the *ss Marine Perch*, from Bremerhaven, Germany, to New York City, New York, the United States of America.

On the same day, a tall, slightly stooped figure made his way through the dusty streets of Dubnitz, Poland, knocking on doors and asking questions in aristocratic-sounding Polish. Everywhere he received the same answer. "The Jews? They're dead. Yes, all. Everyone. A pity, no? Who are you, anyhow, and why do you ask? You're Jewish too, yes?" The final query often came in a menacing tone. From house to house the man went, finally arriving at the gray stone inn on the edge of town, but not before stopping at the hut that had once belonged to Anya Bolyenka, who used to work for the town rabbi. Unfortunately, Anya had left long before, having married a Russian officer in 1941. At the inn the man asked after Antek, expressing such dismay at his death that one would have sworn he was related. Late that evening, he left town and was not seen again.

The local girls giggled about it for days afterward. "He asked me," squealed Katrina, her pockmarked cheeks flushed with laughter, "about that redheaded bitch—you know, the one who came back. I said, 'She? Oh, she's dead.'" Katrina pulled a long face and spoke in a drawling mockery of mournful tones. "'She was shot and burned with the others. I saw it myself. Ask anyone.'"

A tall, blonde girl smiled. "He did, he asked everyone. They all told him the same thing, and then he told my father that he was going back to Russia to find his son, or something. The funny thing is, everyone thought they were all dead. Only you, Katrina, and a few others saw the redhead."

"Or claimed they did," interjected a freckle-faced boy of about twelve. "Katrina," he said to his sister, "come on, you made it up, right? No Jews really survived."

Katrina kicked her brother in the shin, setting him yowling. "Calling me a liar? Christ will strike you for that. I swear in the name of Jesus I saw her, I saw Miriam, the rabbi's daughter. I told her to get the hell out before we killed her, and her brat, too."

"So what?" grumbled her brother. "She's gone now. They're all gone."

"Yeah," answered Katrina. "The one favor Hitler did us." The little crowd dispersed as a Russian truck came lumbering over the hill.

Chapter twenty

Miriam leaned against the ship's railing. With one hand she shaded her eyes. The other clasped Rebecca's tightly. The terrible seasickness that had kept them belowdecks for days had finally passed, and Rebecca was eager to run about and explore, but Miriam was afraid to let her go. The brass deck rails were high enough—there was little danger of the child's falling overboard—but there were so many doorways and staircases, so many places where a mischievous little girl could wander off and suddenly vanish.

"Mama, listen!" Rebecca shouted. "Music!" She wrenched her hand from her mother's grasp and dashed off. Miriam tried to follow but found that her legs were still unsteady. The best she could do was walk quickly, occasionally reaching out to grip the railing as the ship rolled gently from side to side.

Rebecca was squatting at the feet of a young black sailor who strummed a guitar and sang in a deep resonant voice: "You are my sunshine, my only sunshine…" Several passengers clustered around him, all girls in their late teens, and tried to sing along. One of them, a pretty blonde in a brightly flowered dress, laughed out loud as she struggled to pronounce the unfamiliar English sounds. Her smile faded as an old woman, her shoulders wrapped in a thin u.s. Army blanket, approached.

"Sing! Sing!" commanded the woman, pointing a long bony finger at the girl, whose face had frozen into an embarrassed grimace. The sailor lowered his guitar as the other girls fell silent. Turning to the group, she said, "My niece has a lovely voice, no? Sing!" she repeated. "Maybe your mother will hear you. Maybe she's up in heaven, listening to her daughter sing English songs while her own body lies rotting under a Polish swamp." The woman spat and walked on.

Miriam shuddered. Before her eyes, the gentle blue-green swells that stretched to the horizon faded into a vast mound of earth covered by thin blades of new grass—Pan Vorny's meadow. She squeezed her eyes shut, but the image would not disappear. The boat lurched, throwing Miriam against the rail.

"Are you all right?" Miriam opened her eyes. The black sailor leaned over her. She didn't understand the words, but the calm sympathy in his voice was unmistakable. She smiled wanly, took Rebecca by the hand, and walked off. The sailor resumed strumming his guitar. A few voices joined in tentatively, but their hearts were no longer in it and the song soon died away.

Farther down the deck was a row of wooden lounge chairs, on which several passengers now reclined, some dozing, others smoking, chatting, or reading papers. Miriam scanned their faces. Isaac was not among them. She had been looking for him all day, but he hadn't been up on deck once. Nor had he come to the dining hall. Poor Isaac. His ravaged body could not accustom itself to the rich food served on the ship, and he spent most of his time in his bunk. Many times Miriam had asked the stewards if she could go down to him, to bring a cup of clear soup or just to see how he was feeling, but on each occasion they barred her entry, speaking words she could not understand. Finally, one of the other women explained.

"They don't allow women down there. Just like they don't allow men to visit the women. I was sick as a dog for three days and my husband couldn't come even once to see me. They're afraid of what might happen if the men and women were allowed in each other's rooms." She gave a short barking laugh. "As if we had the strength.

Anyway," she added, "you wouldn't want to go down there. I heard what it's like. Two hundred men in one room, triple-tiered bunk beds, everybody seasick, don't ask."

Unlike the men, the women were given comfortable cabins that contained only four beds each. Miriam decided to go to hers now, as it was time for Rebecca's nap.

"Sing me a song, Mama," demanded Rebecca as she curled her small body under the khaki woolen blanket.

"Which song?"

"A song you never sang me before."

"Now that's not so easy. I'll have to think." Miriam closed her eyes. From the depths of her memory a song came back from childhood:

> *There was a tree in the forest,*
> *A tree in the forest.*
> *Then there was an apple in the tree,*
> *An apple in the tree.*
> *There was a peasant in the forest,*
> *A peasant in the forest*
> *Who wanted to pick the apple.*
> *The apple would not fall,*
> *The apple would not fall.*

Her own mother had sung that song, first to Dina and Shlo-imeh, and later, she recalled with a sharp stab of pain, to her own little David. During the short time they had lived together in Dubnitz, before David had fallen from the window…Tears choked her throat so that she could no longer sing. With relief, she saw that Rebecca had already fallen asleep. Wiping away her tears, she took down a book from a shelf near her bed and tried to read. It was a romance novel that one of her roommates had just finished, the story of a Polish countess who runs off with a gypsy who turns out to be a Russian prince. It was foolish nonsense, as Isaac would say, but it kept her from dwelling on her own tragedies and helped pass the long hours at sea. As she read, her eyelids grew heavy and soon she dozed off.

A loud scream followed by a dull thud brought her sharply awake. Miriam sat up, frightened. Who could be screaming? At night people often cried out, or even shouted in their sleep, as their tortured minds spewed up horrible images from their war-torn past. But at this time of day, most of the passengers were either napping or relaxing up on deck. When she had walked down the corridor fifteen minutes earlier, all had been silent. Again she heard it, but this time the scream was muffled. Miriam climbed down from her bunk bed and tiptoed to the door. The hallway was empty, but suddenly she heard a series of slapping sounds. With bare feet, Miriam walked down the corridor. The noise was coming from two rooms away.

Miriam paused just outside the door. Again she heard it, a slap followed by a yelp. Someone was being beaten. A child, perhaps? Without thinking, she pushed against the door. It would not give. Something was in the way. She shoved with all her strength until finally the door opened. The worn leather suitcase that had been pushed against it fell to one side, and Miriam stepped over it into the room.

There were five people inside, all passengers whom Miriam had come to know slightly. Four of them now faced her, glaring defiantly. The fifth, a large and powerfully built woman named Gerda, stood in the center of the group. Her face was bruised and swollen, her arms tied behind her back and strapped to a water pipe with what appeared to be a cotton stocking. One of her captors was holding a strip of cloth, ready to stuff it in her mouth. Another held a leather slipper, which she quickly brought down hard across Gerda's face.

"Stop!" shouted Miriam. "What are you doing?"

"Shut the door," hissed the girl with the slipper. She had spoken to Miriam several times in the dining hall. Her name was Esther and she was only seventeen. "Shut the door, goddamn it!"

Miriam closed the door. "What is this? Why are you doing this? Stop!"

She reached for the slipper but was rudely shoved away. She fell against a bunk bed as the girl continued to rain down slaps on Gerda, who had by now been gagged. Gerda's large, blonde head jerked backward with each blow, banging against the pipe. Miriam now recognized the thuds she had heard earlier.

"You must stop! I'll call the authorities," Miriam cried, backing toward the door. One of the women, a plump brunette named Hana, blocked her path.

"You'll call no one," she said, her voice low and threatening. "If you do, you'll get what she's getting." She jerked her thumb at Gerda. "This big piece of trash, she was a *kapo!* A *kapo!* Were you in the camps?" Miriam shook her head. "A *kapo*," repeated Hana. "A commandant, a collaborator."

With each word, Esther hit Gerda with renewed vigor as the other two watched, smirking. Occasionally, one or the other would administer a cruel pinch. Gerda cried silently, large tears that streaked her face and stained her cloth gag.

"She tortured us," continued Hana. "We were all together in Plaszow concentration camp, near Cracow. She was our block commandant. A Jew, one of our own, right? But oh, how she enjoyed kicking us, punching us with her big fists. Like hammers they were, right, Esther?"

Esther nodded, put down the slipper, and punched Gerda full in the face. Her head hit the pipe with a loud crack and fell forward.

"Stop!" cried Miriam. "You're killing her!"

"Hah!" spat Esther. "It'll take more than this to kill a horse like that." She drew some water from the tap and splashed it in Gerda's face. "Up! Get up, you swine!" Slowly, she began untying the bonds that strapped Gerda's large reddened hands. Finally, she stripped away the gag. Gerda stood before her captors, her broad frame bent and cowering. Then, with a swift jerk of her arm, she flung Esther sideways and burst from the room. Esther, Hana, and the other two women began scrubbing their hands with soap, as if they had touched some loathsome object. "Don't you dare tell," Hana warned as Miriam retreated through the doorway.

Back in their room, Rebecca slept, her lips curled in a thin smile, oblivious to what had transpired. Gerda was not seen again for the remainder of the voyage. It was rumored that she had gotten a job in the kitchen, but no one could be certain.

After more than two weeks aboard ship, Isaac finally recovered from his seasickness and began to enjoy walking about on deck with Miriam and Rebecca at his side. He was noticeably proud of his beautiful wife, whose bright hair and vibrant complexion were enhanced by the salty sea air. He was also violently jealous of the admiring glances she attracted from the crew members and male passengers, insisting that she hold on to his arm at all times and scowling fiercely if anyone smiled in her direction.

"It's not me they're looking at," Miriam contended, trying to placate him. "It's Rebecca, she's so pretty."

"Achh," Isaac would grumble, waving his hand angrily. "Rebecca, Rebecca." With the child he had little patience. Never having had children of his own, he was ill at ease with his stepdaughter, and his frayed nerves could tolerate neither her childish mischief nor her high-spirited prattle. Often he declared that she was spoiled and needed more discipline. Sometimes, when her squeals and shouts were too loud for him to bear, he shouted at her to be still, waggling a finger in her face. Immediately, she would scream and cry, hiding behind her mother's skirt. Then Isaac would be filled with remorse, stalking the deck in tight-lipped silence, his hands clenched behind his back. Later, he would attempt to buy back the child's affection with chocolate or chewing gum, which were sold in the ship's canteen.

Miriam told herself that Isaac would be much better once they were off the boat and living in their own apartment. She recalled the first three months of their marriage, before they had set sail for America. They had lived in a one-room apartment in Warsaw. Isaac rarely shouted at Rebecca in those days. Then again, he had hardly been home, spending his days working at the Joint Distribution Committee and falling into an exhausted sleep right after dinner most evenings. Miriam pictured their cluttered room, the cramped bed they shared, with the frayed curtain she had hung around it for privacy. Not that there was much need for that. Because of his weakened physical condition, their lovemaking had been infrequent and unsatisfying. Isaac would embrace her wordlessly. With a few brief thrusts it was soon over, and he would roll off with a sigh and turn away. Within moments, he was snoring. Miriam wondered if that, too, would change once they were settled. Not that it mattered, one way or the other. She knew it was unfair to compare him to Reuben. It was not his fault that the concentration camp had destroyed his youth and laid waste to his body. Yet she also knew that even before the war, Isaac had not been the type of man who could arouse her physically. When she thought of Reuben, with his tall, strong body and broad shoulders…But what was the use? Reuben was dead. Never again would she lie in his arms.

On the last night of their voyage, Miriam could not sleep. Tossing in her bunk, listening to Rebecca's quiet breathing, she was tormented by fears and anxieties. It was one thing to be a passenger on a ship, warm and snug, rocked by the waves, with no more responsibilities or control over one's fate than a bit of plankton floating on the sea. But once they were ashore, what then? They would begin a new life, alone and friendless in a strange country, sponsored not by relatives or even acquaintances, but by a faceless organization whose name she could not even pronounce. She knew little about their destination, only that they would be housed temporarily in a Manhattan hotel.

Isaac would have to find work. Fortunately, he knew some English, having studied it in the *gymnasium* many years ago. She herself would have to go to school, perhaps in the evenings. During the day, she, too, would find work, maybe caring for other people's children. She would bring Rebecca along, and they could all play together. Isaac had said he didn't want her to work, but even so…her thoughts drifted, forming themselves into a dream of herself standing in her old kitchen in Dubnitz, helping her mother bake poppy-seed cookies for the *Purim* holiday.

"Miriam! Mrs. Fink, wake up!" Someone was shaking her by the shoulder.

"What is it?" Miriam was awake instantly, her stomach clenched in fear. Had something happened to Rebecca, or to Isaac?

Her roommate, Freda Klein, stood over her. "Land!" she exclaimed. "We've spotted the shoreline! You must go up and see. Everyone is coming up." She turned and raced from the room.

Miriam scrambled from the bed, threw on an old cotton dress and her faded woolen jacket, and bent over Rebecca. Awakened by the noise, the child stared at her mother with wide, frightened eyes.

"Come, Rebecca." Miriam wrapped the blankets around her daughter and lifted her from the bed. "Come, we're going to see America."

The deck was crowded with people straining against the rail. Some had stayed up all night, while others, like Miriam, had crawled from their warm beds and now stood shivering in the semi-darkness. Eagerly, they tried to make sense of the gray, inchoate shapes that were massing along the horizon. The ship's lamps made broad paths of golden light that broke up and reconverged on the water's churning surface.

"Look!" someone shouted. All heads turned in the direction of his pointing finger. Off in the distance, the clouds had momentarily lifted. Miriam stared, a sob of wonder forming in her throat. Out of the water rose a huge colossus, a statue of mammoth yet graceful and womanly proportions. Her upraised arm held a gigantic torch, from whose windows streamed beacons of light that illuminated the predawn sky and shone down on the water below. On her head was a crown whose long, pointed spikes radiated outward.

"Mama!" shrieked Rebecca. "It's the queen! It's the queen of America!"

So this is it, thought Miriam. This is she, the famous Statue of Liberty that she had learned about in school. This is the majestic lady whose torch lit up a path for every immigrant, every refugee who, like herself, made his or her way to this new and alien land that promised freedom, freedom to piece together the charred and twisted fragments of their ruined lives and start anew.

Miriam squeezed Rebecca tightly and kissed her forehead. "Yes, darling, this is the queen of America."

Part Three

Chapter twenty-one

R*euben* Zwillinger pulled the wool cap down on his head

Kiev, Russia, 1945

and turned up the collar of his greatcoat, but this did little to protect
him from the damp November chill that penetrated through to his
very bones. He had been standing in the same spot for half an hour
and his shoes were soaked through. Yet he continued to stare at the
somber gray building, examining every inch of its familiar façade, as
if the worn stones could give him an answer, or even a clue toward
solving his problem. Besides, where could he go? He had come, once
again, to a dead end. From here there was nothing left to do but return
to his room, a small bare cubicle that contained a bed, a chair, a pile
of books, and little else. He had no desire to go back there.

In the dim lamplight he allowed his thoughts to drift, carrying him back over these past miserable weeks, to the day when he
had learned that Miriam, his beloved wife, was dead. That insolent
peasant girl with the pock-marked face had been the first to tell him.
"Dead," she had said, shrugging her bony shoulders. "Dead," she had
repeated, taunting him with the flatness of her voice, the mockery
in her cold blue eyes.

At first he had refused to accept it, just as he could not accept the death of his son, his own little David. But the other villagers had repeated the tale; several stepped forward to affirm that, indeed, they had seen it for themselves. Miriam, the rabbi's daughter, they all knew her. Of course it was she, her flaming red hair had blown about her head as she was shot by the German soldiers; she had fallen head-first into the pit.

"There," said the toothless gnome of a man who led him to Pan Vorny's meadow on the outskirts of Dubnitz, the little village of Miriam's birth. "There," he rasped, pointing out over the vast, grassy mound. Reuben had waited alone, long after the man had hobbled away.

In the fading twilight he stood atop the field that had once belonged to Pan Vorny and tried to say the *Kaddish*, the Memorial Prayer, for Miriam, for her family, for all the Jews of Dubnitz, so brutally slain by the Nazis. But the ancient Aramaic words died on his lips. And so he had left Poland forever, returning to Kiev to resume his quest for his son, David, whom he had been told had died three years before.

As opposed to the story of Miriam's death, there were no eye-witnesses to testify to David's last days, no one to say they had seen the child sicken and finally succumb to scarlet fever. Dr. Zamirefsky at Kiev General Hospital had been most sympathetic. Of course he remembered David, the child who'd had the miraculous recovery from a head wound sustained in a fall, was it already four years ago? Little David Zwillinger, who had emerged from a coma crying out, not for his Mama or Papa, but for his hobbyhorse? It had been the talk of the hospital. And then, what a tragedy when the letter came, informing them of the child's death. The doctor sighed and folded his hands. Dr. Karnoshvili, the physician who had saved David's life after the fall? No longer with the hospital. No, he had no idea where he could be found. Perhaps in the Records Department they might know something.

From that point, it had been a wild goose chase. The woman in the records office scrutinized him with eyes that wordlessly told him her opinion of Jews, insisting again and again, "No, we have no idea where Dr. Karnoshvili has gone. He left the hospital years ago, the records were lost. No, we have no letter from the Federenkos, or anyone else for that matter, regarding the death of David Zwillinger. Our files on David Zwillinger end in August 1941, when he was discharged to the custody of his father, Reuben Zwillinger. Dr. Raber, the previous administrator, might have known something, but he died of a heart attack just last month. Too bad. We cannot help you."

As for tracing the Federenkos, that had been nothing more than an exercise in frustration and bitter disappointment. His kind friends, Yuri and Galina Federenko, who had cared for David while Reuben was interned in Siberia, had left the apartment three years ago. Those few neighbors who knew them had no idea where they had gone. And then, suddenly, a ray of hope. A child playing in the courtyard remembered David. "Moscow," he answered. "He took my ball, that David. If you see him, tell him Vladek still wants his ball back."

Now, two weeks later, Reuben had returned, exhausted and broken in body and spirit. For days on end he had sat in innumerable Moscow offices, and had waited in queues in one ministry after another. Finally, in a last, desperate effort, he had walked the boulevards and side streets of Moscow, scouring the city for any sign, any trace of the Federenkos, only to be told, time and again, that he had come to the wrong place.

The sky grew darker and an icy rain began falling. Reuben gave one last look at the building. Inside was the Federenko's apartment, where he had rented a tiny alcove while David lay in the hospital, recovering from his fall. Reuben's thoughts raced back to that terrible day—May 1, 1941. The May Day parade had been scheduled for that morning and he had been forced to march, along with his father-in-law, the Dubnitzer *Rebbe*. Only moments after passing the house he shared with his in-laws, he had been summoned by a frantic group of Hasidim. Little David had fallen from the attic window, fracturing his skull on the stones below. He had apparently climbed up on a chair and leaned out to watch as his Papa marched by. The Dubnitz doctors, limited by lack of knowledge and supplies, recommended that the child be brought to Kiev for treatment. And so he had kissed his pregnant wife goodbye and traveled eastward, his unconscious boy wrapped in his arms.

He pictured Miriam's lovely face as she stood at the railway station, her large green eyes filled with worry. Before boarding the train, he had kissed her, promising that David would get better, and that they would soon return. Miraculously, David had recovered, but was not yet strong enough to travel when Reuben first tried to return to Dubnitz, in the hope of bringing Miriam back. Reuben did not reach Dubnitz. Instead, he was seized as he tried to cross the Polish border. Accused of being a "Nazi Collaborator," he was sent to Siberia. There he remained, barely surviving, while Dubnitz had gone up in flames. And Miriam? Again he heard the voice of the peasant girl: "Her? Oh, she's dead. She was shot and burned with the others. I saw it myself."

Reuben raised his eyes to the windows of what had been the Federenko's apartment. Here he had spent so many happy hours, talking with Yuri and Galina Federenko until the wee hours of the morning, sleeping in the cramped alcove off their kitchen. Yuri had helped him find work in a book depository, classifying and cataloguing hundreds of volumes of Russian literature. What little he had earned helped pay for his bed and his meals at the Federenko's kitchen table. During David's convalescence, they had given Reuben hope for his recovery, and later, when David was discharged from the hospital, they had insisted that Reuben and David stay on with them. When Reuben had left for Poland for the first time, he had felt no qualms about leaving David with the Federenkos, who had no children of their own. Galina's elderly mother, who doted on the child, promised to look after him like her own, while Galina and Yuri worked. Then, when Reuben was arrested, he had managed to get word to them and Yuri had visited him in the dank confines of the Kiev Prison. Kneeling on the grimy stone floor, his earnest, homely face pressed against the bars, Yuri repeated his promise again and again: "We will care for the child. I promise you, Reuben, he will be like our own son."

Through all the terrible years in Siberia, Yuri's promise had sustained Reuben, warming his soul as he pulled potatoes from the frozen ground with bleeding, frostbitten fingers. The knowledge that David was safe and well cared for gave him the strength to keep working, to go on from one day of mind-numbing toil to the next. Night after night, as he lay shivering on his rank straw mattress, he dreamed of his return to Kiev, where he would reclaim David. Together, father and son would travel to Poland, there to be reunited with Miriam, and with the baby he had never seen. And so he had counted off the freezing days and endless, bitter nights, finally returning to find that all of his dreams had turned to ashes. Reuben sighed, shook his head, and started walking up the street.

"Mr. Reuben!" He felt a tug at his sleeve and turned. Staring up at him was a stout young woman, her head and shoulders shrouded in a heavy woolen shawl. "Mr. Reuben, it's you, isn't it? Don't you remember me?" The woman smiled and lowered her shawl somewhat, allowing him to see her face more clearly. It was a plump round face with glowing red cheeks, small black eyes, and an upturned nose.

"Yes, of course I remember you, Nelya, isn't it?"

The woman gave a shriek of laughter. "Nelya? Not Nelya. Yelena, my name is Yelena."

"Oh yes, forgive me. Yelena." Reuben nodded. Although he had forgotten her name, he remembered her very well, and could barely believe his good fortune in seeing her before him. Yelena, a sturdy young woman of peasant background, had worked as a janitor in the building where Reuben had lived with the Federenkos. To earn extra money she often spent her evenings in the Federenko's apartment cleaning and doing the laundry, as Galina Federenko was not a strong woman, and her mother suffered from arthritis. Yelena had always acted like a silly schoolgirl with Reuben, blushing and giggling whenever he addressed her. If, in exchanging pleasantries with her, he made some small joke, she would cover her mouth with her hand and whoop with laughter, her cheeks blazing.

"A real peasant," Yuri would mutter. "Better watch out, Zwillinger, I think she's in love with you." Making sure the women were out of earshot, he would sometimes add, "Why not, she's a tasty morsel, I'll bet." Reuben would smile, but he had no interest in liasons with peasant women. He was a married man, with a beautiful wife who waited for him in Poland, or so he had thought at the time. Besides, the girl repelled him, with her raucous laughter and the warm yeasty smell she exuded as she worked. Now, however, he gazed into her eyes with such intensity that she shivered and stepped backward.

"Yelena," he said, "you must help me."

"Surely, Mr. Reuben. What is it?"

"The Federenkos. Do you know where they are?"

Yelena stared at the man. He looked so strange, standing there in the rain like that, with his coat all soaked and his hat dripping. And his eyes! When had they burned with such fire? Like those of a madman. A chill ran through her body. In the years when she had worked for the Federenkos, she had been infatuated with Mr. Reuben. He was so handsome, so educated, and had such fine manners. Never did he use coarse words with her, or make lewd remarks, as so many of her employers did. What a difference there was between Mr. Reuben and Igor, her erstwhile lover, with his leering grin and uncouth comments. Igor had promised her a wedding, and then left her with nothing but the baby now growing in her womb. Smiling to herself, she recalled how she had once stolen a shirt of Mr. Reuben's from the clothesline, hiding it under her pillow until, one day, it just disappeared. Not long after, Mr. Reuben himself had vanished. Siberia, they had said. How the little boy David had cried for his papa. She had almost felt sorry for the miserable pest. David. She remembered him with distaste, for it was he who had gotten her fired, tattling on her when she borrowed Galina's necklace. No matter. She had soon gotten another job down the street. As for the Federenkos…Yelena frowned. Not too fast, she thought. Take your time and see what this is all about. Perhaps Mr. Reuben would be willing to do something for her, to pay her for what he needed to know.

"I don't know where they are," she lied. "They moved away, years ago, after I stopped working there. Why?"

"It's very important that I find them. Do you remember David?"

"Davidchka? Of course. How could I forget him? A darling child."

"Reuben leaned towards her. "Was he with them when they moved?"

"With them? I don't know. I think perhaps he was. I'm beginning to remember something." She paused and wrapped her shawl tighter around herself. "I must go home," she continued. "It's pouring. Also, I'm starving."

"I'm terribly sorry." Taking her arm, Reuben drew her into a nearby doorway. "So rude of me, you're all wet. Perhaps we could have some coffee."

In the warm and dimly lit café around the corner, Yelena glanced about at all the customers, a smug smile on her lips. *Look at me,* she thought, *having coffee with this fine gentleman. If only one of my friends would come in right now and see.* "Just coffee please," she said haughtily when the waitress, a slight acquaintance of hers, took their order. The waitress raised an eyebrow in surprise but said nothing as she returned to the kitchen. Reuben stared at Yelena eagerly.

"You said you remembered something about the Federenkos—where they might be and whether they took my son with them."

"Yes, yes." Yelena nodded her head, "but it's all very, how do you say, not clear. You know."

"Vague," Reuben prompted.

"Yes, vague. Well, I need some time to think. It's been a few years, you know. And I've worked for many fine families since then, much finer than the Federenkos." When their coffee came Yelena sipped it slowly, extending a stubby pinkie finger as she had seen other women do. "Why do you want to find the Federenkos?" she asked.

"It's very simple. I'm trying to find David, my son. He stayed with them while I was in Siberia, but when I returned I couldn't find any trace of them. The hospital said David had died of scarlet fever while in the Federenkos' care, but they have no proof, no doctor's note, or death certificate, or anything. All they said was that Yuri Federenko had written them of this. But they couldn't even find the letter. It wasn't in their files." Reuben gave a sigh of exhaustion and despair. "I've looked everywhere. I've even searched all over Moscow, but no one knows anything. It's as if they vanished from the face of the earth." He drank his coffee and swallowed hard. "It was bad enough when I found out that my wife was dead, but my son...."

Yelena looked at his face, still handsome and distinguished despite the deep furrows that scored his cheeks and the dark shadows beneath his gray-blue eyes. Something of her old feeling for him came flooding back to her, a raw, physical attraction that caused her to squirm in her seat. Yet combined with this feeling was another sensation, even more exciting than sexual desire and which, though new to her, she recognized as *power*. She, Yelena Bosnov, a poor peasant woman from a tiny village on the banks of the Dnieper, had power over this refined and educated man, because she knew something that he would give all he had to learn. All he had. She glanced at his frayed cuffs, his threadbare jacket. What did he have, anyway? He looked as poor as she was. It's true he was a Jew and many said that the Jews had managed to hide their money before the war. Perhaps there was some secret stash, back in Poland somewhere, the family gold and silver. His dead wife's jewels? And if there weren't? She ran her hand lightly over her bulging stomach and smiled to herself.

Reuben interrupted her thoughts to ask again—"Just what is it you think you remember?"

"You know, Mr. Reuben, I work very hard all day."

"Yes, I know that."

Well, I'm very tired. I can't think straight anymore. But maybe, tomorrow evening—"

"Yes?"

"Meet me tomorrow evening, when I'm finished with my work. Eight o'clock."

"Where? Here, or outside the apartment building?"

"No, no. I will be hungry tomorrow too." She grinned slyly and licked her lips. "Meet me outside the Georgian Restaurant."

Reuben nodded. She had chosen the finest of those few good restaurants that were not destroyed during the war. Still, if she held the key to David's whereabouts he would be glad to take her anywhere.

The next evening Reuben paced back and forth in front of The Georgian, looking anxiously from the face of the heavy brass clock that hung above the door to the faces of the customers as they entered and left. Finally, a stout figure approached, carrying an umbrella. Even from a distance Reuben realized that Yelena had taken pains with her appearance. But when she reached his side he saw that the effect was ludicrous. Her thick, dark hair had been piled up on the top of her head and twisted into a large bun that resembled a round loaf of bread. She wore a quilted jacket of faded black velvet in a style that had not been seen for the last thirty years. Her skirt, of a dull green wool, bagged at the knees but was too tight around the hips, emphasizing her bulging bottom. A white blouse, adorned with yellowing lace at the collar and cuffs, completed the outfit. The first two buttons of the blouse had been left undone, to show off the cleavage of an ample bosom.

Reuben was both amused and oddly touched by her attempts at grandeur. *Poor thing,* he thought, *wearing her mistress's castoffs for a night on the town.* Once at the table his amusement turned to embarrassment as Yelena made every effort to call attention to herself, alternately laughing loudly and whispering, gesticulating flamboyantly, or simpering at him. People stared at them and he caught an occasional titter. Unimportant, he told himself. Who cares what she looks like or how she acts? What is important is that she may know where the Federenkos are. But no matter how he pressed her for information, she refused to tell him anything during the meal. "Wait, wait," she insisted, stuffing a chicken drumstick into her mouth. "Soon enough we'll talk about this. Let me enjoy my food." And she would smile and wink and take another mouthful of *verenniky.* Only after the last drop of tea had been drained from her cup did she discuss the Federenkos.

"Yes," she said. "I believe I know where they have gone."

"Where?" Reuben set down his own cup. "Tell me, please. Where are they?"

"Well, you see, after I left that job for, ah, certain reasons, my friend Violetta started to work for them. Then, when they decided to move, they took her along with them. She cooked for them because the old woman got sick, she couldn't do it anymore. You know, rheumatism, catarrh, this, that and the other. Even when I was there she already had one foot in the grave."

"Yes, but where did they move to? What city?" Reuben asked, his eyes bright with agitation and impatience.

Yelena gave a squeal of a laugh, covering her mouth. "City?" I wouldn't call it a city. Zemelyna. It's more of a village, really."

"Zemelyna? I've never heard of it. Where is it?"

"Oh, it's way out there." She waved her hand casually. "Along the Dnieper."

Reuben frowned. There was something about her story that did not ring true. Why would Yuri and Galina, a typically sophisticated urban young couple who as far as he knew had always lived in big cities, move away to some backwater place in the provinces? Then again, why would Yelena make up such a story? What did it benefit her to send him off on a wild goose chase? He had never wronged her during the time he'd lived with the Federenkos. In fact, he'd had very little to do with her, but their limited contact had always been cordial and respectful. He glanced at her as she toyed with her teacup. Perhaps she was leading him on, giving him false information in order to use him as a meal ticket. Yes, surely that was it. He was being played for a fool and had better put a stop to it now. Pushing back his chair, Reuben signaled the waitress and shook his head at Yelena.

"No, it doesn't make sense. They would never have gone to a place like that. Why are you telling me such stories? Why on earth would they move to Zemelyna, of all places?"

Yelena shrugged her shoulders. "Why? How should I know why? Did they tell me anything? They bought tickets and they went."

Reuben laughed bitterly, wagging a finger at Yelena. "Come now," he said. "What do you take me for? Do you think I was born yesterday? You have no more idea of where they are than I do. Well, your little game is over now. I hope you enjoyed your dinner."

He handed the money to the waitress and stood up.

Yelena jumped to her feet, upsetting the empty teacups and spilling a glass of water. "No, no," she sputtered. "You are mistaken. I am not lying to you. I, I…. why I'll take you there myself."

"Come outside." Reuben took her elbow and guided her past the other diners. "What do you mean?" he asked as they walked along the wide boulevard. A light snow was falling and the sidewalk was coated with a thick film of ice.

"I mean just what I said. I'll take you to Zemelyna. I've been there before, to visit a cousin. You can't go alone, in any case."

"Why not?"

Yelena slipped on a patch of ice and quickly grasped Reuben's arm for support. "They don't like strangers there. They won't help you. You'll never find the Federenkos if you go alone."

"But you said it was a small town. Surely I could find—."

"No, they won't help you. Never. You'll never find them without me."

Reuben hailed a taxi and they climbed in, brushing the snow from their clothing. In the cab, Yelena turned to him. "Look," she said. The strong scent of her musky perfume made him feel dizzy. "Maybe you don't trust me, but why would I lie to you? Think. To go to Zemelyna I must take off several days from my job. When we return, maybe someone else will be working in my place. Then how will I live? Do you think I would risk my livelihood for no reason?"

"Well then, why *are* you risking your livelihood? Why are you willing to take me to find my son? I must tell you, I have no money. I was in Siberia for four years, and now I have nothing but the salary, a pittance really, that I earn in the book depository. I cannot pay you. Tonight's dinner alone cost me more than I can afford."

Yelena shrugged. *And if he had money*, she thought, *would he tell me?* "Your money does not interest me. I am doing this because I want to help you. Because I am a kind person and I like to make people happy. I want to see you and your little boy together again, as you should be. I remember how he cried for you when you were sent away. It broke my heart." She drew a crumpled handkerchief from her pocket and dabbed at her eyes. "Listen," she demanded, as the cab stopped in front of her building. "I must tell my employers that I will be gone for a few days. It's best if I do so after work, tomorrow, so my private clients can pay me before I leave. Then, you must meet me here at eight o'clock and we'll start out."

"What, at night?"

"Yes, there's a train."

They said good night and Reuben watched as she made her way over the icy sidewalk and entered the building. All around it were the ruins of apartment houses that had been leveled during the war.

Snow was falling on the rubble, giving the piles of brick and timber a soft, otherworldly look.

The next night Yelena was waiting for him outside her building. In one hand she held a bulging parcel, wrapped in brown cloth and tied with string. On the ground at her feet was a shabby satchel. Reuben was silent as they rode the streetcar to the railroad station. Exhausted from a sleepless night and a day filled with worry, he asked himself, again and again—What am I doing? Why am I going with this woman? Doubts gnawed at him, and yet he felt impelled by some strange force to believe her, to join her. And, after all, what had he to lose? A few days work at a boring and meaningless job? The students he tutored in the evening would still be there upon his return. And if she were telling the truth, as she swore she was? He pictured his reunion with David, the child throwing himself into his arms. For hadn't Yelena assured him that the child was still alive?

The train was filled with soldiers who spread out their possessions on the seats around them and spent the first few hours of the trip engaged in loud, bawdy conversation, and quarrelsome card games. All of them appeared drunk and occasionally one would leer at Yelena and laugh lewdly when she turned her head away disdainfully. Once again she wore her velvet jacket and lace blouse, but tonight she had put on a loose and shapeless gray skirt. Taking no notice of Reuben's efforts to read his book, she chattered aimlessly about her employers, her friends and her enemies in Kiev, and especially about Alexei, her husband who had died of pneumonia in the first year of their marriage, eight years ago, leaving her a lonely widow. Oh, she had had offers, many offers, but always she refused; she had not yet found the man to replace Alexei. Whenever the train stopped, several soldiers would get off, to be replaced by families of peasants who immediately sprawled out on the seats and went to sleep. Soon, Yelena too was sleeping, her head lolling against Reuben's shoulder while soft snores escaped her parted lips. Only Reuben remained awake, staring at the grimy window. There was nothing new to see, only his own haggard face reflected back at him as the train sped through the black night.

The next morning the compartment was again filled with noise and bustle. The journey seemed endless. At each station more peasants climbed on, shouting at their children and opening up huge hampers of food, which they passed around and devoured eagerly. Yelena too, had brought food for the trip, and she watched Reuben with great satisfaction as he ate the hard-boiled eggs and spicy sausage which she proferred. Later, ignoring her ceaseless prattle, he again turned to the window, watching as the snow-covered fields, dark pine forests, and neat little villages flew by. Always on the horizon, the river crawled, a great gleaming ribbon of silver that sparkled in the sunlight. Late in the evening, Reuben leaned his head against the window and dozed.

"Mr. Reuben, wake up!" Yelena was shaking his shoulder. Slowly he opened his eyes. The train had stopped and people were gathering up their belongings. Somewhere a child was screaming.

"Where are we? Have we reached Zemelyna?" Reuben rubbed the sleep from his eyes.

"No," she giggled. "We are in Varozhni. The line ends here. We must get off." She lifted her satchel and pulled her parcel from under the seat.

Reuben came awake instantly. "What do you mean?" he demanded. "We are going to Zemelyna, not Varozhni." Still laughing, Yelena pulled at his arm.

"Come, get off. We change trains here for Zemelyna. Don't worry so. I've done it many times. I told you, I have family in Zemelyna."

The broken down ticket booth at the station looked as though it had not been in use for many years. Reuben was surprised to see a young man inside, warming his hands over a small kerosene lamp. The man looked up at them and frowned. "Yes? The train to Zemelyna? Not till seven o'clock tomorrow morning." He picked up a pearl-handled knife and carefully whittled at a piece of wood that was carved into the shape of a swan.

"Seven o'clock? What are we supposed to do until then in this godforsaken place?" asked Yelena. "We are from Kiev," she added, with a proud lift of her chin.

"There's an inn back there." The man jerked his head toward the window and turned back to his carving.

The inn consisted of three small rooms above a saloon whose tables were empty save for five or six roughly dressed men who sat silently over their vodka.

"Where is everyone?" Yelena asked the innkeeper, a dour-looking man with an eye-patch and a dirty apron.

"Too early," he responded. "Later the crowds come."

"Well, it's not too early for us. We're exhausted. We came all the way from Kiev."

After bidding good night to Yelena, Reuben entered his room. It was small and bare, but clean. Squinting in the dim gaslight, Reuben examined the sheets, then lifted them, and looked at the mattress. If there were bedbugs, he'd find out soon enough. He lay down on the bed and closed his eyes, but despite his physical exhaustion, his taut nerves would not allow him to sleep. Although he was not much of a drinker he wondered if perhaps a glass of whiskey might help calm him. Pulling on his clothes he went downstairs and downed a shot of straight vodka, then went out to the privy behind the inn. When he returned to his room it was dark as pitch. Someone had closed the curtains and blown out the lamp. Even in a place like this there are chambermaids, he reflected.

Groping in the blackness, he removed his clothes and climbed into bed. No sooner had he drifted off to sleep when he came awake with a start. Someone lay beside him in the bed, stroking his body, twining her fingers in the hair on his chest. When she saw that he was awake, she let out a low, gurgling laugh. Yelena! Reuben tried to climb off the bed, but her arms held him fast, while her heavy legs wound around his own. Panting and giggling, she caressed his body and covered his face with kisses, all the while pressing herself against him, slowly grinding her groin against his until, to his dismay, he found himself responding. Her touch burned him with a white flame that pulsated through his body. It had been so many years, he had almost forgotten what it was like to be with a woman. With a groan, he rolled over onto her, losing himself in the dark, undulating rhythm of her flesh.

In the morning Reuben awoke to find himself alone in the room. His body felt sore and there was a throbbing pain between his eyebrows. Hastily he smoothed the tangled bedclothes, as if to hide the traces of what he had done during the night. The sheets were still damp and the mingled, pungent scents of their bodies wafted up to him when he spread out the counterpane. As he stood at the washstand, peering into the cracked mirror, he pondered what had happened. It's very simple, he told himself. She is a young peasant woman, a lustful creature who wanted a man. And I, for that matter…. He sat down on the bed and shook his head. A terrible thought entered his mind. What if she became pregnant? Forget it, he admonished himself. Surely she would not risk such a thing. Besides, it won't happen again. Today we will reach Zemelyna where she will bring me to the home of the Federenkos and I will tell her thank you, goodbye, and good luck. At that point I will remove David, by force if necessary, and bring him back to Kiev to present the appropriate documents of identification to the Ministry of Displaced Persons. Then I will start a new life, together with my son.

He finished dressing and went downstairs. The saloon had been set up for breakfast and several people sat hunched over the rough plank tables, eating salted herring with their fingers. As he entered the room, he caught sight of Yelena. She was wearing a different dress, made of some shiny red cloth that looked inappropriately festive in the dull light of morning.

"So there you are, my cavalier," she chortled, waving and motioning to the seat beside her. "Come and eat and we'll be on our way. Who wants to hang around here?" She thrust a plate of rolls and herring at him and shouted at the innkeeper to bring tea.

The train, with its usual assortment of peasants and soldiers, puffed and clanked its way into the station, half an hour late. In their crowded compartment, Reuben unfolded his newspaper and tried to read, while as on the previous day, Yelena regaled him with stories about her work in Kiev, and about her childhood. Today, however, she did not talk about Alexei. Every so often she stifled a yawn and snuggled against him, sometimes giving him an intimate smile, or a wink, especially if other passengers were watching. Once she went so far as to slide her hand under the newspaper on his lap and give his thigh a not so gentle squeeze. Immediately Reuben slid away from her, but as there was very little room, he was forced to sit, cramped and cross-legged, with his shoulder pressed against the cold windowpane. Throughout the day no mention was made by either of them of the previous night's events.

It was late afternoon when the train pulled into the tiny depot of the village of Zemelyna. An icy wind blew fiercely across the pink-tinged, snow-covered plain. From the distance came the sound of bells. A *troika* approached, the black horse stamping its hooves and blowing plumes of smoke from its flaring nostrils. Yelena began haggling with the driver, shouting and cursing until a price was set. They climbed in and wrapped themselves in a coarse burlap blanket that bristled with bits of straw and horse manure. Reuben shuddered as memories of Siberia came rushing back at him. What am I doing? he asked himself, again and again. Yelena pressed her thigh against his and he felt the faint stirrings of desire. I am insane, he decided. All my suffering has destroyed my ability to think rationally. He shut his eyes and sat back, blindly allowing the *troika* to propel him onward over the frozen earth.

They stopped in front of a small, thatched cottage. "This is it," said Yelena. "Climb down." A skinny dog rushed out, growling and yapping. "Quiet Blackie." Yelena sent him scurrying with a sharp kick.

"Who lives here?" asked Reuben. Surely the Federenkos had not come to such straits.

Yelena smiled and led him to the door. "You'll see," she giggled. She turned the heavy wooden knob. The door creaked and opened into a small room, lit with a kerosene lamp. A fire burned low on the hearth. Two men sat at a scarred wooden table on which stood a bottle of vodka and an open deck of grimy playing cards. At the sound of the door, the men looked up, annoyed at the disturbance.

"Igor! Vladek!" shrieked Yelena. She rushed toward them as they rose from the table, embracing each in turn. Then, turning towards Reuben, she cried, "Mr. Reuben, don't be shy! Come in! No one will bite you!" With a snort of laughter she pointed at the two dark-haired men whose black eyes stared at Reuben from under heavy, bristling brows with a look of cold hostility.

"These are my cousins, Igor and Vladek. I told you about them on the train, remember?" Reuben did not, but nodded his head as she went on.

"They are like brothers to me, especially now that my parents are dead, right?" She grinned into Igor's face and tweaked his nose, then pulled Vladek's ear. The men smiled in embarrassment and pushed her away roughly. Igor jerked his head at Reuben.

"Who's this?"

"This?" laughed Yelena. This is my fiance, Mr. Reuben Zwillinger." She stretched out the sounds of the last name, Zevee-leen-ger. Igor frowned at the stupified figure standing near the door.

"This Jew is your fiance?"

Moving across the room so that she stood between Reuben and the door, she continued. "Yes, well, I wouldn't have chosen to marry a Jew. But what can I do? One night, when I was cleaning his apartment, he forced himself on me, and now I'm carrying his child."

Reuben stared at her in horror. "Lies," he sputtered as Igor and Vladek rose from their seats and approached him, their eyes bright with hatred, hands clenched into huge fists.

"No, don't hurt him," protested Yelena. "Anyway, it will all be all right since he's going to marry me tonight, make an honest woman of me. Aren't you, my sweetheart?" She squeezed his arm and winked. Reuben stared from Yelena's rosy, smiling face to the scowling visages of her loutish cousins. It was unbelievable, an absolute nightmare. It would have to end.

"No," he insisted, fighting to stay calm. "This is all a lie. She brought me here to find my son. She said the Federenkos were here."

"Nonsense!" burst in Yelena. "What a crazy story. Tell him, is there a Federenko family here, a young couple with a son?"

"Federenko," muttered Igor. "Only Alexander Federenko. He's 79 years old. What is this Jew babbling about?"

"Nothing of importance. The main thing is, I'm to be a bride again! Three months pregnant, but no matter. So that's why we're here, because I wanted to be married in my own village, with my darling cousins as witnesses, yes? And in my own church, just like when I married Alexei; and you be sure to tell Alexei's mother that I am married again, this time to an educated gentleman from the city. No need to mention that he's a Jew. Won't she eat out her liver over my good fortune, the old witch!" She rocked with laughter, her heavy breasts heaving. "And tell me," she went on, "how is Father Dimitri? I want him to perform the ceremony, just like before."

"Forget that," hooted Igor, showing a mouthful of blackened teeth. "Father Dimitri croaked four years ago. And as for the church, it burned down last summer. Whoever wants to pray, goes to the next village, or prays at home. For a wedding, you go to the village hall."

Disappointment clouded Yelena's face momentarily. Then brightening, she announced, "So, let it be the village hall. Religion is for peasants, right?" She nudged Reuben with her elbow and he flinched as if burned. Glancing at a carved wooden clock above the fireplace, Yelena quickly began dusting off her clothes and smoothing her hair. "Is the official still there? Yes? Let's hurry then, before the rooster flies the coop." She jerked her head in Reuben's direction and laughed.

"Don't worry," grunted Vladek. "He won't get away."

One hour later, pale and shaken, Reuben emerged from the narrow stone building that served as Zemelyna's village hall, with Yelena at his side, radiantly beaming.

"So, my darling," she exclaimed. "Now we are man and wife." She laughed and tried to put her arm through his, but he resisted. Vladek and Igor walked on either side of them, never taking their eyes off Reuben. If he were to bolt and run, he knew he would not get far with those two on his heels. Besides, where could he go, in this frozen, backwater place? And what if Yelena really knew where David was, as she swore she did, hissing at him when he refused to sign the marriage contract—"Sign it, sign it, my dear man, or you will never see your son again. I, and I alone, can bring you to him."

They returned to the house. Both the lamp and the fire were out, and a gloomy chill pervaded the room. Vladek quickly had a roaring fire going, while Igor lit the lamp. Yelena opened a cupboard and pulled out a loaf of bread and a hunk of moldy cheese. She bit off a chunk of bread and spat it out on the floor. "Ugh! Dry as dust! How can you live like this? High time you two got married and had someone cook for you." Igor shrugged his massive shoulders.

"I was married," he muttered through a mouthful of cheese.

"You married? When? To whom? Nobody tells me anything! And where is she, anyway?" Yelena glanced about the room as if expecting a woman to materialize from the rough stone walls. Igor shrugged again.

"She ran away."

"Just like that?" Vladek gave a coarse laugh and slapped Igor on the back.

"Yah!" he shouted. "Right after the wedding night! Igor was too much for her. But don't worry, Yelenichka. It won't happen to you." He pointed at the door. "I'll sleep right there tonight, by the door, so your prince won't slip away, like Lydia did."

"And where will we sleep?" Yelena asked, fluttering her eyelids in feigned modesty.

"In the back room there, behind the curtain. No window on that side, so you'll be nice and cozy."

No window, thought Reuben. No escape. Yelena shoved some bread and cheese at him, but he would not eat. Nor would he accept the fiery vodka they jestingly offered in a toast to the bride and groom. When the few cracked dishes had been put away, Yelena motioned to Reuben.

"Come," she said, pointing toward the back room. "We have to talk." Vladek and Igor had started a game of cards, passing the vodka bottle back and forth as they played.

In the back room Yelena lit a candle, dispelling the darkness somewhat, but not the cold. Pulling Reuben by the sleeve of his coat, she led him to a makeshift alcove behind a curtain. On the floor was a plank bed with a dirty straw mattress, beside which stood a rush chair, whose seat was badly in need of recaning. A few nails on the wall held several articles of clothing—a pair of greasy overalls, a woolen shirt with tattered cuffs, and, inexplicably, a silk scarf.

Yelena squatted down on the bed and patted the mattress. "Here, sit."

Reuben remained standing.

"Would you like me to bring a better chair?" Yelena asked. "This one looks like it can't hold anyone."

Reuben did not answer.

"All right, then," she snapped, her eyes flashing in the candle-light. "Don't speak, don't eat, and don't sit down. It doesn't matter. We are married in the eyes of the law, like it or not. And if you are thinking of running away, go right ahead. But, as I said before—you'll never see David again. I know exactly where he is, believe me. And I can also tell you that it would be impossible for you to find him on your own. So that's the way it is, eh, my fine husband?" She gazed at him sullenly. After a moment or two her face softened and she hoisted herself to her feet. Putting her arms around Reuben's neck, she leaned her body against his. He felt her hot breath on his cheek. "Come on," she whispered. "It's not so bad, is it? Last night you didn't think it was so bad." She snickered and licked his ear with the tip of her tongue. "I'll be a good wife to you, you'll see. I can cook, I can clean, I'm a hard worker. I'll be good to the child, too. And maybe we'll have our own child. Who knows? Come," she whispered, "Come and lie down."

Reuben shut his eyes. I am lost, he told himself, as he allowed Yelena's well-muscled arms to pull him down onto the bed. I am lost.

After three weeks of snow the streets of Leningrad were slick and treacherous. An old woman, her head bound in a colorful woolen kerchief, hobbled along slowly, holding tight to a child's hand. It was difficult for passersby to tell which one was preventing the other from falling. The child, a boy of seven, was heavily clad in a coat of dense brown fur, with a matching hat from which a few strands of red-gold hair protruded. As they approached the tall, grayish-tan apartment building, he let go of the woman's hand and walked faster, stopping momentarily to glance at the couple who stood near the door. They were strangers and so he walked past them, eager to go upstairs and eat his dinner after a long day at school. As he was about to step through the door the strange woman said something to the man, who bent down, bringing his face in line with the boy's own.

"David?" the man asked in a hoarse, quavering voice. "David Federenko?"

"Yes, I'm David," the child answered. There was something about the man's bright, burning eyes that frightened him and he moved back toward the safety of his grandmother's stout figure. Then, feeling more confident, he drew himself up to his full height. "I'm David," he repeated. "Who are you?"

Chapter twenty-two

I
Moscow, 1946

n the corner of a small parlor, behind a worn and faded velvet chair, a young boy sat huddled in a blanket, his ear pressed to the wall. He waited, his body tense with anticipation, and then relaxed, as he heard the familiar muffled sounds once again. Soft at first, then slowly rising in volume, until David no longer had to strain to hear, came the strange, sweet sounds of Mr. Bikov's violin. Every evening it was the same—trudge up the grimy stairs after a Pioneer meeting, eat a cold supper of bread and potatoes that Yelena had hastily thrown together, sometimes with a bit of stringy meat tossed in, finish the homework you started at Pioneer's before your group leader arrived, and then settle down by the wall to listen to Mr. Bikov.

"Look at him, shoved up against the wall like a mouse, like a cockroach!" Yelena mocked. "This child is not normal!"

His father was more understanding, and promised to buy him a new radio to replace the one that Yelena had flung to the floor during one of their arguments. But weeks had passed, and no new radio had appeared.

One night, Reuben took David by the hand, raising him from his corner. "Come, David, we are going to visit someone."

"Who, Papa?" David's heart soared. Perhaps they would finally go and see the Federenkos, as Papa had promised when he first took David away.

"Don't cry, David," he had said. "You will see them again. Don't worry." But many months had passed, and still they had not returned to Leningrad. When David pressed his father, he was given answers that grew ever more evasive.

Now he followed his father out into the hall, but rather than walk toward the stairs, Reuben turned right and knocked on the neighbor's door.

"What are you doing?" whispered David, anxiously. "Mr. Bikov doesn't like us. He always complains when you and Yelena…"

Slowly the door opened. A short man with a shock of thick gray hair, wearing a neat, but threadbare suit, peered at them.

"What do you want?"

Reuben put his hands on David's shoulders. "This is my son, David. He would like very much to see you play the violin, but only if it's no trouble."

At first, David only sat and listened. Occasionally Reuben went with him, but mostly he went alone. Curled on the old horsehair sofa, he would close his eyes, while the music took him far away into a land of kaleidoscopic visions. With the music streaming behind his closed lids, he could forget Yelena's harsh voice and painful slaps, the dreariness of his home, and sometimes even the terrible throb of longing in his heart for Yuri, and especially, for Galina Federenko, whom he feared he would never see again.

One warm evening in late summer, when David rose to leave, Mr. Bikov touched his shoulder. "Wait," he said. He walked into the other room and returned, carrying a small violin. "Here," he said, holding it out to David. "Play."

David shrank back. "I don't know how to play."

"Then I teach you."

Two months later, as he read the evening paper, Reuben was interrupted by a knock at the door. He opened it to find Mr. Bikov in the hallway, scratching his head and pacing in an agitated manner.

"David is not home yet. Is something wrong?" asked Reuben.

"My sister is dying. I must go to Minsk."

"I'm so sorry. Please come in." Reuben gestured toward the small room that served as their parlor and dining area. "Is there anything I can do?"

"Yes. You can register your son in the class for musically advanced children under the Moscow Conservatory. Your David has a gift."

Chapter twenty-three

B*Brooklyn, New York, 1952*

ack and forth, back and forth, went the swing, its rusting chains keeping the tempo with metallic groans. The slim child pumped her body; legs out, head back, legs in, head forward. The wind whipped her long red-brown hair across her face, and a strand of it caught on her lips. She brushed it away with her shoulder, not wanting to break the rhythm of the swing. The air was chilly, and the wind blew the leaves and candy wrappers into dust devils that whirled about the legs of the departing children. A few mothers stood near the playground gate, chattering together, laughing and gesticulating. Rebecca glanced at them, and looked away. She knew her mother would not be among them, just as she knew that her mother would soon be at the gate herself, for she never let Rebecca walk home alone. She continued swinging, occasionally glancing at the gate.

The other mothers left with their children. Some of them wheeled baby carriages, the sight of which always gave Rebecca a twinge of envy. For so many years she had begged her mother, "I want a baby sister or brother, like Joanie has, or Debbie, or Ruthie."

"Rebecca, Rebecca!"

The child stopped pumping and the swing gradually lost

momentum. Just as it was about to stop she impulsively jumped off, losing her balance and scraping her knees in the dirt.

"Rebecca!" Her mother's voice was full of anxiety as she came rushing into the playground. "Why did you do that? Why did you let yourself fall off the swing?"

She pulled the girl to her feet, brushing the dirt off her dress, examining her knees and elbows. "Did you hurt yourself?"

From somewhere behind them came a mocking voice: "Did you hoit yourself?"

Rebecca shot a quick glance backward, and turned away, her cheeks blazing. Dominick Magnavito, the fourteen-year-old Italian boy who lived upstairs, was lounging at the birdbath-shaped concrete water fountain with two of his friends. He often taunted Rebecca and the other kids in the building whose parents spoke with European accents. His own parents were American-born, and spoke a loud, casual English, the words pouring out as loosely as if the speakers were chewing gum.

Rebecca herself spoke almost the same way, flattening and nasalizing her vowels in a conscious effort to differentiate her English as much as possible from that of her parents. She was an American. Someday she would have papers to prove it, but no one would ever see them, for no one was to know that she was born "over there," on the "other side." In the old neighborhood, where she had lived between the ages of five and eight, everyone knew it, but here nobody did.

Their yellow brick apartment building smelled of mothballs, for it was late October, and everyone had begun taking their winter clothes out of the boxes and suitcases in which they had been stored. Several girls had come to school that day in lumpy, bright-colored sweaters that their grandmothers had knit for them. Rebecca's sweater came from the store. She had no grandmothers. And her mother didn't knit.

The apartment was warm, the red and white kitchen still steamy and fragrant from the vegetable soup that Miriam had cooked. Rebecca sat down at the gray and white Formica-topped table. Its cold chrome legs felt soothing against her skinned knees.

Her mother put a red place mat before her, and set down a napkin, fork, and spoon.

The soup was tasty and filling. Rebecca ate most of it, but left half an inch at the bottom of the plate. It didn't matter, because Isaac, her stepfather, wasn't home. If he were, he would have thundered, "Finish it! Why you always leave over!" He could not bear to see food left on her plate. When she was younger there would be terrible scenes over this, shouting and recriminations which invariably ended with Rebecca vomiting what little she had eaten on the kitchen floor while her tight-lipped mother held her heaving shoulders, and Isaac stormed out of the room. Now she rarely ate in front of him. Miriam served her early, before Isaac came home. Only on Friday night did they eat together and at those meals she took tiny portions and forced herself to finish.

Miriam was cleaning away the dishes when Isaac's key clicked in the door. Rebecca's stomach tensed. She gathered up her black and white copybooks and brown paper-covered texts, and went into her tiny bedroom. Large crimson roses on twisting green vines climbed the walls on paper hung by the previous tenant. Rebecca hated it, but Mommy said next year maybe they could replace it with something light—pink perhaps, or yellow. She tried to concentrate on her arithmetic homework, but it was difficult. From outside came the sounds of neighbors' radios. "Use Ajax, bumm bumm, the foaming cleanser."

Some of her neighbors had TVs, and Rebecca was occasionally allowed to go to their homes to watch. Daddy would not buy them a TV—ever, not even if he had enough money. He said TV was bad for the eyes, and that it wasted time. A child should study and learn, not watch TV or read comics, or "joke books" as he called them. Rebecca loved comic books and had dozens of them, stashed in a box under her bed. Mommy knew and didn't care. After all, Rebecca was a good student and an avid reader of books as well. She got good grades in everything except arithmetic. Frowning, she chewed on the pencil top, which had long since lost its eraser. "Bring down the zero, carry the one…"

The muffled sounds of her parents' voices came through the

door. At least they weren't arguing. Her homework finished, she put on a white cotton nightgown made silky soft by many washings, and reached above her bed to her bookshelf, bringing down *Chester, the Golden Stallion.*

Anabelle raced through the tall meadow grass as the hailstones pelted her all over.

'Chester! Chester!' she shouted. In the distance she saw him, galloping with a wild grace, heading toward the gate, his golden flanks glistening…'

Rebecca loved books about horses and dogs, and about children who lived in the country. For years her favorite book had been *Rebecca of Sunnybrook Farm.* How amazing and wonderful that an American girl on a farm was also named Rebecca! It was because of that book that she forbade her mother to call her Rivkeh anymore, at least not in public. Rebecca with her mother's guttural "r" was bad enough, but Rivkeh was too much to bear. She read until she grew sleepy, then put on a flannel robe and went into the kitchen to say goodnight to her mother and stepfather.

Isaac Fink sat at the kitchen table, hunched over the newspaper. Miriam sat at the other end of the table, letting down a hem on one of Rebecca's winter skirts. The radio played faintly in the background, soft, nondescript music interspersed with static. Isaac looked up at Rebecca.

"Did you finish your lessons?"

"Yes."

"Um." He went back to his reading.

"Goodnight, Daddy."

"Goodnight."

"Goodnight, Mommy."

Miriam bent down as the child kissed her cheek, then returned the kiss. "Goodnight, my *Shain Kind,* my pretty child."

Rebecca went into her room, wiped the kiss off her cheek with the back of her sleeve, removed her robe and crawled under the covers. "Please don't let them fight," she prayed, staring into the dark, listening to the muted TV, radio, and human sounds that surrounded her, until she fell asleep. Sometime later, she awoke, a sickening spasm gripping her. Their voices came through the wall, her mother's high and strident, her stepfather's deep and rumbling. Fragments of Yiddish words came through, then whole sentences as their voices rose in volume.

"Yah, you suffered! Sure, you know all about suffering! Safety, shelter, food you had! Suffering you say? If you knew what I went through, what Bella went through!"

"Isaac, please, the child…"

"The child! The child! Always the child!"

Rebecca squeezed her eyes shut and pulled the covers over her head. When she could no longer hear their words she began to relax, and to conjure up her own secret world. Once, years ago, she had lived on a farm in Poland. It was during the war, she and her mother had been hiding there. Her mother had told her about it, and she could still remember bits of it too. There had been cows, other children, and another woman, soft and gentle, who never spoke. She could barely picture it, but the idea of herself on a farm made her feel more American, for it gave her a sense of kinship to the blonde children in the books she read, girls with names like Anabelle, or Betsy, or Mary Ellen; boys named Timothy or Christopher. In her secret world, she was like them, only she was not over there in Poland but here in America, somewhere in the Midwest, or even the Far West, where there were lots of horses. She lived in a big rambling house, not a cramped apartment, and she had an American mother who smiled a lot and spoke without an accent, and a tall, strong, real father who loved her. She also had a baby sister named Amanda, with straight blonde hair, and a big shaggy dog named Bones. She went to a public school on a yellow bus that rode past beautiful woods and farmland. Soon it became too hot under the covers, and Rebecca cautiously peered out. Silence. Thank God. She lay back on her pillow and continued dreaming about her secret world until she fell asleep.

After school, in nice weather, Rebecca would go to the playground, and her mother would meet her there on her way home from her job in Greenberg's Bakery. When it rained or was too cold,

Rebecca walked from school to the bakery, where she did her home-work in the steamy back room, feasting on a pink-frosted cupcake or a still-warm poppy-seed roll. Sometimes her mother would give her the best treat of all, a charlotte-rousse. This was a delectable concoction made of a disk of yellow sponge cake in a cylinder of scalloped, white cardboard, topped with a swirl of whipped cream and half of a maraschino cherry. These delicacies could only be had when the boss wasn't there, for Miriam was very concerned that she not be accused of taking advantage. Mr. Greenberg was not overly generous with his help.

Once Rebecca had asked her mother, "Do you like working in the bakery?"

"No, darling. I really don't, truthfully."

"So why do you do it?"

"We need the money."

"Why don't you get a different job?"

"I have always worked in bakeries. In Warsaw we had a book-store, but my English isn't good enough for that here. I have no other experience, except farm-work."

Farm-work. Sometimes Rebecca dreamed of her mother and herself leaving Isaac far behind, going off to mid-America and finding work on a farm. Once she had even broached the subject. Her mother had laughed, dismissing the idea with a wave of her hand.

When they first moved to 49th Street Rebecca became friendly with some of the other children in the building. But because they all went to public school, while she went to *yeshiva*, their after-school paths soon diverged. On Sundays, they, like Rebecca's classmates, often went away to visit grandparents, aunts, uncles, and cousins. Rebecca had no relatives. Once, in fourth grade, Mrs. Castle had assigned them a composition, "My Favorite Relative." Rebecca had promptly invented a cousin, Brenda, who had blonde hair and blue eyes and lived on a farm in Pennsylvania, which Rebecca thought was just near enough to visit but far enough to be "real" country.

Rebecca spent most of her Sundays at home, curled up on her bed, reading. Sometimes she dropped a pink Spalding ball into the toe of a cable-stitched, winter stocking and went downstairs to the courtyard of the building where she would toss the stockinged ball against the wall and catch it as it swung back, chanting to the rhythm—

"Hello, Hello, Hello Sir;
Meet me at the gro-cer,
No Sir
Why Sir?
Because I have a cold, Sir,
Where'd you get the cold Sir?
At the North Pole Sir…"

Occasionally, Ramona Magnavito, Dominick's younger sister, would join her in another ball game. The girls would bounce the ball on the ground to an alphabetical chant, lifting one leg over the ball whenever they said a word with the appropriate letter:

"One day just as I was about to approach my apartment on Avenue A in America I met my Aunt Alice.
Better buy Bond's Bread because Bond's Bread builds better bones.
Can or can't you cook that Chinese Chicken Chow Mein like Cathy can?…"

When Rebecca graduated from Bais Yehudis Elementary School she won two awards—one for "Excellence in Expressive Writing," and the other for "Excellence in Hebrew Studies." As they were leaving the auditorium after the graduation ceremony, Miriam opened her white wicker pocketbook and withdrew a slim black box, which she handed to Rebecca.

"Here, Rebecca. A little present from Daddy and me."

Rebecca opened the box. Inside was a delicate gold chain bracelet, upon which hung a tiny gold heart. Her first real piece of jewelry, not like the string of fake pearls she had bought herself in Woolworth's two years before.

"It's beautiful. Thank you, Ma, thanks Dad." Her throat felt swollen with emotion and embarrassment, she could barely get the words out. She put the bracelet on, glad to have something to do to break the tension. In her stepfather's presence, she always found it difficult to display emotions such as love or gratitude. He was always so formal, so unreachable, and his stiffness with her had increased as she grew older, so that now there seemed to be an impermeable wall separating him from her. He had never been like a real father to her, had never hugged and kissed her, bounced her on his knee, or given her piggy-back rides. He had never even asked Miriam to change Rebecca's last name from Zwillinger to his own, Fink.

When they returned home, Rebecca went straight into her bedroom and turned on the lamp. Stretching out her wrist, she admired the way the links in the bracelet caught and refracted the yellow light. She held the little heart charm up to her face and saw her own eye reflected in it. Looking up, she studied herself in the round mirror that hung over her desk. Oval face, reddish brown hair worn in a page boy cut, with bangs cut straight across her forehead, stopping half an inch above delicately arched eyebrows. The arches were slightly uneven, the left higher than the right. Rebecca needed more practice with the tweezers that she had used for the first time the night before last. The eyes, large and blue-green, her best feature. Everyone told her so. Then the nose, straight, thank goodness, but a bit too long in her estimation. Then her mouth. She frowned, pursed her lips, smirked, then smiled, showing all of her teeth. Her mouth was okay, she decided.

Her mother tapped lightly on the door. "Rebecca, you want to go down for a walk?"

"Soon, Ma."

Her stepfather must have gone to bed. He didn't enjoy strolling on the streets at night, as Miriam and her daughter did.

Rebecca stood up and surveyed herself one more time. Her graduation dress was tastefully simple; white cotton, with a pale pink ribbon at the waist and a few pink roses embroidered at the shoulder. It flattered her slim figure, making her look more buxom than she actually was. She and her mother had taken the subway downtown to buy it, and it cost more than any dress she'd ever had. She reached behind her back, unzipped the dress and stepped out of it, replacing it with a striped cotton sundress that tied at the shoulders. She hung the dress in the closet, then changed her mind and lay it down on the bed. Mommy would wash it in cold water, and iron it, and then it would be put away in the closet. When would she wear it again? Maybe on the High Holidays. Exchanging her white flat pumps for a pair of multicolored striped sandals, she left the room. Her mother waited in the kitchen. A small pyramid of brown and black balled-up socks was on the table. Next to it was a bunch of odd socks, the blacks and browns separate from one another. Miriam held up one hand, which wore a brown sock, and pulled a needle through its toe.

"Oh Ma, I thought you wanted to go downstairs."

"I do, sweetheart. Okay, I'm finished for now. I'll do the rest tomorrow." She bit off the thread, stuck the needle into the pin-cushion, and swept the odd socks off the table into a small wicker basket.

They walked outside, nodding to the neighbors in the courtyard. Although it was nine thirty in the evening, it was still uncomfortably warm. The moist air clung to the buildings and formed dim halos around the street lamps. Insects of every size and description flitted about the lamps, their wings incandescent. The streets were filled with people, sitting on chairs alongside the buildings, or strolling up and down the main thoroughfare looking into the lit-up windows of the closed shops. Those lucky enough to own fans sat indoors, but many came downstairs at night, to escape their hot, often cramped apartments. Nearly every corner held a cluster of teenagers; girls in shorts and halter-tops, with hair falling in waves to their shoulders and shiny, red-lipsticked mouths. The boys wore tight cotton slacks and bright colored shirts. They all leaned against the walls of the buildings, smoking, laughing, and flirting. Rebecca stared at them with longing. Those were the kids from Roosevelt High. Just like the kids in the Archie comic books, these boys and girls hung out together, having fun. She herself had never had a boyfriend, unless you counted Patrick Ferguson, back when she was nine.

"Look darling." Miriam pointed toward a dimly lit shop window, "Such a pretty dress, the sailor one there. It would look so nice on you. Maybe tomorrow you come meet me after work, and we'll go have a look"

It was a cute dress, white cotton with short sleeves and a navy sailor collar and tie. "Sure, Ma, thanks."

Rebecca loved clothes. She had long since resigned herself to her inability to compete with many of her classmates in this regard, but lately her mother had been buying her more new dresses, and spending more on each one, than she had in the past. She wondered why, but certainly had no intention of questioning it. Maybe Mommy had gotten a raise at the bakery? Doubtful. She would have mentioned it. And surely Isaac wasn't earning more. If anything, he was making less now than before, having recently lost his job at the factory where he had worked for the last six years. Instead of rising through the ranks, he had been pushed out by one of the partners, with whom he'd had an ongoing enmity.

Now he had started a new position, which Rebecca suspected paid less than his old one. He came home every evening exhausted, his face pale and drawn. After a light supper he went to bed early, often waking up in the middle of the night because of nightmares or stomach pains, which had returned to plague him after a respite of eight years. The lack of sleep and the frustrations of his new job combined to make him more irritable and short tempered than usual. He railed against everything; his job, his co-workers, the "Jewish anti-Semite" partner who had fired him, and the political situation. The last few years of McCarthyism terrified him, reminding him of Hitler. He had good days when he was calm and quiet, like today, but the bad days outnumbered these by far.

Rebecca had always avoided him but now she found that her mother also seemed only too happy to get out of the house whenever she could, even when he was awake. Late at night, after his screams or groans woke them, she could hear their voices. Her mother's tones would be soft and soothing. Then there would be the sounds of Miriam's footsteps, the running of the faucet, the metallic clang of the teakettle, and the rattle of cup and spoon. Did her mother love Isaac? She could never bring herself to ask.

They walked on, turning up a quiet street of small private

homes made of clapboard, with closed front porches and overhanging, shingled roofs, all built with a vague resemblance to a style Rebecca later learned was Dutch Colonial. They came to their favorite spot, a house whose ground floor had been converted to a dentist's office. The people who lived upstairs were away for the summer. In front of the house, under a leafy sycamore, was a wooden bench. Here they sat, shielded from the street, in darkness and privacy, barely able to see each other. Here was where they talked about things they didn't discuss when Isaac was around.

"Mommy, tell me about Dina."

"Dina. Ah, Dina was a darling girl. Just like you." She reached out and fingered a lock of Rebecca's dark hair.

"But tell me a story about her. You know, something that happened."

Miriam sat back and sighed. The pain she felt when speaking of her family had dulled over the years, and now, when she spoke about them to her daughter, she felt an inner peace. It was the best way she had of keeping their memories alive. Even so, there were things she could never discuss, not even with her daughter. She never described to her the events of her family's death; of seeing Shloimeh and Dina shot down in the street, nor of her niece and nephew left to die in the flames of their burning home. She never discussed what happened in Pan Vorny's meadow, nor her own escape, only that her parents had died, and that she had been spared. And while she had at times described Reuben to Rebecca, she could never mention her little David without tears overflowing into her throat, choking off further attempts at speech.

"Dina," Miriam began, "was full of life, always laughing and joking. At your age she was already worried about who her husband would be. And she was full of mischief. One time when she was maybe ten or eleven years old, she borrowed clothes from the brother of her friend; you should have seen her! Black hat, coat, knee pants and white socks, and she let out her hair like *payes*, you know, by the ears. So like this she went and sat in the study house, swaying her body over a book. Nobody paid much attention at first. Then Feivel, the *gabbai* recognized her. He whispered to our *Tateh* who came over and said,

'What does it say in the Bible, young fellow, about the clothes of a female?' Of course, Dina didn't say a word. So he shouted at her. 'A man may not dress in the clothes of a woman, nor a woman in the clothes of a man!'"

"And what did she say, Ma?"

"She said, 'What about a child?' Well, he couldn't answer so fast. And she jumped up and ran out of the *Beis Medrash. Tati* was angry for a little, but not much. He knew she was only joking."

Rebecca smiled, a pale crescent in the darkness. "Tell me about Shloimeh," she begged.

"Ah Shloimeh, he was the biggest mischief-maker of all. Until later, until the Nazis…" her voice trailed off, then picked up again. "Anyway, once, it happened on a *Shabbes* in the spring, the men were in *shul* for the afternoon, for the *Mincha* Service. It was hot, and they used to hang up their fur hats, their *shtraimlach*, on hooks on the wall, in the hallway. Everyone had his own hook. And they would daven in their skullcaps, their yarmulkas, and later everyone put his *shtraimel* back on.

"So one day Shloimeh, he was maybe six years old or so, decided to conduct an experiment. He climbed on a chair, and took down all the *shtraimlach*, and mixed them all up, and hung them up again. Well, when *shul* ended, what confusion! Nobody could find his *shtraimel*. It took them hours to find them."

"Was Shloimeh punished?"

"This I don't remember."

Rebecca began to feel anxious. She scratched a mosquito bite, shifted on the bench, crossed and uncrossed her legs. There were so many questions she wanted to ask, about the war, about her father, her brother David, their life in Warsaw. Also about her own early years; about the farm in Poland, which she could remember only as a series of blurry pictures like old photographs, and wasn't even sure if they were real or imagined. But, in the past, when she had tried, her mother's face would close off and her eyes would go flat and distant, or even worse, fill with tears. Some things her mother talked about happily—her childhood, and the years she spent on the estate of

Fyedritski during the war. But then the wall would come down, and the discussion would be over.

With her stepfather it was different. He often discussed the camps, usually as a means of reproach. "You think you have a problem?" he'd ask, when she complained of some worry or slight by a classmate, "You don't know what a problem is. A problem is to have no clothes in winter, no food…" Rebecca did not want to hear about the camps anymore. When Isaac talked about them her stomach clenched in upon itself and she had to leave the room. If only her mother would talk more, and he less.

"*Nu*, lets go home." Tension had settled over them like the night's hot moisture. They both rose and walked back up the tree-lined street to the avenue, where the stores and people were. They turned up their corner, past Eddie's candy store where boys harmonized together in slightly flat voices:

"Life would be a dream
If I could take you up
In Paradise up above
And tell me honey I'm the
Only one that you love
Life would be a dream, sweetheart,
Sh'boom Sh'boom, Sh badada dada dadada."

The voices trailed after Rebecca and Miriam as they entered their courtyard. The neighbors had folded their chairs and dispersed, leaving only the aged Mrs. Schneider, who grunted at them and continued staring off at the darkened houses across the street.

Chapter twenty-four

The summer of 1955 broke records for heat and humidity. Seated on one of the yellow wicker benches of the BMT, which always reminded her of giant, flattened ears of corn, Miriam wiped her forehead delicately with a lace handkerchief. The pale-haired girl in the advertisement above the window grinned at her coyly.

Meet Miss Subway
    Lissome Caroline Butkowsky, who hails from Bushwick, Brooklyn, is a secretary for the Bender Trading Company.
    In her spare time she enjoys cooking, roller skating, and listening to…

The train screeched to a halt and Miriam looked out at the sign on the platform. It was not her station. She still had several stops to pass before she reached De Kalb Avenue, where the department stores were. Watching the dark-brown blades of the ceiling fan turn ineffectually, she sighed. If only she had found a dress in her own neighborhood. She hated riding the subway, with its crowds of irritable passengers, its unearthly noises, and its peculiar smell, a mixture of sweat, dust, and juicy-fruit gum. But the local stores were so expensive, and the dresses they carried were too frilly and overdone for her taste. For the wedding of her boss' daughter, Shifra, Miriam wanted something tailored and sedate, appropriate to a very Orthodox affair.

Several people stood on the platform, waiting for the doors of the train to open. One of them, a tall man with thinning blond hair and a neat gray suit, kept glancing at his watch. When the doors opened, he tightened his grip on the crutch he used and limped into the train, taking great care as he stepped off the platform and into the subway car. The moment he entered, a woman stood up and offered him her seat, but he shook his head. It was far easier to stand, leaning on his crutch and holding on to a strap with his free hand, than to ease himself into a seat and then have to get up again. Besides, he hated having to accept help from strangers. Like many amputees, he was fiercely independent. With the help of his crutch and his artificial limb, he could get around almost as well as anyone. He refused to pamper himself, preferring to take the subway, rather than taxicabs.

Adjusting his body to the movement of the train, he surveyed the passengers idly. White people, black people, Spanish people, nearly all with the same tired-looking faces, beaten down by the heat and by the monotony of their lives, exhausted already, though the day had barely begun. Only the high school students showed signs of vitality, laughing and jostling each other as they swung through the train. How he despised them, these roving packs of pimpled boys with long, greasy hair and disreputable clothes, and their sluttish girl-friends who stared cow-eyed at his crutch, or smirked at his limping walk. Sometimes, though, there was a pretty woman, like the slim redhead sitting opposite him. She appeared to be in her late thirties. Not so young anymore, he thought, but then again, neither am I. And she was certainly beautiful, with her shining auburn waves and her fine features. He had not seen her on the train before, yet she looked vaguely familiar. Feeling his eyes on her, Miriam looked up, met his gaze, and froze. Irritated by the noticeable change in Miriam's expression, the man looked away. He had seen that look before. A woman glances up at his handsome face, perhaps with interest, and then suddenly becomes aware of his handicap, with a resulting loss of expression in her face, or worse, a look filled with pity. *Well, it doesn't matter,* he thought, *I'm a married man anyhow.* His lip curled with distaste at the thought of Ingrid, his slatternly wife.

Miriam continued staring at the man. How could it be possible? Yet she was almost sure it was he—Dribber. Dribber, the Nazi monster who had murdered her family, who had burned their house with Bluma and Baruch inside, who had shot Dina and then had forced her parents, Leibel and herself to dig their own graves. Could this be Dribber? Standing before her on a New York City subway train? He was older, of course, but the years had not changed his smooth skin much, nor his even, bland features or the way his mouth had moved just now, that slight, sneering movement of his upper lip. Oh no, she could not be mistaken. Or could she? Was her imagination playing tricks on her, the way it did sometimes in a crowd of people, when for a moment she was sure she saw Dina or Shloimeh amid the sea of swirling faces, only to look again and find she was mistaken?

The train stopped and the man turned, swung his crutch forward, and limped out the door. Miriam rose from her seat but her path was blocked by an elderly woman with a huge suitcase. The doors closed before she reached them. Miriam had barely caught a glimpse of the man as he entered the stairwell when the train lurched forward and plunged, once again, into the blackness of the subway tunnel.

"What stop was that? What stop was that?" she asked the young black woman who stood beside her.

"Pacific. Next stop De Kalb."

"Thank you."

Miriam got off the train at the next stop but found she was too shaken and upset to deal with a shopping expedition. Instead, she crossed over and took the train back home. Unlike the other train, this one was empty. A terrible exhaustion overcame her and she leaned back and closed her eyes. Immediately, horrible visions appeared behind her eyelids, visions she had been struggling for years to obliterate, and her eyes flew open. She had to find him again, to make sure. Today she had not had enough time. The man had been dressed for business, most probably on his way to work. Perhaps he took the same train every day. She would have to return tomorrow, take the subway at the exact same time, sit in the same car. Which car had it been? She could not remember. No matter. She would walk through all the cars, if need be. Her mind raced furiously, making plans. She would tell Mr. Greenberg at the bakery that she couldn't work tomorrow, and maybe not even the next day, just in case she needed more time. She would claim to have some health problem, nothing serious, but one that necessitated seeing a specialist. She would make up the lost hours by working in the evenings. Isaac and Rebecca could be told that the bakery needed Miriam to work overtime, because of pressure related to Shifra Greenberg's wedding. When the train stopped at 50th Street Miriam found herself barely able to negotiate the stairs. Her knees were still trembling.

The next morning Miriam paced the elevated platform nervously. Above the station's overhanging roof the sky was glaringly white, oppresive with humidity that would not condense into rain. The train roared into the station. Miriam stepped in, glancing at her watch. It was earlier than yesterday. Perhaps he would be late, would miss this train, and be forced to take the next one? Perhaps, for some reason, he had left even earlier today, and would therefore have taken the previous train? Then again, maybe yesterday had been a fluke, a special appointment for him, not fitting into his usual, daily routine, and so she would not see him at all. As the train approached his station, Miriam scanned the crowded platform. He was not there. Then, as the doors opened, her eye caught a flash of yellow in the distance. Far down the station she saw his crutch swing forward as he entered the local train, across the platform from her own. She leaped from her seat and rushed out, barely squeezing into the local as its rubber-edged doors closed behind her. Hurriedly, she made her way through the swaying cars, holding her breath with fear as she crossed from one car into the next. One false step and you could so easily fall...

At last she saw him. He was leaning against the doors, propped up on his crutch, reading a folded newspaper. Positioning herself behind another passenger, whose large, stocky frame partially concealed her own body, Miriam studied the face of the man with the crutch. Despite the heat, a chill ran through her. Surely it was he. Surely she knew that face, the short, straight nose, the well-arched blond eyebrows. Still, she could be mistaken. There was only one way to be certain. Heart pounding, barely able to breathe, Miriam moved forward, excusing herself to the other passengers as she squeezed by, until she stood before him.

"Excuse me, please," she said, her voice hoarse with tension. "What is the time?"

The man looked up from his newspaper and eyed Miriam appraisingly. She saw a flicker of something in his gaze, amusement or interest, perhaps? He looked at his watch, then raised his pale blue eyes to meet her own.

"It's eight forty-five, Ma'am," he answered, in perfect American English, the syllables slightly softened by a Southern accent.

Chapter twenty-five

The wedding took place two days later. At the crowded, noisy reception, Isaac quickly disappeared, lost in a group of cronies from the "*shmatteh* business," as they termed the garment industry. Miriam wandered about among the guests, greeting customers whom she recognized from the bakery, and pausing at times to admire Rebecca from afar.

In her sheath dress of aqua silk, with the matching high-heeled pumps that Miriam had finally allowed her to buy, Rebecca looked older than her almost fifteen years. Her figure was filling out, growing more womanly. On several occasions lately, boys had called, their cracking adolescent voices asking for Rebecca. But Miriam would not yet permit Rebecca to date. Plenty of time for that. Turning her eyes from Rebecca, she saw once again the tall man with the dark, silver-flecked hair who leaned against the table and stared back at her, a slight smile on his lips. She had noticed him before, when they first arrived at the wedding. His eyes had met hers as she entered the reception room, and he had frowned slightly, then suddenly smiled, as if he knew her. Probably a customer, she decided, although she didn't remember ever seeing him in the bakery. Now he put down his glass and approached her, his smile broadening.

"Excuse me," he said. "I cannot help but feel that I know you from somewhere. Are you a relative of the bride?"

"No, and not of the groom either. I work at the Greenberg's bakery. Perhaps you've seen me there?"

"No, I'm sure I haven't. I don't live so close to the bakery, so I don't shop there." He studied her face with an intensity that Miriam found disconcerting. Clearing his throat, he asked, "Would you mind telling me your name?"

"Miriam Fink."

He shook his head. "No, I don't know the name. But the face, I'm sure I know the face." He extended his hand. "By the way, my name is Mendel Baumgart."

She touched his fingers lightly. "Pleased to meet you."

He leaned forward. "Did you ever live in Warsaw or Cracow?"

"Yes, I lived in Warsaw before the war."

"Before the war…." The man repeated her words, closing his eyes and fingering his red silk tie. He was expressively dressed, in a highly styled black suit and a cream silk shirt. From his breast pocket an inch of red silk protruded. A dandy, thought Miriam. His face was handsome in the European fashion, with high cheekbones, a long straight nose, and heavy black eyebrows. He opened his eyes and frowned at her.

"I'm beginning to remember something. You worked, perhaps, in a store?"

"Yes," Miriam nodded. "A bookstore."

"A bookstore, a bookstore, of course. On Rymarska Street?"

Miriam gasped. "Yes! That's the one!"

Mr. Baumgart laughed. "I knew I remembered you. You see? And your husband, Mr. ah…"

"Zwillinger."

"Yes, Zwillinger. But," he paused, "didn't you say your name was Fink?"

"Yes. My second husband's name is Fink. My first husband died."

"Oh, I'm so very sorry." Mr. Baumgart's dark eyes filled with concern. "How did it happen?"

"It was in Siberia. He died there, I don't really know how."

"In Siberia? What year?"

"It was in 1944. In December."

"Ah, a great pity… I remember him very well, tall, thin, dark hair, spectacles, yes? And you too. Everyone talked of you, Mr. Zwillinger's beautiful wife." Miriam smiled and waved her hand derisively. Just then Isaac touched her shoulder.

"Miriam, where were you? Come, I want you to meet Fogelman."

Isaac's brown suit was rumpled and there was a stain on his tie. She had neglected to remind him to shave before they left, and now his cheeks were gray with the beginnings of stubble. Miriam looked at him and sighed. *Poor Isaac. How tired he looks,* she thought, *with those dark circles under his eyes. He looks older than his forty-eight years.* Then, remembering her manners, she said, brightly:

"Mr. Baumgart, this is my husband, Isaac Fink." The men exchanged perfunctory handshakes.

"He comes from Warsaw. He knew Reuben," she continued.

"Yes? Reuben was a good friend of mine," said Isaac. "But you, I don't remember. Did you attend the Warsaw gymnasium?"

"No. Actually I'm originally from Cracow. I came to Warsaw later, shortly before the war."

"Well, nice to meet you." Isaac took Miriam by the arm and led her away.

"Who is this man?" he asked. "I don't like him."

"But Isaac, how can you not like him? You spoke to him for two minutes, not more."

"I don't like his type and I don't like how he looks at you… I know the type, believe me." Miriam shook her head and kept silent. Isaac's jealousy was an old sore point between them.

The wedding ended at one in the morning. Miriam had to be

in early the next morning as the Greenbergs were taking the day off to recuperate.

Tired, and with beginnings of a headache, Miriam wished they had decided to close the bakery for the day. Her experience on the subway had unnerved her. Unable to speak about it with anyone, she tried to force it out of her mind, but the man's sneering face returned to her time and again, and at night her sleep was disturbed by terrifying nightmares. Now she concentrated on counting the colorful petit fours she had prepared for a synagogue luncheon. Fraydel, the Greenberg's niece who was supposed to help her today, had called in to say she wasn't coming.

The day dragged. Customers came in and exchanged a few pleasantries, complained about the heat, and left, holding their white-paper packages away from their damp bodies. By mid-afternoon, Miriam's head was pounding. The store was empty. Most everyone had bought their bread for the day, and it was too early for the neighborhood children, who usually trooped in after four to buy cupcakes and charlotte-rousses. Miriam sat down on a stool behind the counter, leaned her head back against the wall, and dozed. She barely heard the door open and close. Rousing herself with difficulty she opened her eyes and stood up.

"Hello Mrs. Fink. I happened to be in the neighborhood."

"Oh, Mr. ah—forgive me."

"Baumgart, Mendel Baumgart. I had to see a customer up the block, Levy, the jeweler. You know him?"

"No, I don't think so." He leaned his elbows on the counter and studied her face.

"Where is Greenberg?"

"They took the day off. Too exhausted after the wedding."

"And so you must work here all alone? No help?"

"The help also didn't come in."

"That's very bad. On such a hot day, too."

Miriam nodded. Baumgart himself did not appear to be affected by the heat. His gray suit was impeccable, his blue silk tie a splash of color against his neat white shirt.

"Well, Mrs. Fink," he said. "I was up all night."

"Really? But the wedding ended at one."

"Ah, not because of the wedding. I had something on my mind."

Miriam smiled to herself. She was beginning to think that Isaac was right, at least in this case. The man was probably what Rivka Greenberg called "a smoothie." Well, it was okay. She was used to being flirted with. Her years in the store had taught her how to banter with men, how to parry their suggestive remarks, how to tease without really leading them on, and how to rebuff without giving offense. "Really," she asked, looking him in the eye. "And what was on your mind?"

"Your husband."

"My husband? Isaac?"

"Not Isaac. Reuben." Miriam's smile faded from her lips.

"Reuben?" she whispered.

"Yes. When did you say he died? December of 1944, you said. In Siberia?"

"Yes."

"How do you know this?"

"The Russian authorities informed me. They sent me his papers."

"What papers?"

"His identification papers. What he had when he died, in Siberia."

"Were there witnesses to his death?"

"What? Witnesses? I don't know, I…" Miriam's legs had begun to tremble. She sat down on the stool and groped for a tissue to wipe her face.

"Mrs. Fink, I don't mean to upset you. Can I get you something, some cold water perhaps? A glass of seltzer from next door?"

She shook her head. The door opened with a bang as a boy of nine, his face grimy with mud and sweat, entered. "Gimme a thirty-five cent rye," he ordered, standing on tiptoe and thrusting four damp coins across the counter top. Miriam wrapped the bread and handed it to him. When the child left, Mr. Baumgart looked at his watch.

"I have an appointment, I cannot stay. But Mrs. Fink, I don't even know if I should tell you this, I don't know why I should upset you, but I couldn't sleep all night over this…" He paused and ran his hands through his smooth, brilliantined hair.

"Yes, go on," urged Miriam. "You must tell me. What is it?"

"Mrs. Fink, I think that your husband did not die in Siberia."

"Did not die? But the papers…"

"Papers mean nothing, Mrs. Fink. Look," He glanced again at his watch. "I must go, I am already late for my appointment." Reaching into his vest pocket, he removed a small, cream-colored card.

"Mrs. Fink, here is my card. Please call me at the second number, anytime after nine at night. I must discuss this with you."

Miriam took the card. 'M. Baumgart, Fine Jewelry.' Underneath was an address and two phone numbers. He walked to the door of the store, then turned to her abruptly. "Mrs. Fink, I believe I saw your husband, in Warsaw, in 1945." Then the door closed behind him and he was gone.

Miriam sat on the stool, her heart pounding. She wanted to run out after him, but her legs had turned to stone. With trembling fingers, she placed the card in her purse. For the rest of the day she could think of nothing else. Could it be possible that what he said was true? That he had seen Reuben in Warsaw, after the war? She herself had left, but her name, and Isaac's, had been listed with the Joint Distribution Committee. Surely Reuben could have found her through their records. If he was alive, then why hadn't he? But of course, things were so confused after the war. Names were changed, records were lost.

The moment she entered the hot, stuffy apartment she went to her dresser and opened the top drawer. Reaching under a bunch of letters, she pulled out the heavy manila envelope that contained Reuben's papers, as well as the letter she had received from Dr. Raber, the administrator of Kiev General Hospital, informing her of Reuben's death. The letter clearly stated that Reuben had died in 1944, in Siberia. His papers were all there as well, written in Russian and stamped with a government seal. His own signature was there. Her heart tightened, as it always did whenever she looked at the familiar handwriting.

At nine o'clock Isaac was still sitting in the kitchen, reading the newspaper. She could not call Baumgart with him sitting there. At nine fifteen Isaac rose and went into the bedroom. Miriam went to the phone and touched the receiver just as it began ringing. Rebecca grabbed the received from her hand.

"It's for me, Ma. Hi Leah! Did you get the red shoes?"

Miriam sighed. Rebecca could talk for hours. Perhaps she should say something, tell her she needed the phone. Her daughter would think it odd; Miriam rarely chatted on the phone at night; she did not have many friends and those she had she preferred to call in the early evening, while she was preparing dinner. Finally, at nine thirty, Rebecca hung up and went into her room to finish her homework. Miriam fished the card out of her purse and slowly dialed the number. He picked up on the fourth ring.

"Hello. Mendel Baumgart here."

"Hello. This is Mrs. Fink."

"Mrs. Fink?"

"From the bakery."

"Ah, Mrs. Fink. I think of you as Mrs. Zwillinger, actually. Unfortunately, Mrs. Fink, I cannot speak with you now. Relatives have come to visit, unexpectedly. Perhaps tomorrow…I'll tell you what, Mrs. Fink. Perhaps you can meet me for lunch tomorrow, or for coffee, and we can discuss this matter. I have to be in the neighborhood. I can come to the bakery again, or meet you at a restaurant on 13th Avenue."

The bakery. Rivka Greenberg would be back tomorrow. And as for a restaurant—no. The neighborhood was like a small town in many ways. How would it look if one of her customers happened to see her, having lunch with a strange man? People were so quick to gossip.

"I'm sorry, I can't do that. I can't talk in front of Mrs. Greenberg. It wouldn't be…You must understand. And I can't have coffee or lunch with you. Everyone knows me…."

"Well then look, Mrs. Fink. You are married again; perhaps you should forget the whole thing. After all, even if your husband is still alive, what good does this do you now? Only trouble, only trouble.

Probably I shouldn't have said anything. Well, it was nice meeting you again. Goodbye."

Miriam stood in front of the tall building, staring at the brass numbers above the door. Yes, this was the right place. The windows flanking the doorway blazed with diamonds; rings, bracelets, necklaces and earrings were arrayed on platforms of black velvet, the better to emphasize their dazzling beauty. She hoped he would keep the appointment; it had been made through his secretary. It would not be easy for her to take time off again, to go all the way into the city.

The elevator was crowded with men, many of them dressed in hasidic garb. Baumgart had worn a skullcap at the wedding, but at the bakery his head had been uncovered, she mused. The office was on the fifth floor. She opened the door and found herself in a small room, its walls painted a drab brown. Behind a desk sat an equally drab young woman, with stringy hair and a bad complexion. She looked up from her typewriter.

"Yes?"

"I'm Mrs. Fink. I have an appointment."

"Okay. Go right in."

Mr. Baumgart stood up as she entered. His office was also small and plain, its pale beige walls unadorned.

"Mrs. Fink. So good to see you. Please sit down." He motioned her to a chair. "No trouble finding the building, yes?"

"No. Your directions were very good."

"Some coffee, perhaps?"

"No, thank you, really—"

"Nonsense." He pressed a button on his desk and picked up the phone. "Lena, some coffee for us please, with cream and sugar." He turned to Miriam. "You take cream and sugar, yes?"

"Yes, that's fine, thank you." Pressing her hands together, she looked at him. "Mr. Baumgart, I am not in the habit of traveling into the city to meet with men in offices. Please tell me what news it is you have about my husband, Reuben. I have to know. I cannot just leave it. It's true, it might make trouble, but, well, trouble is no stranger to me anyhow. So now, please tell me."

"I'm so sorry to hear that you have troubles. I noticed at the wedding that Mr. Fink is much older than you are. Also, he doesn't look well. No, I could see right away that things are not so good with you…" His voice trailed off. Rising from his seat, he walked over to a pile of brown-wrapped parcels that stood beneath the window and took one of them.

"Mrs. Fink, can you please do me a favor?"

"A favor?"

The door opened and Lena entered, set down a tray of coffee with two cups on it, and left.

"Yes, a favor," Baumgart repeated. "Look at this." He unwrapped the parcel, removing a blue velvet oblong box. This he opened, and turned to face her. Inside was an exquisite diamond necklace, made up of large and small stones in an intricate design.

"Beautiful, isn't it?" He smiled at her.

"Yes, it's very beautiful."

"Could you please stand up?"

"Stand up?"

"Yes. I want you to try it on."

"What? Try it on? Oh no, please. No."

"Why not?" He came out from behind his desk and stood in back of her, the necklace in his hand. "I need you to try it on, to model it. It's for an important customer, a very wealthy woman from Argentina. I have to be sure it's the right length. I thought of trying it on Lena, but, somehow…" He frowned and shook his head. Before she knew what was happening he had fastened the necklace about her neck.

"Come, look," he said, motioning toward an oval mirror that hung on the wall.

Confused and disoriented, Miriam followed him to the mirror. In it she saw her face, pale and frightened-looking, and below it the necklace, its glittering elegance looking totally out of place above the prim white blouse she wore. "Take it off," she demanded. "Take it off."

Baumgart reached behind her and unfastened the clasp, allowing his hand to linger on her neck, to lightly caress the skin above her collar. "Mrs. Fink, you were made for diamonds."

Turning from the mirror, she tried to move away, but he was too quick. Wrapping his arms about her, he pushed her roughly against the wall, pressing his mouth hard upon her own so that she could not cry out. Desperately she tried to turn her face away, to free herself from the headlock in which he held her. She felt his teeth biting her lips, the salty taste of his tongue as he tried to force it between her teeth. Miriam wanted to shout for help, but when he stopped kissing her, he positioned his arm so that her face was pressed against his shoulder. Miriam felt as if she were suffocating.

"Mrs. Fink, dear Miriam," he whispered, tightening his grip while she struggled against him. "You are so beautiful, so lovely… please don't fight me. I could make you so happy…"

With all her strength Miriam turned her head, wrenching her face free. "Let me go," she gasped. "Let me go or I will scream! I will call the police!" Baumgart dropped his arms.

"Don't scream," he said. "Although it wouldn't matter. Lena is out to lunch and the walls are soundproof." He smiled, straightening his tie as Miriam grabbed her purse and made for the door.

"Mrs. Fink," he said. "Miriam, please forgive me. Please don't leave."

Miriam turned the door handle, but the door did not move.

"Automatic locking device," said Baumgart, still smiling. "Security feature. Mrs. Fink, please sit down." He bowed gallantly, waving his hand toward the chair.

"Let me out," Miriam hissed. "You are despicable. Luring me here, pretending you had information about Reuben…"

"What, 'luring you'?" He sat down behind his desk and opened a gold-toned box, removing a slender cigar. "You came here on your own. It was you who phoned here, yes? To make an appointment with me." With a gadget that resembled a tiny guillotine, he trimmed the cigar, placed it between his teeth and lit it. "I know that you enjoyed it, no matter what you may say now." He lowered his eyelids and smiled. "And why did you say 'pretending' I had information'? I *do* have information. But never mind, since you are in such a hurry to leave…" He pressed a button on the desk. "There. Now the door is unlocked. You are free to go."

Miriam stood at the door, he hand on the brass knob. "What information?"

"Mrs. Fink, please sit down. Don't worry, I won't touch you again."

Miriam sat down opposite him, grateful for the massive desk that stood between them. He pointed at the tray that Lena had brought earlier.

"There—you can drink your coffee. It's still hot."

"No, thank you. I don't want it. Look, Mr. Baumgart, if you have something to tell me, then please tell me. If not, then let me go. I did not come here for you to play with me. I am a married woman. I have no interest in 'fooling around,' as they say."

Baumgart leaned back in his chair. "Mrs. Fink, forgive me. I won't bother you again. I lost control before, it's true, but this is because you are such an extraordinary woman. I see many beautiful women in my work, but few who are so beautiful and also so unhappy as you."

"I'm not unhappy."

"Let's not play games. You yourself said it before; you are no stranger to trouble and anyone can see this, anyone with sensitivity to people, that is. In any case," he said, taking a sip of coffee, "I believe I saw your husband, Reuben Zwillinger, in a café in Warsaw in 1945."

"You say you 'believe.' Are you not sure?"

"Well, I'm not a hundred per cent sure. I didn't speak to him, you see. It was in a café that was frequented by displaced persons, Jews who had survived and were looking to find each other; you know how it was. I was sitting at a table, and I saw this man come in. He looked around for a minute, and then he went out again. At first I didn't realize who it was; I hadn't seen him since before the war, and people change. But later it came to me, I thought to myself that maybe this was Zwillinger, from the bookstore."

"And?"

"And what?"

Miriam leaned forward, nearly upsetting the coffee that stood before her on the desk. "And did you find out if it was him? Did you look for him?" Baumgart sighed and shook his head.

"I was busy looking for my own family, which I didn't find, by the way. No, I didn't see him again, I didn't see anyone from the old days, except Shapiro. Did you know Shapiro, the milliner? They had a large factory, a—"

Miriam cut him off. "But is this all you can tell me? Nothing more? Only that you thought you may have seen my husband, but you aren't sure? You don't know anything else?" Her voice shook.

"My dear Mrs. Fink. This is very important information. This means that your first husband is perhaps still alive, after all this time."

"Yes? And what can I do now? Can I find him, based on such 'information,' as you call it, that someone *thinks* they *may* have seen him in a cafe in Warsaw in 1945?"

"Well, Mrs. Fink, there are agencies, organizations…"

"What organizations?"

"You can contact, perhaps, the International Red Cross. They find people all over the world. Here, I'll write it down for you." He took a scrap of paper from his desk and wrote "International Red Cross" in backward-slanting, European handwriting. Miriam took the paper and stood up.

"All right," she said, then hesitated. She was about to thank him, but it didn't seem appropriate, considering what had happened earlier. She walked to the door.

"Goodbye Mr. Baumgart."

"Goodbye, Mrs. Fink. I hope you find him, though what you will do, if you should be successful, I really wonder. You are married, maybe he is married—ah well. Life is full of complexities." He laughed as he rose and held the door for her.

It took Miriam two weeks to compose the letter to the International Red Cross. Each day she sat down to write it, only to tear up the paper and throw it in the kitchen wastebasket. Baumgart was right. What was the use in complicating her life? She was married to Isaac. It was true that their relationship was not a loving one. Isaac had never been an affectionate or demonstrative husband. From the beginning he had been irritable and contentious, often finding fault with her cooking or with her behavior toward Rebecca, whom he felt was spoiled beyond reason. Always worried about Miriam's appeal to other men, his jealousy and suspicions had increased over the years, especially as his own sexual potency had diminished. Two years before, after one of their brief lovemaking sessions, Isaac had suffered a mild heart attack. Fear of a recurrence had left him unable to perform sexually ever since. Now, when they lay in bed at night, more often than not, they argued. Isaac was worried about money. His heart condition had caused him to cut down his working hours; as a result his salary was even lower than before. Last night he had demanded that Rebecca leave her *yeshiva* high school, to save on the tuition.

"I should throw away money to send a girl to *yeshiva*, when education is free in this country? She went to *yeshiva* elementary school; for a girl that is enough."

"Isaac, she must go to *yeshiva*. My parents would have wanted it. My father—"

"Your father. I suppose her own father would have wanted it too. I suppose Reuben was very religious, concerned about *yeshivas*..."

"He *was* religious, he—"

"Hah! Reuben religious. 'After death we say they are holy,'" Isaac scoffed, using a well-known Hebrew phrase based on chapter headings in Leviticus.

That morning, after Isaac left for work, Rebecca burst out, "Why do you two have to fight all the time? I hate it! Every time I go to sleep I have to hear your voices, yelling and arguing. I can't stand it! Why is he always picking on you? It's bad enough how he picks on me, but on you? You do everything for him! He's such a creep!"

"Don't speak that way about your father," Miriam admonished.

"He's not my father," Rebecca retorted. "He's my stepfather. He's never been a real father to me. He's never cared for me at all. And now he wants to take me out of school, away from all my friends. Some father! Why do we have to put up with it? Don't you hate it too? Don't you hate him? I wish we could just leave!"

Miriam shook her head. "Hate him? No, I don't hate him. And how could I leave him? He saved us when we had nothing, not a penny; he took us with him to America, to make a new life. So how can I leave him now? He's a sick man, Rebecca, that's why he acts the way he does."

Rebecca had glared at her mother, despising the weakness in this woman who had survived the Nazis only to tie herself to this loveless tyrant of a man.

After Rebecca left for her job as a junior counselor in a local day camp, Miriam once again sat down and tried to write the letter, consulting the dictionary when she was unsure of the spelling. This time she did not rip it up. Instead she put the letter in an envelope on which she printed the name and address of the International Red Cross. There was a mailbox around the corner; she hesitated for a moment, then dropped it in and walked on to the bakery.

The summer dragged on, day after day of searing heat that baked the cracked pavement of Brooklyn's streets and faded the striped awnings on the store fronts from bright blue and orange to tired green and beige. Each afternoon, as she turned the tiny key to the battered mailbox downstairs, Miriam's heart tightened. Would there be an answer? But every day brought the same bills and advertisements. As the weeks wore on, Miriam reconciled herself to the idea that it could take a long time before she received a reply. Reuben, if he were alive, could be anywhere, possibly even in America. It could take the Red Cross months, even years, to locate him. And suppose he were dead, after all, as she had always believed? Even that could take time to validate. Possibly the records in Kiev were misplaced, or even lost. Eleven years was a long time.

Chapter twenty-six

The heat broke. Evening brought cool breezes that hinted of autumn. Fewer people came downstairs at night to sit outside their apartment buildings, and those who did wrapped themselves in stretched-out cardigans or khaki cotton windbreakers. As the days lengthened, the air grew crisp and soon the sidewalks were covered with waxy yellow leaves that would soon shrivel and turn brown, resembling tiny, clutching monkey hands. Rebecca went back to her Bais Yehudis High School, and Miriam spent long hours baking round raisin *challahs* and honey cake in preparation for the Jewish New Year. Isaac alone had less work to do than before. Moshe Fogel, his employer, had gone away to the Catskill Mountains for the last two weeks of August. When he returned, he gave Isaac a long look and pronounced, "Isaac, I can see you are not a well man. Truthfully, I worry about you. God forbid, something could happen to you on the job."

"What can happen?" Isaac had protested. "How strenuous is it to oversee workers in a tie factory? This is not bricklaying, Moshe. The doctor says I can work, so why are you worrying?"

But Fogel was not convinced. One week after his return from White Lake, he introduced Isaac to a pale, gangly youth of about nineteen in an oversize gray suit cut from a fabric that resembled cardboard. "Isaac, this is my nephew, Sheldon. You take him around with you, show him the ropes." At lunchtime Isaac cornered Fogel, whom he had known for a dozen years.

"Since when do I need an assistant?"

"What assistant? You are teaching him the business. Starting next week, you work three days, he works two. "Isaac," he lay a heavy hand on his employee's shoulder, "you are a sick man. Be happy I don't tell you to stay home altogether."

Choking with rage and humiliation, Isaac could not answer. All afternoon, he seethed inwardly, occasionally darting looks of contempt at Sheldon, who smiled back affably and made inane comments about the patterns—"So this is paisley? Looks like fish to me."

It doesn't matter, Isaac decided. He would show Fogel. He would find another job, a better job, one that paid much more. He could use the two "days off" Fogel had now given him, to comb the want ads and walk the streets, until he found something to his liking, a job to match his managerial skills and years of experience. After all, who understood the garment industry better than Isaac Fink? In Poland, before the war, he had owned a dress factory. Not a big place, but certainly a lot better than Fogel's Neckwear. He had lost it, of course, along with everything else. And here in America, bad luck continued to plague him. Riding home on the subway he decided he would not tell Miriam what had happened. He did not want to see the pitying look in her eyes, the look that said, "You are a failure."

For the next few weeks, Isaac spent his free days job hunting. In the morning he would scan the papers, then present himself at various offices in the garment center, only to be told that the job was filled or that he was under or even overqualified. The days grew cold and a bitter wind blew through his worn overcoat, chilling him as he walked the rainswept streets.

One day, after being turned down from a job in a Brooklyn clothing store, he passed a library on his way to the subway. Without knowing why, he made his way up the wide, stone steps and went inside. A feeling of warmth and peace enveloped him as he sat down and began reading a Yiddish newspaper that someone had left on a table. From that day on, he gave up looking for another job. Instead, he spent his free days at the library, reading old newspapers and Yiddish literature. There was a timelessness about the old Yiddish classics that was especially comforting to him. He saw himself as the hero of a Yiddish tragedy, stalked by misfortune, misunderstood by friends and family. Someday, he was certain, his luck would change. A business opportunity would present itself, he would recover his wealth, his health, and his strength, and he would show Miriam that he too, was a man among men.

Miriam. He pictured her as he had first seen her, a young beautiful woman, full of life, tossing her glowing auburn hair as she smiled radiantly at her new husband, Reuben. Isaac's own wife, Bella, would nudge him in the ribs with her elbow, jerking her head at the Zwillingers. "Look at them, the two lovebirds! Did you ever see such a thing?"

Now Miriam was his, and she was still beautiful, though the years had dulled the vibrancy of her hair, and her smile was thin and tight. He remembered how she looked when he found her after the war at the offices of the Joint Distribution Committee in Warsaw. Unlike so many of the survivors, she was blooming, her cheeks full and bright with health. She had been working on a farm and had not known the horrors of the concentration camps. And yet she had looked so forlorn, standing there with the child in her arms. And so he had married Miriam, because she was all alone, she and the child. He had held her in his arms, on his cramped iron cot, and made love to her, while she lay so still, with her eyes far away, gazing past him, into the darkness. And later, in her sleep, she had cried out, "Reuben! Reuben, my darling!" Night after night she had called for Reuben, but Isaac never told her.

During the day, calm and quiet, Miriam tended to his needs, and to those of the child. They had traveled to America, and she had learned English, and had gotten a job. She was a good wife, he could not complain. She worked hard, kept the house spotless, and cooked well. She was also lovely to look at, too lovely perhaps. All the men stared at her, and that worried Isaac, because he knew, in his heart, that she did not really love him. Miriam loved the child, doted on her and spoiled her, but the light in her eyes when she looked at Rebecca was not there for him, nor had it ever been. With Bella it had been different. Bella had been no beauty, but she'd had fire in her eyes, and in her heart as well. In bed she would poke and prod Isaac, tickling and scratching him till he went mad with desire. Then she would wrap her legs around him, gasping out her passion until it was spent. And in Bella, his seed had flourished. It was not his fault that she had miscarried three times. The doctors said it had something to do with the shape of Bella's womb. And yet the fourth time the womb must have righted itself, for Bella grew fat and round, glowing with fecundity, like a ripe melon. She had been eight months pregnant when the Nazis dragged her away from him on the platform at Auschwitz. That was his last memory of Bella, clawing and spitting like a tigress, her huge belly poking out of her coat, while two tall Nazis pulled her by the arms into a crowd of terrified women and children.

In the early years with Miriam, Isaac had wanted a child of his own, a namesake, someone to replace the ones that had been lost. Miriam had borne Reuben two children and had miscarried once, in between, but with Isaac, she never even became pregnant. Her body, so still and silent under his, rejected his seed, so that it could not take root. Now, of course, all that was over, finished. Sometimes, late in the night, she still cried out in her dreams, "Reuben!" And it felt like a knife in Isaac's heart.

One morning, as he sat in the library, Isaac was seized by a terrible spasm of coughing. He tried desperately to catch his breath, or clear his throat, but the coughs would not subside. The few old people who frequented the library looked up from their newspapers in alarm, while the librarian, a pinched-faced woman with tightly curled white hair and frameless glasses, frowned. The coughing finally stopped, leaving Isaac weak and shaken. Each breath seemed to sear his raw throat. After a few moments he decided to go home, rather than risk another fit. Wrapping his woolen scarf tightly around his neck, he leaned into the damp wind as he walked the two blocks to the subway. Once on the train, he sat shivering, until he reached his station. *What's wrong with me? I must have a fever*, he thought. *The minute I get home I'll get right into bed.*

He entered the lobby of his building and immediately felt a little better. The familiar combination of cooking smells and burnt cinders from the incinerator comforted him. The superintendent had waxed the linoleum floor and it gleamed like marble. Near the staircase, the mailman was busy stuffing letters and *Reader's Digests* into the last row of mailboxes. Heaving his sack to his shoulder, he nodded at Isaac as he shuffled by on his way to the next building. Isaac grunted a greeting and glanced at his mailbox. Might as well bring up the mail. He opened the box and removed a single letter, in a long white envelope. The return address said "International Red Cross." Why would they be writing to him? Must be something to do with his work after the war, when he was employed by the Joint Distribution Committee. He was about to put it in his pocket when he noticed that it was addressed, not to him, but to Miriam. Inexplicably, his hand began to shake. Miriam rarely received mail, aside from coupons and advertisements for women's magazines. Should he open it? Miriam might be annoyed.

He remembered an incident from last summer, when Miriam had accidentally opened a letter addressed to Rebecca. The girl had shrieked and cried, accusing her mother of prying, of not letting her live her own life. Her own life, at age fourteen! He recalled Miriam's pleading, her protestations. "It was a mistake, Rebecca. The envelope said 'National Foods,' so I thought it was for me."

Rebecca had narrowed her eyes. "Suri's father works for National Foods, that's why she put it in that envelope. Next time look at the mailing address."

The child was spoiled. Spoiled and willful, but that was another story. He gazed again at the envelope in his hand, and began opening it. It was as if he could not stop himself. If Miriam complained he'd say he'd thought it was for him.

Fighting to steady his trembling hand, he read:

Dear Mrs. Fink:

With regard to your request for information concerning the whereabouts of Mr. Reuben Zwillinger, we require the following information, without which we cannot proceed with our investigation:

1. The date of birth and place of birth of Mr. Reuben Zwillinger.
2. The maiden name of Mr. Zwillinger's mother.
3. The exact date on which he was last...

Isaac's eyes misted and he stopped reading. *So this is it,* he thought. *This is what I get from her. I save her from starvation in Warsaw, I put a roof over her head, I bring her to America, she and her child, and this is how she repays me. Ten years of struggle, fighting to make ends meet, running here and there, trying to earn a good living, ruining my health. All for her and for the child. And to what end? Now that I am sick, now that I can no longer hold down a decent job, this is what she does. She looks for* him. *After all these years, she is still looking for* him, *hoping, against all the evidence—the papers she has that say he is dead—still hoping that she will find him. Still hoping that one day he will come back and rescue her from Isaac Fink, the failure.* Bitterly he crumpled the letter in his hand, squeezing it into a ball of damp paper. Slowly he walked across the lobby to the incinerator room. As he pulled open the trap door leading to the incinerator duct, he hesitated momentarily, and then tossed the letter in, watching as it was sucked downward by a gust of hot air. The envelope followed, gently floating down as he closed the door.

Chapter twenty-seven

D*avid's* eyes swept across the crowded lecture hall, searching

Moscow, 1959

for the 'princess.' There were several pretty girls in the class, scattered about among the homely ones, like gold amidst the dross. But this one was exceptional. Each time she entered the room, all of the boys' heads turned, all of their eyes followed her as she gracefully made her way down the rows and slipped into her seat. Even flat-faced Bolek, David's study partner, was not immune. On the first day of the semester he had nudged David and pointed, "A beauty, hah? But kind of cold-looking. An ice-princess. How'd you like to warm her up?"

Ever since that day, David found himself staring at her during class and looking for her elsewhere on the campus as well. It was not just her flawlessly chiseled features, and the smooth blonde hair that swept across her shoulders like fine-spun gold. Nor was it her tall, slender figure, so graceful and well-proportioned that even the drab clothes she wore looked almost elegant. What attracted David most was the puzzling sensation of familiarity that he felt whenever he looked at her. He had seen that girl somewhere before, but he could not remember where. She had not been in any of his previous classes at Moscow University. Nor had he known her in the gymnasium or in elementary school. Perhaps he had seen her at Pioneer meetings long ago? Some day, he vowed, he would gather up the courage to speak to her. Having grown up without a mother or sisters, David was shy with women. Although many girls were attracted to his handsome features and red-gold hair, at the age of twenty-two he had had few serious relationships.

One afternoon, on his way to class, he spotted her in the corridor. She leaned against the wall, twisting a strand of her hair between her fingers as she chatted with another student, a short plump girl with coarse features. As he approached her, David's heart began to pound. His legs felt tense and wooden. Speak to her, you fool, he admonished himself. But he couldn't. Then, just as he was about to pass by, she looked directly at him.

"Excuse me, but isn't that book, *Theories of Harmony*, by Svanovec?" she asked, indicating the heavy volume he held pressed against his chest.

"Yes, it is. Why do you ask?" He felt himself blushing furiously.

"I've been looking everywhere for that book. I need it for a paper I'm working on, but the library hasn't had it in weeks."

"You may borrow mine if you like." He held out the book, grateful for the opportunity to help her in some way. Her friend looked at her watch. "Goodbye Marina," she said. "See you tomorrow." She walked away, joining a small group of students at the end of the hall.

Marina examined the book. In the corner of the frontispiece he had written his name, 'David Zwillinger.' The girl's eyes narrowed as she read it, then widened as she looked up in his face. Suddenly her lips parted in a delighted smile. "So it *is* you, after all," she laughed. Impulsively she leaned forward and planted a kiss on his cheek. David jumped back, putting his hand to his face as if he had been struck.

"Who *are* you?"

"I'm your cousin, Marina Bosnov. Don't you remember me?"

David stared at her in confusion. From the far distant past came the memory of two flaxen braids, and of mocking laughter. "My cousin?"

"What a dummy you are. You *are* David, aren't you?"

He nodded. All around students were rushing past, jostling him as they went by. Their class was scheduled to begin in a moment.

"Well, then," she continued, "you really should remember me. I mean, it's been maybe, oh, twelve years, but even so. I remember *you*. Of course, I wasn't as little as you were then, so maybe it's easier for me. I was about nine years old. You were maybe seven or eight. I used to come visit you; we came maybe three or four times, all told, but I recall you very well. My mother would take me to visit her sister-in-law, my Aunt Yelena. Your stepmother. Then your parents got divorced and Yelena came to live with us. In fact, she still lives with me."

"Yelena! Then you are Yelena's niece! I believe I do recollect something…"

"Well, it's probably not a good memory," Marina laughed. "I used to tease you quite a bit, as I recall. I was jealous of you because you had a papa and mine was dead. So I teased you, and you would cry. What a baby you were. But," she paused and looked David up and down, "you've grown up, I see."

From that day on David and Marina were inseparable. They would meet after class and study together and in the evenings they would sit in the shabby cafeteria, drinking coffee and gazing into each other's eyes. At night they would steal off to the tiny room of Marina's friend, Sonya, who would tactfully leave them alone for an hour or two. Soon everyone knew they were in love. Everyone except Reuben. When Marina told Yelena about her relationship with David, the old woman had cursed and spat.

"Whore!" she shouted. "Jew lover!"

"And what were you, auntie?" Marina had retorted, prompting her aunt to strike her across the face. But, with the help of her daily pint of vodka, Yelena soon lost interest in the affairs of her niece.

When the year ended, David graduated from Moscow University with a degree in music, while Marina, who had started school a year late, completed a degree in mathematics. That night, as he reached for her in Sonya's lumpy bed, Marina turned away from David. The smooth skin of her shoulders gleamed white in the moonlight that filtered in through the dusty windowpanes.

"What is it darling?" David asked, trying to enfold her in his arms even as she slid away from him.

"What is it?" Marina sat up. Her long blonde hair hung like a curtain over her creamy breasts. "It's this. I cannot continue making love to you, night after night, when you behave like a spineless coward."

"A coward?"

"Yes."

"You mean because of my father?"

"Yes, exactly. How perceptive you are."

David sighed. That afternoon he had confessed to her his inability to tell Reuben about their relationship. Now he sat up in bed, smoothing the tattered blanket across his knees. "Marina dearest, please try to understand. My father has been having such a difficult time lately. Not that he's ever been really happy in all the years I can remember, but lately, somehow, it's gotten much worse. One would think, after all these years, that he would have gotten over my mother's death, but he never has. And now, it's as if the old memories have returned to haunt him. I think it started after he caught pneumonia this winter. He couldn't work and he was left alone all day, with his thoughts. He was always a brooding type and being by himself isn't good for him. For many years he rarely spoke about my mother, just as he almost never mentioned his first wife, Pola. She was always a shadowy figure to me, someone I could never picture. When I was young, after he got me back from the Federenkos, he talked to me a lot about my mother. He would describe her to me in great detail, how beautiful she was, her red hair and green eyes…I think it was an effort on his part to make me forget about Galina Federenko, whom I thought of as my *real* mother. After a while, though, he stopped talking about Miriam—that was my mother's name. Sometimes I would mention her to him and he would get this terribly hurt look in his eyes and change the subject. But in the last few months he's been talking about her again, saying things like, 'If only Miriam had lived.' Once or twice at night I thought I heard him crying, but I wasn't certain. I didn't want to embarrass him, so I never mentioned it."

"But what has all that to do with us?" Marina asked petulantly.

"Don't you understand? I don't want to upset him further. If I told him I was in love with Yelena's niece…You know how he feels about Yelena. He despises her. He despised her all the while they were married, if you could call what they had a marriage. God, even now, when I think of the fights they had, she always blaming him for her miscarriage early on, and the way she treated me, pulling my hair out by the roots, almost strangling me once when I called her a fat pig—"

Marina gave a bark of laughter, then became serious. "Well then." She climbed off the bed and began pulling on her clothes. "If you cannot tell him about us, then there's no point in continuing our relationship. So, Davidchka," she ruffled his hair with her fingers, "goodbye."

"What do you mean, goodbye?" David stood up and as he did so, the blanket fell off, exposing his nakedness. Feeling vulnerable and ashamed, he began dressing hurriedly.

"Here, look at this." Marina switched on the lamp and handed him an envelope. In the dim light, David's eyes could not focus on the small print.

"What is this?" he asked.

"A letter. From Odessa. I've been offered a position there, teaching mathematics in a gymnasium.

"Odessa?" David grabbed Marina by the shoulders. "You cannot go!"

"Can't I? Why not? I'm a free agent."

"No. You belong to me. I love you." Clutching her to him he kissed her lips until she stopped resisting. "Marina," he breathed. "Marry me. Tell me you'll marry me. Say yes. I'll tell my father tonight. Please say yes."

Marina sighed deeply. "Yes," she whispered.

Chapter twenty-eight

M*iriam* leaned into the oven, checking on the *rugelach*. That afternoon the baker, Lapidus, had left them in too long and they had burned. His carelessness resulted in a violent argument with Mrs. Greenberg, culminating in his immediate dismissal when he called her a *"farshlepte krenk,"* the Yiddish term for a protracted illness. Later Mrs. Greenberg phoned Miriam in tears:

Brooklyn, 1960

"Please, you *must* come in tonight. Not only do we have to bake the cakes for the Krupnick *bar mitzvah*, there's also the Anshei Brody Sisterhood. Bernie is coming in to help, but Shifra is still away on vacation; I couldn't even reach her. And I've got to go to my nephew's wedding; my sister's boy, up in Poughkeepsie. Please Miriam," she pleaded. "I'll pay you double."

At first Miriam said no. She wanted to spend more time with Isaac, who was not well. Lately his angina had worsened so that even a short walk left him pale and breathless. But money was scarce and the offer of double pay was too attractive to refuse. The doctor had urged Isaac to retire, and while he had insisted that he was well enough to work, Miriam knew that it was only a matter of time before Isaac's job would be given to Sheldon Fogel, the boss's nephew.

Bernie, the daytime baker, was a gangling young man in his thirties, with a mop of unruly black hair and a large, good-humored face. "Listen to that rain," he said, as he sifted powdered sugar over a tray of cookies.

"How's Ellen feeling today?" Miriam asked. "Everything all right?"

"Oh yeah, she's okay. It's harder for her this time, what with David always underfoot, but she's all right. She just can't wait till it's over. But I tell her she doesn't know what she's in for. Better enjoy it now while there's still only one to deal with. David'll probably really be jealous too, once the baby comes. Right now he's king of the castle."

Miriam smiled and turned away. Bernie's words brought back the discussions she and Reuben had often had about their own little David, so many years before. She had worried that David would be envious of the child she was carrying, but Reuben had not been concerned. "He'll soon learn to love the baby," he had predicted. Miriam sighed. Too much dwelling on the past might turn her into a depressed, bitter woman, like her upstairs neighbor, Mrs. Bialystok, who constantly talked about what might have been, if only there had been no Holocaust. Better to follow the advice of that popular singer, the one who warbled "Count your blessings," on Rebecca's radio. The loud ringing of the telephone interrupted her thoughts. Wiping her hands on her apron, she moved towards the phone, but Bernie had already picked up.

"What? Are you sure? Oh my God. Every ten minutes? I'll be right there." He hung up the phone and threw off his apron. "I'm sorry, Mrs. Fink, but I gotta run. Ellen's having her pains. I can't believe it, she's still got five weeks to go."

"Don't worry, Bernie. Everything will be fine. I'll manage okay. We're almost done anyway."

"Thanks, Mrs. Fink. Bye." He rushed out, slamming the door behind him.

"Good luck," Miriam called after him. She worked for another half-hour before checking the clock. It was ten fifteen. Gazing through the shop window she saw that the rain was still falling heavily, though with less fury than before. The pale neon signs of the stores illuminated the rain-slicked sidewalk. The street was deserted, save for the occasional car that drove slowly past, windshield wipers swishing silently. Leaning on the counter in front of the bakery, Miriam weighed the cookies and dropped them into the paper boxes that Bernie had made up several hours earlier. Just as she finished tying the last box Miriam jumped, startled by a loud jangling noise from the back room, where the ovens were. It sounded as though a pan had fallen.

"Bernie, is that you?" she called, walking through the door that led to the back room. Strange, she thought. She did not remember turning off the lights when she finished the baking. Maybe Bernie had done it before he left. Squinting in the darkness, she could barely make out the outlines of the ovens and tables. Feeling along the wall, she flipped the light switch, blinked in the sudden brightness, and gasped. A man was standing in the room. He was tall, with a blonde crew-cut, and his wet clothes were plastered to his muscular body. In one gloved hand he held the large bread knife that Miriam herself had sharpened the day before yesterday.

"Who are you?" Miriam asked, fighting to stay calm. "What do you want?"

"Open the register," the man said in a voice hardly above a whisper. He looked young, twenty at most.

"I can't," said Miriam. "I don't have the key. Besides, it's empty. The owner took the money out already."

"Cut the crap," said the man, his voice shaking. "You're the owner. I seen you in here before."

"I'm not. Really, I just work here. The owner left."

The man moved closer, pointing the knife at Miriam. She could see the blade trembling in his hand. *He's afraid,* she thought.

"Open it," he said hoarsely, jerking the knife towards the register.

"I can't," Miriam insisted.

"Open it, or I'll cut up that pretty face." Grabbing Miriam with one arm, he held the knife to her cheek. All at once the telephone rang. Startled, the man moved the knife and Miriam twisted from his grasp, throwing him off balance. He fell against her, heavily. She felt a searing pain in her breast. From far away she heard the sound of her own voice, screaming. Then, she knew nothing.

Rebecca held the receiver to her ear. The phone rang six, seven, eight times. Finally, she hung up and turned to Isaac. "No answer. She must be on her way home."

Isaac grunted and went back to his bedroom. Rebecca sat at the kitchen table, reading a novel. She was tired but didn't want to go to bed before her mother came home. She needed to ask her advice about a problem she was having at work. True, it was only a summer job, but there were still four weeks left to the season. Mommy was good at understanding people; she would help her solve the problem with her boss.

As time passed Rebecca began to feel uneasy. Her mother should have been home by now. She tried the bakery; again, no answer. Mommy usually came home in a taxi when she worked late. It was still pouring out. What if there'd been an accident? But that was unlikely; it was only a few blocks, after all. Perhaps she should call Mrs. Greenberg. It was so late though; maybe they'd be annoyed. Never mind, she'd try anyway. But there was no answer there either. The Greenbergs were not home. Pulling aside the drapes, Rebecca peered out the living room window. The street was empty. I'd better get over there, she decided, thinking of all the times Miriam had met her at school when she was a kid with boots and an umbrella so she wouldn't get soaked walking home. Taking a heavy black umbrella from the closet, she put on her raincoat and left the house.

When she arrived at the bakery, the door was locked. "Ma!" she called, banging on the door. No one came. Inside it was dark, except for the light-blue neon sign in the window. Pressing her nose against the glass, Rebecca looked in. She saw no one. Then, as she continued to stare, something odd caught her eye. Protruding from under the counter, lying on its side, was a woman's crepe soled shoe. The kind of shoe her mother wore to work.

When the surgeon finished examining Miriam, he turned to his interns and shook his head. "I doubt we can save her," he said.

The surgery took four hours. Four hours during which Rebecca alternately paced back and forth in the hospital corridors, pestered the doctors and nurses with questions they could not answer, and cried on the plump shoulders of Mrs. Greenberg. Isaac had gone home after two hours. The strain was too much for him. Rebecca promised to call as soon as she knew anything.

When not comforting Rebecca, Mrs. Greenberg cried herself, hiding her eyes with her hands and sobbing, "Why did I make her stay late? Why?" over and over.

Finally, the surgeon emerged from behind the double metal doors of the operating room. He had removed his mask and there were red marks on his face where it had pressed too tightly into his cheeks.

"We've done all we can," he told Rebecca gently. "Your mother has lost a lot of blood. We hope she'll recover, but right now we can't be sure of anything. At this point we also don't know whether or not there was any brain damage as a result of the loss of blood. We'll know a lot more in the next twenty-four hours. In the meantime," he touched her shoulder, "try to be strong. Where is your father?"

"He had to go home. He has a weak heart." The surgeon shook his head.

"Well then, you'll have to be strong for both of them."

The days passed slowly. Miriam lay still and silent in the hospital bed as each shift of nurses came and went, murmuring softly to Rebecca and Isaac as they sponged Miriam's forehead or changed her intravenous tube. Isaac generally spent a few hours at Miriam's bedside before returning home, pale and exhausted. Rebecca rarely left her mother's side. All day she would sit by the bed, holding her mother's hand, gazing at her white, waxy-looking face. Sometimes she would speak to her:

"Mom, Mommy, can you hear me?" But there was no response. Often, Rebecca would lower her head to her mother's bed and cry silent, bitter tears. "Mommy," she would plead, "don't die. Please don't die."

She tried to imagine what life would be like without her mother, but it was too awful to contemplate. Although she was nineteen and no longer a child, she still depended on Miriam for so many things, both practical and intangible. Despite her frequent complaints that her mother was too protective, too given to worrying, she secretly enjoyed the fact Miriam cared so much about her. *It's all so unfair,* she thought, anxiously watching as the blanket that covered her mother's chest rose and fell with each weak breath. *Look at the life she's had. Losing her whole family, going through the war in hiding, and coming back to find out that the husband and son she adored were dead. She almost didn't find me, either. And look at her life in America; slaving away the years in the bakery, never having enough money, putting up with all of Isaac's griping and complaining, without ever complaining herself. And putting up with me as well,* she reflected. *I haven't exactly been the ideal daughter. In high school I was always nagging, always wanting more sweaters, more dresses, another pair of shoes, even though I knew we didn't have the money. Even now I argue with her too much, always trying to prove that I'm right, that I know better because I'm an American and she's just an old-fashioned woman from Poland.* Rebecca sighed. Part of her problem in getting along with her parents, she knew, had to do with her own feelings of guilt and lack of self-worth. Even without Isaac's frequent reminders, she often thought of what her parents had gone through. Nothing she did, nothing she could ever do, would possibly make up to them for what they had already lost, even before she was born. *If Mommy lives,* she vowed, *I'll be a better daughter. I'll try to please her more and to argue less. I'll help more in the house.*

One day her thoughts were interrupted by the entry of a policeman, who identified himself as Lieutenant Dunne of the 66th Precinct. "Has she said anything yet?" he asked.

No," Rebecca answered. "Have you been able to piece together what happened?"

"Only that there were signs of a struggle; things in disarray, pans and cookies on the floor like you saw, the bruises on your mother's neck and arms, in addition to the stab wound. We have the knife, of course. The bakery owner identified it. But there were no prints on it. That's really all I'm able to tell you. If you need to reach me, or if she wakes up, or says anything in her sleep, let me know." He handed her a card with his name and phone number.

At night Rebecca returned home to prepare supper for Isaac. Each evening his greeting was the same— "How was she when you left?" and Rebecca would answer, "no change." Isaac would sigh and lower his eyes. Although he said nothing, Rebecca could see that he blamed himself for what had happened. If he weren't such a failure as a provider, Miriam would not have had to work in the bakery. Seeing his gray, careworn face and the anguish in his deep-set eyes, Rebecca felt her heart twist with pity. She wanted to reach out and touch his hand, to comfort him in some small way. Yet she found herself unable to do so. An impenetrable wall separated her from the man she called "Daddy," a wall that had been erected long ago, in her early childhood years.

Miriam stood on the platform, watching as the train grew smaller and smaller. The people around her moved away, talking and gesticulating as they left the station. The sky darkened and light rain began to fall.

"Come Miriam," her mother said. "Come home."

But Miriam did not answer. Instead, she lifted her skirts and started running swiftly down the tracks, following the train. As she ran, her swollen belly began to shrink, growing smaller with each step until it was flat again, like that of a young girl. She ran on and on, growing not wearier, but stronger. She felt she could run forever, with the damp wind singing in her ears. Soon she saw the outline of the train, but a great river separated her from it. Raising her arms, she leaped towards the water and was amazed to find herself flying, effortlessly skimming over the waves. Now she could see the train clearly. A face stared at her from one of the windows. It was Reuben, and she waved her arms excitedly, trying to get his attention. "Reuben!" she cried. "Wait for me, Reuben!"

"No, dear. It's me, Hazel," the night nurse said cheerily, and hurried out to tell the doctor, "She's coming around."

Miriam came home two weeks later. For three additional weeks she stayed at home while Iris, the practical nurse provided by the Greenbergs, ministered to both her and Isaac's needs. Then, for another two weeks, she and Isaac took care of each other, the nurse having left abruptly for a better-paying job. However, instead of growing closer to each other through mutual dependency, Isaac and Miriam found that their forced proximity led to tensions that grew worse with each passing day. Isaac alternated between anger and depression over the fact that Fogel had told him not to return to work. For hours he brooded in tight-lipped silence, while Miriam waited, nerves on edge, for his next outburst, which could be triggered by anything from a newspaper headline to the tight skirts Rebecca wore to her classes at Brooklyn College.

Finally, Miriam could tolerate it no longer. On a foggy morning in early fall, when the air was fragrant with falling leaves and impending rain, she rose, put on a bright blue dress that hung loosely over her gaunt frame, and announced, "I'm going back to work."

"What, are you crazy?" Isaac protested.

But Miriam was adamant. She felt perfectly fine; the doctor had given her a clean bill of health. If she stayed home another day she would go crazy. She simply could not stand being cooped up with nothing to do.

"You cannot go back there!" Isaac shouted. "I'm afraid to let you go! What if he comes back? Aren't you afraid yourself?"

"No. He won't come back in broad daylight. The place is too busy. Besides, they put in a whole alarm system, chains and bolts, the Greenbergs told me. And I'll never work there alone again, and certainly I won't ever work late. So it's all right. Don't worry about me, Isaac. It's you we have to worry about."

And so Miriam returned to the bakery, working steadily for four days until summoned home by a phone call from a neighbor. Isaac had collapsed outside the door of their apartment. Mrs. Greenberg drove Miriam home, arriving there just as the ambulance pulled up. It was too late. Isaac had died instantly of a massive heart attack.

Chapter twenty-nine

Davis slammed his half-finished mug of tea onto the table and glared at his wife. "Why don't you let me finish speaking? I can barely start a sentence before you interrupt me. I said it would only be for three days."

The woman raised a slender wrist to her forehead, wiping a strand of long blonde hair away from her eyes. "Three days, ten days, it doesn't matter. You promised me we would paint the apartment next week. Always there's a new excuse, a new reason for postponing it. I tell you I can't live like this anymore!"

"Lower your voice, Marina."

"Why?" She gestured toward the faded blue curtain that served to partition a section of the room. "Your father isn't in."

"The neighbors—"

"Who gives a damn about the neighbors? Do they give a damn about us? They know our whole story anyhow."

"Yes, because of your constant yelling."

"Yelling? Who wouldn't yell in my situation? Stuck in this dump of a room, sharing this excuse for a kitchen with the Yacheslavs, and then having your father snoring away behind that curtain all night."

"Don't start on my father again, please. It's enough."

"Enough? It's never enough. When I think of how he treats me, it's a miracle I haven't gone completely crazy."

"How does he treat you? He treats you with the greatest respect. He never says a—"

"Never says a bad word? Oh no, of course not. He barely says a word to me at all. But it's his eyes, it's all there in his eyes. I'm not blind." She tossed a dishrag onto a rack above the sink and continued. "Ever since we got married, it's been there, the hatred, the contempt! He thinks I'm not good enough for his darling son. He can't stand the sight of me because I'm *her* niece. She said it herself. She says the reason I haven't gotten pregnant is because he has cursed me with his eyes."

"Ahh, peasant nonsense." David drained the mug and rose from his chair. "In any case, there's no point in discussing it further. I'm flying Sunday night; we'll play two concerts in New York, and I'll be back here on Wednesday. Most wives would be thrilled for their husbands to be able to go to America."

"Don't tell me about most wives. Most wives don't have to put up with what I put up with."

As the plane taxied down the runway at Kennedy Airport, David could not contain his excitement. Turning to his seat partner, he blurted, "I still can't believe it, Sasha. To this day I can't understand why they chose me to go in place of Presser."

His companion smiled cynically. "Why do you think?"

David's brow furrowed. "I don't know. It was a last minute decision apparently. Last Monday Grimkov told me to prepare my papers, that I would be playing in place of Presser. He never said why, and I didn't ask."

Sasha leaned over and spoke into David's ear. "Presser's out."

"Out? What do you mean?"

"He's out of the orchestra. We won't be seeing him for a while."

David's blue eyes widened in surprise. "Presser? Him, too?"

"Yes, Presser. Just like Nemlich and Kremenev. If you apply for a visa to Israel, then you're out of the orchestra, and Presser is out of Moscow as well." His black eyes narrowed, scanning the passengers around them. "And now let's not discuss it anymore, eh?"

David finished the last note with a flourish and lowered his violin. The soloist, Yuri Jillinski, bowed deeply as the concert hall resonated with applause. David watched the members of the audience rise from their seats and file slowly out of the auditorium. Here and there he could pick out a face—a fat matron, heavily rouged, whose hat tipped sideways, nearly covering one eye, and behind her, a tall gentleman in a black evening suit and derby hat—they looked like characters in a comic opera.

Someone bumped against him roughly. "Hurry up, Zwillinger, goddamn you. The van is waiting. Do you want us to miss the plane because of your daydreaming?"

David grunted, snapped his violin case shut, and left the stage. It was no use talking back to Radek and subjecting oneself to further abuse. The cellist had had it in for him since the day he joined the orchestra. Still, he did not take it personally. Radek hated all Jews, not just David Zwillinger.

When he walked through the stage door that led out onto the street, David was momentarily blinded by the bright sunlight. "This way, this way," called Sasha, pulling him along by the elbow. The musicians walked forward, then stopped. A small crowd of young people blocked their path.

"What's this?" laughed Sasha. "Are we such celebrities?"

Suddenly several people in the group surged forward and began shouting angrily at the performers. The musicians stared at them in confusion. Several members of the crowd raised placards, on which was written, in both English and Russian—"Let My People Go!" One young man thrust a leaflet in David's face.

"Let Jews out!" he shouted. David turned to Sasha. "Who are these people?"

"American Jews. Haven't you heard about this?"

"About what?"

"This, these demonstrations. A group of American students have formed an organization. They are trying to embarrass the Russian government into letting Jews go to Israel." He reached down and picked up a leaflet.

"See?" he pointed. "The Student Struggle for Soviet Jewry."

The students linked arms and began chanting—"Let my people go! Let my people go!"

From out of nowhere two policemen appeared, their horses stamping their hooves and shaking their huge heads.

"Cossacks!" jested Sasha. "Now we're in for it!" But David did not laugh. Silently following as the police escorted his group to the waiting van, he watched as the crowd of students moved back but continued to chant. *Unbelievable*, he thought. *Jewish students in America care so much about us? Enough to risk being arrested by the police?* He shook his head in amazement as he climbed into the van.

On the other side of the street, a Rock Hudson-Doris Day comedy had just ended. Groups of people left the theater, shading their eyes as they emerged from under the marquis.

"So what did you think of it, Ma?" asked Rebecca.

Miriam smiled. "It was quite funny, wasn't it? I really enjoyed it. Look over there, Rebecca. What's going on?" She pointed across the street, where a group of people were shouting angrily at a cluster of young men in evening clothes, some of whom were carrying instrument cases.

"I don't know. Some kind of demonstration." Rebecca shrugged. Gazing at the placards they waved, she read aloud, "Let My People Go—Oh, I know what it is. It's that organization that tries to help Russian Jews. This must be a Russian orchestra or something. You, know, that impresario, Sol Hurok, is it? He brings over these Russian musicians and dancers." She glanced at her watch. "Come on, Ma, I've got to get home." Arm in arm, the two women walked down the street toward the subway.

Chapter thirty

Brooklyn, New York, 1968

"Evenin', Miz Zwillinger."

"Good evening, Charlie." Rebecca smiled at the doorman as he held the door open for her. When she entered her apartment, a small gray and white cat leaped from the sofa and began rubbing against her legs, purring so that his whole body vibrated. Scooping him up, Rebecca nuzzled the triangular face and put him down again. He followed as she went into the kitchen to prepare his food.

Thank God for you, Ringo, thought Rebecca, as she dumped a can of fishy-smelling cat food into a small red bowl and set it on the floor next to a bowl of water. Although she had been relieved when Trudy, her roommate of two years, had left for a commune in California, divesting the apartment of several Mexican pillows, Indian throw rugs and Moroccan incense burners, not to mention a vast collection of pipes and bongs for smoking grass, the apartment did get lonely at night. The cat was company, if nothing else, and if he didn't speak, he also didn't invite to his bed a steady stream of long-haired young men who leered at Rebecca and left the bathroom door open while they peed. The odd thing about Trudy was that she had seemed perfectly respectable when she'd first moved in, after answering Rebecca's ad in the *Times*. But over the two years they had roomed together, Trudy had become progressively freakier, letting her hair grow down to her backside and filling the house with sitar music, fragrant smoke and an assortment of stoned boyfriends. Not that Rebecca minded smoking a joint now and then herself, but there was a limit. After Trudy left, the quiet and the extra space seemed worth the increase in rent, and Rebecca had decided not to look for another roommate. As she was eating her supper of cottage cheese and crackers, the phone rang.

"Hello?"

"Hey babe, how's my girl?"

"Hi Eddie. I'm fine. What's doing?"

"Nothing much. Hey, can I come over?"

"Sure. What time?"

"In about an hour or so."

"Okay. See ya."

She hung up the phone and hurriedly tidied up the kitchen. Eddie hated slovenliness. Until Trudy moved out he never spent more than a few minutes in the apartment, but now he came over so often the new doorman thought he was one of the tenants. By the time the buzzer sounded Rebecca had changed into a striped mini-dress and dangling silver earrings. Eddie walked in carrying a brown paper bag which crackled as he embraced her. His kiss tasted of breath spray.

"Hey, wow. I love your perfume!" he exclaimed, setting the bag down on the kitchen table. "I once went out with a girl who wore the same perfume as my Aunt Gert. What a turn-off. This girl was really good-looking too—don't get upset, this was years ago. Anyway, we were at a party and the whole time while we danced I felt like I was dancing with Aunt Gert, who's sixty-five years old and weighs three hundred pounds." While he spoke he removed two round, foil wrapped objects from the bag, along with a sheaf of paper napkins.

"So what happened?" asked Rebecca, shooing away the cat, who had climbed onto a chair and was now poised to spring on the table.

"Nothing. I never asked her out again. I don't think she liked me anyway."

"Maybe your aftershave reminded her of her Uncle Bernie. What did you bring, for God's sake?"

"Roast beef on club." He opened a twist of waxed paper and lathered mustard on both sandwiches, carefully putting the soiled paper back into the bag.

"Oh, Eddie. I've been eating all day. Besides, I'm supposed to be on a diet. I told you."

"Diet, shmiet," Eddie said through a mouthful of food. "You don't need to diet. I like my women a little *zaftig* anyway."

Later they went into the bedroom and made love by the flickering blue light of the TV screen. Eddie had turned off the sound, substituting the dreamy songs of Simon and Garfunkel on the stereo. When it was over and he had gone home, Rebecca felt, as always, a sense of loss and despair. Besides being witty and fun to be with, Eddie was an expert lover, who knew exactly what to do to heighten and prolong her pleasure. Unlike the two other men she had had sexual relationships with, Eddie was patient, considerate, and inventive without being crude.

Rebecca still laughed when she thought of their first time. They had dated eight times before she consented to go to bed with him. Not that he wasn't nice looking, with his curly hair and round, choirboy face. But he had seemed so shy and innocent, not the type she was usually attracted to. Still, he was friendly and funny, in addition to being the son of Mr. Kramer, her boss at Kramer Imports. So she started dating him on the rebound, after Sidney Kuperman had dumped her for a wealthy girl from the Five Towns. Sidney was black-haired and sexy looking, but he made love like a speed-racer. Afterwards he would smirk at her and ask, "How was it?" to which Rebecca always lied and said "Great, Sid."

Eddie had surprised her. Now, after four months of seeing him almost daily at work and at least two evenings a week, she had begun to hope for something more. Did she love him? She thought she did, although not the way she had loved Monty Fleischer, the bastard. The thought of Monty still sent a stab of pain through her chest, even after all this time. They had met at a party, when Rebecca was twenty-two and beginning to worry about her single status. He had attracted her with his blond, all-American good looks; a Richard Chamberlain type except that Monty was Jewish, of Hungarian extraction. In addition, he was a second year medical student. Rebecca could not help but be impressed, thinking of her friends' envy, her mother's pride. Marriage to a doctor was every Jewish American girl's dream.

They dated regularly for three years; they talked of marriage once he became 'established.' Clearly he could not afford to take a wife while in school or even during his internship. He was in debt, his parents had little money, he was the oldest of four children, the family had staked all its hopes on him. Rebecca understood. Patiently she picked him up every day in her eight-year-old dented Rambler, no matter how late it was, and drove him home to the roach-infested apartment he shared with three fellow med students. Sometimes she even cleaned the apartment and did his grocery shopping. He was so busy, there were many exams, lab work, hours spent on rounds in the hospital, sleepless nights. When he took her, on occasion, to a movie, he often fell asleep, his blond head sagging back against her shoulder. In the gray light of the theater she studied the planes of his wide high-cheekboned face and her heart would fill with love and pity. Her mother loved him too.

What high hopes Miriam had had, baking him chocolate cakes, Linzer tarts, chocolate chip cookies with walnuts, his favorite kind. Rebecca was still living at home then, sneaking in late at night after she and Monty had made love in his tiny, crowded bedroom, with Rebecca holding her breath, hoping his roommates wouldn't hear through the paper-thin walls. That bastard! It had taken her two whole years of dating before she had finally given in to his persistent, almost nagging demands to "show him she *really* loved him."

Her reticence was partly due to vestiges of guilt from her days at Bais Yehudis High School, where her teachers preached constantly about the virtues a religious Jewish girl must possess. Of these, modesty and chastity were foremost. "God sees what you do in dark hallways!" thundered Rabbi Stein, her Bible teacher, every Monday morning, referring to the Saturday night dates that some lucky few in the class may have had that weekend.

Listening to him, Rebecca would shiver self-righteously. Not for her the dark hallway, the pawing hands of some pimply teenager from Boys Yeshiva High School. She was a 'good' girl. But as the Bais Yehudis years receded, so did Rebecca's religious fervor. In college she began to question God. Watching her mother's lips move soundlessly as she lit the *Shabbes* candles every Friday night, Rebecca wondered at the depth of Miriam's faith in a God who had allowed her entire family to be slaughtered. Slowly her own level of observance diminished. While she still considered herself orthodox, she found excuses for not attending synagogue on Saturday mornings, and began ordering salads and tuna sandwiches to eat with her friends in the non-kosher college cafeteria. Yet, in the area of sex, she remained steadfast. Before Monty, no boy had gotten farther than necking with her. As soon as his fingers traveled tentatively toward her breast, or slipped lightly beneath her skirt, she would push the fellow away. If it meant the end of a budding relationship, she did not care. She was saving herself for the man who would truly respect her, who would wait until they were properly married before demanding her body.

But Monty! With Monty it had been different. They were in love, they would surely get engaged soon. She was twenty-two, no longer a child. Most of her friends were married, and others had started to sleep with men. It was time. Their ensuing sex life was nothing spectacular, she knew that now that she had Eddie. Looking back on it now she remembered her vague feelings of disappointment, her frustration at not being truly satisfied by him. But at that time she hadn't really minded. Had he given her an engagement ring, it would have mattered even less. Instead, he had strung her along for a whole year more, only to abruptly tell her, on New Year's Eve of all times, that it was over, that she no longer 'did it for him.' Who *did* 'do it for him,' she later found out from one of his roommates, was a lab technician from Iowa named Hillary Bates.

The room felt hot. Rebecca got out of bed and opened the window. Down below, traffic streamed by on Ocean Parkway, a steady procession whose red and white lights temporarily mesmerized her. It was only ten-thirty, and she felt restless. Turning up the volume of the TV, she listened briefly to a description of the day's battles near the Mekong Delta, then flicked through the other channels before turning off the set. By the light of the streetlamp outside her window, she brushed her hair, peering at her shadowy reflection in the three-way-mirror above her vanity table. She was still pretty. Men always stared at her when she walked by. Although she could lose a pound here and there, her figure was basically fine, a perfect size eight. So why, at age twenty-seven, was she sitting alone in her apartment, while most of her classmates were married, many with children? As for Eddie—would he ever marry her? He never brought up the topic. Even Rebecca never mentioned it, out of fear that what happened to her friend Leah Steinberg, would happen to her. After dating Herman Krochmal, a CPA from Long Beach for five months, Leah had insisted that he declare his 'intentions.' "I'll have to think about it," he said, and walked out of Leah's door, and out of her life as well.

Everyone at the office teased Rebecca about her relationship with Eddie. Even his father, Mr. Kramer, 'The Boss,' called her "*Maideleh*", and sometimes pinched her cheek with paternal fondness when he passed her desk. But what did it all mean? What if Eddie, like Herman, had no 'intentions'? What if no one ever married her at all? The future stretched before her, year after bleak year; long days spent working at unsatisfying, 'nowhere' jobs, longer nights alone in a silent apartment. She was already an old maid, a spinster, shoulder-length hair and mini-skirts notwithstanding. Last week she had discovered her first gray hair.

"Ma!" she had complained on the phone, "I'm getting gray already. It's not fair! You don't even have gray hair!"

Miriam had laughed. "Of course I have gray hair. They color it for me in the beauty parlor. What did you think?"

Of course. Since she had bought her own bakery several years earlier, Miriam had become a 'fancy lady', touching up her hair, dressing in svelte suits and wearing jewelry and perfume every day. She even had a boyfriend, Mr. Geldzahler, who owned the liquor store across from the bakery. A tall, spindly fellow with a bristling mustache, Mr. Geldzahler appeared promptly at seven every Sunday evening, a small bouquet in hand, to take Miriam to dinner at the local dairy restaurant.

"So, when are you getting married, Ma?" Rebecca would ask, half in jest and half in dread of the cadaverous Mr. Geldzahler.

"After you," her mother always answered. Some months before, Miriam had explained to Rebecca why she would not marry again. She had had several chances in the years since Isaac's death; one or another widower introduced to her by Mrs. Elfenbaum the landlady, or by customers in the bakery. She would date them for a month or two, sometimes even longer, but when they pressed for a commitment, she ended the relationship.

"Why don't you marry him, Ma?" Rebecca would ask and Miriam always answered "It's not for me. I've had enough already." Her face, still youthful-looking and attractive, would take on a veiled, closed-off look, and the discussion would be over. But last fall, while commiserating with Rebecca over the loss of Sidney Kuperman, Miriam smoothed her daughter's hair away from her face, as she had done when Rebecca was a child, and said: "I know you are feeling miserable now, because of this business with Sidney, and even more because of all the good years you threw away with Monty. I know it still hurts you, this business with Monty, that you probably never got over. But I believe that what is destined, 'bashert' as we say, is 'bashert.' Monty was not your 'bashert,' and neither is Sidney. Even if you married one of them, it wouldn't have worked, because they weren't destined for you."

"Oh Ma, come on," Rebecca burst out, pulling away from her mother's caress. "Don't give me that destiny stuff. You think I believe that story about an angel announcing every baby's destined mate forty days before the baby is born? What about you? Who was your destined one? Was it Isaac? Was it my father, Reuben? Or was it that first one, the Hasid, whatever his name was, that you finally told me about at the age of twenty-five, though what the big secret was I'll never understand? Look," Rebecca went on." If I had married Monty, you would've been thrilled. You would've said he was my 'bashert.' And the same goes for Sidney. Whoever you marry is your destined one, just by virtue of the fact that you married him, whether it works out or not. If your marriage is lousy, then you were destined to have a lousy marriage, that's all. I mean, like, why don't you marry Geldzahler?

Is it because he's not your 'destined one,' or because you don't want another crummy marriage, like the last one? That's the real reason, anyone can see that; don't give me this 'destiny' baloney."

Miriam had nodded her head. "Yes, of course. You are right about that. I don't want to marry Geldzahler, or anyone, because I know what a good marriage is and what a bad marriage is. With your father, Reuben, I had a wonderful marriage. I loved him, he loved me, we were…" Her voice broke and she brushed away a tear. "I miss him still, Rebecca, to this day. And with Isaac, well, you know how it was with Isaac. So this is why I say, I'm better off alone. Look at Geldzahler, look at any man I might meet. Geldzahler lost his children in the war. He had a sick wife. For many years he took care of her, till she died. He himself is not a well man. Many of us refugees have health problems. Stomach pains, heart trouble, nightmares, nerves, whatever. And the older we get, the worse it is. Isaac was a bitter man, and also a sick man, and I took care of him for years, but now I want to live my own life. These last years I've finally been happy by myself. I go to the store, I see people, I come home, I do what I want. For the first time in my life I'm my own boss. It's true I get lonely at times. Maybe if I met someone whom I could really love…" Her voice trailed off.

"So why wouldn't you even go out with Mr. Levine, the insurance man? He's an American. He doesn't have all these problems that Isaac and the other refugees have." Miriam looked at Rebecca as if she were some strange, misshapen bird that had suddenly flown in her window and perched on her kitchen chair.

"An American? Rebecca, you don't understand. Since when do I have something in common with an American? I should marry a man who watches football and baseball? And what does an American know about me? Talk to an American about the war, they say, 'What? We also suffered! We didn't have any sugar, we didn't have any chicken!' Americans."

So Mom was happy, all by herself. But of course, unlike her daughter, she had had her chances; she'd never frowned at herself in the mirror, wondering why she was left out of the marriage market. *If only Eddie would propose,* Rebecca thought. Eddie was funny, smart, nice-looking, rich, tender, great in bed. Often, lately, he told her that he loved her. He didn't seem to have anyone else. Be patient, she admonished herself. Don't pressure him or you'll lose him, and then where will you be? Going to singles dances with Leah Steinberg, that's where.

Rebecca climbed into bed. With sleep came her oft-recurring dream of being lost in the subways. The dream had many variations, but always the same theme. Rebecca was on her way to meet a man. Who? Eddie? Monty? Sidney? It was never clear. She took train after train, changing in dark, deserted stations, sometimes going out onto empty streets lined with shuttered factories. Bulky, sinister human forms huddled in doorways, people she could not ask for directions. Down a long flight of filthy stairs she ran, her anxiety mounting, only to board the wrong train once again. Sometimes the dream fell apart at that point, resolving itself into a more pleasant one, or just a period of dreamless slumber. More often she awoke, her heart pounding and her blankets and sheets twisted and damp with sweat. Tonight she was lucky; the dream ended and she drifted into a blurred series of childhood images that relaxed her once again. The next morning Eddie stopped by her desk.

"Rebecca, you busy tonight?"

"Busy? No. Why?"

"Come have dinner with me. Okay?"

"Sure, okay. Where do you want to eat?"

"Wherever. Feinblatt's."

Feinblatt's was a kosher restaurant with well-prepared traditional food and no atmosphere. It was filled with loud-talking men from the garment center, and religious, long-sleeved office girls whose demure hairdos would soon be replaced by marriage wigs worn in exactly the same style. Eddie and Rebecca sat down at a small table in the rear. A broad-backed waiter in a soiled red jacket lurched against their table.

"What'll you have?" Feinblatt's was known for its Hungarian stuffed cabbage. They both ordered it along with chicken soup and salad. The waiter picked up the menus and left.

Eddie could not sit still. He folded and refolded his napkin, rearranged the cutlery and shifted about in his chair.

"What is it, Eddie? Is something the matter?"

"What? No. Why?"

"You seem so nervous tonight. Is it the Goldman order?"

"The Goldman order! What sons of bitches those Akahari guys are! Did you see today's cable?"

"No, Lorraine took it in. She didn't have a chance to tell me. She left early, to have her root canal done."

"Oh yeah. Well it's on Dave's desk now. Listen, the bastards sold the whole order, all eighty-five tons of it, to Konidaris."

"To Konidaris! Why? Didn't they get our purchase order?"

"Sure they got our purchase order. But now they claim his broker, that schmuck Zanides, had confirmed his order first. He must've sucked off the whole company to get it."

Rebecca shook her head. "Damn. What will you tell Goldman?"

"Nothing yet. I'm working on a deal with Molloy. I'll figure it out somehow." He settled back in his chair but remained fidgety throughout the meal.

Later, in Rebecca's apartment, he put Beethoven's Pastorale on the stereo, and motioned for her to sit beside him on the sofa. When she did, he put his left arm around her while fumbling in his pocket with his right hand. After a moment he produced a tiny, blue velvet box.

"What's that?" Rebecca asked, her throat tightening.

"Open it."

Inside was a large pear-shaped diamond, set high on a platinum ring, and flanked by two tiny oblong baguettes.

"Eddie! I can't believe it!" She put it on immediately. To her dismay, her finger was too thin for the ring. It would have to be returned for a smaller size. For the moment however, she took enormous pleasure in turning it about on her hand, watching its facets refract the light from her living room lamp and scatter it across the ceiling in dozens of tiny yellow-white dots.

Taking her face in both his hands, Eddie kissed her and whispered, "Are you happy?"

"Yes," she breathed. "Are you?"

"Delighted!" he said. "I wanted to do this long ago, but somehow the time wasn't ripe. My Dad kept saying, 'Wait, get to know her better, don't make a mistake…'"

"What does he say now?" Somehow it disturbed her to think that old Mr. Kramer was in on the decision.

"He's thrilled! Whaddya think? He always liked you. 'Ah nice Jewish goil'."

"Oh Eddie. Your father doesn't talk like that."

"Maybe not, but he thinks like that. Anyway, babe, he's really happy. It's too bad my mother didn't live to see it though. Her only son, finally tying the knot. She would've been so excited. Or maybe she wouldn't have. She was very possessive. She was so possessive she sewed nametags on my band-aids. She hated this girl, Natalie, that I went out with when I was twenty or so. She called her 'Natalie the *Nafka*'. That means whore."

"I know. I speak Yiddish, too, remember? What happened to her?"

"Who, my mother? She died when I was twenty-one. I told you that."

"No, to Natalie."

"Who the hell knows? Probably heads a Hadassah chapter in Cedarhurst or wherever. Hey!" Eddie leaned forward. "Bring out some wine! It's a celebration!"

Rebecca bought in a bottle of pink Chablis and two crystal wineglasses. Snuggled together on the sofa, they sipped at the wine and made wedding plans. Much later, they went into the bedroom and made love. As the sky turned from gray to mauve, they fell asleep, their arms and legs intertwined.

At seven in the morning Ocean Parkway was already thrumming with traffic. Rebecca groaned and covered her eyes with the blanket. There was a sour taste in her mouth and her head ached. Too much wine, too little sleep. Slowly her brain came alive, like a damp, ungainly butterfly struggling out of its cocoon. The ring! There it was, in the box on her dresser. Thank God she had had enough sense to remove it, or it might have rolled off among the tangled bedclothes. The apartment was quiet except for the early morning sounds that filtered through the walls; toilets flushing, doors closing, the faint hum of someone's radio or TV. Where was Eddie? She sat up in bed.

"Ed? Eddie?" There was no answer. Ringo padded in, mewing softly. He tensed his legs and sprang up on the bed, rubbing against Rebecca's knees and purring. Rebecca stroked him, detached his claws from the bedspread and lowered him to the floor, where she found a folded piece of paper.

Babe—had to leave. Dad's calling at seven. See you at work—Love ya—
Eddie

She smiled. He must have left it on the pillow, but her tossing about had knocked it to the floor.

The sun streamed in through the window. It promised to be a beautiful day.

Chapter thirty-one

F
Queens, New York, 1971

orest Hills was a wonderful neighborhood for young married
couples. Several of Eddie's friends lived there, and besides, it was
the perfect compromise, since Rebecca hated the noise and dirt of
Manhattan, and Eddie despised the provinciality and inconvenience
of Brooklyn. Nobody lived in the Bronx, and Staten Island was even
worse than Brooklyn, according to Eddie. Rebecca had been to Staten
Island only once; its empty marshes and tract-housing developments
held no appeal for her. Anyway, it was all temporary; very soon they
would begin house hunting, Eddie promised.

Rebecca smiled down at the twins. They were so sweet, with
their soft pink and white skin and tiny, delicate features. They had
named the boy Robert, Reuvain in Hebrew, for Rebecca's father,
whom he was said to resemble. Like his grandfather, Robert had
black hair and deep-set, gray-blue eyes, which Rebecca hoped would
not change color. The girl was called Sarah, after Eddie's mother, but
in looks she favored Miriam's side of the family. The faint tendrils of
hair on her downy scalp had a reddish cast, and her long-lashed eyes
were a clear blue-green.

It had taken Rebecca two years to conceive and the twins still

413

seemed like an absolute miracle. Although she often felt exhausted they were wonderful company, especially when Eddie was away. Lately he traveled a great deal—to Spain, Italy, even to Japan. When she complained about the length of his trips, which often lasted several weeks, Eddie reassured her that this, too, was temporary; later on they would hire someone they could trust who would take over the traveling. But right now, with his father's ulcer acting up, it wasn't possible. Besides, the business was doing well. That was the main thing, wasn't it? And didn't she love the things he brought her? Silk nightgowns from Paris, Italian sweaters and shoes. Even if these didn't fit properly he'd only been off by half a size. Still, it would be nicer if he were around more, to share in the joy of the children, and to help out with the night-time feedings. The maid Yvonne was a wonderful help during the day. Cradling the babies to her enormous bosom, she crooned Jamaican lullabies in a thin reedy voice that seemed to come from some invisible wraith up near the ceiling of the room; certainly not from this solid black giant of a woman in her starched white uniform. But promptly at six o'clock every day, Yvonne kissed the twins and departed for her home in South Ozone Park. There was no room in the Kramer apartment for a live-in maid. After making sure the twins were asleep, Rebecca picked up the phone and dialed her mother's number.

"Hello?"

"Hi Ma. How's everything?"

"Everything is fine. Have you heard from Eddie?"

"No. But it's probably hard to get through. And then there's the time difference."

"Where is he now?"

"In Tokyo, I think. Maybe he'll call tomorrow."

"How are my beautiful grandchildren?"

"Fine, perfect. I just wish they'd start sleeping through the night already. It's getting harder and harder to feed both of them at once at three in the morning. And when they wake up at different times, it's really impossible."

"Are you sure you won't change your mind and come here?"

Rebecca sighed. "Thanks Ma, but it's really easier for me to stay home right now. You're busy all day in the store and Yvonne won't come to Brooklyn. Maybe we'll come and stay next time, when the babies are older." Robert rolled over in his crib, opened his eyes, and let out a wailing cry. "Ma, I gotta go. Robbie's up. I'll talk to you soon. Bye." She replaced the receiver and hurried to prepare a bottle. As she cradled Robbie against her body, listening to the soft, contented sounds he made as he sucked, Rebecca thought of her own mother, and of the joy that suffused Miriam's face when she held the twins. Yet occasionally, Rebecca caught a sudden shift in her mother's expression as she gazed at the babies, a barely discernible shadow that passed over her face. Even as she smiled, a trace of sadness would appear in her eyes, and at the corners of her mouth. Remembering, Rebecca felt the familiar guilt that had been with her since childhood, whenever she thought about Miriam's past.

What did her mother feel when she held Robert or Sarah in her arms? Was she remembering her own little David, the beautiful first-born son who was to disappear from her life at the age of three, never to be held by his mother again? Or was she thinking perhaps of the infant Rebecca, whose babyhood Miriam had shared with, and finally relinquished to, a half-wit peasant on a dirt-poor Polish farm? Thinking about her mother's life always gave her a feeling of inadequacy. What did any of her own problems or disappointments amount to, compared to what Miriam had suffered? How could she complain to her mother about Eddie's long absences, or the difficulties she had caring for two babies, when her mother had lost everyone except Rebecca? *She* was the only one left to comfort her mother and give her *naches*, pleasure.

As a child Rebecca had bitterly resented the burden her mother's suffering had imposed on her. For years she had been afraid to do anything that might anger or hurt her mother, while in her fantasies she created a different identity for herself, one in which she was the child of American Christians. In high school, she had rebelled secretly, letting her Hebrew grades slump, and even sneaking out once to see a movie with Michael Cimino, an Italian boy from around the corner. When Michael squeezed her breast in the elevator, she had refused to see him again. At Brooklyn College she had done well enough, maintaining a B average. As an education major she had discovered, while student teaching in her senior year, that she had neither the interest nor the patience for dealing with large groups of bored and restless children. After graduation she had taken a series of secretarial-type jobs that afforded little room for advancement. Although Miriam never commented on it, Rebecca knew that she had disappointed her mother by not becoming a teacher. But perhaps now she had made up for it somewhat, by marrying a wealthy man and producing these beautiful twins.

Robert finished his bottle with a satisfied burp. Rebecca placed him on the changing table and removed his diaper. As she sponged his bottom, she heard Sarah sobbing in the other room. Quickly she fastened a new diaper on Robert and placed him in his crib. She picked up Sarah and hurried to heat up a bottle. Robert, unhappy at being left in his crib, wailed angrily. Impatient for her bottle, which was slowly warming in a pot of hot water, Sarah added her own cries to Robert's. With all the noise Rebecca almost missed the sound of the phone ringing. Holding the screaming Sarah in the crook of her arm, she picked up the phone.

"Hello?"

For a moment there was only static. Then she heard Eddie's voice. "Hello, Rebecca?"

"Yeah, Eddie?"

"Yeah, it's me. What's going on there? I can hardly hear you."

"I know. Both kids are screaming."

"Well, can't you take the other phone? I'm calling all the way from Japan, for God's sake."

"I can't. I'm in the middle of preparing a bottle. Sarah's hungry and I don't know what Robbie's problem is."

"Well, can't you put them down for a second so I can talk?"

"Okay, wait a minute." She put Sarah in her crib and popped a pacifier into her mouth, but the baby spat it out and continued screaming. Meanwhile, Robert's face was purple and his cries had accelerated into shrieks. Rebecca lingered for a moment, holding the phone near the door of the nursery. *Let him hear what it's like,* she thought. In the bedroom, she picked up the blue princess phone beside her pillow.

"Okay, Eddie, I'm back, but they're still screaming."

"Okay, I'll make it quick. Listen, Beck, I'm really sorry, but I've got to stay on an extra week or so."

"What? Why? You promised you'd be home next Tuesday."

"Yeah, I know, but it's taking longer than we thought to close the deal. Yamoshi is giving us a rough time."

"Oh, Eddie." Tears filled her eyes. "I miss you."

"Yeah, well, I know, honey. I miss you too. How are the kids? Besides all the hollering right now, I mean."

"They're fine, but they're a handful, especially at night, after Yvonne leaves."

"Yeah, well, I'll help you out more when I get back. Listen I gotta go now. Love you."

"Love you, too." The phone clicked off. She replaced the receiver and went back into the nursery. Both babies were still crying. Lifting Sarah from the crib, she carried her into the kitchen. Damn! She had forgotten to turn off the flame under the bottle. By now the milk was scalding. Plunging the bottle under the cold-water faucet, she crooned to Sarah, rocking her against her shoulder as Robert howled in the background.

Eddie returned two weeks later, his face gray and haggard-looking. Giving Rebecca a perfunctory kiss, he threw himself onto his easy chair, letting his briefcase slide to the door.

"Eddie, what's wrong. You look terrible."

"Where are the kids?"

"Sleeping. Talk low. What happened?"

"We lost the deal."

"What deal?"

"'What deal,' she says. What deal have we been talking about all these weeks? What do you think I was in Japan for, my health? The Yamoshi deal. Sold it to that low-balling bastard, Evans."

"Oh."

"'Oh.' That's all you can say. 'Oh.'"

"Oh, that's awful, Eddie."

"Damn right it's awful. It's worse than awful. You don't know the half of it. The whole Oppenheimer line depended on it. My father's fit to be tied. I thought he'd have a coronary. All this right on top of losing the Austrian deal last week."

"The Austrian deal?"

"Yeah, you remember, I told you about a shipment of merino... ah, what's the difference. It's gone, down the drain. Get me a Coke or something, will you?"

"Sure." She leaned over Eddie and kissed him lightly on the forehead but he shrugged her away. "Just get me a cold drink."

Returning with a frosted glass of cola, Rebecca said, "I guess this means we can't look at houses next week, after all."

"Houses!" Eddie exploded. The Coke sloshed over the side of the glass, leaving a dark stain on the carpet. "Is that all you can think about at a time like this? Houses? You think I can ask my father for a loan *now*? Are you out of your mind?" His voice rose sharply.

"Eddie, shush, the kids. I didn't mean...." It was too late. Loud wailing, pitched high and low, like a two-part harmony, came from the nursery.

Eddie shook his head. "Shit. No peace."

For the next few weeks Eddie left the house early and returned late, often coming home with a stack of papers over which he pored until past midnight. When the babies cried, Rebecca had to shut them in the bedroom with her, so that Eddie wouldn't be disturbed. The second night that he was home, both babies awoke at four in the morning, screaming. Rebecca touched Eddie's shoulder gently, then prodded him when he didn't respond.

"Eddie, can you give me a hand? The two of them are crying."

"Goddamn it, Beck, I'm exhausted. How did you manage while I was away?" He rolled over and buried his head in the pillow.

From then on Rebecca did her best to manage without Eddie, but her resentment grew. Eddie didn't seem to notice. He went into the office even on weekends. "Just till this crisis ends," he promised. "After I get back from Spain things'll be a lot calmer."

"Spain? You didn't tell me."

"Sure I did. I must've. I fly to Spain on Tuesday."

Two days before Eddie's departure Yvonne gave notice that she was leaving. Her father had taken ill and she had to go back to Jamaica to help care for him. Rebecca was devastated. Frantically she called household employment agencies, which sent a series of women, some capable and efficient, others lazy and incompetent. All left within a few days, for one reason or another. In desperation, Rebecca phoned her mother, who closed the store, packed a few things, and arrived in a taxi. Rebecca cried with relief when she saw her. For the rest of the week Miriam helped care for the twins, while Rebecca continued searching for a new housekeeper. When Miriam left, unable to keep the store closed for so long, Rebecca still hadn't found anyone she felt she could trust. Eddie returned a day earlier than expected. Rebecca answered the door in a stained housecoat, her hair plastered to her face in damp strings.

"Beck," he cried, giving her a hug. "Get dressed. We're going out to dinner at seven thirty with a new client. Vic Sharrer from United Mills. Put on something nice, okay?" He slid his suitcase through the door and removed his tie.

"Eddie, I can't." He frowned at her.

"What do you mean, you can't? Ask the girl to stay late. We'll pay her extra." Rebecca shook her head in exasperation.

"Eddie, there is no girl. I haven't found anyone yet."

"Then call a kid from the building. Lenore, or whatever her name is." He took off his jacket, tossing it over the arm of the sofa.

"Eddie, I can't go out tonight. Robbie has a fever and sore throat and Sarah's been crying all day. I think she's probably coming down with the same thing."

"Do you mean to tell me you can't leave the kids for a few hours because of a little fever? After I've been gone for eight days? Christ. Give 'em some aspirins or something."

Rebecca bristled. "Give 'em some aspirin," she mimicked.

"Are you making fun of me?" Eddie's voice took on a quiet, menacing tone. "Because if you are I have news for you. I won't stand for it. I work my guts out flying all over the place so you and the kids can live in this," he waved his hand at the living room set, "this showy apartment, with a maid and whatever else your heart desires. I bring you presents from Europe, from Japan, the best of everything, and this is what I get? You can't spend time with me the first night I'm home?"

"Stay home tonight and I'll spend time with you. I just can't go out." Rebecca fought to keep the tears from falling.

"Stay home? Fat chance. Forget it. I'll go myself." He walked into the bedroom, slamming the door. Some time later he emerged, shaved and showered, in a new suit and colorful silk tie.

Rebecca sat on the sofa, the twins on her lap, as Eddie rushed past her and out the door without a backward glance. Cuddling the children against her chest, Rebecca could no longer stem the tears. *He didn't even look at them,* she thought, sobbing. *Eight days away from home, and he didn't even look at them.*

Eddie came home after eleven. Rebecca lay in bed half-asleep, having dozed off during the eleven o'clock news. She heard him close the door of the room and snap off the TV. With her eyes shut she burrowed deeper into her pillow. Eddie turned on the lamp and began undressing. *Very considerate,* thought Rebecca. *He sees I'm asleep and still turns the lamp on.* The bed creaked as he slid across the sheets.

"Beck," he said softly, touching her shoulder.

"Hmmm?"

"Listen, I'm sorry about before. It was a rough flight. But the dinner went great. Hey, is your diaphragm in?"

He must be kidding, thought Rebecca. She groaned and shook her head, her eyes shut against the yellow lamplight.

"I'll get it for you." He left the bed and went into the bathroom. In a moment, he was back.

"Rebecca, you up?" She opened one eye.

"Eddie, I'm so tired, and I'm still upset from before. I really can't. Please."

"Tired, hell. I fly back from Spain and go out to dinner till eleven, and she's tired. Okay. Don't do me any favors."

He turned off the lamp and climbed back into bed, his back to her. Silently she waited for his breathing to become flat and shallow. As she stared into the fuzzy darkness her body slowly lost its tension and she drifted into the clouded semi-consciousness that heralded sleep.

As the weeks passed, Eddie became more and more preoccupied with his work. Complaining that the house was too noisy, he stayed late at the office most evenings. When he returned home Rebecca was often asleep. He barely saw the twins, who sometimes cried when he picked them up, as if he were a stranger. His trips abroad became more frequent, sometimes lasting as long as three weeks.

Little by little, Rebecca began to enjoy the time he was away more than the time he spent at home. When Eddie was out of town her life took on a steady pattern. She had finally secured a good housekeeper, a Barbadian woman named Constance, who had a warm and easy relationship with both Rebecca and the twins. The four of them co-existed in a cocoon that revolved around the children—their meals, their naps, their outings, their bedtime. Rebecca had also made a few friends among the mothers who sat in the park on sunny afternoons. When Eddie returned he struck a jarring note in the rhythm of her life, disrupting Rebecca's schedule by demanding her time and attention. Since she now had Constance, he could neither understand nor sympathize with her fatigue in the evenings. In addition, when she told him stories of the twins' escapades, his lack of interest was evident. She, in turn, found it difficult to concentrate when Eddie discussed his business deals with her. Slowly their resentment of each other grew, as their separate orbits widened, shutting each other out.

One week before the twins' first birthday, Eddie announced that he was flying to Italy in two days.

"But Eddie! The twins' party! You said you'd be here!"

"So postpone the party. I'll only be gone two weeks. What's the big deal? The kids don't know the difference anyway."

"I can't postpone it. I've sent out invitations, my mother's coming, and your father with Carmela, and a bunch of my friends—Eddie, you said you'd be here for the party, you promised!"

"What are you getting so worked up about a goddamn kids' party for?"

"Goddamn kids' party! Right! That's all they mean to you! To you they're nothing but goddamn kids anyway!" Her anger and resentment boiling to the surface, she pointed her finger at him and shouted—"When did you last do anything for the kids? When did you ever give one of them a bath, a bottle, or even change a diaper? Never, that's when! Even on weekends, you're always too busy to bother with them. To you they're just nuisances, they get in your way. All you care about is your work. Can't even be home for their first party. Why can't you be more of a father? Susan's husband, Ricky—"

"Oh, so here we go again." He put on a whining, falsetto voice. "Ricky bathes his kid! Ricky diapers his kid! Ricky does the dishes! Ricky mops the floor! Well, I'll bet Susan puts out a lot more for Ricky than you do for me. Why should I help you, anyway? You have Constance."

"Constance, sure! Constance leaves at six o'clock. And she's off on weekends. Do you know what it's like chasing two babies around all day?"

"Lots of mothers do it and they don't give their husbands such a pain in the ass! That's all you are to me anyway, a pain in the ass! You might as well know it right now. Always tired, always nagging, complaining."

"I do not!"

"Not much you don't. All that matters to you about me is the money I make. Well then, you can have it. I don't give a shit. I'm leaving. I'll send you a check in the mail."

He stormed out, slamming the door so hard the crockery in the breakfront rattled.

In the early weeks of their separation, Rebecca was sure Eddie would return. In bed at night she lay awake, half expecting, half dreading, the click of his key in the lock. Several times his father called, to ask how she and the children were. Once he even came to see the twins, with his twenty-four year old girlfriend Carmela in tow. Their visit was intensely uncomfortable for everyone. The children showed little interest in their grandfather but were fascinated by Carmela's amber beaded earrings, and kept climbing up on her lap, trying to pull them out of her ears. Mr. Kramer hemmed and hawed about Eddie:

"He's a good boy, but you know, it's hard for him, the job, the kids, and all. I mean, it's not that he didn't try…"

"He was never around long enough to try. You always sent him off to Milan, or Dresden, or wherever."

"Ah, Rebecca, don't be like that. Things'll straighten out, he'll be back. I try to talk to him, but Eddie, well, he's got his own mind. You know, I also traveled when I was married to Eddie's mother, and she took it okay. When Eddie got older she used to come along sometimes. You could do that too, maybe, later on."

Rebecca sniffed.

"Anyway," he went on, fidgeting with his tie while Carmela brushed off her peach silk sheath dress which was crisscrossed all over with wrinkles and smudges from the twins' climbing, "the money's coming in, isn't it? I mean, he's sending you money, ain't he?"

Rebecca nodded, embarrassed at having to admit her complete financial dependence on a man who no longer lived with her, no longer loved her, or even cared enough to visit their children.

"Well, okay then. Let me know if you need anything."

He kissed her on the cheek and left, a short, stocky man with gray hair, a gray suit, a gray foulard tie, and grayish stubble forming on his jaws. Carmela's spike heels clickety-clicked down the hallway as Rebecca locked and bolted the door. On the kitchen counter she found an envelope with the Kramer Import-Export Co. imprint. In it were three crisp one hundred dollar bills.

When Rebecca called Miriam that evening she knew something was wrong as soon as she heard her mother's voice. Instead of her usually cheerful "Hello," Miriam picked up the phone with a quavering "Yes? Who is it?"

"Ma, what's wrong?" Rebecca felt her stomach tighten.

"Oh, Rebecca. I didn't want to worry you; it's nothing, really."

"What's nothing? What happened? You sound terrible."

"It was this afternoon. I stood up on the stool to get down a tin of flour and somehow the stool tipped over and I fell. But it's nothing serious."

"Oh Ma, how awful. Are you in pain?"

"Yes, not so much, really. The doctor at the hospital gave me some painkillers."

"Hospital? You went to the hospital?"

"I wouldn't have, but Lucy, my helper, insisted. She called me a cab, so I went to the emergency room."

"And what did they say?"

"After they x-rayed my leg, they told me I had a bad sprain."

"Well, I guess we can be grateful it's not broken. But why were you climbing on a stool? That's what Lucy's there for. Anyway, what's happening now? Can you walk?"

"Not really. They gave me crutches. But it's very difficult. I'll have to get used to them, I guess. Listen, don't worry about me, Rifkaleh. I'll be all right. How are the children?"

"But Ma, you can't stay there alone in your apartment, on crutches. How will you go up and down the stairs? How will you even get around the house? You've got to come here and stay with us. How long do you have to be off your feet?"

"The doctor wasn't sure. Two, three weeks, maybe less."

"Oh God. What about the bakery?"

"That's a problem. I can't leave Lucy there alone. I'll have to close it for a while. To tell you the truth, Rebecca, I could use a rest from the bakery anyhow. I'm getting tired of it all. I've been thinking of getting a buyer and selling it altogether. Maybe I'll do something else. Open a bookstore, maybe."

"Whatever the case, you've got to come stay with me for a while. Call Lucy and tell her, and then pack a suitcase. I'd come myself to get you but the kids are asleep already. It's best I call you a cab."

"Rebecca, are you sure you want me there? I'll just be in the way."

"No you won't. The kids will love it and you'll be company for me too, especially in the evenings. I'm calling the cab right away. Bye."

Rebecca sighed. More problems. Still, it was true about the kids and she, too, would enjoy having her mother around. She'd been feeling guilty lately about not seeing her often enough. And certainly her mother was in no condition to stay alone. She'd sounded awful.

When the cab arrived Rebecca hurried downstairs to help her mother into the elevator. Miriam's face was pale as she pulled herself forward on the stiff wooden crutches. Her left leg was encased in bandages.

"Oh, look at you, Ma!" Rebecca cried. "Imagine even thinking of staying alone. Did you call Lucy?"

"Yes. I told her to close the store after tomorrow; she'll tell the bakers and the suppliers. It'll be okay."

On Monday evening of the following week, Miriam retired early. A late-summer storm was on its way, with a resulting drop in air pressure. Miriam wiped her brow and complained of the pain in her ankle. "It must be the weather," she said. "The doctor told me it might hurt when the weather changes." She took a painkiller and hobbled off to bed.

Rebecca chain-locked the door and settled down on the creamy velour club chair in her living room. She needed some time alone to resolve the many problems that had plagued her all day. On a simple, day-to-day basis, she could cope with her life as it stood right now. Her mother was here, she had Constance, the kids were fine. Eddie's check came regularly, so there were no money problems. But under the surface, everything was a mess. Since he'd left, Eddie had only called twice. Their conversations had been terse and strained. Eddie had asked about the children and then hung up. So far, he had not mentioned divorce. Unsure of her own feelings, Rebecca was afraid to bring up the subject. Did she want Eddie back? She thought of their courtship and the first few years of their marriage. Tears filled her eyes and she felt a strong urge to call him, to say: "Eddie, remember how it was, on Ocean Parkway? Remember, before the twins? Wasn't it fun? Wasn't it good, then?" But then she imagined Eddie's response and all the hurt returned. Eddie would say it was she, not he, who had spoiled everything. She who had destroyed his love by her constant nagging, her chronic fatigue, and her always putting the kids first.

Fragments of their many arguments echoed in her ears. Eddie's voice, harsh with anger, "What a pain in the ass you turned out to be!" No, she would not call Eddie. Turning on the lamp that stood beside her chair, she reached for the novel she had started the night before.

The house was nearly silent. The vague droning sound of apartment life, along with the faint traffic noises of Yellowstone Boulevard, were masked by the steady hum of the air conditioner. Rebecca's eyelids had just begun to droop when she was startled awake by the trill of the downstairs buzzer ringing through the intercom in her tiny entrance hall.

"Damn!" she muttered. "I hope it doesn't wake the kids." Tensely listening for any sound from their room, she tiptoed to the intercom. Mercifully, the twins stayed quiet.

"Yes? Who is it?" Rebecca called softly into the white disc of the receiver. The hoarse, heavily accented voice of an old woman answered.

"Zwillinger?"

"Yes," Rebecca answered. Both her married and maiden names were written on the downstairs mailbox, since she still occasionally received mail addressed to Rebecca Zwillinger.

"Zwillinger?" the voice repeated. "Reuben? David?"

A chill of fear went through Rebecca. "Who is this?" she gasped. Crackling static came through the receiver, then nothing at all. Dropping the receiver so that it swung on its wire like a pendulum, Rebecca rushed to the door. Who could it be that was ringing downstairs at this hour, nine at night, asking for her dead father and brother? For surely that's whom she meant, Reuben and David Zwillinger, dead nearly thirty years, indirect victims of 'The War.' Her mother always called it 'The War,' talking about it as if it had happened yesterday. At the door of the apartment, Rebecca stopped. The keys! She couldn't just leave the apartment unlocked, for anybody to get in. Where was her pocketbook? Walking as quickly and as silently as she could, she searched her bedroom for her bag, finally locating it on the floor of the closet. The keys were another matter; they seemed to be stuck in the lining and wouldn't come loose. Frustrated, she ripped the keys free, ran to the door and locked it behind her. The hall was very quiet, except for the usual television noises. The elevator was not in use, but neither was it at her floor. Rather than wait, she hurried down the stairs, her sandals clacking loudly on the worn marble.

The lobby was empty. The white plaster statue of some nameless goddess stared at her with calm blank eyes. Rebecca rushed through the entrance doors and out into the courtyard. A few fat drops of rain splattered on the warm concrete. Within seconds, she reached the street. A block down, barely visible, the small, bent figure of a woman could be seen, walking slowly towards the lower-numbered streets.

"Stop!" Rebecca cried as she ran after her, oblivious to the sudden thunderstorm that soon soaked her thin summer dress and plastered her hair to her forehead.

Over several cups of tea that Miriam served with trembling hands in Rebecca's brightly lit dinette, Mrs. Abramovich told her story. Rebecca listened, frozen in her chair as the woman spoke in Russian-accented Yiddish:

"I live here, in Forest Hills, only three months. I was lucky to get out of Russia, with my son, Yuri. My son Gregor, they did not let go. He had a job once, in a government bureau; they said he knew secrets. So they made him stay." Rebecca fidgeted impatiently. She didn't want to hear about the woman's son and his difficulties, but couldn't risk offending her either. Sensing the discomfort of her audience, Mrs. Abramovich continued:

"But you don't want to know about this, about my Gregor. So tonight I was visiting my friend Julia, who lives in this building, but she wasn't home. Then I saw the name on the mailbox next to the bell there—Zwillinger. I can read English because, of course, I grew up in Poland, and the letters are the same, you know. And I remembered, I knew a family, Zwillinger, an older man and a young man, his son. They lived near me, in Moscow. Mr. Zwillinger had lived before in Kiev, but he was sent right away to Siberia, and it was lucky, because otherwise, who knows? Maybe today he'd be lying in Babi Yar, with the others. But he lived in Moscow, and he had a nice young son, David, with such golden, reddish-golden hair, so handsome." She looked at Miriam. "Are you all right?"

Miriam's face had turned ashen. "Go on," she whispered.

Mrs. Abramovich squinted at Miriam, cleared her throat and continued. "They lived next door from me, for a while. But then we moved, and later they also moved to another apartment, I don't know where. My Yuri has a nice family, so he moved to a bigger place, and I didn't see the Zwillingers any more. Still, when I saw the name, I thought, 'Who knows? Maybe they got out too.' So I took a chance, I rang the bell."

"Why did you go away so quickly? Why didn't you wait, or come up?" Rebecca asked.

"Well, I hear your voice, a young woman, American. I thought, nah, this is not the same family. There are maybe many Zwillingers in New York. So I left."

Miriam leaned forward in her chair. "Tell me," she said, in a voice that was now strangely loud, "What did the father look like, this Reuben Zwillinger? I mean, when you first met him?"

Mrs. Abramovich closed her eyes and reopened them, took a few swallows of tea and pursed her lips. "Well, I knew him maybe five or six years. He was tall, a little bit stooped, maybe; you know, we all suffered in the war, maybe he had trouble with his back. And he was balding, but his hair was dark. A nice-looking man. That's all I remember. Oh, and he wore glasses. Yes. That's all. I'm sorry I can't remember better."

Rebecca looked at her mother, who was nodding her head with such conviction one would think Mrs. Abramovich had produced a photograph, rather than this sketchy description that could have been anyone.

"Ma! How can you be sure it's them?"

"Oh, I'm sure it's them. Reuben was already balding when we were separated. And he was a little stooped, too, even before the war. And David, he was blonde, reddish-blonde, like an angel…" Her voice broke and she began to cry softly.

Rebecca awkwardly put her arm around her mother's shoulder.

"Rifkaleh, you must go to Russia."

The late morning sun slanting through the blinds formed broad white stripes on the Wedgwood blue carpet and across the plump shoulders of the little child who lay quietly, playing with a toy car. Rebecca shifted her gaze from her son to her mother. Miriam looked haggard and worn despite the cheery colors of her floral housecoat and the hectic spots of color on her cheeks. Had the wrinkles under her eyes always been there? The sharp creases along her mouth? Rebecca had never noticed them. I probably look like hell myself, she thought. In their excitement over Mrs. Abramovich's story, neither had slept much the night before.

"You must go." Miriam repeated.

"Me? How can I go? I'll never be able to find my way around in Russia, of all places. Besides how can I leave the twins? It would make much more sense for you to go. After a few weeks, when your leg heals…"

Miriam shook her head. "No, Rebecca. This cannot wait. This Mrs. Abramovich has already lived here, in New York, for several months. Even before she came to America she had not seen Reuben and David for several years. She said they had moved away." Moving closer to her daughter, she took her hand and held it firmly in her own. "Rebecca," she pleaded, "please try to understand how I feel. After the war, when I received the letter from Russia telling me that Reuben and David were dead, it was as if some part of me died as well. I had lost so much already; my parents, my brother and sister killed before my eyes…if not for you, I doubt I would have had the strength to go on. But, thank God, I did have you to take care of, and so I did go on, and I managed to make a new life for myself, with you and with Isaac. But you know very well, Rebecca, that my life with Isaac was not a happy one. It wasn't Isaac's fault; he was a good man, but he suffered always with his own memories, his own horrors. Maybe if I could have loved him more."

She stroked the soft skin on the back of Rebecca's hand and went on. "But it was as if a part of my heart had closed off when I lost Reuben and David. I was able to love you but there was no more room for Isaac. Now," she continued, tightening her grip on Rebecca's hand, "now when I hear that the husband I adored with all my heart, and the beautiful little boy I loved so much, they whom I never stopped mourning for more than twenty-five years—that they may still be alive! After all this time! Rebecca, darling, this cannot wait. If not for this ankle, I would go myself. This very minute, I would fly...." Her voice broke.

Rebecca looked at her mother's beautiful but anguished face and at the tears that glistened on her cheeks. Throughout her own life, behind all of her meager accomplishments, there had gnawed at her the dark, insidious feelings of guilt and inadequacy. Compared to the sufferings her mother had endured, her own problems shrank to petty insignificance. And what value did her own few, small triumphs have, compared to those of her mother, who, after staring death in the face, had found the courage to go on, rebuilding her life and raising her child on alien shores? All through the years Rebecca had wondered, would she, if faced with the same challenges her mother had confronted, have overcome them with the same courage, the same quiet strength? Now her mother was providing her with a challenge of her own. She tried to picture herself stealing through sinister Russian streets, searching for a father and brother she had never known. She could not envision it. In her mind's eye, she saw only her mother, bruised and bloodied, fighting her way through the Polish forest, her body heavy with the burden of her yet unborn daughter.

"All right, Mom," she whispered. "I'll go. I'll arrange for Constance to stay here and I'll go to Russia."

The visa arrived within a week and final preparations were made. On the morning of Rebecca's departure Constance arrived promptly at six, to find Miriam and Rebecca bleary-eyed and exhausted. The twins had awakened them twice during the night, and in their nervous excitement they had been unable to fall back to sleep. Instead they had talked until dawn, with Miriam begging Rebecca over and over to be careful, to take no risks, to keep in touch with the American Embassy, to call whenever she could. Rebecca peeked into the nursery, where the twins now slept peacefully. Then, once more, she hugged and kissed her mother, who was crying softly. Finally, with a quick peck on Constance's cheek, she lifted her two small suitcases and went downstairs, where the taxi was already waiting.

Chapter thirty-two

Though the takeoff was uneventful, Rebecca felt a mounting tension. Again and again she read a note she had taken from the home of Mrs. Abramovich's son, Yuri. A tall, heavyset man of thirty, with thick black hair and kindly features set in a florid face, he painstakingly drew her a map of the Moscow neighborhood where Reuben and David Zwillinger had lived. With a red pen, he marked the crude map with circles and x's.

"Here is Archipova Street. Here is synagogue, number eight Archipova. Here this is Petrovskije, number 64, where they lived with us in same building." His English, although heavily accented, was surprisingly good.

At Heathrow Airport, after a brief stopover, Rebecca boarded the Aeroflot plane for Russia. As soon as she was seated, her flight bag stuffed into the too-small luggage rack, she felt she had made a grave mistake. Perhaps she could still get out, spend an hour or two in London and catch a return flight to New York? But the plane was already taxiing down the runway. A blonde stewardess, slightly plumper than her American counterparts, stood up in the aisle. While a female voice overhead described the airplane's safety features in three

431

languages, the stewardess pointed to escape hatches and displayed an oxygen mask in a graceful, ballet-like pantomime. The plane was half-empty. Many of the passengers had the careworn expressive faces of Eastern Europeans. An enormous lunch was served, most of which Rebecca could not eat. Aeroflot did not provide kosher meals. Even if it did, she had no intention of advertising her Jewishness.

The announcements jolted her awake. First in Russian, then German, then French, and finally English. "Please fasten your seatbelts. We are preparing to land at Sheremetyevo International Airport."

The plane touched down with a gentle bump that set Rebecca's heart racing. There was no turning back. Buttoned up in her all-weather coat and clutching her flight bag, she walked haltingly down the metal staircase. The steps were still slick from the morning rain. On the airport bus she huddled between two sleepy-eyed East Germans who leaned across her to carry on a heated argument. Rebecca turned her head from one to the other in disgust. Their breath stank of coffee and bad teeth.

Rebecca had barely stepped off the bus when a stout young woman in a shapeless gray suit approached her. "Your name, please," she demanded, scowling slightly.

"Rebecca Kramer."

"Yes. Kramer." The woman ran a plump finger up and down a list of names. "Yes," she repeated, "National Hotel."

The cab ride from the airport should have been relaxing, but Rebecca felt tense and exhausted. Although her passage through customs had been swift and uneventful, she could not rid herself of a feeling of dread. The countryside sped by; pine trees, an occasional log cabin, later a huge monument of some sort, followed by more and more tall buildings. One or two of these were old and ornate relics of the pre-revolutionary period, but most were new and plain looking, made of dull yellowish brick. A cold rain was still falling, and the overall scene was gray and depressing.

As the cab approached Moscow proper, the city took on a different look. The cab driver pointed out the golden domes of the Novodevichi Monastery, rising like jewels across the Moscow River. This was the Moscow Rebecca had pictured, a city of soaring spires and golden onion-shaped domes. She had not expected the innumerable dun-colored, graceless apartment houses that lined the broad streets, block after block, along the Leningrad Highway. Central Moscow did not disappoint Rebecca. Here were the grand old buildings she had imagined, similar in appearance to those on Park Avenue or Central Park West. As they neared the city center the driver cleared his throat and announced "Gorkovo." Rebecca consulted her guide-book. The highway had become Gorki Street. When the driver pulled over, Rebecca instinctively fumbled in her purse, then remembered the first and last cab trips had been paid for as part of the Intourist package. She climbed out of the cab, waved at the driver who carried in her bags and said *"Spaseeba balshoye,"* as her guidebook had instructed. The driver grinned broadly.

Only as the cab pulled away did she look up. Directly opposite her was the walled fortress, the famous Kremlin. All of her guide-books had not prepared her for the sight. Breathless, she stared at the imposing, crenelated wall and then beyond, to the graceful spires and gold and silver domes of its majestic churches. So this was the Kremlin. Behind those walls Nikita Khrushchev had bellowed hatred for America in the years when Rebecca, as a thirteen-year-old child, had cowered under a desk in a Brooklyn classroom while air-raid sirens howled. In her early childhood years she had learned to differentiate between the monsters of the past, the Germans, and the monsters of the present, the Russians. The former had killed her father and brother, not to mention her grandparents, aunts and uncles, while the latter kept their dreaded bombs poised, ready to drop at any moment on the heads of American schoolchildren. As Rebecca watched, the rain slowed to a drizzle. The elegant spires and domes of the Kremlin rose out of the mist like a cluster of fairytale castles. And why not? Rebecca had long since learned that beauty and cruelty can coexist in perfect harmony.

The National Hotel was one of the best in Moscow. Rebecca knew she was very lucky to have been placed here by Intourist. They could have just as easily put her in the Tolstoy, which her guidebook described as seedy and run down. Travelers had no choice as to where they would be billeted. The Russian equivalent of a bellhop emerged

433

from the hotel, escorted Rebecca inside to the 'Service Bureau' and left her there. Rebecca smiled at the young woman behind the desk and received a wan twitch of the lips in return.

"I'm Rebecca Kramer. K-r-a-m-e-r. May I have my room key?" The woman nodded. After twenty-five minutes of anxious waiting as the woman tried to determine which accommodation had been reserved for Mrs. Rebecca Kramer, Rebecca was finally taken to her room. The porter set down her luggage, nodded and disappeared. The room was large, with a high ceiling, and slightly shabby, but did have elegant, turn-of-the-century furniture pieces. Thick draperies of maroon velvet surrounded the windows. In the small, black and gold marble bathroom, Rebecca took a long, relaxing bath, letting the warm water ease away the tension in her limbs.

Dressed, with her hair freshly combed, she felt much better. Leaning into the oval mirror, she applied deep pink lipstick. *Striking*, she thought. *I'll show those Muscovites what an American woman is supposed to look like.* Minutes later, she wiped the lipstick off. No use in calling attention to herself, after all.

At six o'clock Rebecca left the room key with the *dezhurnaya*, the corpulent 'floor lady' who squatted sphinx–like at her desk near the stairs.

Out on the street, Rebecca lost her courage. The street was vast, wider even than Queens Boulevard. An endless ribbon of cars streamed past, while masses of people trudged by in all directions, jostling her with their elbows and shoulders. A thin gray rain was falling. Rebecca made her way to the curb and tried to hail one of the passing taxis. One by one they drove past, ignoring her frantic waving and calling. Even those whose green lights were on, indicating that they were free, did not stop. Then she remembered—the Service Bureau would call her a cab, as her guidebook advised.

Wet and hungry she went back into the hotel. The Service Bureau's evening clerk, who looked exactly like the morning clerk except she had darker hair, was being besieged by a group of Eastern European tourists who leaned across her desk, shouting and gesticulating. To all their cries and complaints, the clerk calmly repeated the same phrase. Curious, Rebecca thumbed through her guidebook, trying to match the listed transliterations to the sounds the clerk was making, but the phrase did not seem to be included. Finally the tourists departed, muttering and grumbling. In response to Rebecca's request, the clerk phoned for a cab.

Fifteen minutes later Rebecca stepped out of the rain and into the warm and crowded Zikov Bazaar where she ordered cucumber salad and jellied fish. Before arriving in Russia she had carefully made note of those restaurants which served good vegetable and fish dishes. Keeping somewhat kosher would be difficult, but not impossible. While waiting for her food she alternately read her guidebook and watched her fellow diners, all of whom looked Russian. She assumed this boded well for the food; it was generally said that restaurants frequented by locals served the best fare. When her meal arrived she ate slowly, savoring each mouthful. Neither cucumber salad nor jellied carp were dishes she enjoyed at home, but she was very hungry, and the food was well prepared, if a bit salty. The restaurant was bathed in a warm amber light that shone from the gilded lanterns that hung above each table. The walls were festooned with tapestries of intricate Russian scenes. In one a peasant stabbed a boar with a long spear while his comrades clapped and shouted. In another a young couple wearing traditional costume marched in what looked like a wedding procession, the woman draped with garlands of flowers and fruit. The once rich colors of the tapestries had faded to a dull patina that blended well with the amber warmth of the room. Violin music began playing—the slow, heavy strains of a vaguely familiar Russian melody.

Couples slowly got up from their tables and began to dance, languidly swaying and bumping into one another. The men all wore shabby brown or gray suits and were either tieless or sported equally drab and colorless neckwear. Most of the women wore dowdy dresses of cheap looking fabric. At one point, as she ate her dinner, a man leaned over and asked her to dance, but she demurred. *That's all I need*, she thought wryly. *A Russian dance partner to brighten up my evening.* Both her mother and Yuri Abramovich had warned her to avoid strangers. "Anyone can be KGB," Yuri had intoned. "Anyone."

After dinner, unable to catch a taxi, she walked the eight blocks back to the hotel. The cool, moist air refreshed her after the smoky warmth of the restaurant. The rain had stopped and the streets had a freshly washed look. She looked at her watch. It was only nine o'clock, but she felt pleasantly sleepy. She would go upstairs and read a bit before going to bed. As she approached the brightly lit Hotel National, a heavy-set man walked past briskly and disappeared into the doorway of an apartment building. Rebecca's heart began to pound. She could not be certain but she felt quite sure that it was the man who had asked her to dance. Had he followed her? She glanced about in all directions. People strolled casually along the streets, heading homeward after a long day. Perhaps the man lived nearby. Perhaps it wasn't even the same fellow. Even as she reassured herself, she quickened her pace, nearly running the last block to the hotel, as passersby watched curiously.

Back in the safe confines of her room, Rebecca laughed at herself for being so paranoid. After all, the guidebooks did warn that single women in Moscow are often approached by lonely, well-meaning men; that it was perfectly proper for strangers to ask each other to dance. Still, she could not shake off the feelings of dread that engulfed her as she tossed about on the bed, unable to sleep. The thick bed curtains seemed to be closing in on her and she pulled on the heavy tasseled rope, opening them wider. She thought of Robert and Sarah, far away in her modern New York apartment with their grandmother and Constance. Did they miss their Mommy? Were they crying for her? And how was her mother coping with them, now that Rebecca was away? *"Untern yiddeleh's vigeleh shteht a klohr veiss tzigelleh..."* (Under my little one's crib stands a snow-white kid). She heard her mother's voice, the age-old Yiddish words lilting through the nursery as she sang the twins to sleep.

The next morning, after a troubled night, Rebecca rose at eight and dressed carefully in the navy suit she had worn for important meetings at Kramer's Import and Export Company, years before. Pulling her hair into a tight ponytail she examined her image in the mirror. Severe, business-like, but still pretty. Today she would begin her search. After drinking a cup of bitter coffee she approached the Service Bureau. The woman at the desk glanced at Rebecca without recognition, despite the fact she had admitted her to the hotel the day before.

"Excuse me please, do you have a telephone directory?"

"You want to call American Embassy? Consulate?"

"No, a—friend, who lives here." The woman sniffed and shook her head.

"No. Only official directory for embassies and consulates. No private numbers. Yes?" She was already addressing a group of British tourists who stood behind Rebecca, waving maps and spiral notebooks. Rebecca tapped one of them on the shoulder. A thin young woman with pallid, pockmarked skin and mouse-brown hair turned and frowned at her.

"Excuse me, but do you have any idea where I can get hold of a telephone book?" Instantly the whole group burst into laughter.

"Telephone book?" snickered a tall thin man wearing a violently colored, decidedly un-British looking necktie. "Why, they're scarce as hens' teeth, as you Americans would say. Can't seem to find one anywhere. Can't imagine what the Russians do when they need someone's number."

No telephone books. Rebecca sank down into a soft chair in the hotel lobby, and folded the paper on which the name Zwillinger had been written for her, in Cyrillic letters, by Yuri Abramovich. Replacing it in her purse, she sighed heavily. With any other country, if you wanted to find someone, you went first to their consulate in America. Then, if that didn't help, you went to the ministry of whatever, some government department in the country itself, and they would help you track down your long-lost relative. But not here in Russia, and certainly not if the person you were looking for happened to be a Jew. No, here you had to do just the opposite. She remembered Yuri Abramovich's words, and the concern in his deepset black eyes:

"Be very careful who you ask anything. Stay away from any government officials. If you ask anyone in any official capacity about a Jew, right away that Jew is suspect, right away he will be followed, questioned, harassed. I cannot even give you the address of my brother, because he is already under surveillance. I don't want to give him more problems. But here, I will give you some names, people to contact. Go to their homes in the evenings, make sure you are not followed." And he had given her two names and addresses, which she had tucked into a zippered compartment in her wallet, behind her photos of the twins.

Now she opened her wallet, to check if the paper was still there. It wasn't. She thumbed quickly through the photos, catching a glimpse of two smiling babies, taken in the early years before everything went wrong with her marriage. Not there. Perhaps it was in another compartment. Anxiously, she shuffled through her driver's license and credit cards, then searched among her rubles, dollar bills and traveler's checks. The folded yellow paper was not there. Could she have accidentally thrown it away when, in preparation for her trip, she had cleared her wallet of old supermarket receipts, movie stubs, bank statements, shopping lists and other frayed bits of graying paper that had accumulated over the last several months? Or maybe it was upstairs, among the travel vouchers and other important papers that were in a drawer in her room? She rushed into the elevator, colliding with a rotund woman in a forest green suit who grumbled at her in a Slavic tongue.

Retrieving the key from the impassive floor-lady, Rebecca re-entered her room, where she ransacked her drawers and suitcases to no avail. The paper was gone. She was on her own. *What will I do now*, she wondered. She could not call Yuri Abramovich in America and ask him again for the names and addresses. All the phones were tapped. Never mind. She still had the address of the building where Reuben and David Zwillinger had lived. She would go there tonight. In the meantime, since nearly everyone in Moscow worked during the day, she would do some sightseeing. Through Intourist, she had booked several English-speaking tours. Today's was the Kremlin. Slipping into her sensible crepe-soled shoes, she glanced once more about the room and went out. At six, she returned to the hotel and went to the Restaurant Nationale for dinner. As it was fairly early, she found a seat at an empty table. Immediately, she was joined by a small tour group, who regaled each other all through the meal in the rhyming, singsong cadences of the Hungarian language.

Finally, at seven thirty, Rebecca set out. Darkness had fallen, and the Moscow streets were bathed in artificial light. Rebecca had no time to admire the majesty of the Moscow night. Huddled in the back of a taxi, she silently rehearsed what she had to do. The cab rode slowly down the broad boulevards and turned off into a neighborhood of drab apartment blocks. A sleety drizzle made the slick streets shine like patent leather.

"Petrovskije 64" grunted the driver, pointing.

"*Spaseeba*", said Rebecca, handing him several rubles. Yuri had taught her a few basic Russian words. Her guidebook also contained a glossary, in which important words and phrases were transliterated.

As she walked up the gloomy staircase, a young man hurried past, glancing back at her briefly before continuing down the stairs. The apartment was on the sixth floor. Her heart pounding from the climb, as well as from excitement, Rebecca paused before the door. Unlike some of the others, which held small name plaques, this one was unadorned, its paint slightly grooved and pitted. Hesitantly, she knocked. Nothing happened. She knocked again. This time she heard footsteps approaching from within.

"*Dah?*" said a gruff voice.

"*Zh...Zhdrahstvwytye,*" ventured Rebecca, her tongue struggling with the complicated syllables of a Russian "hello."

The door opened and a man peered at Rebecca. Her heart sank. This middle-aged man with his blond hair and porcine features obviously had no connection to her father or brother. Still, perhaps he did, for some reason, know the previous occupants of his apartment. She held out the paper on which "Zwillinger" was written in Russian. "*Gd'yeh?*" (where) she asked, pointing to it. Squinting at the name, the man shook his hand. "*Nyet.*" He muttered a few words in Russian and started to close the door.

"Please! Do you speak English?"

"*Nyet,*" he said again, and the door slammed shut, the sound reverberating through the quiet hallway.

Rebecca looked at the other apartment doors. Surely there was a neighbor who still remembered the Zwillingers. Because apartments in Moscow were hard to come by, people didn't move around much. Screwing up her courage, she rapped lightly at the next-door apartment. No answer. She tried the apartment on the other side. A squat, apple-cheeked woman with pin curls in her hair opened the door. Rebecca showed her the paper. Without a word, the woman closed the door. *So that's how it's going to be*, thought Rebecca. There was one more apartment on the floor. Rebecca knocked tentatively.

The door opened and a teenage girl stared out at her with deep-set black eyes. Her dark, curly hair fell to her shoulders. Rebecca's heart gave a leap. Jewish! This girl was obviously Jewish. There was no mistaking the intense expression in those long-lashed eyes, the slight bump on the bridge of the nose, the quizzical lift of the eyebrows.

"Do you speak English?" Rebecca asked.

"Yes. Not so very well."

"Please, can you help me? I'm looking for somebody." She held up the paper.

"Please to come in."

Rebecca followed the girl into a square room that looked taller than it was wide, due to the high ceiling. Two other rooms led off from it, one of which appeared to be the kitchen. The room itself was crowded with dark, heavy furniture. There were two beds with ornately carved headboards, a matching bureau, a wooden table with four chairs, and in the corner, a small desk at which sat a girl of about twelve, apparently doing homework. The child looked up at the visitor curiously, and Rebecca saw the older sister's expression reflected in her softer, more rounded features. The older girl motioned Rebecca to a chair.

"Who are you looking for?" she asked, slowly and carefully enunciating the English words.

"A man named Reuben Zwillinger. And his son, David Zwillinger."

"You are American, yes?"

"Yes. I'm sorry." Rebecca smiled and held out her passport, thankful that she'd remembered to redeem it from the Service Bureau earlier that day. "I'm looking for my relatives. I'm Rebecca Kramer and I'm Jewish, from New York. Here's my passport so you'll see I'm telling the truth." Miriam had cautioned Rebecca not to say that Reuben was her father, for fear that the shock would be too great were he to find out that his daughter was alive and looking for him. Instead, she would first find him and personally break the news as gently and gradually as possible. The girl looked at the passport and shook Rebecca's hand.

"I am Alla, and this is my sister, Maya. But," she pointed to Rebecca's paper, "I do not know this name."

"How long have you been living in this apartment?"

"Four years. Before we moved here we shared apartment with two other families, on Kujbyseva. Now is better."

"Here we have hot water," chimed in her sister, with a gap-toothed smile. Rebecca smiled back, mentally comparing the girl with her American counterparts. Imagine one of them being delighted about such a commonplace necessity as hot water.

"The Zwillingers," she explained, "used to live in this building nine, ten years ago. Then they moved away. The other neighbors say they don't know them. Can you think of anyone who might remember them, or who might have some information?" Alla pondered for a moment, then nodded.

"I will give you a name. It is the cousin of my friend. He knows many people in the Jewish community. Maybe he can help you. But," she added, "you must be very careful. This man is under suspicion. Often he is followed by KGB. Wait, I will get you his phone number." She went into the other room and returned with a tattered copybook, from which she copied the number with a stubby pencil. "I write many numbers in secret—ah, ah—" she stammered.

"Code?"

"Yes, code. I will write this number in code too. Add two to the first two numbers and one to the rest. Please remember this. Call and ask for Dima."

"Dima?"

"Yes. Is Dimitry. Same name. No. Wait." She held up her hand. "You cannot call him. KGB will hear your voice, English, that is the end. Okay. Wait here. I call him."

Rebecca swallowed. So it was true about phones being tapped. "But are you sure?" she asked. "Won't you be putting yourself in danger? I don't want to cause you any trouble—"

"No, is all right."

Again she went into the other room. Soon Rebecca heard her speaking in low-pitched Russian. Maya looked up at her and smiled, then returned to her homework. In a moment Alla returned.

"You must meet Dima tomorrow night, eight o'clock, at the Museum of Literature. You have guidebook? You will find there the address."

"But you said this on the phone? How can you be sure we won't be followed?"

"We have, how you say again, code. We have different ways to say things what we mean. But even with, if someone is following you, go back to hotel, where you are staying." Alla glanced at her watch. "Please forgive. Is better you go now. Please forgive, I did not give you any drink or food. But soon comes my father. Please you go now." Rebecca clasped the girl's hand. "Thank you so much. Thank you for your help."

Alla waved her hand. "Is nothing. Go now."

Later, at the hotel, Rebecca looked up the address of the Museum of Literature in her Baedeker. 38 Dimitrov Street. And wasn't the man's name Dimitry as well? It would be easy to remember. Closing the book she fell into an exhausted sleep. When Rebecca awoke, her room was so dark she was sure it was the middle of the night. Surprised to find that her watch read seven thirty in the morning, she pulled the window drapes aside and found that a dismal rain was falling. Forget Lenin's Tomb, she thought. She would have to go to the Service Bureau and book a different tour. Unfortunately, this proved to be a problem. The only other tour available was to Gorky Park, a far worse option in this weather.

"But it's raining," protested Rebecca. "Rain is nothing," snapped the Service bureaucrat.

Later, as the rain turned to sleet, an Intourist guide radiating robust Soviet health led Rebecca and three other tourists across Red Square. Shivering in her damp raincoat, Rebecca looked with dismay at the endless line of tourists, all bundled in their dark, drab clothing, who awaited entry to the mausoleum.

As if reading her thoughts, the guide proudly announced, "We do not wait. Foreign visitors are privileged to enter first." Briskly ushering them to the front of the line, she pointed to the squat, reddish stone crypt.

"In here is buried our greatest leader, Vladimir Ilyich Lenin. His remains are preserved for all to see. Do not, please, make noise inside. Please give up your camera when it is taken from you. Please keep your hands from your pockets."

Two by two they filed past a pair of expressionless guards and descended a stone staircase. The temperature dropped abruptly and Rebecca rubbed her frozen hands together, careful not to put them in her pockets. Absorbed in her own thoughts, Rebecca was unprepared for what she saw next. In a glass coffin, lit with pink neon light, lay a smallish, rather nondescript figure looking peacefully at ease in a dark suit, his pointed beard neatly combed. The absolute ordinariness of the man made her want to giggle, but she bit her tongue and clenched her fists, fighting the urge. All around her people gazed solemnly down at the man in the glass box. Rebecca was glad to be led out onto an avenue shaded by trees, their branches dripping with rain.

"Here were buried many Russian heroes," explained the guide, "Josef Stalin, our cosmonauts Vladimir Komiarov and Yuri Gagarin, the writer Maxim Gorki, John Reed…"

John Reed? Rebecca had never heard of him.

"…the American communist," explained the guide, looking at her watch. "Ah! Time to see the Changing of the Guard," she announced, with great excitement.

"Haven't you seen it before?" asked a frail looking elderly man in Rebecca's party. Earlier he had explained to Rebecca that he was a reporter for his hometown newspaper, the *Winterton Gazette*.

"Oh, many, many times, hundreds of times," gushed the guide, beaming with anticipation. Rounding the mausoleum, they watched silently as a quartet of fur-hatted loden-clad guards with fixed bayonets and gleaming boots goosestepped about in flawless precision.

An ancient fear spiralled its way up from Rebecca's stomach, lodging somewhere in her chest. Nazis, Cossacks, she thought. An image of blood spattered snow flashed in her brain. She was grateful when the tour ended. Back at the hotel, she took a hot bath and prepared herself for the evening's encounter.

At eight o'clock it was still raining, but the air had turned colder and the streets were covered with slush. Rebecca nearly slipped as she walked from the streetcar stop to the museum entrance. It would be nice, she thought, to talk to Dima inside the museum, where she could warm up and dry off. But when she reached the gray stone building only a few lights shone dimly from the windows, and the iron doors were shut. Worse yet, no one stood waiting for her. She leaned against the door, looking at her watch and trying to remember what her guidebooks had said about Muscovites. Were they prompt, or tardy? Were Moscow Jews in a separate category altogether? German Jews were impeccably punctual, Polish Jews notoriously late for everything. As she gazed down the street, a dark figure materialized out of the mist and sleet. He approached, head bent, walking quickly. At the museum entrance, he stopped and scrutinized Rebecca.

"*Vremya pazhalsta?*"

"I'm sorry. I don't speak Russian."

"American?"

"Yes."

"Rebecca Kramer?" He pronounced it Krah-mer.

"Yes. Are you Dima?"

"No. I am Ilya. Dima cannot come this evening. He sent me instead. Listen carefully. If you want information about someone in our community, come to this address tomorrow evening at eight. Perhaps they can help you. Here." He handed her a folded piece of paper. "Memorize now the address." Rebecca unfolded the paper and mouthed the words silently, "Chochlovskaja 18, apartment six. Chochlovskaja 18, apartment six."

Ilya nodded, ripped up the paper and shoved the tiny pieces deep into the pocket of his overcoat. "Good night," he said, with a brusque nod, before trudging off into the sleet.

Bitterly disappointed, Rebecca boarded a streetcar to return to the hotel. Each day that passed without concrete information was a day wasted, and she had been here three days already. The whole thing was beginning to feel like a grade B spy movie. As the streetcar rattled along, she composed a mnemonic to help her remember the address, and repeated it to herself over and over. Chocolate-sky, 18-6, Chocolate-sky, 18-6. It was the best she could come up with.

The next morning Rebecca awoke to find that she had overslept. It was nearly eleven o'clock. No matter. She had reserved the day for shopping, so there was still plenty of time. After a light lunch she proceeded to one of the Berioskas tourist shops listed in her guidebook. Here she pondered the array of Russian souvenirs, finally choosing several amber necklaces, some red and gold *khokhloma* bowls for the apartment, and a few sets of brightly painted nesting dolls to give as gifts. Finally, almost as an afterthought, she chose a carved bone sailing ship for Eddie's father. For a moment she had the urge to buy something for Eddie. Picturing his face, she felt a combination of resentment and pain. Did she still love him? It was hard to say. There were too many conflicting emotions, and too much else going on in her life right now for her to assess or analyze the scope of her feelings for Eddie.

"Anything else, please, Miss?" the clerk asked, adding up the combined purchases.

"No, that's it, thank you." She paid and left the shop, spending the remainder of the afternoon walking about on Kalinin Prospect, until it was time to prepare for her 'appointment.' Returning to her room, she bathed, dressed and went downstairs to have the Service Bureau call a taxi. The hotel lobby was filled, as usual, with an assortment of tourists and foreign dignitaries. Many of the men stared unabashedly at Rebecca. Cool and aloof, she walked past them, ignoring their frank appraisal but secretly pleased; the time she had taken with her toilette had been well spent. Suddenly, she began to feel self-conscious. It would be better not to be noticed at all.

One man in particular seemed to be staring awfully hard. She glanced back, frowning slightly so as not to encourage him. Just a plain looking, middle-aged man in a dull brown suit, with no tie. A shabby fedora hat of an equally dull color shaded his eyes. Totally nondescript, yet there was something familiar about him. Where had she seen him before? When she looked at his face, he quickly averted his gaze by looking at his watch. Even the gesture seemed familiar. She looked away and continued walking, then casually glanced back over her shoulder. He was still watching her. In addition, he was no longer leaning against the wall, but had moved forward in the same direction she was walking. Puzzled and disconcerted, Rebecca walked through the lobby doors as the doorman, smiling and bowing, held them for her.

Once again the night was damp and cold, and Rebecca was grateful when the taxi arrived promptly. As she stepped into it, she glanced back at the hotel entrance. Just inside the doors stood the man, smoking a cigarette. Was he watching her still, or was he, too, waiting for a cab? The taxi smelled of dampness and old cigarettes.

"Chochlovskaja," said Rebecca, and handed him a paper on which she had written "14," deliberately giving an earlier number, so as not to get out directly in front of the actual address.

Eighteen Chochlovskaja was a large gray apartment building of pre-war vintage. Two men in bulky overcoats stood outside talking. When Rebecca brushed past, they fell silent and regarded her coolly. Avoiding their eyes Rebecca walked up the narrow stairs. At apartment six she stopped. She could hear noise coming from within; the low-pitched hum of conversation, coupled with the tinkling sound of a piano. It took several loud knocks until the door was opened by a plump, redheaded young woman.

"Hello, do you speak English? I am Rebecca Kramer from America, I was sent here by Ilya, to meet Dimitri. I'm looking for David and Reuben Zwillinger…"

The girl smiled and held up her hand. "Please, slowly, slowly. My English is not so perfect."

"I'm sorry, I'm just so nervous." Rebecca held up her passport, displaying her photograph for the redhead and the group of young people who had approached, attracted by the sound of an American voice.

"Come in." The redhead drew her into the large, crowded room. "Take off your coat. I am Hannah, and this is Moshe and Yossi, and Rena." She pointed to each of the friendly, curious faces that clustered around her.

Hannah drew her further into the room where a group of young men and women stood around a piano. All turned their heads to stare at the newcomer, but Rebecca noticed only the pianist. Even from a sitting position he appeared tall and well built. His broad shoulders and heavily muscled arms looked out of place behind the elegant grand piano. But what struck Rebecca most was his hair, soft masses of coppery-golden curls that hung low over his forehead, so different from the clipped, dark hair of most of his comrades. His large, light colored eyes locked with hers momentarily, then he turned his head and resumed playing the song she had recognized from outside the door. It was "Jerusalem of Gold," one of her favorite Hebrew songs from the Six Day War.

"Attention, *chaverim*," called Hannah, using the Hebrew word for friends. "We have here an important guest, Rebecca Kramer from America." Leading her to the piano, Hannah proceeded to introduce her to the rest of the assemblage. "Rebecca, I present to you Moshe, Sara, and Avram." All three smiled and shook her hand. "And this," said Hannah, indicating the pianist, "is Itzik."

Itzik? Rebecca felt a stab of disappointment as she shook his fine-boned, long-fingered hand. Somehow, with that hair... but of course he wouldn't be David. It could never be that easy. Besides, David would be at least ten years older than this fellow.

Moshe, heavy and dark, with beetling brows that shaded burning black eyes, leaned towards her. "Are you journalist? With Jewish newspaper? *Mizrachi Woman, Hadassah?*"

"No, no."

"What organization, then, you are represent?"

"No organization. I came on my own."

Sara, a bright-faced girl with straight black hair that hung below her shoulders, stepped forward. "But you came to see us, yes? To speak with us? To tell our story? And when you go back you will speak to the media, to the Student Struggle for Soviet Jewry, to the newspapers? Everyone who comes here must bring back our story."

"Of course," Rebecca agreed, feeling guilty. How could she tell them that she had come for her own reasons? "Of course I will tell everyone your story, all of your stories."

"All of our stories is one story," said Yossi. Slight and bespectacled, he looked like a typical rabbinical academy student. "Persecution, discrimination, refusals. You are maybe active in New York Coalition for Soviet Jews? You know Gedalia Cohen, Mordechai Fisher, Shira Weber?" Rebecca, blushing with embarrassment, shook her head.

"No, sorry. I don't know them."

Hannah came to her defense. "She says she comes alone. She is looking for someone. Let us listen to her, and then she will listen to us."

Over cheese sandwiches and raisin wine, Rebecca told them of her meetings with the Abramovichs, and of her mother's strong conviction that Rebecca's father and brother, Reuben and David Zwillinger, were alive today, in Moscow. Halfway through her story, Rena, a tiny, bird-like girl with a sharp nose and quick, spirited movements, began nodding her head excitedly.

"Yes? What is it? Do you know them?" asked Rebecca, as all eyes focused on Rena.

"Go on, continue," urged the girl, her black eyes sparkling. "I will tell you in minute."

When Rebecca finished, Rena jumped up, clapping her hands triumphantly. "I know them, I know them!" She cried. "They used to live near us, on Stretenskij."

Rebecca stared open-mouthed at the eager faces around her. Suddenly the room began spinning before her eyes and she lurched forward, clutching the arm of her chair.

"Are you all right?" asked Hannah.

"Yes, it must be the wine."

A black and red lacquered tray was put before her. "Here, have, please, a sandwich, another one."

"Oh, no thank you." She reached out and touched Rena's arm. "You say you know them? Reuben and David Zwillinger? Are you sure?"

"Yes, yes. The older man, he walked so." She bent her narrow back slightly and strode purposefully about the room. "And the son, tall, handsome, reddish hair."

"Like this?" Rebecca pointed to Itzik.

"Yes. Like this, like Itzik's hair, maybe a little ah, not so dark, more light, maybe."

"Do they still live there, on Stret, Stret…"

"Stretenskij. No. They left, maybe three years ago. When the son got divorced."

"Divorced? You mean he was married?"

"Yes, yes, married."

"Did they have children?" Rebecca felt a sudden twisting in her chest. She pictured a bright-haired niece or a nephew perhaps, her own flesh and blood, living here all this time unknown to herself and to her mother.

"No, no children." The niece and nephew faded into shadowy fragments, leaving behind an equally shadowy figure, their mother.

"What about the wife? Does she still live there?"

"I don't know. I have not been back there in more than year."

"And you don't know where the father and the son moved to?"

"No. But wait." Rena frowned, crinkling her eyes, then smiled again. "Could be the wife, she is still there. Or the neighbor knows. Was her friend."

"How can I get there?" Rena glanced at her watch.

"Not tonight. Is too late. Tomorrow night, I take you there. We find the wife." The group bubbled with excitement. Everyone had suggestions, advice. Rena beamed, obviously delighted to be part of this adventure.

"All right, comrades," boomed Moshe, his deep baritone putting an end to their spirited conversations. "We have here important opportunity," he continued, "to talk with American guest, who can help us, just as we can help her. Now," he said, focusing his smoldering gaze on Rebecca, "you will hear our stories. Here." He removed a small notepad and a stubby pencil from his pocket and thrust them at Rebecca.

"You must write what we tell you, but do not write our names. Only use initial, any initial, the names do not matter."

"I'm happy to do it," said Rebecca, placing the notepad on her knee like a stenographer. "But what if I'm stopped at the airport, with this notebook? Won't it be confiscated?"

Moshe shook his head. "You tell them is personal diary."

"But if they read through it? Can't I get into trouble, or get you into trouble?"

A spark of contempt flashed in Moshe's black eyes. "You will not use our names, as I told you. But if you are afraid, do this. Read the notebook, once, twice, in the hotel, then tear it up. We want you to remember the story, to know it here," he pointed to his temple. "When you come back to New York, you will go to Coalition for Soviet Jews. You will speak to Mordechai Fisher, tell him what we told you."

Rebecca nodded, flooded with shame at having shown reluctance to help them out of fear for herself. For two hours, she listened and wrote, as they poured out their stories:

Hannah: She had grown up a loyal and devoted member of Pioneer, the official communist youth movement, and later was a member of Komsomol, the communist organization, but after meeting Rena at the university, Hannah had begun attending services at the Moscow Synagogue. There she met the others, and had begun to feel what it really meant to have a national identity as a Jew. For the last several years she had met with increasing frustration at her job, where she was denied promotion after promotion in favor of other, less deserving, but non-Jewish workers. When she applied to leave for Israel, she was expelled from the Komsomol, and soon after, demoted to a much lower position at her job. Finally, she was fired altogether. In the meantime, her visa had been refused three times.

Itzik: A talented pianist who had been denied a place in a music school because his father, now dead, had been labeled a Zionist, and had served time in a labor camp. Itzik himself was now being followed, hounded by the KGB. Three weeks before they had broken into his apartment, looking for Zionist literature. Disappointed at finding none, they knocked over the furniture and smashed the dishes before leaving.

Moshe: Older than the rest, he had served time in a labor camp, and viewed the scars on his hands as badges of distinction. Removed from his position at the university, he was told he would never be allowed to leave for Israel. Nevertheless, he applied every few months, in the meantime spending his time with Jewish students, teaching them Hebrew and Jewish history.

Rebecca listened, and wrote on into the night. Occasionally, she asked a question, "Why do you apply for the visa, if you know you will be refused?"

"Because it is our right, according to the constitution of the Soviet Union, as well as according to international law. We have a constitutional right to return to our religious homeland, Israel. Eventually, some of us will be allowed to leave. Many have already left."

"Why do so many come to America?"

"No one knows what is in the heart of another, nor can anyone judge another's actions in this regard. Perhaps they were not true Zionists. Perhaps they tried life there and found it too difficult. Then again, you"—Moshe pointed at Rebecca—"you have the freedom to move to Israel, yet you choose to live in America. What we want is our freedom to choose. We are not viewed here as true Russians; we are identified as Jews on our identity cards. Why then, should they keep us?"

"They love us," joked Sara. The others laughed bitterly.

It was midnight when Rebecca got up to leave. Hannah phoned for a taxi and explained, "We would walk you down, to wait with you, but is not good for us, too dangerous."

"Dangerous?"

"Yes. KGB are downstairs. They watch all the time this building. Is not good for us to be seen with you here."

Rebecca swallowed hard. "What about tomorrow? How will Rena go with me to find David Zwillinger's wife?"

Rena stood up. "Don't worry. I will meet you there, at the address. Here, I write it down for you. You memorize, then tear it up." Rebecca looked at the address: Stretenskij 29.

Outside the building, the pale glow of the streetlamps cast eerie shadows along the dark street. Occasional cars rode by, sometimes slowing down as they passed Rebecca, but none carried the taxi's little green light in the corner of the windshield.

Suddenly a man stepped out of the darkness and stood beside Rebecca. "*Dobry vyecher.*"

Rebecca nodded. Afraid to look at him, she continued scanning the street, praying for the arrival of a taxi.

"*Kak vasheh eemyah?*" Rebecca shook her head.

"Ah. You don't speak Russian. You speak English, yes?" Glancing up at him, Rebecca felt a chill pass through her body. The broad, flat, face, the small gray eyes, the angle of the hat brim. This was the man she had seen earlier in the hotel lobby. Even then he had looked familiar. Had he been following her? Where? When? And where in God's name, was her taxi?

The man lit a cigarette. "You are visiting friends?" he asked, blowing a cloud of smoke into her face. Rebecca nodded and began walking away, in the direction from which she hoped the cab would come. The man followed close behind. Touching her arm lightly, he asked, "Who are these friends?" Rebecca turned to stare at him. Slowly, anger overcame her fear. What right had he to question her? She was, after all, an American citizen.

"Who are these friends?" he repeated. She jerked away from him.

"Don't you dare touch me. I'll complain to the American Embassy!"

"Oho! I am terrified with fear! You know, of course, that if you are doing something illegal, your embassy will not help you."

"I'm not doing anything illegal."

"No? Perhaps you are changing money, smuggling literature?"

"No."

"May I see, please, your passport?"

"No."

"No? Then I have no choice but to arrest you."

"Arrest me! What for?" To her great chagrin, Rebecca felt tears fill her eyes.

"For traveling with no passport. For dealing in illegal activities. For abnormal sexual behavior."

Rebecca gasped. Could he really arrest her? Why not? This was, after all, Russia, not Ocean Parkway.

"All right. Here's my passport." She opened her purse. Immediately he reached over and pulled the little blue notebook out from between her make-up case and manicure set.

"What is this?" He thumbed through the pages, stopping here and there to mouth some of the words that she had written, words dictated to her by Hannah, Moshe, Sara, Itzik. Rebecca thanked God inwardly for her awful handwriting, and for her new friends' warning that she not use names. The man shoved the notebook into the inside breast pocket of his overcoat.

Taking her passport, he glanced at the picture, then at her face. "Rebecca Krah-mer. Hm. Very pretty in picture. In life, not so pretty."

You sonofabitch, thought Rebecca. Bristling with anger, she glared at him, biting her tongue. He leaned toward her, again blowing malodorous cigarette smoke into her eyes.

"I give you friendly warning. In Russian jail you are less pretty. No cosmetics allowed. Stay away from these so-called 'refuseniks.' They are nothing but ungrateful malcontented scum. They are only using you to try to get sympathy. They care nothing for you, for your safety. See, already you have nearly been arrested, only because you are dealing with scum. What do they want? Do you know?"

Rebecca stared at him. Stamping his cigarette into the ground, he went on. "They want capitalist garbage, color television sets! They care nothing for you, nothing for Russia, nothing, especially, for Israel. They care only for color television sets. Believe me. Stay away. I warn you. Now go."

He thrust her passport back at her, and turned off. Rebecca began walking swiftly, and then running, in the opposite direction. Faintly she heard his voice again. "I warn you."

On and on she ran, sobbing with fear, not knowing where she was going. Finally, miraculously, a taxi appeared, its tiny green light a beacon in the distance. Rebecca fell into it, grateful for its dank-smelling warmth.

Back in her room she sat up, wrapped in her robe and shawl, as well as all of the blankets from the bed. Still shivering, she copied down, as best as she could remember, the stories of Hannah, Moshe, Itzik and the others, on her delicate, rose-embossed stationery.

Rebecca awoke early the next morning, with a heaviness in her limbs and an icy feeling of dread in the pit of her stomach. Recalling last night's experience, she shuddered. *Don't dwell on it*, she told herself, *or you'll become paralyzed by fear. You are here on a mission and you must continue until you accomplish it.* Peering between the heavy draperies, she gazed at the street below. Several elderly women were just finishing their street-sweeping. She tried to picture her own mother in a babushka, bent over a broom and large dustpan, sweeping last night's debris from the sidewalks, but she couldn't. Her mother had lately become so stylish and elegant, it was even difficult to picture her at the ovens in the bakery she had so recently left. Leaving the window, she bathed and dressed. An Intourist guide was to meet her at ten, to lead her and a few other foreigners on a tour of some of Moscow's more impressive museums. Rebecca looked at her watch. Only seven thirty. She had no desire to leave the warm confines of her room, which had become home to her, the one safe haven in a hostile and threatening place.

Then again, was her room really safe? Hurriedly she searched her drawers, and rifled through the dresses hanging in the closet. Everything seemed in order. Or was it? Frantically, she tried to remember whether she had laid her possessions in just that way—hairbrush, comb, wallet, tickets, guidebooks, postcards. She could not recall. She thought of the *dezhurnaya*, the placid mountain of a woman who sat all day just outside, in the hall. Could Rebecca piece together enough Russian words to ask if a stranger had entered her room? Probably not. And even if she could, wasn't it possible that the *dezhurnaya* was in cahoots with the KGB? And the little Kalmuk chambermaid could be, as well. Or was she just being paranoid? No. Last night's encounter had not been paranoia. It was certainly possible that her room had been searched. But what if it had? She had nothing to hide. Unlike other Jewish visitors, she had brought no prayer books, no *mezuzahs*, or phylacteries. All she had was the name Zwillinger, written in Cyrillic, on a folded paper in her raincoat. Or was it? A rush back to the closet confirmed that it was.

Leaving the room, she felt a wave of panic. What if she were followed again? Could she really be arrested? Who would get her out? Nonsense, she admonished herself. Pull yourself together. She thought of her mother, fleeing from the Nazis, hiding wounded and pregnant behind the very trees where Nazi soldiers lurked. The old familiar mix of guilt and shame burned through Rebecca's chest. Her mother had risked her life for her. She could not disappoint her now.

Even had she not been nervous and preoccupied, Rebecca was sure she would have found the museums tedious. The Russians, or at least Intourist, seemed to have a one-track mind. They were positively obsessed with communism. First it was the Lenin Museum, a celebration of the life of the God of Russia, filled with exhibit after exhibit of books and documents, newspaper clippings, old pictures and memorabilia. All of these were described with starry-eyed reverence by the worshipful Intourist guide. By the time they had been through the Museum of the Revolution and the Museum of Marx and Engels, Rebecca could barely contain her impatience. Finally, pleading illness, she left the tour at the State History Museum and wandered off into Red Square, where she spent the time idly snapping pictures of St. Basil's Cathedral, a brilliant phantasmagoria of vari-colored, multi-shaped domes that looked like a magic castle out of Disneyland. Later, as she sat in her room preparing herself for tonight's meeting, the phone rang.

"Hello?"

"Hello, is Mrs. Krah-mer?" A young, tremulous voice asked.

"Yes, who is this?"

"Is Regina. I cannot come. Sorry. Good-bye."

"Regina? Who?"

The phone rang off. Regina? Who was Regina? Suddenly Rebecca remembered. All of the young people she met last night had given themselves Hebrew names: Itzik was really Igor, Moshe was Mikhael, Hannah was Dunya, and Rena was Regina. So Rena would not accompany her this evening. Scared off, no doubt, judging by the tone of her voice. She would have to go alone, there was no choice.

455

Opening her map, she found Stretenskij Boulevard, and copied it carefully in Cyrillic letters, adding the number twenty-three, which would be close enough to twenty-nine to prevent her losing her way in strange streets. Rather than asking the Service Bureau to call her a cab, Rebecca left the hotel and walked down Gorkovo Street, often looking back to see if she were being followed. In their dull overcoats and shabby fedoras, almost any of the men who strode along behind her could have been KGB agents. Still, it was a relief not to see her "friend" from last night. Several dark, checkered cabs went by before Rebecca finally flagged one down. Midway to their destination, the driver turned around.

"You American?"

"Yes. How can you tell?"

"I can tell. I can tell French, German, American, I can tell all." Rebecca smiled and looked out the window. She was in no mood to make conversation with taxi drivers.

"You like Russia?" he persisted.

"Oh yes. It's wonderful. A wonderful country."

"*Da*, wonderful, wonderful." He turned away and said nothing more for the remainder of the ride. Somehow she felt she had offended him, and compensated by giving him an overly generous tip, which he acknowledged with a wink.

In front of 29 Stretenskij, Rebecca paused and looked about. There were several people on the street. Three men and two women walked along slowly, with blank, tired faces, probably returning home after a long day's work. No one seemed to be watching as she entered the building. The apartment was on the fourth floor. Rebecca climbed the stairs awkwardly, tension stiffening her joints. More than once, she nearly stumbled. When she reached apartment fifteen she rushed forward and knocked vigorously, for fear her courage would fail her.

From within the apartment Rebecca heard a woman's voice, shouting some Russian words. Rebecca waited. If only Rena had come with her! Then again, Rena had assured her that Mrs. Zwillinger spoke English. Light footsteps approached, and the door opened. Rebecca stared. A tall, slim woman stood before her. Strikingly beautiful, with straight, upswept blonde hair and a glowing pink and white complexion, she appeared to be about Rebecca's age, or perhaps a year or two older.

"*Da?*" Her large blue eyes scanned Rebecca's face questioningly. With a sigh, Rebecca shook her head. Surely, this was the wrong place. This woman was obviously not Jewish. But perhaps she knew who Mrs. Zwillinger was.

"Do you speak English?" she asked.

"Yes." The large eyes narrowed as the woman took a step backwards.

"My name is Rebecca Kramer. I come from America." The woman nodded, but made no move to invite her visitor in.

Suddenly there were heavy footsteps and another figure appeared on the threshold. An old woman, in a dark red babushka and a white apron, peered at her. Short and squat, she had the round fat face of the typical Russian peasant. The two women spoke briefly in Russian. The older woman had apparently asked a question of the younger one, and had received a curt answer in return. Both then resumed staring at Rebecca.

"I'm from New York, from America," Rebecca repeated. "I'm looking for a family named Zwillinger." She drew the folded paper with its now smudged Cyrillic characters from her pocket and held it out. The younger woman took it, nodded, and handed it back.

"This is family Zwillinger."

"What?" Rebecca suddenly felt weak, and pressed her hand against the doorjamb for support. "You are Zwillinger?"

"Yes."

"You are the wife of David Zwillinger?"

"Yes. I was. Not more. Divorced."

"Can I come in?" Rebecca stepped forward, but the two women did not move from their position in the doorway.

"Is better not," said the blonde.

Rebecca's knees felt hollow. If only she could sit down. "I don't mean you any harm," she said, smiling in what she hoped was a pleasant and reassuring manner. "David Zwillinger, and his father Reuben, are my cousins. So," she smiled even more broadly at the younger woman, "we were cousins, too, at least by marriage." Stupid of me to qualify it, she chastised herself, but went on, "Here, look at my passport, you see who I am." She held it out. The women glanced at it perfunctorily, and the blonde one stepped forward.

"They are not here."

"Where are they, then? I must speak to them, to find out if it's really them, if they are really my cousins. We heard about them in America, and my mother would be so…"

"Not here," the woman repeated coldly, cutting Rebecca off.

"But if I could speak to them? Can you tell me where, or at least give me some information?" She gazed past them, into the dim foyer of the apartment.

The woman did not budge. Resigned to having to talk in the hall, Rebecca spoke as rapidly as she could. "Is this the Reuben Zwillinger who came from Warsaw? And then went to Kiev when his son, David, was hurt in a fall, right before the war?"

Across the hall, a door opened slightly, then closed again with a soft thud.

"Ssshhh!" The young woman hissed at Rebecca, pulling her into the apartment. She shut the door.

"We talk here, then you go."

"I need to know if it's the same people, the ones I said, who came to Kiev…"

"Talk slower. I cannot understand."

"The father, Reuben, came from Warsaw," Rebecca spoke slowly and carefully, struggling to retain her self-confidence under the scrutiny of the womens' cold, suspicious eyes. "Before the war he lived in Dubnitz, and then, when his son, David, was about three or so, he, the son, that is, fell out of a window. The father took David to Kiev, but then the Nazis came. No one knew what happened to them after that. Later, when the war ended, the family was told they had both died. But then recently, in America, someone from Russia told us they had known them in Moscow."

"Who? Who told you?"

"A woman, Mrs. Tarnov." Yuri had told Rebecca not to give

their real name, for fear of reprisals against his brother, Gregor, who still lived in Moscow.

"We don't know her." At this point the older woman once more asked a question. With a sigh of impatience the blonde turned to her and spoke rapidly in Russian, translating the conversation. The old woman stiffened. Clenching and unclenching her fists, she scowled at Rebecca, her angry eyes like tiny currants in her suet pudding face.

"Is something wrong?" Rebecca asked. "I didn't mean to upset her. Please, just tell me if I've come to the right place, and where I can find my cousins, and I'll never trouble you again."

The younger woman stepped forward, crowding Rebecca into a small narrow square of space just before the apartment door. "Is right place," she said. "This Reuben, this David, this is their story. Kiev, Siberia, yes. But is too late. Now they are gone."

"Gone? Gone where?" Suddenly the old woman, who had been frowning fixedly at Rebecca, began shouting furiously, at which point the blonde seized the matron by the shoulders and spoke forcefully to her in Russian. Immediately the old woman stopped shouting and shuffled off, disappearing into the dim interior of the apartment.

"She does not like foreigners, Americans," explained the blonde woman. She brushed a stray hair from her forehead. Rebecca noticed that her fingernails were bitten to the quick.

"I'm sorry. I didn't mean to upset her. But you said they are gone? Reuben and David Zwillinger? Gone where? Where are they? Have they left the city?"

"Yes. They've left the city."

"Have they moved somewhere else? To another city? Please tell me. I'll travel all over Russia. If I have to. It's very important that I find them. They're my mother's only cousins. She's very anxious... you know how people are when they get old..." she faltered. She knew she was rambling, but the woman's eyes were so cold, so strange. "I'm sorry," she went on, "that I upset your mother like that. But if you'll just tell me where to find them, I won't disturb you any more. Can you give me, perhaps, their address?"

The woman's lips curled into the semblance of a smile. "I have no address."

"No address?"

"No. They are not in Russia."

"Then, where…"

"In Israel. They are in Israel. And that," she pointed at the old woman, who had returned and was standing at the end of the hallway, leaning against the wall and watching them, "is not my mother. Is my, how you say, mother-in-law. David's stepmother." Turning, she translated in rapid-fire Russian, and the old lady cackled and spat, rubbing her plump hands together.

David's stepmother. Something exploded in Rebecca's brain, sending whorls and spirals of flashing light flying across her field of vision. Fighting to stay calm, she leaned against the doorjamb. "Can I, can I please sit down?" Reluctantly, they led her inside to a threadbare sofa of a faded murky color that had perhaps, once, been green. There she sat, spellbound as the shadows deepened, while Marina Zwillinger stared into her eyes and told her story.

Chapter thirty-three

On the flight home, as her fellow passengers dozed around her, Rebecca could not sleep. Over and over she heard the story as it was told to her in the gutturally-accented Moscow University English of Marina Zwillinger, in the gloomy parlor with its faint mildew smell. Again and again, over the toneless drone of the airliner, the words sounded in her brain until their rhythm was one with the beating of her heart. Once home, she waited until the twins were asleep and then, holding her mother's light, fine-boned hand, she retold the story, her voice at times unconsciously taking on the halting measures of Marina's own.

"Reuben Zwillinger was deported to Siberia in September of 1941, shortly before the Nazis occupied Kiev. He was very lucky, Marina said, to have been deported, or else he would very likely have been murdered at Babi Yar. Meanwhile, David was with a Russian family, I think she said the father was a friend of Reuben's, or something. At some point they became afraid that Reuben would reclaim him, so they told the hospital that David had died of scarlet fever. Then they left Kiev and moved to Leningrad. Then later, I think it was in 1945, Reuben was allowed to leave Siberia and he went back to Kiev, to look for David, but he couldn't find him. The hospital said David had died of scarlet fever, but he didn't accept it, really. Then, I think, he went to Poland, to look for you, and he was told that you had died, as well."

Miriam began to cry, silently. She detached her fingers from her daughter's hand and fumbled in her pocket, removing a crumpled, pink tissue.

"Are you all right, Ma?"

"Of course. Go on. Don't stop. Go on."

Rebecca picked up a yellow plastic truck from where it lay on the coffee table, idly turning it about in her hands as she spoke. "He went back to Kiev, then, to continue looking for David. He tried to trace the family that had adopted him, and he didn't find them, but he found their maid. I mean, the woman who used to be their maid. Well, she was a Russian woman, from some backwoods place, and she had been fired by these people, and I guess she saw an opportunity. Anyway, she, well, I guess you could call it blackmail, though the way Marina told it she tried to make it sound better. This woman said she knew where David was, and she would take Reuben to him, but first, well…"

She paused and stared into her mother's eyes, before going on. "She said she wouldn't take him there unless he married her first."

Miriam gasped. "Married her? Your father married a Russian peasant?"

"Apparently that's what he did; he had to. Marina said that the old woman, her name is Yelena, she told her it was a great love story; that he fell in love with her after, or while she was helping him to find David, but, of course, later the truth came out that it was really blackmail, the whole family knew it."

"And did you see her? This woman, this, this…"

"Yes. A real peasant, Ma, like I said. Short, really fat, a round face, pug nose, the whole thing."

"I cannot believe it. And David? What happened to David?"

"Well, this Yelena took Reuben to Leningrad and they found David; somehow they were able to prove that David was really Reuben's son, and they got him back. Then they moved to Moscow, where Yelena had a sister-in-law who was working for some other family. That's where Marina, David's wife, comes into the picture. Ma, are you sure you're okay? You look terrible. Maybe you should take something."

"No," Miriam shook her head. "It's just the shock. Go on."

"Okay, so, Marina. Marina is the one who told me the whole story—David's wife. She was Yelena's niece, so she and David played together when they were little kids, in Moscow. They were like cousins, you know. Before the divorce."

"Divorce? What divorce?"

"Reuben and Yelena; they got divorced about a year or so after their marriage. Marina said they never got along at all. She said Reuben looked down on Yelena, complained that she forced him, tricked him into marrying her. And Yelena felt that he only used her to find his son, and then dumped her."

"And then?" Miriam twisted the tissue between her fingers, forming it into a thin, damp spiral.

"And then, well, they just lived in Moscow, David and Reuben together. Reuben had some kind of job in one of the ministries, I forgot which. Economics, or Languages, or something. And eventually, David went to the university. That's where he and Marina met each other again."

"And got married? Also a *goya*?"

"Yes, of course. She said they remembered each other, and then they fell in love. David was some sort of musician, a violinist, I think she said. But then he became interested in Judaism, and it was all spoiled. Those were her words—'it was all spoiled.'"

"Spoiled? Why? What happened?"

"He applied to go to Israel, and she had no interest in that of course, so they started fighting. But I'm sure there was more to it than that."

"Did they have children?" Miriam's eyes were bright with tears.

"No. No children."

"And now?" Leaning forward, Miriam clutched her daughter's arm. "Now they are in Israel? Both of them?"

Rebecca nodded. "Both of them."

"But where? Where in Israel?"

Rebecca leaned back against the creamy beige couch cushions, pressing her shoulders into their downy softness as if trying to escape into them.

"Where?" her mother repeated.

"That's just it. I don't know."

"You don't know? You got so far and this, *this* most important thing of all, *this* you don't know?" A bright flush rose in Miriam's cheeks. "How come you don't know this?"

Rebecca bridled. "Look, Ma, I did the best I could, for heaven's sake! Marina said she hadn't heard from them since before they left. She thought they had gone to some place in the north, she wasn't sure where."

"Yah. She didn't want you to know."

"Whatever. But I also went back to see these, these refuseniks, you know? And they didn't know either."

"Well." Miriam sat up, shoved the shredded tissue back into her pocket and wiped her palms on her skirt. "You know what must be done now, yes?"

"Go to Israel."

"The sooner the better."

"Ma," Rebecca said, dropping her voice to a whisper in response to a soft whimper from the children's room, "I can't go running off to Israel now. I just got back from Russia, for God's sake. How can I leave again?"

"All right. We will talk in the morning. Goodnight, Rifkaleh. You did very well." Miriam pressed her daughter's arm and Rebecca smiled wanly.

Early the next morning, the phone rang, waking Rebecca. Groggy from jet lag, she could hardly grasp the receiver.

"Hello?" her voice was a hoarse croak.

"Hi."

"Eddie? What do *you* want?"

"I want to know how your trip was."

"It was fine."

"Did you find them?"

"Yes." She yawned into the phone. "Look, Eddie, I'm tired. I can't talk now."

"You found them? Where are they?"

"They're in Israel."

"Israel! Fantastic! So what are you going to do now?"

Rebecca sat up. The fuzziness of sleep began to dissipate, leaving the sharp prick of anger instead. "I don't believe you care."

"I do care."

"Yeah Eddie, I see how much you care. You don't even ask about the kids. When was the last time you came to see them?"

"As a matter of fact, I came twice last week." Rebecca paused. Her mother hadn't even told her.

"I didn't know that. So, what did you think of your kids?"

"I love my kids."

"Sure," Rebecca sniffed. "Listen, Eddie. I really have to rest. Call me tomorrow."

"I can't. I'm going to Hong Kong tomorrow."

"Okay, Eddie."

"Listen, Rebecca, I'd like to—"

"Sarah's crying," she lied. "I have to go." She put down the receiver and climbed out of bed. She had no patience for Eddie now.

Miriam opened her eyes. "Who was that?"

"Eddie. You didn't tell me he was here last week."

"I didn't have a chance."

"What nerve he has. Thinks he can just abandon us, show up whenever he wants and run off again."

Miriam nodded sympathetically, but she was unable to concentrate on anything that her daughter was saying. Her brain kept flitting back to yesterday, to Rebecca's story about Reuben, and David, her darling son. Picturing Sarah's curls, she remembered little David, his reddish gold ringlets bouncing as Reuben carried him piggyback around their Warsaw apartment. She recalled the strength of Reuben's shoulders, the curve of his intelligent forehead. She thought of her last days with them, David lying unconscious on the hospital bed, his frail body so light that he seemed to be floating on the ragged mattress, with his golden head swathed in bandages and his pinched face so white and unresponsive. Reuben had kissed her goodbye at the train station as she stood weeping, her stomach swollen with their daughter, Rebecca, the daughter he would never see.

"Rebecca!" she said. "We must go to Israel."

"Ma. I can't go to Israel now."

Miriam stood up slowly from her seat at the table. Quietly she walked toward her daughter. "Rebecca," she said. "I cannot wait any longer. I told you this before you went to Russia. If not for my leg, I would have gone with you. Now that I can walk again, we must go to Israel immediately to find them. Rebecca, you never knew your father or your brother, but to me, it's as if I said goodbye to them yesterday, because I've carried them in my heart all these years. No," she shook her head. "We cannot wait."

Chapter thirty-four

Reuben smiled across the table at the woman who sat opposite him. "I know, Aliza," he said. "I've heard all the arguments. It's just that I'm not sure I can spare the time. Things are very busy, right now, in anticipation of the tourist season...."

"Nonsense!" she exclaimed. "Menashe can spare you for a week or two. The factory won't collapse. Besides, don't you have some vacation time owed you?"

"Well, yes, although..."

Aliza reached out and pressed Reuben's hand with her well-manicured fingers. "Look, let me deal with Menashe. He and I are old friends from the early years. Sometimes I think he'd like to be more than friends, but of course he knows I'll never let him step out of line. With you, however, it's another matter." She laughed coyly and squeezed his hand again. "So don't worry about a thing," she continued, smoothing her light brown hair away from her forehead. "I can book us a flight for next week. What day did you say David was leaving for reserve duty?"

"Next Wednesday."

"So why should you be alone? You'll come with me; we'll stay at my brother's house on Sierra Bonita Avenue. He has a lovely home with six bedrooms, so there's plenty of privacy. Or, if you insist, I can book you into a beautiful hotel, there's one right nearby, practically around the corner."

Reuben glanced at Aliza and laughed. Her plump, good-humored face was alive with purpose. "And what makes you think I can afford to stay at luxury hotels in Los Angeles, California?" he asked. "I'm lucky if I can afford the plane fare."

"So then it's settled. If you can't afford the hotel, you'll stay at my brother's. Don't worry, you won't feel embarrassed. He knows I'm a big girl. I wheeled him in the carriage when he was a baby. Who'd have guessed that sickly, whining child with the runny nose would grow up to become a millionaire? And I, whom everyone called "the Contessa," ends up working as a bookkeeper in a luggage factory. Ah well, such is life, eh Reuben?" She rose from her chair, sidling past the table until she stood behind him.

"Come," she said, tapping him lightly on the shoulder. "Time to go." Arm in arm they walked through the winding streets until they reached Aliza's apartment on the ground floor of an old Arab house built of yellowish stone. "Coming in?" she asked, still clinging to his arm.

"Well, I really shouldn't. I have so much...."

"Come on." She unlocked the door and pulled him into the foyer. On the wall hung a large framed photograph of a short man with brawny arms and a cynical smile; Aliza's late husband Dov, a former resistance fighter who had died of cancer two years before.

"Some tea?" Aliza asked as she hung their coats in the carved wooden wardrobe that stood against the wall.

"No thank you."

"All right, then." She took his hand and without further talk they walked down the narrow hall and into the bedroom, where they undressed and made love silently, in the dark. It was Reuben who insisted on the darkness. Afterward, Aliza lit a cigarette, its glowing end barely illuminating the outlines of her face.

"Going so soon?" she asked, as Reuben hurried into his clothes.

"Yes."

"You dash away as if the house were on fire. Do you have another appointment?"

"No."

"Then stay awhile. It's early yet."

"No." He opened the door of the room and turned to her. "Goodbye, Aliza."

"See you tomorrow then."

"Yes."

Avoiding the crowded bus, Reuben walked home, savoring the damp night air that cooled his flushed cheeks. He could not explain to Aliza why, on the few occasions that they had made love, he had, each time, felt the need to flee, to escape into the night like a criminal. Surely Aliza was not to blame. She was a wonderful woman, warm, good-natured, attractive. She also tended to be somewhat domineering, always telling him what would be best for him. This trip to Los Angeles, for example. She had first broached the subject two weeks before, bursting into his tiny office at the luggage factory where they were both bookkeepers.

"Listen, Reuben," she had exclaimed. "I'm fed up with this job. Working like a dog six days a week, having to take abuse from everybody. I should have left six years ago. The only reason I stay is because of you."

Reuben had smiled with disbelief. His relationship with Aliza was of a mere three months duration, while only yesterday Aliza had been awarded a small plaque to mark her tenth year at the factory. Her tenure at the job had nothing to do with him and he knew it.

"So," she went on. "I have an idea. In three weeks I have vacation. I've told you about my brother, Henryk, who owns a jewelry store in Los Angeles. Well, he's always inviting me to spend some time with him and his family. He has a beautiful home; after all, he's a millionaire many times over. For years he's been telling me to come visit, maybe even stay there, but of course Dov wouldn't hear of it and then, after he passed away… well, I don't like to travel alone.

"But if you would come with me! Oh Reuben, we could have the most wonderful time! No, don't say anything, let me finish. Hen-

469

ryk has a very large jewelry emporium and he mentioned to me that he may have some positions open, maybe even a managerial job. Right away I thought of you! Just picture yourself, Reuben, the manager of a big thriving jewelry store, in a beautiful American city…"

"Aliza, what kind of fairytales are these?"

"No fairytales, Reuben. Remember Krasnov? He left for America four months ago, and now I hear he's already in business for himself!"

"Yes, probably driving a taxicab. Aliza, I'm perfectly happy here in Jerusalem. I struggled very hard to get here, to get this job… I'm not going to run off to America now. Besides, what would I tell David? You know how Zionistic he is. It's out of the question." He laughed sardonically, opened up a folder, and began copying numbers onto the page in his neat and precise handwriting.

"Well then Reuben, come for a vacation. Just spend a week or so. Henryk said we'd have a car and a driver at our disposal. And Reuben, if you're worried about the airfare…" She paused and ran her hand down the arm of his jacket, "I'll pay for it. A loan. You could pay me back some other time. Don't be embarrassed. Think about it, okay?" She leaned over, kissed the top of his head lightly, and left the cubicle.

Later that evening, Reuben had a long talk with David. "Aliza wants me to go with her to California," he announced, scanning David's face for a reaction. There was no discernible change, save for the slight elevation of one eyebrow.

"When?" David asked.

"In two, three weeks, or so."

"What for?" Both eyebrows raised.

"For a vacation, she says." He felt no need, at that point, to mention the part about her brother Henryk's possible managerial position, since he was sure that this was merely one of Aliza's fantasies.

"Sounds like a good idea," said David. "I wish I could come with you. California!" He picked up his violin case and swung it past his legs as if hitting a golf ball. "You'll have to buy a new wardrobe," he joked. "Knee-length shorts, plaid, of course, and some of those flowery shirts. Seriously, are you planning on going?"

"Not really. For one thing, the ticket is too expensive, and for another, she expects me stay with her, at her brother's house. But those are not the main reasons why I'd rather not go."

"So what is the main reason? It seems to me you could use a vacation. Even if it is expensive. We have enough money, we can manage. You haven't had more than two days off since you started at the factory. What is it, ten months already?"

"Yes, about ten months."

"So, you're entitled to some time off. And as far as staying at her brother's, if it doesn't bother her, why should it bother you?"

Reuben sat back in his chair and gazed at his son without responding. The light from the parlor lamp fell across David's features, imparting an added touch of softness to them. In the pale golden glow he resembled his mother so much that it pained Reuben to look at him, and he averted his eyes.

"Papa," David said. "Are you embarrassed to go away with Aliza because of me? You mustn't be. Aliza is a fine woman, Papa. I like her. I've always liked her. She's funny. She makes you laugh. In Russia I never saw you laugh. And more important, she's also a kind person. Remember last month, when I had the flu and she brought me chicken soup? For the first time in over twenty years I felt what it must be like to have a mother. I know it sounds maudlin, but," he shrugged, "that's the way I feel."

Reuben shook his head. "But, you see, David, that's not the way *I* feel."

"What do you mean?"

"Aliza is not your mother. She isn't 'like' your mother. It's true that I'm happier with her than I've been with any other woman since Miriam was…. since I lost your mother."

"Any other woman?" David interrupted. "As if you had so many. The only one I can recall besides that bitch Yelena was Sonia, that sad-faced widow whom you saw for about three weeks. A short-lived passion. Of course Aliza's not my mother. It's unrealistic for you to expect her to be. And it's also unfair to Aliza. She obviously cares for you, but you have an idealized picture of someone else in your mind, and no one can ever measure up. As a result, you deny yourself happiness, and you deny Aliza happiness as well."

Reuben sighed. "I suppose you are right, but on the other hand…David, it's very hard to explain to you how I feel. You can't really understand, although I know you try, because your own marriage was…well, it's no secret that you and Marina were not happy except maybe in the very beginning. Your mother and I, we had something so… ah, well. Of course, you are correct. It's not fair to expect someone to measure up to that. But I must be fair to myself, as well as to Aliza. When I try to become close to Aliza, I mean close in an emotional, spiritual sense, it's as if there is a barrier there, and that barrier is the memory of your mother. It's funny. I loved Pola, my first wife, but once I had Miriam, I almost never thought of Pola. I didn't even feel guilty about it. It was as if my life with Pola was a book that had ended. But now, even after so many years, Miriam is still very real to me."

"Papa, you're talking yourself into a problem that doesn't exist. All Aliza wants right now is for you to go on vacation with her. Maybe she's not the love of your life, but truthfully, isn't it a bit late for a new 'Grand Passion?' After all, you're sixty-six years old. So go to California, have yourself some fun, and don't take the whole thing so seriously. So you won't be close in an 'emotional, spiritual sense.' Things could still be a lot worse, as you well know, Papa, *'Yihiyeh Tov'* he asserted, using the popular Israeli expression—it will be good. Rising from his chair, David walked to the telephone that hung on the wall in the hallway and dialed a number.

"Hello, Shira?" he smiled broadly at the receiver. "How are you? Of course I remember. Ha ha." Reuben listened to the echo of his son's laughter in the quiet, dimly lit apartment and closed his eyes.

The next morning, shortly after entering the factory, he knocked on Aliza's cubicle.

"Hello, Reuben." She gave him a delighted smile, as if they had not seen each other in weeks. "How are you feeling this morning?"

"Fine, Aliza. May I sit down?" He squeezed into the narrow alcove and slid into a rickety folding chair.

"So, Reuben?"

"So, I've decided to come with you, to California."

Aliza threw her arms around his neck. "Oh, Reuben! The

minute I awoke this morning I knew this would be a good day," she cried. "Now I must make the arrangements. What day is David leaving for the reserve duty?"

"Wednesday."

"Okay, so you'll want to spend Tuesday with him. I'll try to book a flight for Wednesday night, or Thursday. Well tell Menashe as soon as I can arrange it."

Chapter thirty-five

The plane glided toward the runway and then bumped the ground—a slightly rough landing. As Rebecca sighed with fatigue and relief, the passengers around her began applauding. A song filled the cabin. The El Al passengers, young American boys in knitted yarmulkas, lissome girls with long, shining hair or voluminous curls, black-garbed, bearded hasidim, their wives elaborately coiffed in heavy marriage wigs, aged European Jews with wrinkled faces and sardonic eyes, all joined in the song: *"Heveinu Shalom, Shalom, Shalom Aleichem*! ("We bring peace unto you.") Miriam slipped her arm across Rebecca's shoulders and hugged her, her green eyes filled with tears. Rebecca smiled at her mother. Softly they added their own voices to the traditional Jewish song of welcome.

Lod Airport's arrival area was crowded and noisy. European and American tourists, loaded down with Japanese cameras and matching sets of sleek, blue-gray Samsonite luggage, collided with returning Israelis carrying well-worn, brownish-yellow valises and stained khaki duffel bags. Children were everywhere, some with pale, almost translucent skin and silken sidecurls, others with unruly black locks and darkly glowing suntans.

After passing through customs and claiming their baggage, Rebecca and Miriam went outside and hailed a Jerusalem-bound taxi. The dark-skinned taxi driver spoke Hebrew in curt, guttural barks. A small circlet of orange beads hung from his rear view mirror. Was he an Arab? Rebecca felt a slight prickle of excitement, even fear, on her skin. She looked at the other passengers, a family of four who laughed and chattered incessantly in French, totally unconcerned, not even looking at the scenery. But no, he was not an Arab after all, for up there clipped to the sun visor was a photograph of a wraith-like Moroccan saint, his shell-like skull draped in a flowing robe, his sunken eyes staring out knowingly above a hawk nose and scraggly white beard. Squinting, she was able to read the Hebrew inscription "Our holy saint and teacher, the Baba Sali, Rabbi Israel Abu Hazeira."

Rebecca looked at her mother. There were dark circles under Miriam's eyes, and her face had a tense, feverish look. "Why don't you try to sleep a little, Ma?"

"Sleep? I am seeing Israel for the first time. I cannot sleep." She turned back toward the window. Rebecca too, watched as the taxi left the sleepy little town of Lod, with its adobe houses and muddy streets, and made its way up the Jerusalem–Tel Aviv road. Behind them, in the distance, were the soaring skyscrapers of Tel Aviv, the 'New York' of Israel. Hopefully, they would visit Tel Aviv at some point during their trip, but Rebecca could not be sure. Unlike her trip to Russia, this one was not very carefully planned.

The road was narrow and curving. Often the driver swerved sharply, cursing in the Arabic of his native Morocco, as a tour bus or army truck came careening at them from around a bluff. Rebecca stared out at the scenery. They were near the Mediterranean coast, and the ground was flat and sandy, covered with tall reeds or thick tangled vines of ocean-loving plants stretching and twisting towards the water. Later, the beaches curved away as they approached higher ground. Here the soil was gray and rocky, but in the distance one could see broad stretches of rolling grassy areas that looked like farmland. Every so often, they came upon the charred hulk of an army truck or a rusted tank; a silent memorial of some recent or long-past battle.

The taxi climbed higher. Soon it wound its way through a forest of pine trees that grew along both sides of the road. An image flashed through Rebecca's mind: her fifth grade teacher, Mrs. Rosenbaum, wiry gray hair pulled into a large braided bun at the back of her neck, blue veined hands trembling as she passed around the little aqua and white charity box, "Give money girls, money for the *Keren Hakayemet*"—the Jewish National Fund." On the first day of the Jewish month the box would be opened and all the nickels, dimes and pennies emptied out in a pile on her desk, to be counted and sent away to Israel. The money paid for the trees; tall green pine trees, to make Israel green, to "make the desert bloom," as the slogan said. The forest thinned out. Stretching away beyond them were gently rolling hills, terraced in reddish-yellow stone. Miriam caught her daughter's hand and pointed:

"Look, how beautiful."

"Yes, Ma. The Judean Hills, I think those are called."

As Jerusalem came into view, Rebecca and Miriam looked through the smudged cab windows. Block by block the city unfolded before them, broad boulevards turning into narrow, winding alleyways; tall, modern apartment buildings flanked by squat stone houses with tiled roofs. Everywhere were gardens; each apartment house, each private dwelling, even the drab office buildings, all were surrounded by small plots of land on which a profusion of flowers grew. It was November, and in New York nothing flourished but a few scraggly chrysanthemums, hardy enough to have withstood the early frost. But here Rebecca saw deep blue morning glories and red, pink, and white roses. Bougainvillea in voluptuous shades of vermillion hung heavily from terraces and archways, while giant Roses of Sharon climbed along the beige stone walls.

The driver stopped the cab in front of The Maccabee, the moderately priced hotel which Miriam and Rebecca had chosen based on the travel agent's recommendation. The hotel was modest and unassuming, a square building with an unadorned facade, save for a three-foot high brass candelabra over the entrance. Their room was crowded but clean, containing two large beds, a desk-bureau combination, and a pair of vinyl-covered chairs, all colored the same dull greenish-blue. After unpacking, Rebecca sat down on her bed and looked at her mother, who had kicked off her shoes and was now stretched out on her bed, eyes closed.

"Ma," she said, softly. "Are you awake?" Miriam's eyelids fluttered open.

"Yes?"

"Ma, you're exhausted. Look at you. I know you want to get started now, right this minute, looking for my father. You want me to start phoning people, making inquiries, right?" When Miriam did not answer, Rebecca went on, "But listen, Ma. Tomorrow we're going straight to the Jewish Agency. First thing in the morning. I don't think we can do much tonight. You're tired, I'm tired; I hardly know what I'm saying, I'm so tired. Are you hungry?"

"No."

"Ma, you hardly touched your food on the plane."

"Even so, I'm not hungry."

"Well, neither am I. I'm too exhausted. We haven't slept in twelve hours, really. Let's go to bed, and tomorrow we'll get an early start." Rebecca wriggled out of her pink sweater-dress and crawled under the covers. Within minutes she had fallen into a deep, dreamless sleep.

Miriam lay awake, staring off into the gray-green room. Vague images of faces she had seen on the plane or in the airport terminal formed in her mind. Dim and blurry at first, they slowly became sharp and focused, as if seen through opera glasses, before fading away again. The last image was one of a young Hasid, who had sat across the aisle from her in the airplane. Off and on throughout the trip he prayed quietly from a holy book, his bony shoulders swaying back and forth. In her mind's eye Miriam saw him again, the pale, waxy complexion, the black beard and earlocks framed by a round black hat. Half-awake, she heard his chant, soft and low, in the hum of the tiny refrigerator beside the bed:

"All prepare to accept God's chosen, Berish Sonnenblatt, God's own anointed, the Messiah, son of David…"

She jerked awake. Why think of Berish now? Instead she forced herself to remember Reuben, young and strong, working in his well-appointed bookstore, and little David, laughing on his hobbyhorse, until her eyelids slowly closed and she drifted off to sleep.

At nine the next morning Miriam and Rebecca sat on hard plastic chairs in a large anteroom, nervously waiting to see an official of the Jewish Agency. Across the room a door opened and a young woman barely out of her teens, with strikingly beautiful features and straight black hair peered out. "Who is first?" She asked in accented English.

Miriam and Rebecca rose and walked toward her.

"Come this way, please," she said, directing them toward a desk at which a harried-looking man wearing a worn blue suit and no tie sat. Yellow file folders, various Hebrew and English newspapers, pamphlets, letters and other papers were strewn helter-skelter across the top of the desk.

"Yes? Can I help you?" The man looked up.

Rebecca took a step forward. "We called yesterday. Zwillinger."

With ink-stained fingers the man thumbed through a well-worn date book. "Zwillinger, Zwillinger. Sorry. I don't see it. Whom did you speak to?"

"I don't know his name. I didn't write it down. I told him we were looking for Russian Jews named Zwillinger."

"Ah, yes. Okay." He turned and slowly pulled out a drawer from the file cabinet behind him. Removing a file, he ran his finger up and down several pages. "Here it is. There are three Zwillinger families. Which one are you looking for?"

"Reuben and David. *Re-oo-vain ve Da-veed.*" said Rebecca, hoping that the Hebrew pronunciation would make them easier to locate.

"Yes. Here it is. Reuben and David Zwillinger, arrived in Israel June 1971, sent to absorption center Bet Akiva, Kiryat Hayovel."

Rebecca and Miriam stared at the man, then at each other. It's so easy? wondered Rebecca. In Russia you had to search for people in secret, sneaking around in dark streets, using code names and addresses, and even with all those precautions, the KGB harassed you and threatened you with arrest. But here in Israel you could go right to a government agency, give them a name, and someone says, 'Yes, here they are.' Amazing!

The man removed his glasses and wiped them with a handkerchief. There were tiny half-moons of reddened skin on either side of his nose. Carefully, he replaced the glasses and wrote down an address on a yellow card. "Here," he said, handing Rebecca the card. "You can take the number eighteen bus, if you want to go now. It's right outside."

"Rebecca." She touched her daughter's arm. "I'm afraid."

"Well, do you want to wait? We don't have to go right now. We really should call first, anyway."

"Yes. First call."

They found a phone booth and Rebecca inserted an *asimon*, a round token with a hole in the center used for Israeli telephones. She dialed the number.

"Damn. The line is busy. Should we try again later?" Miriam hesitated. "Later, I don't know. No." She shook her head. "I cannot be afraid now. I went through so much in my life, I can get through this, too. I'm here already, why should I wait? Let's go."

They climbed aboard the red and white Egged bus, paid the fare and sat down. The driver informed them that Kiryat Hayovel was on the outskirts of the city, and that therefore the ride would take some time. Miriam stared out the window, but Rebecca could see from her mother's tense, pinched lips and by the way she twisted a shred of tissue between her fingers, that her thoughts were not on the passing street scenes. Rebecca herself could not think about the reunion that possibly lay ahead. There were too many unknown factors involved, too many emotion-laden issues. Instead, she looked at her fellow passengers, keeping her expression impassive so as not to catch anyone's eye. Directly across from her sat a young soldier, a boy of about nineteen, in rumpled khaki fatigues. Although he appeared to be asleep, with his long-lashed eyes closed, and his lips slightly parted, he clutched the sub-machine gun that leaned between his knees with tense fingers. His darkly handsome features and thick black hair, combined with the army uniform, gave him a look of sexy masculinity; yet, as the sunlight fell across his face Rebecca saw the softness of childhood still clinging to his curved cheeks.

The bus left the crowded streets of the city and began climbing a winding road that ascended higher and higher. From the window, Rebecca saw a great open field, covered with scraggly vegetation; purple thistles and yellow wildflowers. Gray-shouldered ravens pecked about in the road, flying up with hoarse cries of protest as the bus rumbled past. Stretching out beyond the field was a neighborhood of modern apartment buildings. Plain and stark in their architecture, the buildings were brightened only by the multicolored laundry that flapped on the many clotheslines strung across the terraces. Yet as the sun shone upon the yellow stone, touching it with a warm golden glow, the neighborhood, with its pine trees and neat little gardens, took on an ethereal radiance that made it truly beautiful.

The bus wound its way higher, passing vast apartment complexes of stone, and cement high-rises, and new looking playgrounds where small children scrambled over concrete and wood sculptures and fanciful slides. Finally, the driver called out "Bet Akiva." Rebecca tapped her mother on the shoulder. "Ma, here it is. The absorption center."

They made their way down the crowded aisle and left the bus. Facing them was a wide, three story building made of beige stone and black marble. The words "Bet Akiva" were engraved into the stone in both Hebrew and English.

Rebecca and Miriam approached the desk clerk, who looked up at them with bright black eyes. Rebecca spoke in Hebrew, slowly and carefully, embarrassed by her accent and limited vocabulary. She hadn't used the language since her high school years at Bais Yehudis. "We're looking for relatives. From Russia. Reuben and David Zwillinger. The Jewish Agency said they were here."

The woman nodded. "When were they last here?" she asked in softly-accented English. "I don't recognize the name."

"I don't know that, either. They came here in June of 1971, I think."

"Ah. I wasn't here then. Okay, let me look it up." From behind the desk the woman drew out a heavy spiral notebook, frayed at the edges. She opened it and leafed through several pages.

"What was the name you said?"

"Zwillinger. Reuben and David."

"Yes, yes. They were here, it is correct." Rebecca looked at her mother, who had gone pale. The clerk frowned at the notebook. "It says they left, in September 1971."

"Left?" Miriam leaned over the desk and squinted at the paper. "Left for where? Where are they now?"

"I'll check to see if we have another address. Usually we have something, to send mail and whatever." She rifled through several folders, then shook her head. "No. I don't see anything. Sometimes they don't leave us any address. Did you say they were Russians?"

"Yes, from Moscow."

"Well, there are organizations here, for the Russians. Or, you can go directly to the Department of the Interior. They can help you even if the people left Jerusalem, they have records for the whole country." She looked at her watch. "They're closed now, but they'll open again at four. Maybe you go there."

Rebecca thanked her for her help, and noted the address of the Department of the Interior. Turning to leave, she found that her mother was no longer standing behind her, but had moved away and was now seated in an aqua vinyl-covered easy chair, her head thrown back. She bent over her. "Ma, are you feeling all right? Do you want to rest here for a while?" Miriam turned to her daughter. Her face had regained its color but her eyes looked flat, their green color faded and bleak.

"I can't believe we are sitting in the same place where they were living," she said and sighed deeply. "We come all this way and now they are not here any more."

"But Ma, we'll find them! We'll go to the Department of the Interior as soon as it reopens. Look," she glanced at her watch, "it's almost lunchtime, you're tired, let's just take a cab back into town, instead of the bus, and we'll have lunch. After you eat, and rest for a while, you'll feel much better about everything. Okay?" Miriam nodded but did not move.

"They were here," she repeated. "Here, in this place." Slowly she stood up, and took her daughter's arm. "Okay. We take a taxi."

After a brief altercation with the Kurdish cabdriver who claimed his meter was broken, Rebecca and Miriam settled back to discuss their plans. "We can eat at the hotel, or someplace close by," suggested Rebecca. Miriam nodded and looked out the window. Suddenly she sat up.

"No. I want to go to the *Kotel*. The Wailing Wall."

"What? Now? We haven't eaten!"

"I'm not hungry. I want to see the *Kotel*. Tell the driver." Rebecca stared at her mother in consternation. What was this sudden fixation with the Wailing Wall?

"Tell the driver," Miriam insisted. "Or if you don't want to, if you are so hungry, then I'll go myself." She leaned forward *"Ich vil geyn zum Koisel!"* she announced, addressing the driver in Yiddish.

"Ma, for heaven's sake," whispered Rebecca. "He doesn't know Yiddish. He's a Sephardic Jew. I'll tell him in Hebrew." Haltingly she explained the change in destination to the driver, and agreed to his new price. She had no idea what the price should be anyway, and what did it matter? Her mother was determined to go. The cab sped through winding back streets and alleyways. Rebecca, gazing impassively out the window, suddenly caught her breath. Rising above the hotels, offices, apartment buildings and bustling stores of modern Jerusalem were the ancient, crenelated walls of the Old City. Touching her mother's arm, she pointed towards them, but Miriam was already staring, transfixed, with tears coursing down her cheeks. Moments later they paid the driver and made their way down from the Lion's Gate, one of the seven that led into the Old City, stopping briefly while a portly soldier with a flowing black beard examined the contents of their purses to ensure that they carried no hidden weapons or explosives.

As they walked on, Miriam looked straight ahead and did not speak, but Rebecca stared with interest at the passing throng of people. A large, noisy family of Oriental Jews walked by, heading in the opposite direction. Apparently they had been celebrating a *bar mitzvah*, for among the gaily dressed relatives was a young boy, clad all in white, with a richly embroidered yarmulka on his head. On either side of him were his grandparents, an old and frail couple who hobbled slowly along the stone path. The woman, in her bright scarves and shawls, was bent almost in two.

A group of hasidic men followed, their somber clothing a sharp contrast to the happy smiles on their faces as they hurried past. Leading them was an elderly hasid with a long white beard. The men who flanked him watched solicitously as he walked, occasionally reaching out to touch his arm reverently, making sure he did not stumble on the worn stones. As they passed, they began to sing with deep, resonant voices. The melody was unfamiliar to Rebecca, but she remembered the words from her Bais Yehudis days:

Rejoice ye with Jerusalem and be glad with her, all ye that love her…

On your ramparts, oh City of David, I have appointed watchmen, all day and all night.

Rebecca and Miriam continued downward, to a huge open square, where more people milled about, many in army uniforms. Three American men walked by, sporting conical paper yarmulkas on their heads. Further down, Rebecca saw a man handing out similar yarmulkas from a large wooden box. And at last, there it was, before them, the Wailing Wall, the only remaining portion of the *Bet Hamikdash*, the Holy Temple of Jerusalem which had been destroyed by the Romans some two thousand years ago. The wall was massive, yet somehow it seemed smaller than Rebecca had expected. Rebecca had seen pictures of it, yet no picture conveyed the essence of the Wall itself. Stark and plain, it was, like everything else in Jerusalem, made of golden-beige stone, with large oblong stones from the bottom to about two-thirds of the way up, and smaller, brick-like stones near the top. Many of the crevices between the stones sprouted long, hairy tendrils of a rock-growing plant.

As they drew closer, Rebecca saw that tiny white pebbles seemed to be protruding from every crack and cranny in the wall. Many had also fallen to the ground and lay in the cracks between the wall and the floor. Rebecca knew what they were; everyone had heard about them. They were *kvitlach*, the Yiddish word for notes or, more accurately, requests. Ever since the seventh of June 1967, when the Old City was recaptured from the Jordanians by the victorious Israeli Army, people had been writing down requests and prayers on tiny wads of paper, and inserting them into the Wall. Obeying a strange impulse, Rebecca bent down and picked up one of the many that had fallen out. Opening it, she read the Hebrew words "May it be thy will, oh Lord, that my son, Yehoshua Zevuluni, be returned to me from his army duty, safe in body and in mind." Ashamed at having read a note not meant for her own eyes, she refolded the paper and shoved it into a tiny space between two stones, where it fit snugly. Turning to look for her mother, Rebecca saw that she too was inserting a note in the wall. Miriam caught her eye.

"You should put one in too," she urged. "Put in a *kvitel* for the twins, that they should stay well. And for yourself, too. It can't hurt." She handed Rebecca her pen and a small scrap of paper, torn from the *Jerusalem Post* that they had purchased earlier. Rebecca shrugged. Like chicken soup, it couldn't hurt, and maybe it would even help. Using her handbag for support, she wrote awkwardly in Hebrew, which seemed more appropriate than English for prayer. "Dear Lord, please keep me and my children well and help me find happiness." As an afterthought, she crossed out 'happiness' and substituted 'contentment,' which sounded less selfish. She plugged it into a chink beneath a smooth stone whose corners had long since worn away, uttering a silent prayer that her request would be granted.

The Wall was, after all, such a holy place, perhaps prayers left there had a better chance of reaching God's eyes or ears. She pictured a tall blonde angel, the kind one usually saw on Christmas cards, complete with a halo and great white bird-wings. The angel was collecting all the *kvitlach* in a large blue-gray mail sack, soon to be whisked heavenward for God's perusal. God would be sitting at a huge mahogany desk, like the one her father-in-law had in his office. Next to the desk was a large waste paper basket. Which prayers would God read and grant, she wondered, and which would go into his 'circular file'?

"Nu, Rifkaleh, we can go now. You are hungry, right?" Rebecca turned. Although her mother's voice was calm and her features composed, her face was again wet with tears.

After a meal of spicy shishlik and rice, served along with a salad in which tomatoes, cucumbers and onions were cut into infinitesimally tiny pieces and jumbled together, they made their way back to the hotel for a rest. As they walked up a narrow road that led to the main thoroughfare on which their hotel was located, Rebecca noticed two Arab women seated near the intersection of the streets. In their long black dresses embroidered with red and gold thread in chain stitches and floral patterns, and with filmy white scarves draped about their heads and shoulders, they looked too elegant to be squatting down on the dusty sidewalk. Before each one was a rectangular open basket. As Miriam and Rebecca passed, one of the women hissed at them. Pointing at the dates and figs before her, she said in broken Hebrew, "Please madam, one lira."

Rebecca shook her head, but Miriam stopped and removed a wrinkled note from her purse. Bending down, she handed it to the older of the two, a tired-looking woman with dark, rough-hewn features, and received a small parcel of figs in return.

"What did you buy figs for, Ma?" asked Rebecca as they walked on. "Figs will give you diarrhea."

"Well maybe I won't eat them then. But I felt for this woman, I don't know. She looks to me like a grandmother, like I am."

Farther down the street they passed a low stone wall, atop which were three rolls, each speckled with sesame seeds. "Look Ma," Rebecca pointed out. "I heard about this. The Israelis don't throw bread away. Whatever's left over, they put on a wall, for the poor."

Miriam set the bag of figs beside the bread and they continued on.

When they returned to the hotel, Miriam and Rebecca lay down on their beds, but found they were too restless to sleep. After half an hour they left the hotel and took a bus to the center of town, then walked several blocks to the office of the Ministry of the Interior, which was located on the third floor of an unprepossessing building. The waiting room looked like a small classroom. Each chair had a little desk affixed to it, the kind Rebecca remembered from Brooklyn College. Fortunately, there were only four people ahead of them. There were two girl soldiers, looking casually sexy in their khaki uniforms, their long legs stretching languidly into the aisle. Across from them, with his eyes carefully averted, was an elderly hasid. A few seats away sat a young man in a tattered T-shirt and faded jeans. A blue satin yarmulka looked oddly out of place above his long, tangled ponytail. Unable to sit still, he constantly crossed and uncrossed his legs and drummed his fingers on the desktop. Every few moments he jerked his head round and stared at the doorway. Finally, he got up and left. The girl soldiers giggled as the door closed behind him.

Half an hour later all of the desks were occupied. Several more people stood in the aisles, including Rebecca, who had given her seat to a very pregnant Yemenite woman. A short man with a bristling mustache emerged from the room at regular intervals, and everyone tried to get his attention by waving, calling, or standing up. Ignoring them, the man chose people according to the numbers they had been given when they first came in.

Rebecca and Miriam were ushered into a small office that smelled of cigarettes and old newspapers. A plump woman in her mid-thirties smiled at them.

"Yes, can I help you?" She asked in Hebrew. Once again Rebecca explained that they were looking for their relatives, Reuben and David Zwillinger.

"Zwillinger—please write it down."

Rebecca wrote it in English, then hesitated. "I'm not exactly sure how it's spelled in Hebrew."

Frowning at the English name, the woman chewed her pen, then wrote a Hebrew name and showed it to Rebecca, who nodded. "That looks about right." She showed the paper to her mother.

"No," said Miriam. "I'll give it to you in Yiddish." She took the pen and slowly wrote the name. The Yiddish name contained several more letters than the Hebrew.

"Try them both," suggested Rebecca. The woman brought the paper into another room. After several moments the door opened, but a different woman emerged, bustled past them and went into the outer office.

"I wonder what's taking so long?" asked Rebecca. Miriam

shrugged, nervously biting her lips and toying with the strap of her handbag. "Maybe there are a lot of them, Zwillingers."

"Named Reuben or David, in the same place?"

"Maybe they don't live together. Who says they have to live together?"

The door opened again, and this time the first woman came out. Her face had a harried look, and a few bits of dusty fluff clung to her hair.

"I'm sorry," she said. "I'm having some difficulty finding them. I tried the name with a *zayin* and with a *tzadi*," she explained, mentioning the two Hebrew letters that could have been used in Zwillinger, "but I have no Reuben or David. There is an Abraham, and a Ruth, and a Eugene, also a Moshe and a Ronen, but these two names I don't have. But this doesn't mean it's hopeless. We have just moved our office, so the records are in boxes, it's very difficult. Can you come back later, perhaps?"

Miriam sighed and Rebecca shook her head. "Please, I've been all the way to Russia, only to find out they're in Israel. This is very hard on us, especially my mother. This is her husband and her son we're talking about. She hasn't seen them in over thirty years, she was told they were dead. Now we know they're alive, we've come this far, can't you help us?"

The woman looked from Rebecca to her mother, who was leaning on the desk. Miriam's face had crumpled and her body sagged, as if she had suddenly grown much older. "You know what?" said the woman. "I'll try to find it now. Don't worry. Maybe you want to sit down, have some tea?" Coming out from behind her desk she found Miriam and Rebecca some chairs and brought over a thermos and two cups, and left to continue her search.

When the woman returned, carrying a sheaf of paper. She smiled tentatively. "I think I found something. Look here."

She pointed at one name—David Zvi. Then, further down the list—Reuben Zvi. "Look," she said, "The same address—17 Hapalmach."

"But what does that mean?" Rebecca asked, "Reuben and David Zvi?"

"They changed their name," said the woman. "Shortened it. That's why they were in another file. It should have been cross-referenced, but things are not always so efficient here. And, of course, since we moved, a lot of things are out of order, or piled under other things where they shouldn't be. But I'm sure these are the right ones." She copied the names, along with the address and phone number onto a sheet of paper and handed it to Rebecca. Turning to Miriam, she said in English, "Your husband and your son?" Miriam nodded.

"How beautiful. How wonderful," the woman continued. "I wish you all the best." She beamed at them as they rose from their chairs.

"Thank you so much," said Rebecca. She nudged her mother, who was staring at the piece of paper on which the names, address, and phone number had been written.

"Thank you," whispered Miriam.

"It's nothing," the woman demurred. And please, if it really is them," she touched Rebecca's sleeve, "will you come back and let me know?"

"Of course."

Too nervous to wait for a bus, they took a taxi back to the hotel and rushed up to the room.

"Okay, Ma, are you ready? I'm going to call." Reaching for the phone she noticed that the message button on its base was illuminated. Who would have called here? She felt a pang of fear. Had something happened to the twins?

"Ma there's a message. I'd better see what it is first." She dialed the desk.

"Yes, Mrs. Kramer, there is a telegram for you. We'll send it right up."

A swarthy young man in a dark red jacket knocked on the door and handed Rebecca an envelope. With trembling hands she opened it:

Rebecca—stop—Call me—stop—urgent—Eddie.

"What is it?" asked Miriam. "Is anything wrong? Are the kids okay?"

"I don't know. It's from Eddie. He says to call him. It's urgent.

Oh God, if anything happened to the babies I'll never forgive myself. Traipsing all over creation looking for long lost relatives, and my own children left behind…"

She let Eddie's phone ring ten times before finally hanging up. "He's not home. I'll call Constance." She dialed her home number but there was no answer.

"Maybe call Eddie at the office," suggested Miriam. "What time is it over there?"

"Oh, right, right! The time difference! We're seven hours ahead over here. I'll call the office." Again she dialed the operator and gave her the number.

After several seconds of crackling and whistling, the nasal twang of Eddie's new secretary announced, "Kramer Import-Export, can I help you?"

"Pauline? Let me speak to Eddie."

"Who's calling please?"

"Pauline, it's me, for heaven's sake. Rebecca Kramer."

"Oh, sorreee. One moment please. I'll see if he's available."

Eddie picked up a moment later. "Hello?"

"Eddie, it's me. I got your telegram. What's wrong?"

"Rebecca! Is that you? Pauline didn't even tell me. How are you?"

"Eddie, What's wrong? Are the kids okay? What happened?"

"Nothing happened. Everything's fine."

"But you sent a telegram! You said it was urgent!"

"It *is* urgent. To me, anyway. Listen, Rebecca, I…I was over to visit the twins yesterday. It was a beautiful day, so I took them out to the park. We had a great time together and they seemed so…so happy to be with me. When I left, I said to myself, where are you going *shmuck*? Those beautiful children are your own kids! You should be with them, and with your beautiful wife, too, not living alone in a studio apartment! Rebecca, I can't tell you how terrible I felt."

"Eddie—"

"Please, Rebecca, let me continue. It isn't easy for me to say this. I've been… I've been doing a lot of thinking. I know I haven't been in touch with you as often as I should have been, but believe me, you were on my mind every minute; you and the kids. Look Rebecca, there's no way I can excuse what I did, walking out on you, turning my back like that. I was a real rat, I know. But I just couldn't deal with it. I guess I wasn't ready to be a father, even though I should have been. And then to have two at once, plus all the pressure at work…" He paused and cleared his throat. "I know now I should have taken more interest in you, in the kids, but at the time it was just too much for me. Still, as I said, there's really no excuse for it. But Rebecca," She heard the sharp intake of his breath before he continued. "The main thing is I still love you. I want to come back. I'd like for us to try again."

"Eddie." Rebecca fought against the tears but they came anyway, flowing down her cheeks. Miriam looked at her daughter with alarm. Rebecca quickly shook her head to indicate that nothing was seriously wrong. Without a word Miriam left the room, gently closing the door behind her.

"Rebecca," Eddie said softly. "What do you say?"

"Eddie," she repeated, her voice choking on a sob. "I don't know what to answer. I'm afraid… afraid that if you come back" she paused, trying to gain control over her voice. "I'm afraid that all the problems will start again—Robbie and Sarah will begin to get on your nerves, and the next thing I know you'll be off to Italy or Japan for three months…"

"No, Rebecca. I've talked to my father. We're revamping the whole operation. From now on I'll only take two trips a year, short trips, two or three weeks at most. And when I go, you'll come with me. So what do you think?"

"Eddie, I just—I don't know what to think. I'm too confused. There's so much going on, I can't…Eddie, I'm sitting here in Jerusalem, about to call my long lost father and brother—"

"What? You found them?"

"Not yet, but almost. At least, we have their address, if it is them. My mother is on pins and needles. I was going to dial their number when I saw your message. So now, in the middle of all this—"

"Rebecca, I hope to God you find your father and your brother. I sincerely do. For your own sake as well as for your mother's. But it's

491

us, you and me, that I'm concerned about right now. And of course, Robbie and Sarah, too… Rebecca, I love you. I miss you. I've missed you all this time. Don't you love me anymore? You used to, once."

His voice had a tender quality that she had nearly forgotten. Hearing it, she began to cry again. "Oh, Eddie…"

The door opened. Miriam put her head in, looked at Rebecca, and silently withdrew.

"Eddie, I can't talk right now. My mother is a nervous wreck, she keeps coming in and—"

"I'll call back tomorrow. Think about what I said, okay? I love you, Rebecca."

"I…I love you too, Eddie."

Rebecca replaced the phone. Her knees trembled as she opened the door. Miriam stood at the end of the long corridor, anxiously peering out the window. When she heard Rebecca, she rushed towards her.

"Rebecca, what is it?"

"Oh, Mom…" Awkwardly, she put her arms around her mother and began to cry. "Mom, Eddie wants me to take him back."

"But, Rebecca darling, that's good news. I thought something terrible had happened." She smoothed the hair from Rebecca's face and wiped away the tears with a tissue from her pocket. "What did you tell him?"

"I didn't give him an answer yet. I was in shock, I didn't know what to say. He's going to call tomorrow."

"Do you want him to come back?"

Rebecca absently brushed at the wrinkles in her skirt. "I think so, but I'm not sure. I'm so afraid…Eddie promised that things would be different, that he would have less pressure…he'll hardly have to travel anymore. But I'm worried that after a while things will fall apart again. I was so hurt when he left, so angry at him. Especially when all those weeks went by and he hardly called. I'm not sure I can trust him anymore. I need time to think, to sort everything out in my mind."

Miriam nodded. "But Rebecca, please, think it through very carefully. Remember, you must also consider the children. They need a father. And it won't be easy for you either, alone with two babies. If Eddie says he'll change, then maybe you should consider...But," she shook her head, "I shouldn't be telling you how to live your life. I can give advice, but this is something you really must decide for yourself."

"I know, Mom." Rebecca well understood her mother's reluctance to advise her. Years before, when Rebecca had been dumped by Monty Fleischer, Miriam had told her the story of her disastrous first marriage. Now she saw again in her mother's eyes the painful memories of a daughter forced by her parents to marry the wrong man. Turning her gaze from her mother's face, she noticed the slip of paper beside the telephone.

"Mom," she said. "We have to try the number from the Interior Ministry."

After studying the number, Miriam began dialing, but stopped after three digits. "Rifkaleh, my hands are shaking. Please, you make the call."

Throughout the rest of the evening Rebecca dialed the number again and again. Each time there was no response.

"They must have gone out to some late night function," she finally said to her mother who, though obviously exhausted, was pacing about the room, still fully dressed. "It's after midnight. Why don't we go to bed and I'll try again in the morning."

They undressed and turned off the lights. "Goodnight, Mom," Rebecca called out softly. "Try to get some sleep."

"Goodnight, Rifkaleh."

Rebecca lay on her pillow, staring up at the dark ceiling. Eddie wanted her back. As she recalled the sound of his voice, so tender and loving, a warm feeling filled her body. Not so long ago, she had been very much in love with Eddie. In the dim greyness of the room she saw his face; his soft brown eyes and innocent, choirboy smile. Happy memories, long buried beneath layers of resentment, forced their way back into her consciousness—Eddie, snuggled beside her on the living room sofa, tunefully translating the words of the TV commercials into Yiddish until she was weak with laughter. Eddie, with his arms full of flowers, surprising her on her 'un-birthday,' when she turned twenty-nine and a half. Eddie in bed, his arms wrapped tightly around her moist body, bringing her to a breathless, frenzied climax as the rain streamed across the windowpanes. What had happened to spoil their love? How had they allowed the day-to-day pressures of life to mushroom into the malevolent cloud that finally descended upon them, smothering the joy they had taken in each other? She recalled the cold glint of anger in Eddie's eyes, the once compassionate voice turned harsh and sneering. But was it Eddie alone who was to blame? Hadn't she, too, been at fault? How many nights had she turned from Eddie's embrace, claiming she was too tired, despite the fact that Constance had done most of the work that day? How often had Eddie returned from a business trip, his shoulders slack and his face taut with fatigue, to be greeted, not by a joyful hug or a sympathetic smile, but by a litany of complaints about the various problems she'd encountered while he'd been away? When Eddie had tried to involve her in his business, how had she responded? By nodding her head mindlessly, because her thoughts were elsewhere. It was true. She was too wrapped up in the kids. Eddie worked hard. He too, deserved her attention. It wasn't his fault that he had such a hectic work schedule.

Today Eddie had promised to change. Well, she too would have to change. But was it worth it? Did she really want Eddie back? She pictured her life as it had been these last few months; the long empty nights, the days with little to look forward to. The children were forgetting what it meant to have a daddy. No. She could not go on this way. Her mother was right. Of course she would take Eddie back. Beneath all the hurt feelings, the old love still remained. Smiling into the darkness, she closed her eyes and drifted off to sleep.

Miriam lay awake in the silent room, pondering the problem that both she and Rebecca had avoided discussing for weeks, though it hovered in the air above them, palpable as the Jerusalem fog. If the Reuben and David Zvi whose number they had just dialed were truly her own Reuben and David, what then? What would she do? And what would they do, about her? Rising from the bed, Miriam snapped on the lamp. The familiar room, with its featureless furniture and dull colors, calmed her. Rebecca stirred in her sleep and moaned, throwing a forearm across her eyes. Miriam turned off the lamp. Quietly, she drew a chair to the window, and parted the curtains just enough to see out. The window faced the back of the hotel. The street was dark and silent. A skinny cat with light colored fur slunk past a row of parked cars and leaped onto a trashcan. Surprisingly, there was no accompanying crash of metal. The stillness remained unbroken. Far away, beyond the rooftops of the hotels and apartment buildings, the moon shone, cold and insistent, illuminating the ancient stone walls and the modern housing developments alike with a pale silver glow.

"Rebecca, are you up? Rebecca, wake up."

Rebecca rolled onto her stomach, winding herself into the tangled bedclothes. With a groan, she burrowed her head under the pillow.

"Rebecca, it's already a quarter to seven."

"What?" She struggled out from under the covers. "What time is it?"

"A quarter to seven."

Rebecca sat up and pushed the hair back from her face. "Did you call them, Ma?"

"No. Do you think we should call this early?"

"Sure. What if they leave for work?" She rushed into the bathroom, then emerged, wrapped in a fleecy robe.

"Okay, Ma. Here goes."

The phone rang four times. On the fifth ring, a young woman's voice said, "Allo?"

Rebbeca paused. Who could this be? A wrong number? Or did David have a new wife?

"Hello." she answered. "Is Reuben or David Zwill—I mean Zvi there?"

"Ah, no English."

Switching to Hebrew, Rebecca tried again, this time pronouncing the names slowly and carefully. Seated on the other bed, her mother stared at her with wide, frightened eyes.

"May I please speak to Reuben or David Zvi?"

"Sorry. Not here."

495

"They don't live here?"

"Yes, they live here. But they're not here now. They just left for work."

"Both of them?"

"Yes. Both."

"Where do they work?"

The woman on the other end giggled nervously. "In the city. I don't know where."

"Don't you have a number?"

"No." More giggles.

"Who is this?"

"Mila."

"Mila?"

"Mila. The helper."

"Helper? Dimly Rebecca realized that 'helper' must be the Hebrew term for a cleaning woman. Bais Yehudis had not equipped her for day-to-day modern Hebrew.

"What time will they be home?"

"At seven thirty, eight o'clock. Do you want to leave a name, a number?"

"Yes, ah, no. No. I'll call again." She put down the phone. Her mother was still staring at her with eyes round as glass marbles.

"Ma, they're not home."

"Not home? Who was that?"

"The cleaning lady. They won't be home till seven thirty, eight o'clock, tonight."

"You are sure it's them? The right family?"

"It's Reuben and David Zvi anyway. God, if only I'd gotten up earlier. But you were up. Why didn't you call?"

"You know I cannot call. I cannot. If I heard their voices, either of them, I wouldn't.... I wouldn't be able to speak."

"The cleaning girl didn't even know where they work. Damn! Now we'll have to wait until this evening." Miriam nodded silently. In the pale light of morning, with disappointment settling over her even features, she appeared to age before Rebecca's eyes.

"But Mom, listen! I do have good news!"

"Yes, what?" Miriam's voice was listless.

"I've decided. I'm going to take Eddie back."

Miriam leaped from her chair, all traces of sadness gone from her face. "*Mazel Tov*, darling!" Clasping Rebecca in her arms, she kissed her on both cheeks. "*Mazel Tov!*"

Rebecca reached for the phone. "I'm going to call him right now and tell him. Why should I wait until he calls me?"

"You are right, Rifkaleh. Don't delay." Miriam went into the bathroom, locked the door, and took a lengthy shower. She emerged just as Rebecca was putting down the phone.

"Ma, I told him!"

"Oh darling, I'm so glad. What did he say?"

Blushing like a new bride, Rebecca wiped a tear from her eye and smiled. "He said he loves me. He said he can't wait till I get home. Oh, Ma!" She hugged her mother tightly, breathing in the sweet fragrance of her after-bath cologne, before finally releasing her.

"Now," she said, "let's decide how to spend the day." Leafing through a pile of travel brochures, she pointed at a colorful photograph. "How about the Israel Museum and the Knesset? And maybe the Dead Sea Scrolls, afterward?"

At six-thirty, after a Yemenite dinner which both of them left virtually untouched, Rebecca announced, "Okay. It's time we went back to the hotel and called."

"No." Miriam looked into her hand mirror and reapplied her lipstick.

"No?" Rebecca asked, signalling the waitress for the check. "Why, 'No'? If we don't call soon we might miss them again."

"That's it. Better we don't call. I can't stand any more of these calls; this agency, that agency, the cleaning woman, the whole business. We go over, straight to their apartment. You have the address?"

Rebecca opened her purse. "Yes. 17 HaPalmach. I remembered it anyway. But how can we do that, just show up like that?"

"Why not? We go there, we see them, we talk, we see what's what. No more telephones." She powdered her nose with a trembling hand. "How do I look?"

Rebecca looked at her mother. "Beautiful," she said.

They left the restaurant and caught a taxi. As it rumbled through the darkened streets, Miriam squeezed Rebecca's hand. "Rifkaleh, I'm afraid."

"Don't be afraid, Ma."

The cab stopped in front of a four-story apartment building, identical to the others on the street in its simple, pale, stone facade, and flower-laden terraces. Some of the windows glowed with warm, yellow light while others were black and vacant-looking. Spicy cooking smells wafted through the air. The evening chill frosted the breath of the people hurrying past.

Still holding hands, Rebecca and Miriam entered the building. The lobby was no more than a large empty room paved with speckled mosaic tile. Along one wall, four baby carriages were lined up, one behind the other, like a fanciful train. Above them hung a sign with the Hebrew word "shelter", and an arrow pointing downward to a small staircase. On the opposite wall was a row of gray metal mailboxes. Scrutinizing the names, Rebecca pointed triumphantly when she found the correct one—Zvi, 6, awkwardly written in Hebrew script.

Apartment six turned out to be on the third floor. With icy fingers, Miriam pressed the doorbell. A soft ringing sound could be heard through the door. Again and again she rang, but no one answered. Rebecca looked at her watch.

"It's only seven fifteen. It's probably too early. Let's wait downstairs."

As they turned toward the staircase, the door to an adjacent apartment opened and a wizened old woman peered out at them. "Are you looking for Weiss?" she asked, in Polish-accented Hebrew.

"No, for Zvi," answered Rebecca.

"Zvi!" The woman laughed hoarsely. "Are they expecting you?"

"No."

"I should think not, because they just left, not more than five minutes ago, maybe less. Mr. Zvi is going on a trip. To America! But hurry, maybe you'll still catch them downstairs." She withdrew her head into the apartment and closed the door.

As they raced down the three flights of stone steps, Miriam's newly healed ankle throbbed with pain, but she paid no attention. Once outside the building the two women looked frantically up and down the dark street. Half a block away two men emerged from beneath a shadowy eucalyptus tree and climbed into a taxi.

"Reuben!" Miriam shouted, breaking into an awkward limping sprint. "Reuben, wait!" Her voice was lost in the roar of the engine as the cab pulled away from the curb and disappeared around the corner.

"Ma!" Rebecca rushed up. "Was that them?"

"I couldn't tell for sure. I think so. One was an older man, the other looked like—"

"A soldier. I saw him. What do we do now?" Miriam turned and waved at another taxi that had just rounded the corner.

"Lod Airport," she told the driver, as she and Rebecca climbed in.

"How do you know they're going to Lod?" asked Rebecca.

"Where else could they be going? They're on their way to America! Please, tell him to hurry." The cab sped through the dark winding streets and made its way to the Jerusalem–Tel Aviv road, where it picked up speed, slamming mercilessly around the sharp, downhill curves. Miriam and Rebecca clung to each other, too nervous to speak.

Please, Rebecca prayed, *don't let us get killed in an accident. Not now!*

At the airport Miriam and Rebecca fought their way through the crowd until they reached the departure area. Due to a baggage handler's strike, the terminal was in chaos. Hordes of people milled about, gesticulating and shouting. Rebecca nearly lost sight of her mother in the crush as a large contingent of hasidim trouped by, escorting their *rebbe* on his return voyage to Brooklyn.

"Ma, we'll never find them in this mob." Rebecca clutched her mother's hand as Miriam's eyes darted about, searching every face.

"Look, Ma, I have to go to the ladies' room. The minute I get out I'll have them paged." She hurried away.

Miriam had scanned the faces of nearly a dozen middle-aged, European-looking men when she caught her breath. Not more than three feet away, a tall thin man leaned against the wall, reading a Russian newspaper which partially obscured his face. From what she could discern, he appeared to be in his mid-sixties and he was bald, with thin gray hair at his temples. He wore horn-rimmed eyeglasses, and as he read, he absently rubbed one side of his eyeglass frame with a slender finger. The simple gesture, long buried under countless treasured memories, pierced Miriam's heart. On frozen, unsteady legs, she forced herself to approach him.

"Excuse me, please," she began, her lips barely able to form the Yiddish words.

The man lowered his newspaper. Miriam gazed past the misty lenses of his glasses to the gray-blue eyes, surrounded by a fine web of wrinkles, that stared back at her curiously. She opened her mouth to speak, but no words came. Instead, the entire airport, with all of its bustling customs agents and noisy passengers, began to spin before her eyes like a kaleidoscope. The man reached out and grasped her arm, gently steadying her as she swayed before him.

"Are you all right?" he asked.

The voice had not changed.

"Reuben," she whispered. "Reuben, it's me."

"You?" He looked at her uncomprehending. "But who are you?"

"Reuben, Reuben." She began to cry. "I am Miriam. Miriam, your wife. I've been looking for you…"

"My wife? Miriam? But Miriam is dead!" With trembling hands he removed his glasses, wiped his lenses quickly with his handkerchief and replaced them. Lowering his head, he studied her face, carefully scrutinizing each feature in turn; the large, green eyes that glistened with tears, the gently curved, high cheekbones, the small, straight nose, the delicate lips and the straight, even teeth. Finally, he returned again to the eyes. Only then was he certain. These were the eyes he had never forgotten, the eyes that had burned their way into his soul like glowing coals. The memory of their green fire had warmed him throughout the endless Siberian nights, and had tormented him with longing through all of his nights since.

"Miriam," he whispered. "But you were shot! They told me you had died!"

Smiling through her tears, Miriam shook her head. "No. I was shot, but I didn't die. I lived. And when they told me you were dead, I went to America."

"I? Dead?"

"Yes. They sent me papers. They said you had died in Siberia and that David had died of scarlet fever. Look." She drew a manila envelope from her purse and handed it to him. Slowly he removed a few yellowed documents and a cracked, faded photograph.

"My God," murmured Reuben. "My papers." Opening one, he read: 'It is with great regret that I inform you of bad news regarding your husband, Reuben Zwillinger....'

"My God," he repeated, as tears streaked his face. "Miriam. Alive. Alive after all this time. Are you really my Miriam?" He lifted her chin and stared into her eyes once more.

"Yes, yes, Reuben," she answered, weeping."I am your Miriam. I have always been your Miriam. All these years I've never forgotten, I've never stopped..." she reached up and lightly touched his cheek, "loving you. Oh Reuben!" she cried. "Tell me I'm not dreaming."

"My darling, Miriam," he breathed. "This is the best dream." Then, catching her in his arms, he whirled her round and round in a wild embrace, finally kissing her lips with all the passion of old love too long denied.

A plump woman, her light brown hair pinned into a neat chignon and her arms laden with suitcases and parcels, rushed toward them. "Reuben! What—" She stopped short and turned to the equally encumbered young soldier behind her. "David!" she cried. "What on earth is going on here? Who is that woman with your father?"

David stared, transfixed, at the bizarre tableaux before him. Without thinking, he put his arm around Aliza's shoulders, as if to protect her from the sight of his father in the arms of a stranger. An unexplainable fear filled his body.

"Papa," he whispered. "Papa, who is this?"

Reuben raised his head and looked at his son. "David...David, this is your mother."

"My mother?!"

"Yes, this is my wife. My Miriam."

Shrugging off David's arm, Aliza stepped forward. "Your wife? What do you mean? Since when do you have a wife?"

"Since before the war. We lost each other in the war. I thought she was dead."

"And now you found her? Here? After all these years?"

"She found me. Just now...I...I cannot believe it myself, but it's true. Aliza, I'm sorry. I'm sorry for everything..."

"Sorry? Don't be sorry." She fixed Miriam with a penetrating look. "Your wife! Well. So I'm to travel alone, after all. Just this morning I said to Menashe, 'If Reuben changes his mind, he'd better have a good excuse.' Your wife," she repeated, shaking her head. "Well, goodbye, then. Good-bye and good luck to all of you." Hoisting her suitcases she turned and took a few steps before looking back. "Reuben," she called. "Tell Menashe goodbye for me. I won't be returning."

From overhead came an announcement: "Will Reuben and David Zvi please come to the El Al security office." The announcement was repeated twice before David noticed it.

He pointed up at the loudspeaker. "They are paging us."

Still locked in Reuben's arms, Miriam gazed up at him. "It's Rebecca," she said. "She told me she would have you paged."

"Rebecca?" Reuben asked. "Who is Rebecca?"

"Our daughter. Rebecca is our daughter. I was pregnant when you left for Kiev—" Stopping in mid-sentence, she pointed at the young soldier with the red-gold hair who stood before her, his handsome face drained of color.

"Is this David?" she gasped. "Can this be my little boy?" Without waiting for an answer, Miriam broke from Reuben's arms and embraced David fiercely, her tears staining his khaki uniform.

"Will Reuben and David Zvi please come to the El Al security office." The Hebrew words resounded through the airport once again.

With their arms around each other, Miriam and Reuben walked through the airport terminal, while David followed behind, shaking his head in wonder. Rebecca ran up to them moments later, her dark hair flying.

"Mommy!" she shouted. "You found them!"

Seated on the red plastic chairs in the Departure Area, the Zwillinger family watched the El Al passengers line up to board flight 206 to New York. This was the flight Reuben would have taken; the first leg of his journey to Los Angeles. But now Reuben would not be aboard. Instead, Rebecca was flying home. El Al had agreed to allow her the use of her father's ticket. Once in New York, she would pack up Eddie and the twins, and the four of them would return to Israel for a family reunion. It had all been arranged by Rebecca in a breathless phone call to Eddie, only moments before.

Rebecca cried as she kissed her parents and brother good-bye before disappearing into a long line of passengers.

Reuben put his arm around Miriam. "I still cannot believe it," he said. "That you are really alive! That you've been looking for me! Tell me the story again. I was too much in shock before to absorb it."

Miriam leaned her head against his shoulder. "It was your neighbor, Mrs. Abramovich, from Moscow." She repeated the story once more, from the woman's ringing of the doorbell, through Rebecca's trip to Russia, and up to the very moment she herself had spotted him at the airport, reading a newspaper. Turning to David, she asked, "David, do you remember anything about me at all?"

David shook his head. "No. I wish I could, but I remember nothing from before the war."

"Never mind," said Reuben. "You will soon get to know her. Miriam," he murmured, his lips brushing her forehead. "You must never leave me again."

"Never," Miriam whispered. "I will never leave you. Nothing will separate us, ever again."

She kissed Reuben's lips, then reached out and clasped David's hand. Silently, the three sat together, the older couple gazing into each other's eyes, while the young soldier beside them looked through the window at a silver plane soaring gracefully toward the western sky.

Acknowledgments

I wish to express my gratitude and appreciation to the many people who helped me as this book made its way into print.

To Joan Goldberg, who read and edited the manuscript in its earliest incarnation, and encouraged me to go on. To Jean Naggar, for all her efforts. To Irving Louis Horowitz, for his expressions of confidence and invaluable assistance. To Luther Wilson and Yashka Hallein, for publishing the first edition of *The Chimney Tree*. To Zack Dicker, for his wise advice, and for the party!

To Naomi Ragen, for her kindness and generosity in recommending The Toby Press. To Matthew Miller, for giving this book new life, and for enabling me to finally answer the question, "When is the sequel coming out?" To Deborah Meghnagi, for her careful and thoughtful editing of the manuscript.

To my many friends who are children of survivors, and to their parents, who shared their stories with me as I was growing up. To my children, for their patience and good cheer while this book was being written. Finally, to the love of my life, my husband Willy, who from the day he asked "Why don't you write a book?" has been at my side every step of the way, and whose boundless energy and enthusiasm inspired me to keep on going no matter what. He is the most wonderful husband, guide, mentor, agent and best friend a woman could ever ask for.

Helaine G. Helmreich, 5 May 2003

About the Author

Helaine Helmreich

Helaine Helmreich was born in postwar Brooklyn, New York. She attended Brooklyn College and CUNY Graduate Center. Inspired by the many stories she heard growing up in a neighborhood of Holocaust survivors and their children, she began writing *The Chimney Tree* while spending a sabbatical year in Jerusalem.

The fonts used in this book are from the Garamond family

Temple Israel
Minneapolis, Minnesota

IN MEMORY OF
HAROLD FRISHBERG
FROM
GEORGIA & IVAN KALMAN